WE WERE IN BED, ASLEEP, WHEN THE ALARM SOUNDED

Joslyn, who usually wakes up faster than I do, got the computer to decode the alert before I was even in my flight chair. "It's a courier drone!" she said.

We approached the drone slowly. The only thing in it was a great black message cylinder. It was pointed right for the hatchway joining us to the drone; all it needed was a good push from below to send it through the lock into *Stars*.

A giant, booming voice suddenly shouted out from a speaker by the overhead hatch. "THIS IS A WAR EMERGENCY SITUATION," it roared. "TRANSFER THE CYLINDER TO YOUR SHIP WITH ALL POSSIBLE SPEED. DO NOT DELAY FOR ANY REASON . . . DELAY FOR NOTHING . . . HURRY. HURRY. THIS IS A WAR EMERGENCY SITUATION. THAT IS ALL."

What had we gotten ourselves into? War emergency situation?

What war?

Ours, as it turned out.

ROGER MACBRIDE ALLEN

THE TORCH OF HONOR

A BAEN BOOK

*To Dad—my mentor
colleague—and friend*

THE TORCH OF HONOR

This is a work of fiction. All the characters and events portrayed in this book are fictional, and any resemblance to real people or incidents is purely coincidental.

A Baen Book

Baen Enterprises
8–10 W. 36th Street
New York, N.Y. 10018

First printing, February 1985

ISBN: 0-671-55938-9

Cover art by Alan Gutierrez

Printed in the United States of America

Distributed by
SIMON & SCHUSTER
MASS MERCHANDISE SALES COMPANY
1230 Avenue of the Americas
New York, N.Y. 10020

In Flanders Fields

In Flander Fields the poppies blow
   Between the crosses, row on row,
      That mark our place; and in the sky
      The larks, still bravely singing, fly
Scarce heard amid the guns below.

We are the Dead. Short days ago
We lived, felt dawn, saw sunset glow,
   Loved and were loved, and now we lie
   In Flanders Fields.

Take up our quarrel with the foe:
To you from failing hands we throw
   The torch; be yours to hold it high
   If ye break faith with those who die
We shall not sleep, though poppies grow
   In Flanders fields.

          John McCrae

PRELUDE

April, 2115

The Finns knew the Guardians had won. It was over. The Guardians had taken the planet's surface, and now the surrender of the great satellite Vapaus would go into effect in a few hours. The Guardians themselves had caused a delay of the surrender by insisting it be negotiated strictly in English. The Finns, desperately playing for time, stalled for as long as possible, taking hours to search for the English-speaking officer they could have produced in moments.

The time was put to urgent use. The last, the only hope, thin though it might be, was the League. Word had to be sent.

Six of the last torpedoes were stripped of armament. Light-speed-squared generators and radio beacons were installed. Recordings that held the vital knowledge of the anti-ship missile system, and what little information the Finns had on the Guardians, were placed aboard.

Word had to get through.

The Guardians had not yet closed the ring around Vapaus. Three tiny one-man ships were launched from the Forward airlock complex, each with two torps strapped to jury-rigged harnesses amidships. The little ships launched at six gees, to fly straight through the Guardian fleet. The enemy's radar was too good to be fooled by any feinting maneuver; speed was the only protection.

It was not protection enough. The lead ship was destroyed in seconds by laser fire from a troop transport. The Finnish pilot's last act was to blow the fusion engines; the resultant explosion created a plasma that jammed every radar screen and radio within a thousand kilometers. That gave the two remaining ships their chance as they flashed into and beyond the gathering fleet.

They dove down to lower orbits, rushing to get the sheltering bulk of the planet between themselves and the enemy's radar before it could recover from the explosion the Finns' lead ship had died in.

They fell toward the planet, gathering speed for a gravity-assist maneuver. One hundred eighty degrees around the planet from the satellite Vapaus, they both changed course, maneuvering violently, one coming about to fly a forced orbit straight over the planet's North Pole, the second heading over the South Pole.

As soon as the ships had reached their new headings, they cut their engines for a moment, and each released a torp. Then the two ships and the two released torpedoes ignited their engines and flashed on into the sky, the torps holding course, the ships again changing their headings.

The southern ship was caught and destroyed by a Nova fighter scrambled from the planet's surface. The northern ship released its second torp and came about, one final time, to act as a decoy for the torps.

Soon, all too soon, another fusion explosion lit the sky, marking the point where a Guardian missile had found the last Finnish ship.

The Guardians tracked only the last torpedo launched, and they were able to destroy it.

Of the six torpedoes, two now survived, undetected. Engines still burning, they curved around the world in exactly opposite directions, one over the South Pole, one over the North, their courses bent by the planet's gravity until they came about to identical bearings.

The torps cut their engines precisely over the Poles, just as they reached escape velocity.

Each now rose on a straight-line course starting from a point directly over a pole and parallel to the equator, the paths of the torps also parallel to each other.

Engines stopped, they rushed through space, coasting, trusting to the cold and dark of the void to hide them.

Hours after launch, when they were hundreds of thousands of kilometers beyond the orbit of the moon Ku, celestial trackers on each torp examined the starfield. The maneuvering thrusters fired fussily and touched up the torps' headings. The two torps were now on precise headings for the Epsilon Eridani star system, where the English had their colony world, Britannica. The torpedoes were still far too close to New Finland's sun to go into light-speed-squared. For long weeks they coasted on into the darkness, while behind them, the Guardians worked their horrors on the Finns.

On one torp, the power system failed and the torp became another of the useless derelicts in the depths of space.

But the other torp, the last one, held on to life. And at the proper moment, the light-speed-squared generator absorbed nearly all the torp's carefully husbanded power and grabbed at the fabric of space around the torpedo.

The last torp leaped across the dark between the suns.

Soon after, with weak batteries, the radio beacon barely detectable, the torpedo drifted into the Epsilon Eridani system.

Just barely, the last torp made it.

PART ONE:
AN EMPTY GRAVE,
A HOLLOW WORLD

CHAPTER ONE

January, 2115

A cold, drizzly rain spattered the faceplate of my pressure suit as the chaplain droned through the funeral service, there at the edge of the empty grave.

The metal and rubber arm of my helmet's windshield wiper slithered back and forth across my field of vision, clearing the rain away. This was probably the only world humanity had bothered to settle where a pressure suit needed a wiper. We all had them, the wiper blades endlessly waving, side to side, like the mouthparts of giant locusts.

They were gone, dead, missing in the depths of space. Sixty of our classmates. Their ship simply vanished en route back from one final training cruise. There had been exactly one hundred of us when we had started out. Of course there had been other losses to our ranks— other accidents, candidates who had been dropped—but now there was this. There were only 34 of us left to stand on the miserable plain.

"Vanity, vanity, saith the preacher," intoned our chaplain. "We bring nothing into this world, and we take nothing out." The words might as well have been a recording. The chaplain's voice made me think of dried-out toast. He talked on in gravelly, portentous tones, plucking old morsels from half the books of scripture, a

7

shopworn service to be dragged out for all funerals and sad occasions. "What is man, that thou are mindful of him?" he asked, his voice rising for a moment, and then sliding back down to a low grumble.

A light blinked on the telltale board inside my helmet, and I kicked my radio over to a private channel.

"Mac, this man is awful. Can't we make him be quiet, so we could at least stand here and *think*?" Joslyn asked. She and I had been married by the same chaplain three months ago. He had taken two minutes over our vows and 45 minutes on a rambling sermon that put half the congregation to sleep.

"Just keep your suit radio cut off," I suggested.

"But then I could still see his great jaw flapping. And now he's glaring at us. Best we listen. Oh, Mac, they deserve a better send-off." She slipped her gauntleted hand into mine and we switched back to the general circuit.

"Dear Lord, we commit to your care and keeping the immortal souls of these, the departed. We pray you to welcome and cherish the souls of Lieutenant Daniel Ackerman, Lieutenant Lucille Calder, Lieutenant Commander Joseph Danvers. . . ."

Nice touch, I thought. He's got them memorized in alphabetical order.

The empty grave was a regulation hole, one meter wide, two meters long, two meters deep. I looked up into the sky through the gloomy overcast at the blue-and-white globe that hung there. It was there, on the planet Kennedy, that the tradition of the empty grave had arisen. There, during the Fast Plague, it had been rare to have a body to put in the ground. The corpses had been viciously infectious. The only sure way of sterilizing the remains was to destroy them in the fusion flame of a grounded spacecraft. That was what happened to my parents' bodies—I remember the patches of dim incandescence in the cleansing flame. There was a an empty grave there, on Kennedy, a meter by a meter by two meters; on top of it a granite cover slab that bore their names.

There have always been a lot of funerals without bodies at the edges of civilization, I suppose. There still were. A ship doesn't come back. Somebody pushes the wrong button and a ship explodes. People get eaten. There are lots of ways.

Finally, the cover slab with sixty names on it was carefully set down over the grey concrete shell that defined the grave. A few centimeters of dirty water were trapped in a puddle in the bottom.

We trooped back to the pressurized quarters and the wardroom. There was to be a reception there.

Joslyn and I hung back. We stood on the surface of the moon Columbia a while longer. When humanity came to this system, this, the planet Kennedy's only large moon, had had a wispy methane atmosphere and a lot of water ice locked up in polar icecaps. Now the engineers were hard at work in a dozen projects to remake it into a better place. Some day their work would be done and this world would live. Already, the air pressure was up to a third of what Earth's was. But it was still a dank, miserable bog of a world, cold and moody, the air poisonous. It rained too much.

Silently, I bid our comrades a last farewell, and we went inside.

Once in our quarters, it took us a while to get out of our pressure suits and into our dress uniforms, with the grim addition of an issue black armband.

I struggled into the midnight-black, high-collared, rather severe uniform of the Republic of Kennedy Navy. Joslyn, a native of the Planetary Commonwealth of Britannica, was thereby a loyal subject of the King-Emperor of Great Britain. Her uniform was a deep navy blue, with a lower collar, far fewer buttons, and a better cut. Both of us wore the insignia of the League of Planets Survey Service, a starfield superimposed on a rectangular grid. Both of us were lieutenants, assigned to special training classes at the League of Planets Survey Service Training Center on Columbia.

Joslyn checked her appearance in the mirror. She said she was five foot seven and I was six four. *I* said she was 170 centimeters and I was 193. She was slender, well-muscled and strong. Her face was oval, her lips full, and she had a full set of dimples when she smiled. Her hair was a shade between brunette and blonde. She grew it long and braided it. It was long enough to hang to the small of her back. Now she had the braid coiled on top of her head. She pulled her tunic straight and checked her profile, giving me a smile and a wink in the mirror. She might be slender, but even in a dress uniform, she was definitely female. She satisfied herself as to her own appearance and turned to me. She patted my tunic smooth and brushed some lint from my sleeve.

"You'll do," she said, "but if they ever put padded shoulders in those uniforms, you'll never fit through the doorway." Suddenly, she threw her arms around my neck, pulled my head down, and gave me a most unmilitary kiss. She looked me in the eye and sighed. "Mac, I do love you so."

I tickled her under the ear and smiled back. "Never mind that stuff. You sure I look okay?"

"Oh, you'll do. That is, if one likes Greek gods."

I looked in the mirror and shrugged. I've always felt I looked like a refugee from a comic book. Broad shoulders, plenty of muscles, I suppose, kind of a narrow waist. My face is long and lantern-jawed. I've got light blonde hair and the blue eyes to go with them. My smile is a little uneven, but it's friendly enough. My arms and legs are long, my hands and feet big. I take the largest size they issue in practically everything.

Growing up, I was the kid who tripped over his own two feet and tended to smack into walls. My body got bigger than my coordination could handle for a while there. Nowadays, Joslyn can escort me to the dance floor in perfect safety; I can even waltz. Nonetheless, in regulation formal dress I look about the size and shape of the angel of death.

We headed to the wardroom.

We, the survivors, should have been able to gather quietly together, drawn to each other by the bonds of comradery that linked us one to the other, and to the dead.

But the government representatives here had to be treated diplomatically. Some were from nations and planets that opposed the Survey, others from places that were footing the bill. Captain Driscoll had to invite them, and many had come.

Joslyn went off in search of drinks. I stood there and scanned the crowd for a friendly face. Pete Gesseti caught my eye and came over.

Pete works for the Republic of Kennedy State Department, and is one of those rare people who can actually make you believe that the bureaucracy knows what it is doing. He is intelligent, open, and calm. A friendly warning from Pete has kept plenty of people out of trouble. Pete knew my father—and kept *me* out of trouble.

If not for Pete, I'd probably be just another of the orphan punks that cause Hyannisport police to travel in pairs.

Pete is of medium height, his brown hair retreating toward baldness, his face permanently calm.

He came over and shook my hand. "This isn't the right sort of occasion, but I haven't seen you since. Congratulations on your commission, Second Lieutenant Terrance MacKenzie Larson, sir."

"Thanks, Pete."

He raised his glass to me and took a sip. Joslyn returned and handed me my drink. "Two more congratulations. Or three. On *your* commission, Lieutenant Joslyn Marie Cooper Larson. On your marrying him. And on his marrying you. Cheers."

We clinked our glasses and smiled. Pete went on. "Sorry I missed the wedding. I understand the Reverend Buxley was spellbinding. I couldn't get leave."

"We understand, Peter. It was pretty short notice," Joslyn said. "Once we decided to marry, we didn't see much point in waiting."

"The wedding aside, at least you didn't miss a trip to someplace worth going," I said.

"True, I guess. Though the League should have picked someplace a lot better than this to train you kids. And I have a sneaky idea that putting you in this hole was the deliberate policy of certain people who want the Survey to fail, if you're interested in a little paranoia."

"What?"

"Mac—tell me this: How does Columbia rate as a training base for a space-going operation?" Pete has a tendency to snap from one subject to another quickly. He takes some keeping up with.

"Well, okay—not so great."

"Make that terrible. You guys should be in free orbit. That way, if you want to train in your ships, you just hop out the hatch and go to it. Here, since your ships aren't designed to land on a surface, you lose a lot of time taking shuttle craft back and forth. Makes schedules impossible. Even having to fly through this atmosphere is worthless as training. It's a freak since the terraforming engineers started tinkering with it. It hasn't stopped raining here for years, which must be great for morale. The air would kill you, so you have to wear suits. The methane leaks in anyway, and stinks to high heaven. The whole atmosphere is in transition: All kinds of crud precipitates and ruins equipment. . . ."

"Okay, you've made your point. It's not such a great base. So who is it that got the base put here?"

"You kids are lucky this is my third drink or I'd still be a fairly discreet diplomat. People who wanted the Survey to fail. Those people had friends who arranged for some misguided members of the Kennedy Chamber of Commerce to lobby for you to be based here—if you follow that. They would like the Survey to fail because the British donated the ten long-range frigates you'll be flying, because your commander graduated from Annapolis, and because the reports are to be published in English. They think the Brits and the Yanks are plotting to lay claim to all the best real estate out there. Note Britannica, Kennedy, and Newer Jersey are the prime planets so far—Europa, for example, isn't all *that* habitable. There are some grounds for being suspicious. Anyone you met at this reception speaking French, or German, or Japanese, for example, would probably be just as happy if you had all been on the *Venera* when she went poof."

"You're not suggesting the *Venera*. . . ." I began.

"Was nuked on purpose? No. But it has crossed my mind that your friends aren't dead."

"Pete—you're going too fast. We're at their funeral, or didn't you notice?"

"Hmmmm. Look, I'll finish the thought and then forget I said anything. But the *Venera* fits a pattern. In the last ten years or so, there have been at least 30 cases in which something like this happens: a proven, reliable ship takes off, on a well-known route. A number of highly skilled people are on board. Some evidence—in the manifest, say—is sometimes found to suggest that someone bribed their way on board, or stowed away, or whatever. The ship vanishes. No wreckage, no explanation. The ship ends up listed Lost With All Hands, and they put the files away. I get a funny feeling sometimes that someone is setting up shop on some backwater planet. Needs more skilled people than he's got, so he kidnaps the talent he needs. Now *forget* I ever said that, because I'd hate to fib and deny any such idea ever went through my head." He sipped his drink.

I stood there, too surprised by the idea to react. Joslyn wasn't going to let the subject drop, though. "Peter, if you believe that, why aren't you out organizing a search party?"

"Joslyn, please—okay, I know that look. I give up. I guess I've gone far enough that it doesn't matter. Listen. One: No way to prove it. Two: I could not face giving all but certainly false hope to thousands of people who are relatives and friends of people lost on unaccounted-for ships. Three: As the saying goes, it's a big galaxy. We've been in star travel for 100 years, and have yet to visit a tenth of the star systems within a hundred light years of Earth. Four: Sooner or later, we will stumble across them—next year, next millennia—if we keep looking for habitable planets. If something like the Survey gets off the ground and is out there doing the looking. I spend a lot of government time on the Survey. My superiors complain about it at times. So let's leave it alone and talk about the weather. Has it stopped raining yet?"

"Not for another fifty years or so," I said. "We get the message." We murmured something in the direction of a goodbye and circulated among the guests. I went through the motions, mostly on automatic.

My head was whirling with confusion. I had never paid much attention to politics. It had never occurred to me that someone would think ill of the Survey, let alone try and throw monkey wrenches at it. And past that, way past that, the wild thought that all those people might still be *alive.* . . . I understood why Pete wasn't wholesaling his theory. I had known him all my life, and it had taken a funeral that might have been mine and a few drinks too many for him to mention it to me. How could he ever bring himself to suggest it to strangers?

And then there were the rumblings that the Survey Service was to be stillborn. We had yet to send a single ship out on a survey mission. Ours, the first class of the Service, had been about a month from graduation when the *Venera* was lost. I had figured the loss would slow us down to a crawl, but could it really stop us? With all that to worry about, it was a lousy party, even for a funeral.

Some hours after, I was alone in the view room. An overhanging roof shielded the oversize view window from the worst of the rain so that it was possible to see something of the dismal surface of Columbia, and of her sullen sky. Now it was night, and Kennedy gleamed boldly down through the high cloud deck.

I looked up again at the sullen sky, and thought of the stars behind the dirty clouds.

So many stars. . . .

In the vicinity of Earth's sun, the star systems are about five light years apart, on the average. That works out to about 64,000 stars within a hundred light years of Earth. Our home solar system is a good sample of what you can expect to find in an average star system—nine or ten good-sized planets, 40 or 50 noticeable satellites, and a few trillion pieces of sky junk from the size of a rogue moon down to individual atoms and elementary particles.

There's plenty of variety that goes past the average to the incredible. If every human alive now, in 2115, were put to work as a scientist or an explorer, and passed their jobs along to every one of their descendants, it would still take a thousand years to get together a basic catalog of what we know is out there to learn within that 100 light years.

Consider the infinite variety of Earth—the geology, the hydrology, the atmosphere, the biology, the physical reality of our ancestral home. Multiply it by the number of worlds waiting to be found, and you'll begin to understand the problem.

Exploration is not something to do out of idle curiosity. Knowing what is out there is an urgent need, and getting more so every year.

Around the beginning of the third millennium, the experiments were performed that took faster-than-light travel from an impossibility to a laboratory trick to a way to haul freight. Humanity, barely staggering into the third thousand years alive, found that the stars had been dropped in its lap.

The explorers went out.

Some of them came back. The settlers followed in their paths. More than once, settlers went out blazing their own trails. Very few of that number were ever heard from again.

Yet, by the year 2025, the United States Census Bureau estimated the off-Earth population as over 1 million for the first time. Ten years later, the figure was twice that, and the pace accelerating. By 2050, rapid emigration and high birth-rates had pushed the minimum estimate to 10 million. Even to this day, the Census people try to keep track of it. At the moment, the best guess is 85 million people. That is, 85 million, plus or minus 20 million!

The colonists went out, poorly organized, often toward nothing more definite than the hope that they might find a place to settle and live. Few managed that. One job of the Survey was to find these people, and to establish a reliable catalog of habitable planets, so the next generation of colony ships might go out with a better chance of survival.

And we were to locate bounty, the incredible riches that literally hang in the sky. What new mineral, born in exotic heat and pressure, waited for uses to be found and a market established? Where were mountain-sized lumps of pure nickel-iron, orbiting in darkness, waiting for a factory ship to take possession? Where were the lovely green worlds waiting for people to come and live on them? What new plants, new animals, would be worth exporting?

Surely it must have been obvious to everyone there was a need to explore. Just as obviously, it was a job for the governments of humanity to take on. Obvious to everyone except the governments, that is. Governments are supposed to lead, but they have been following the people ever since our race entered space in a big way.

The first crunch came in the 2030s or so. By that time, there were a good half dozen colony planets—and a bad dozen. Nations and consortiums that certainly could not afford to do so established colonies anyway. True, the founding colonies had done great good for the nations that could afford the great capital expense. But a poor nation goes bankrupt long before its colony starts to pay any returns. The pattern was repeated many times. The nation, or the colony, or both, would collapse, and people would start to die. To the richness of space we brought war, riot, pestilence, and starvation. It happened in a dozen different ways on a dozen different worlds.

The big nations, and the healthy colonies, many of them completely independent by this time, got tired of bailing out the failures after a while. The United States, the Asian and European powers, the strong colonies—Kennedy, Britannica, Europa, New Alberta, Newer Jersey, and the others—came to the conference table. By every means possible, they coerced the little and the weak to join them—The Estonian Republic, The People's Federal Protectorate of Chad, Uruguay, colonies like New Antarctica and High Albania, the O'Neill colonies, the self-contained (and self-righteous) free-flying colonies in orbit around Earth.

Some big countries were part of the problem: China had pulled off some truly remarkable failures in space by this time. Many of the smaller nations and colonies were among the most responsible members of the conference: Sweden; Singapore, and her "daughter," the O'Neill colony High Singapore; Portugal; Finland; and New Finland were strong backers of the enterprise.

The delegates bickered. They threatened each other. They indulged in back-room deals that are still causing scandals today. But they managed to come up with a treaty.

So, on January 1, 2038, at 0000 hours GMT and Zero hours Accumulated Stellar Time (AST), the League of Planets came into being and its founding document, the Treaty of Planets, came into effect.

By 0000 hours GMT on January 2, or 24 hours AST, the League was evacuating the hapless residents of New Antarctica and treating them for frostbite.

The delegates came up with a system that works. Its basic tenet sets the right of a human being to live over the right of an idiot to run a government as if it were a family business.

When the League came into being, ground rules were

set up for the founding of colonies. Folks could still bug out and vanish if they wanted to, but fewer people did so by accident. Fewer people starved. When the Fast Plague came to Kennedy, the Interworld Health Organizations (which is one of the pieces of the League that actually predates it, somehow—like the International Court of Justice at The Hague) came in, and their aid saved us. There is no possible question on that point. That's why the Republic of Kennedy is very pro-League.

There are other good things. There are fewer tinhorn dictators taking over small colonies with still-weak governments. Trade is reliable, not for gamblers anymore.

I stood there and looked out at the gloomy night. It occurred to me that I must have been pretty naive to think that politics wasn't going to affect the Survey— not with a history like the League's.

I must have been there for nearly an hour, nursing a drink. An orderly came for me.

"Lieutenant Larson?"

"Mmmmm?"

"Excuse me, sir, but Captain Driscoll's compliments, and could you come to her office right away?"

I followed the young man along the well-known route to Driscoll's office.

The orderly led me into the office and vanished. Joslyn was there already—and so was Pete Gesseti. As I came in, Driscoll was just handing him back a sheaf of papers. He slipped them back into a folder marked REPUBLIC OF KENNEDY STATE DEPARTMENT CLASS A CLEARANCE ONLY***TOP SECRET.

I exchanged glances with Joslyn, but she just shook her head. They hadn't told her anything yet. Pete's expression was one of pure bemusement, a bad job at a poker face.

Driscoll ignored me for a moment and simply sat there, staring into space, chewing on the end of a pencil. Gillian Driscoll didn't do that sort of thing much. A good loud voice that expected to be obeyed was more her style.

She was a small, rather compactly built woman—one who punched out walls when she felt frustrated. Her face was round, and a bit plain. Her skin had a rough, windblown look to it. She kept her hair cut short to the point of severity, for the sake of convenience. She was capable of using makeup artfully, though, and had presented a pretty picture in her full dress uniform earlier in the evening. She fought a tendency to plumpness when she got stuck behind a desk for any amount of time. That wasn't one of her current problems: she led the courses in hand-to-hand combat and survival training. She was of Irish descent, more or less, and her blue eyes and red hair came with a button nose to prove it.

Now she was in standard-issue sneakers and coverall. She seemed to come to herself, and saw I was there. "Mac. Good. Sit down. We've got to do some talking here."

I sat down.

Captain Driscoll drummed her fingers on the the desk and muttered darkly to herself for a moment. Then she spoke up. "Pete, you tell it. Let me hear it again. Maybe I can think a bit."

"Right," Pete said to her, then turned to Joslyn and myself. "First off, do you know how the Survey Service got hold of the ships you are supposed to fly?"

"Donated by the British, right?" I asked.

"Not exactly. You've got ten ships designated as Survey Ships. They used to be long-duration patrol frigates, the plan being to have enough of them to be able to send one or two into a trouble spot and have the ships' firepower hold things together until the political types came in and tidied things up. Now His Majesty's government contracted for 100 such ships with Imperial Shipyards, with a clause calling for an additional ten to be built. H.M.G. thought the extension clause was *activated* by notification, Imperial thought it was *cancellable* by notification. The contractor was a dozen light years from the purchasing office. The upshot is that the Brits got ten more ships than they wanted, and the bill for same.

Turns out they didn't even need the hundred original ships. However, the International Court at The Hague ruled for Imperial, once it got that far. So the Brits had the ships with no budget for operating them, and no use for them anyway. So they leased them to the League for a pound a year. Think of it as their taking a tax loss. Now. In the five years since they got stuck, the British have lost a few ships through accident, and on top of that, they now have more real estate to cover. They decide maybe they could use ten more ships after all. The current lease expires in about 45 days—Earth days, whatever the hell that is in hours."

"To conclude the story and bring you right up to date, your friend Mr. Gesseti has just broken a number of laws, regulations, and treaties to show me a diplomatic message intercept sent from London to the British Embassy on Kennedy," Driscoll said.

"Some of the back-room boys cracked their diplomatic code a while ago," Pete said. "We pulled it off the relay satellite, picked it up, and read it before the British did—fortunately for you people," Pete explained, without a hint of shame. "London was telling the embassy to sort of turn cool on the Survey people. They're pulling their liaison officer soon, and they're thinking of taking the ships back, if politically feasible."

"The cable predates the loss of the *Venera*," Driscoll pointed out. "With the British supporting us at the League, we could weather the loss of personnel. With our establishment intact, it wouldn't be 'politically feasible' to grab the ships this close to graduating the first group."

"But, as things stand now, you're screwed," Pete said blandly.

"So what do we *do*?" Joslyn asked.

"Do. What do we do?" Driscoll pulled open a drawer, extracted a bottle and glass, and poured herself a drink. "We take our 34 surviving crew members, put them on the ten ships that are supposed to have crews of nine each, and send them out before the League bureaucracy has time to cut our head off."

"Ma'am. With all due respect, that can't work!" I said.

"Mac, you may be right. But unless the survey ships launch *now*, they never will. We have to get them out of orbit and at their proper work."

"But can't you rush the next class though? Or use the instructors?" Joslyn asked.

"The very first things I thought of. The second class—hell, those kids haven't even been *inside* one of the survey ships yet. Most of them haven't done the survival course yet, none of them are checked out on astrogation to the point where I'd trust them completely even on the Kennedy-Britannica run, let only on a trip between two poorly-charted stars. They aren't anywhere near trained. And the instructors, strangely enough, are even worse. They're all specialists. Scanlan is the best fusion-reactor and power system expert in 30 light years—but she's never even been in a pressure suit. Jamie Sheppard is turning you all into experts on your pressure suits, but he doesn't know a damn thing about piloting. No. It's you. Your class. Or we don't go."

There was silence for a moment, and then Captain Driscoll spoke again. "One more little problem: ten doesn't go into 34. Also, some of the kids aren't quite good enough for three to be a safe crew. But you two." She paused. "I'm sending out two crews of four. Three crews of three. And one crew of two. You two. You're married, so you're supposed to be compatible. Our hottest pilot and a young man who's been at the head of every class he was ever in, what they call a 'born leader.' Joslyn, you're now a First Lieutenant. Mac, you have the rank—brevet—of commander, and as soon as I sign this piece of paper, you are the skipper of League of Planets Survey Ship 41. You launch in no more than 200 hours—before the damn pols can react to the loss of the *Venera*."

Shock was scarcely the word. Me? Skipper? Launch in 200 hours? The Brits pulling the rug out from under us? I looked around the room in a daze, until my eye met Pete's.

He just grinned. "Congratulations, again."

"Peter, this was your idea," Joslyn said accusingly.

"Wrong that time, Joslyn," Driscoll said. "I worked it out myself. But let's just say his handing me that cable made my conclusions inevitable." For a moment there was a smile on her face. Then, suddenly, she seemed smaller and tireder than I had ever seen her.

"You won't even ask us to volunteer?" Joslyn asked her.

"Would you have?"

Joslyn looked to me, I to her. Her face betrayed an attempt to look only to the rational, to look carefully at what was best, whatever her feelings. I could see the decision she reached, and nodded my agreement, imperceptibly to anyone but her. "Yes," she said, simply.

Captain Driscoll rose. "Then let the record show such. Lieutenant Cooper. Commander Larson. I ask you freely to volunteer for the hazardous duty in question. Answer upon your honor." Her voice took a hard, formal tone.

Self consciously, I stood as well. "I so volunteer," I said hoarsely.

Joslyn remained seated and looked carefully at each of us. "I, too, so volunteer."

There was a long pause. I felt then, and felt for a long time afterward, that things had come too fast. Now our lives were staked to the Survey. LPSS 41 *could* be handled by two people, but it would be very close indeed. The silence held for a long time.

"Well, thank God for that," Pete declared, snapping the tension. "Now maybe you can serve *all* of us a drink, Captain."

"An excellent suggestion, Mr. Gesseti." Driscoll pulled out three more glasses and poured.

Pete took his glass and raised it. With a twinkle in his eye, he offered a toast. "To secrets. And to knowing when to have them, and knowing why to keep them."

"To secrets," the rest of us repeated, and then we all

drank. We were conspirators now; for whatever reasons, we had just agreed to hijack our own fleet.

"One more point," Pete said. "Mac, I don't want to see you piloting a nameless number through space. You have to name it."

"Her," Joslyn and Driscoll corrected in unison.

"So I do," I said. I had to think for only the briefest of moments. "My friends, I ask you to drink to the League of Planets Survey Ship *Joslyn Marie*."

"Mac!" Joslyn cried, very much taken aback. "Don't you dare!"

"Quiet there, Lieutenant," Driscoll said. "Never argue with a man when he's putting your name in lights."

And so, we drank to the newly christened ship.

Joslyn got her revenge on me, though. The people from the planet Kennedy are edgy about being called "American." Objectively, of course, if we aren't American, we're doing a damn fine imitation. Anyway, a week later I discovered that someone had christened the *Joslyn Marie*'s three auxiliary craft *Stars*, *Stripes*, and *Uncle Sam*. Worse, *Stars* had gotten a paint job consisting of huge white stars on a blue background, *Stripes* had been covered with red and white stripes, and *Uncle Sam* had both. The first time I brought the newly emblazoned *Stars* down to the surface of Columbia, it seemed to me as though a stunned silence hung over the ground crew. I ignored it as best I could and went looking for Joslyn, wondering if I could clap her in irons for artistic insubordination. It promised to be an interesting trip.

CHAPTER TWO

The next morning a "Revised Crew Lists" notice was posted. The first lines read:

LPSS 41 "Joslyn Marie"
Larson, T.M. Cmdr. (commanding)
Larson, J.M., 1st Lt.
Volunteer Crew—Billet Complete.

Driscoll had found Girogi Koenig willing to command LPSS 42, and the two empty billets needed to "complete" the crew were filled within four hours of their being posted.

The rest of the ships were listed as well, initially with no crew other than commanders. In 12 hours, LPSS 43, 44, 45, 46, and 48 were listed as Billet Complete. In 30 hours, all ten ships were so listed. As nearly as I could figure, every single person volunteered—and volunteered for the ship that Driscoll intended him or her for. Certainly, the ships with crews of four each had one of the lowest-ranking members of the surviving class aboard, with some of the higher-ups there to back them up. The three-crew ships were staffed by the middle-ranking class members. All the scuttlebutt I could pick up indicated that Driscoll hadn't coerced anyone else into volunteering. I guess she knew her command.

Survey base was soon filled with the roar of launching

auxiliary craft ferrying supplies, instruments, luggage, and incidentals up to the orbiting ships. The parts depot was stripped bare in 50 hours, until the base XO ordered all spares returned to the depot for proper distribution. While I can say that the loyal crew of the *J.M.* returned nearly everything we hadn't installed yet, I can't speak for the other ships. A few aux craft made the run to Kennedy for long-store food that didn't taste like cardboard. We all chipped in on that one.

Every comm channel was jammed with carefully censored goodbye messages to every planet in the League—and none of the messages explained why we were launching so suddenly.

Driscoll was trying to keep the loss of the *Venera* under the tightest wrap possible for as long as possible. She knew perfectly well that there would be a leak sooner or later. Regret-to-inform 'grams had already gone out to the next of kin, of course. These said nothing more than that a son or a daughter, a niece or a nephew, a grandchild, a spouse, had died in the honorable performance of his or her duties. No mention of how, or when, or where, simply a statement that, owing to circumstances beyond human control, the body could not be returned for burial.

If word leaked, and someone higher up bothered to see what was going on at Survey Training Base, you could bet the launching of the Survey Ships would have been stopped cold. For good.

There was hope, there was a reasonable chance, that the risks Driscoll was running could pay off. The Survey Ships could, in theory, be operated by one person—if everything worked perfectly—and two or three could handle the job under a great many circumstances. A crew of nine was a safety measure, a morale improver, a redundancy system. The mission rules for a crew of nine required that at least three people remain aboard and retain at least one auxiliary ship while the others were on an exploratory job. Now that rule was out the window, or else no one could ever have left the ships. So were a lot of similar regs. All was now up to the commander's discretion.

Driscoll called all the commanders to a meeting to cover such points. Her basic orders were quite simple: gather and return to base as much information as possible without risking your command. Bring the ship back in one piece. Find some nice real estate, poke around a little, learn what you can out there—*but bring that ship back*!!

The first explorations of the League of Planets Survey Service were going to be *good* publicity. That was a direct order.

The astrogation section was working around the clock, cooking up courses for us. Interstellar travel was a game of three-dimensional billiards, using the gravity field of one star to whip the ship around and accelerate it toward a new target. The trick was to get the ships not only to the right star, but with a manageable relative velocity, and more or less in the plane of the planetary system (which could be roughly determined by using the Doppler-shift measurements of the star to figure the plane of the star's rotation, which rotation was, God willing, the plane and direction the planetary system moved in). It was a tricky way to fly, but we didn't have the fuel to do it any other way.

Then came the physical checkout of the ships themselves. That was what kept me awake nights. Had I or had I not gotten a proper reading on the fuel pump pressure in the number three oxy tank? Did that overvoltage mean anything? What about the air plant? One bright point was that we ended up spending most nights on the *J.M.*, which meant working and sleeping in zerogee. That helped a lot.

The ship was soon in fine fettle, but would it stay that way until we got back? The astrogation team had given us a course that would have the *J.M.* light years from the nearest shipyard for the next 13,000 hours—about a year and a half, Earthside. Joz and I checked out every primary, secondary, and tertiary backup system every step of the way, then put the diagnostic computer programs through their paces just as thoroughly. *Then* we used the diagnostics to check all our handiwork. Slowly, we squeezed the bugs out.

By the time Joslyn closed down the last access panel and wiped the grease off her nose with an even greasier hand, we had a taut ship. We were proud of her. "Mac," Joslyn said, "I think I can forgive your naming this old girl after me. She is a love."

"I agree. But I'm sure you're a lot more fun on a date." I was mighty happy with both Joslyn Maries. The one with the nice smile cuddled into my arms and gave me a happy kiss, then settled herself over my lap (it would have been into my lap, but we were in zero-gee at the time. Nice thing about zero-gee: laps don't get tired). I stretched out on my command couch and peeked around Joslyn to see a green board. The ship behind that board was a beaut.

The *J.M.* was about 90 meters from stem to stern. At the stern were the three great fusion rocket engines and the support gear for them. Directly forward of the engines was a central core hydrogen tank surrounded by six strap-on fuel tanks. The strap-ons were not to be jettisoned; the *J.M.* could sidle up to a space-going hunk of ice—a comet or whatever—and tank up by extracting hydrogen from it. Above the tankage section was an exercise deck. Like the rest of the ship, it was a cylinder, 15 meters in diameter. Its hatchways were set in its centerline, about which it spun to provide a simulated gravity to exercise in. Above this were two decks of staterooms—plumbing, a galley, a library nook, an entertainment screen, and so forth. The topmost deck was the command center, where Joz and I were now. Here were control centers for the planned nine crew members, most of them redundant in one way or another to the primary command chair, where I sat. Joz was to have the pilot's hotseat when we were maneuvering.

Above our heads were the main docking and extra-vehicular-activity airlock sections. Docked nose-to-nose with the *Joslyn Marie,* and thus flying stern-first when docked to the main ship, was the large, blunt-cone shape of the large ballistic lander, *Uncle Sam.* Access tunnels led from here back down the length of the ship to the docking ports of *Stars* and *Stripes,* which sat atop the number one and number four outboard fuel tanks. Unlike *Uncle Sam,* they rode the *J.M.* right side up, sitting, inside additional bracing, on their own landing gear.

The *J.M., Uncle Sam, Stars,* and *Stripes* were all armed with torpedo tubes and powerful laser cannon. We carried sensitive telescopes, radio gear, and detection devices of all sorts. There were dozens of internal and external inspection cameras all over the ship, wired into the command center video screens. Pressure suits, maneuvering units, a washer and drier, climbing ropes, a biological lab, workshop space, what seemed like an extra ship in spare parts, and a great deal more were tucked inside the hull here and there.

She was a good ship.

We sat there, admiring her, for a long time. For me, at least, that was the moment she stopped being a piece of metal for holding the vacuum out, and became my home. And now she was ready to fly.

Driscoll called us into her office for a brief set of final words before we launched. She was tired, very tired, and certainly more frightened than we were. She welcomed us to her office, sat us down, and politely offered us a drink, which we politely refused. She didn't seem to know where to begin for a long time. She hemmed and hawed about little things, the details of what would come next, all the time toying with the pencils and papers on her desk.

Finally, she plunged in. "Damn it. Do you kids know how much I love you?" she asked. "I hope not. They told me at command school that you're not supposed to know. Of course, they also told me that I'm not supposed to love you, either. I'm so proud of you. You've truly taken on the world, the galaxy. And you're going to go out there and break your back trying to wrestle with the unknown. You might die out there, struggling and fighting with the cold and the heat and the vacuum and the loneliness, and yet die well, with your spirit and your heart intact, without fully knowing what it is you are dying for. You can't possibly know. You're too young, too brave, too sure."

She paused, and sighed deeply. She threw back her head and stared at the ceiling for a time before she continued.

"The best clue to what it is all about that I can give you is this: only if you *do* die with your spirit and your heart intact will you have died well—and dying well simply means that you have *lived* well. But I don't truly believe you will die—you are both survivors. If there comes a time when you feel you can't go on, remember that; you are survivors, and use that fact to find the tiny shred of endurance, of courage, of strength you forgot you still had." She paused, and smiled, and we saw that her eyes were shining. "And that's all I have left to tell you." She led us to the door, embraced us both for a moment, and then we took out leave.

A few hours later we were at our command chairs, and a powerful tug was thundering along behind us, providing us the velocity we'd need for our first jump without having to touch the fuel in the *J.M.* tanks. This freed up our fuel for later use and thereby increased our range.

Faster-than-light drive moves a ship at the square of the speed of light. It's usually referred to as C^2, pronounced "cee-squared." C^2 gets you from the solar system to Proxima Centuri in about 105 seconds. That is, it would if anyone had any reason to go to Proxima Centuri. Of course, one has to use the C^2 drive well outside the gravity well of a solar system, or end up far, far, far away from the intended destination.

There are other catches, as well. The jump between "normal" space and C^2 takes a big jolt of power. If, God forbid, anything went wrong with your power supply and you got stuck in C^2, well, the edge of the universe is over that way, and no one knows exactly what happens once you get there. Certainly, ships have been lost that way. Less catastrophic, but still very dangerous, is inaccurate astrogation. An error of .09 seconds in coming out of C^2 would put you roughly as far from your target as Saturn is from the Sun.

Navigation computers are good enough these days that pilots can feel safe with about a half-billion-kilometer miss-factor. The *J.M.* would shoot for about three times that, as we were headed into territory not as well charted as that on the regular space lines. Also, if we came out over the pole of the target star, as we hoped to do, we would have the best vantage point for us to look for planets.

Most star systems (including Earth's) have the plane of rotation of their planets in the same plane as the equator of the star in question. So, if you looked at, say, the Solar System from the plane of the Sun's equator, the planets, asteroids, and what have you would be moving in orbits that would be seen edge-on from where you stood. If you watched the Earth for a year—that is, one orbit—it would simply appear to move in a straight line from one side of the sun to the other, and then back again, moving once in front of the Sun's disk, and once behind it. From a point far enough away to observe the entire orbit, the change in size of the Earth's disk as it moves toward and away from you, inscribing a circle seen edge-on, would be difficult to measure accurately. Seen from the north or south polar regions, however, the orbits of the planets would be laid out before the observer face-on and so would be easy to observe. This in turn makes it easy to measure motions of planets and other bodies and put together reasonably accurate charts and ephemera of their orbits.

What all this boils down to is that it is best to come in over a star system and look down on it, rather than come in at the side and see it edge-on.

Fine. It has been found that planets usually rotate in

the plane of a star's equator. So how do we determine where the equator is? One star seen from another is a featureless dot of light.

The standard technique is to use the Doppler effect. Light of a given frequency has a higher *apparent* frequency when it is moving toward you, and a lower apparent frequency when it is moving away from you. The light doesn't change, the way you perceive it does. Obviously, one side of a rotating object will be moving toward you and the other side will be moving away. The difference is measurable over stellar distances. Very careful measurements can usually yield the plane of rotation, and thus the equator and poles, within about ten degrees or so.

Ten degrees is a lot. Stack on top of that the fact that the actual distance to a target star is rarely known to any degree of accuracy, and you'll see that there is a certain degree of luck in Survey work. Get bad data, use it to put your ship in the wrong plane, and you'll have to waste fuel getting the ship to where it was supposed to be. Waste too much fuel and you come back early, or not at all. It is possible to "mine" hydrogen fuel from an ice moon, but finding suitable ice is rare, and the process is a long and tedious one.

You come out of C^2 with precisely the heading and velocity you start out with. The stars orbit the center of the galaxy, just as planets move about a star. Thus, they move relative to each other. A typical velocity difference would be on the order of about 70 kilometers a second. A ship travelling from one star to the other would have to match that velocity shift.

The tug was boosting us up to our required velocity, so that we could match speeds with the star we were shooting for first. Once there, we would make any adjustments needed to our speed and heading, and begin the search for planets.

We cast off from the tug and were on our way. Five minutes later the *J.M.*'s computers decided were in the right place at the right time and booted us into C^2, and we were off into untravelled regions.

For 4,000 hours or so, say six months, the *J.M.* did her job. We visited a half dozen star systems, each magnificently different from the others, each a sore temptation to stay and explore and wonder at for a lifetime, at least. The only thing that kept us from staying was the promise of fresh wonders in another part of the sky.

Not only a universe of wonders, but the woman I loved to share them with me. Those were the days of my greatest happiness. Each day I woke to challenging, satisfying work that was not only fun but useful, vital. Each day was spent with someone I not only loved, but liked. Each day was a new adventure.

Each day, every day, was *fun*.

Imagine yourself standing on a tiny worldlet of tremendous mineral wealth left there by some quirk of the way worlds are born. Imagine staring up at the sky at a world ten times the size of Jupiter, knowing that the violent storms you see in its roiling sea of clouds are the birthpangs of a star, its thermonuclear furnaces just flickering into life. Joslyn and I stood in such a place, and knew others would follow, rushing to extract the treasure beneath our feet before the fireball came to full life and expanded out into space, leaving nothing but cinders where we stood. The end for that world will come in a human lifetime, or perhaps twice that.

Imagine two worlds the size of Earth's moon that revolve around each other, separated from each other by less than 3,000 kilometers. Tidal forces have spawned endless earthquakes and utterly shattered the surfaces of the twin worlds. We named them Romulus and Remus. One day they will smash into each other and leave only rocks careering through the void.

Imagine a world where the air is fresh and sweet, and life very like that on Earth fills the seas and skies and land. There I found—something. I say it is a piece of worked metal. Joslyn thinks it is a chance piece of nature's work, a glob of alloy spat out of a volcano and shaped by the caprice of water and weather. Humanity will settle there soon, and I hope some child born there will dig one place, dig another, and one day prove that ours are not the only minds to have touched that place.

Joslyn and I lived to wander the sky and do as we pleased. It was the happiest time of our life together.

And then they found us.

We were in the vicinity of our sixth target when they did. We had been there for about ten days. We were just about finished with the location-and-orbit survey search for major planets, and were ready to start down from our perch far above the star's north pole to take a close-up look at some of the better real estate we had spotted.

We were in bed, asleep, when the alarm sounded. It was the general-alert buzzer, which meant the emergency was rare enough that it didn't rate its own alarm code.

Joslyn and I scrambled out of bed, bounced off a few bulkheads, and made our way to the command deck. I fumbled a hand to a switch and killed the alert buzzer.

Joslyn, who usually wakes up faster than I do, got the computer to decode the alert before I was even in my flight chair. "It's a courier drone!" she said.

"*What?*"

"You heard me."

"Yeah, but it doesn't make any sense." Courier drones were *expensive*, and the odds of one finding us all the way out here were remote, at best.

"Tell the drone that. Get on your board and pull a printout of the drone ops manual, will you?" Joslyn was studying her screen, trying to squeeze more information out of the words on it.

I typed in a few commands and a book-length manual buzzed its way into the line printer's hopper. I instructed the computer to convert the courier's beacon signal into something we could use.

"So when is it going to transmit its message to us?" Joslyn asked.

I looked at my screen and whistled. "Never. Don't ask me why, but there's a security block on all the information aboard except the beacon."

"Can we get it to home in on us?" Joslyn was thinking like a pilot—if the drone did the maneuvering, that would save on our fuel.

"The decode of the beacon signal shows tanks nearly dry."

"Oh, wacko. It can't get to us?"

"Not unless you want our grandkids to pick it up. That 'nearly' dry is close to being 'completely'."

"They shouldn't be, with a direct boost from base."

"I'll bet you who fixes dinner it isn't a direct boost. I think it tried our last survey system first, then headed here."

"Mac! Do you have any idea how difficult it would be to program a drone to do that? The search gear it would need? The instruments? The power? It would have to be *huge*."

"I know, I know, I know. That's why this is a manned ship we're flying. But we left the last system a week ahead of schedule. We're still supposed to be there. And the heading that thing's on is almost exactly the heading *we* used to come from there—and about 120 degrees away from where it would be on a direct boost from Columbia."

"Bloody. You're right. The velocity is all wrong for Columbia, too."

I stared at the screen full of numbers. "Get some rendezvous data. Give us a set of three trajectories—reasonable economy, mid-range, and minimum time. I'll make coffee."

"We'll need it," Joslyn said, and started plotting courses.

Fifteen minutes later she had some rough figures to show me. "One percent of our fuel gets us there in a month. Five percent gets us there in five and a half days." She paused.

"And what's the minimum trajectory?"

She bit her lip. "Thirty-six hours. Fifteen percent of our remaining fuel."

"Is that assuming we fly the *Joslyn Marie*?"

"Oh, goodness no! All of these are assuming we fly *Stars*. She seems to fly a trifle more efficiently than *Stripes*."

"Fifteen percent . . . damn. Okay, feed the minimum time course to *Stars'* computer. I'll start a systems check on her." I started for the airlock level.

"Mac!" Joslyn called. "We—we can't lose that much fuel! We do that and we might as well pack up the rest of the mission!"

I sighed. "Joz—I know you're the pilot. You're in charge of flying the ship without wasting fuel and keeping our options open. Driscoll put me in command, so I have to be in charge of choosing which options we take. Now, whyever base sent that drone after us, they judged it more important than our mission, or else they wouldn't have sent it."

"But what could they have to say that would be important enough to send a drone after the ship?"

"I don't know. But if it's so important that it was worth tracking us across two star systems, it's certainly urgent. The party's over, Joz. The real world just caught up." I went below to start on powering up the lander.

What *could* be imporant enough? I simply couldn't think of a single possibility. I did a rough guess in my head on what the drone would cost, juggling the figures as I worked. The answer was impressive. For a robot ship smart enough to scan one system, search it, and then reject it, plus the computers to hack a course to another system, plus the engines, the fusion plant, the C^2 plant, the communications gear—probably more than the *Joslyn Marie*, since it would be a custom job, not mass-produced like the *J.M.*

Getting the *J.M.* for this job was a miracle. What was big enough to *spend* that kind of money?

Three hours later we cast off from the *Joslyn Marie*,

leaving her powered down to wait for our return. *Stars* was a trim little ship, and Joslyn even let me do the flying, for once. I lined us up with the gyros to save fuel on the attitude jets, just to keep on Joslyn's good side.

The course was a hair-raising one. We had to blip into C^2 for a few milliseconds, pop out and change our heading, then into C^2 again. All this to avoid falling into the local sun, which was dangerously close to what would be a direct course to the drone. Then a long cruise while we gunned out fusion engine in earnest and lined up for the final jump to the drone's position and velocity.

It was a dull 36 hours, besides the few minutes required now and again to monitor the ship and guide the computer through the course. It was not made any more pleasant by the fact that Joslyn was mad at me. While she understood the need to get to the drone fast, she didn't have to like it, and she couldn't yell at the base personnel who had sent it out after us.

Well, she didn't exactly yell at me, either, but the effect was the same: what she did was barely speak to me at all. I was left without much to do besides trying to figure out what the drone was. And I still didn't get anywhere with that.

By the time we were within visual range of the drone, I was more than glad of the change of pace—to say nothing of going out of my mind with curiosity.

Stars didn't have all the fancy optical gadgets we had on board the *J.M.*, but she carried a pretty fair long-range camera. As soon as there was the slightest hope of picking up the drone with it, I brought it to bear. And got one of the great shocks of my life. Drones are usually about the size of a torpedo—maybe five meters long, and most of that fuel tanks. This thing was the size of the *Joslyn Marie*. Most of it fuel tanks. The only cargo seemed to be in a blister on the apex of the drone. Huge arrows, painted on the hull, pointed to it.

"It must have five times the fuel capacity of the *J.M.*," Joslyn said, her voice betraying as much shock as I felt. Surprise had evaporated all her annoyance with me.

"If they burned all that fuel getting here, they must have tracked us through *three* star systems. . . ."

"If not more. And at high acceleration, too. See all the structural bracing?"

"Yes. The aft end is pointed along the direction of flight, too. It must have burned its last fuel slowing to a velocity we could match. One thing on the bright side—if the drone has scavenger pumps, we could take the last of its fuel for *Stars'* tanks."

"Even if that monster's tanks are down to one percent, that'd be enough to top us off. Here's hoping, Mac, what could it *be*?"

"We'll know soon."

We approached the giant ship slowly. As we closed to within a hundred meters or so, Joslyn pointed to one side of the screen. "There! A fuel hose waiting for us. They did think to set up a scavenger."

"Good. Maybe we'll have some fuel when this is over. Whatever it is."

I switched on our fueling system and forgot about it. It was an automatic that was supposed to call to a fuel system at a commercial port and request fueling. The port's robots were supposed to come and tend to the ship without bothering the crew. The home office had been kind enough to arrange that kind of service out here.

We came in over the docking port and swung our topside around to meet it, so that the two ships came together nose to nose. I made the docking run on the first pass and activated the capture latches to hold us solidly to the other ship.

We got out of our crash couches and climbed over each other getting to the nose airlock door, both of us burning with curiosity. I cracked open a bleeder valve to match our ship's air pressure with the drone's cabin pressure. There was a brief *wooshing* of air, and I swallowed to make my eardrums pop. At a nod from me, Joslyn undogged *Stars'* hatch, and then opened the drone's hatchway, a meter or so beyond it.

The drone's hatch swung open, revealing the interior. Since the ships were docked nose to nose, we were looking straight down from the top of the drone's cabin. The only thing in it was a great black cylinder, exactly the size to fit through the airlock passage. It was pointed right for the hatchway joining the ships; all it needed was a good push from below to send it through the lock into *Stars*.

We kicked off from the hatchway and drifted into the drone's cabin, staring at the cylinder. It was big, and its base was heavily braced against acceleration.

Joslyn hung in midair, fascinated. "My God, it's like a totem pole ready for—"

But a giant, booming voice suddenly shouted out from a speaker by the overhead hatch. "THIS IS A WAR EMERGENCY SITUATION," it roared. "TRANSFER THE CYLINDER TO YOUR SHIP WITH ALL POSSIBLE SPEED. DO NOT DELAY FOR ANY REASON. THE MOMENT AUTOMATIC REFUELING IS COMPLETED, CAST OFF AND RETURN TO THE *JOSLYN MARIE* AT MAXIMUM SPEED. DELAY FOR NOTHING. YOU MAY EXAMINE THE CYLINDER EN ROUTE. HURRY. HURRY. THIS IS A WAR EMERGENCY SITUATION. THAT IS ALL."

I clapped my hands over my ears and heard the great voice that way. The moment it was over, Joslyn and I looked at each other in something close to shock, and instantly got to work on the cylinder. That wasn't the sort of voice you argued with.

There was a very simple, straightforward quick-release device holding the cylinder to its bracing, and a diagram painted on it in bright red paint, showing how to use it. I pulled at one lever, Joslyn at the other, and the cylinder popped off its moorings with a deep *sprung*. A spring-loaded pusher had been cocked underneath it, and gave it a gentle shove toward the overhead hatch, moving it at about half a meter a second. I kicked over to one side of the cabin, scrambled up a set of handholds, and beat the cylinder through the hatch by only a few seconds. I cleared the hatchway and got to one side. As the cylinder came through *Stars'* hatch, the forward end of the great black shape sprouted a set of legs, a tripod, that swung into place and locked, forming a solid support for the thing. The legs touched *Stars'* inner hull and I heard a *thunk, thunk, thunk*—electromagnets coming on to further brace our new cargo.

Joslyn came into *Stars'* forward cabin right behind the cylinder, squeezing past it as she sealed the hatches. The cylinder was a good eight meters long: it took up the entire height of the cabin, with just room to get around it to go out the nose hatch. Someone had done very careful planning—apparently down to figuring out which ship type we'd use.

Just as Joslyn dogged the inside hatch, a speaker hooked into the cylinder came on, cued by radio from the drone. It wasn't quite as loud, but that voice still had authority. "REFUELING IS COMPLETED. CAST OFF. GET UNDER WAY. GET UNDER WAY. THAT IS ALL."

But Joslyn was already at the command seat, working the joystick. She snapped *Stars* through a tight head-over-tail loop and gunned the engine, bathing the drone's cabin in fusion flame, vaporizing part of it. The robot ship was a derelict now, and she wasn't going to waste time being careful of it.

I held on as best I could through the loop, and made it to my own couch as she started the main engine and we set out home. I looked at the base of the cylinder that sat in the centerline of our lander.

What had we gotten ourselves into? War emergency situation?

What war?

Ours, as it turned out.

Joslyn got us under way as quickly as possible, and we did the post-maneuver checkouts in record time. Twenty minutes after casting off from the giant drone ship, we started to take a good look at the cylinder.

The first thing I realized was that it was not quite as awesome an object as I had first thought. Underneath an outer sheath, much of its bulk was padding and bracing against acceleration. We set to work taking it apart.

Inside the packing material were a few odd-looking pieces of equipment and a set of very standard magnetic recording disks, each marked with a large red numeral. Joslyn pulled the one marked "1" out of its jacket and set it into *Stars'* playback unit.

"Mac—I'm almost afraid to play this thing."

"It's to late to chicken out, Joz—run it."

She pressed the play button. The main screen came to life, first displaying the flag of the League of Planets, and then dissolving to Pete Gesseti's face. Pete? What was he doing in a communication from base? Why not Driscoll? I looked hard at his image on the screen. He was tired, his clothes looked slept in. For the first time in my life, I looked at Pete and thought of him as . . . old. Something more than six months' time had aged him.

But it was his eyes that drew me. They spoke of anger, determination, and some odd hint of faith.

Pete began to speak. "Mac, Joslyn. Hello. They asked me to do this because you both know me. Maybe it'll sound a little better from me, though it can't sound very good.

"We—the League, all the members, everybody, are at war. Not with each other. With someone from outside. Human, descended from Earth, speaking English. A heavy military force has attacked . . . no, they haven't attacked. They've *conquered* the planet of New Finland.

"The Treaty of Planets requires that the members of the League come to the aid of New Finland. Period. No ifs, and, or buts. The other members of the League have an absolutely binding legal and moral duty to come to the assistance of our sworn allies. We have to help them. And we want to. We need to.

"Maybe this isn't official policy, but it's fact: if the

League doesn't fulfill its commitment, it will fall apart. At best, it will become a useless debating club. No one could rely on it. It isn't healthy now. Worse since you've been gone. There are too many bad little signs—infighting, petty squabbles, minor, pointless defiances of the League. Ugly, mean, little things.

"The League has *got* to hold together, because we don't have anything else. If it goes down, it'll go down the way the League of Nations went down. Straight down into war.

"None of that is pretty, but you need to know how much is riding on this. How much is riding on you."

Pete, or rather the recording of Pete, paused and frowned. He sighed. "It's this way. The New Finns are settlers from a group of people who were leaned on a lot by a big, dangerous neighbor—the old Soviet Union. So they settled far out from everyone else, where no one would be near enough to bother them. They are right at the limits of the physical area of space humanity is known to have colonized.

"The only thing we knew for a while was that we had lost contact with the New Finns. Then a small message drone popped into normal space in the New Britannica system. In it was a message from a group of New Finns who lived on the planet's large artificial satellite, Vapaus.

"They reported that the invaders called themselves 'Guardians,' and that these Guardians were in the process of setting up an anti-ship missile system around the New Finnish system. The Guardians had developed a rather simply gadget which detected the very specific burst of ultraviolet and X-ray radiation a ship coming in from C^2 gives off, and hooked it up to a missile with a C^2 generator of its own.

"The effect is that if a ship appears inside the Guardian-held New Finnish system, it will be detected, and destroyed within seconds of being so detected.

"There are already a number of civilian ships missing that were due to call on New Finland. We assume the missile system got them.

"The one ray of hope from the New Finns' message was that the missile array was not completely deployed. At the cost of the lives of several of their men, they came up with the deployment schedule for the missiles.

"If a ship enters the N.F. system from a certain direction by a certain time—670,716 hours Stellar Time, or noon GMT on July 8, 2115, Earthside, it should be able to enter the N.F. system without being destroyed."

Pete swallowed hard. "The only ship, the only people we've got with the slightest hope of getting there on time—well, the ship is the League of Planets Survey Ship 41, *Joslyn Marie*. Your ship is fast. New Finland happens to be out the way of your survey. You're it.

"You have got to go in there."

Pete suddenly looked, not worried or afraid, but embarrassed. "Okay, that's *that* part of it. What you've got to do once you're there is *really* crazy.

"Bell Labs, on the mining satellite Lucifer. They came up with something about the time the *Joslyn Marie* was launched.

"A matter transmitter."

"Oh, boy," I said. A *matter* transmitter?

"They say—well, they say it works on the same principle as the C^2 generator, except with the force, or the field, or the power, or something, rotated through 90 degrees. I'm a paper pusher; I don't understand it. Now this next is the nutty part."

He paused. "They have a lot of faith in it. In the same package where you found this recording, is the receiver, or at least the core of it, for the matter transmitter. You're supposed to get to the planet's surface with it, assemble the receiver on a precisely predetermined spot— and they'll transmit 5,000 troops to you from a light-month away."

"Good Lord!" Joslyn cried, drowning out Pete for a moment.

" . . . means they'll have to transmit the troops, or the signal carrying the troops, a standard month—30 Earth days, 720 hours—*before* you receive it. Which boils down to mean the troops will be transmitted to you before you could possibly build the device to receive them."

"Joslyn," I said, "this is insane. How could it work?"

"Mac, I don't. . . ." Joslyn trailed off to listen to Pete.

"There are more recordings that give you the technical grounding for all this. Some other gadgetry. Learning sets for the Finnish language." Pete's image fumbled with some papers.

"Mac, Joslyn. I dunno. It seems crazy from this end— but not as crazy as it must seem to you. We are very frightened. These Guardians simply took New Finland. Maybe they could just take us. The message from the Finns say that's the way they're talking. We have to stop them. The guys in the lab came up with the transmitter, and the brass came up with this plan. We're going to put it all in the fastest drone ever made—actually the fastest ship ever made. We're going to try and find you in three different star systems. The drone will launch and cruise at accelerations that would kill a man in minutes.

"There isn't any way for you to send a message saying 'Yes, we got the drone's signal and the cargo and we'll do it.' There isn't enough time. So they'll send the troops no matter what, just hoping you've picked up the ball.

"In other words, if you do it, 5,000 men are taking a tremendous risk. If you don't, and the signal isn't received, they're dead.

"It is all on you. You are the only chance those troops have to live, and maybe the only chance the Finns have to regain their liberty." He paused and lowered his voice. *"And I have a very strong, gut feeling that this has something to do with what I said after the third drink at the funeral."*

My stomach did a flip-flop. The Guardians? They hijacked the *Venera*?

"I have no logical reason, no evidence. But I have a very strong hunch I'm right. If I am, and it is true, our friends won't be on New Finland. They, and others caught the same way, will be back in the Guardians' system, forced to fill in for those who went to war on New Finland. I warned the people who asked me to do this I'd have some cryptic ways of convincing you." There was a bare, brief hint of a smile on his face for a moment.

"Listen, you two. There's a very old poem, from long ago and far away. It's the last way I have to ask you to do this thing, to fight this war for us. Part of it said:

" 'Take up our quarrel with the foe.
　To you, from failing hands we throw
　The torch, be yours to hold it high.
　If ye break faith we those who die,
　We shall not sleep. . . .'

"The torch be yours," Pete repeated. His voice came close to cracking. I was as close as he had to a son, and he was called upon to send me out to war—to die, perhaps. No, the odds were too bad. To die, probably.

"Gesseti out."

And we were on our own.

CHAPTER THREE

The spanner nearly jumped out of my hands again, but this time I kept it under control at the cost of a set of rescraped knuckles.

"Damn!" I yelled, sucking at the reopened cuts. "This is not my idea of a good time."

We were working on one of the torpedoes in the airlock and workshop deck of the *J.M.* Two things made it tougher. The first was that most of the handtools aboard the *J.M.* were intended for use in zero-gee. This meant a tool had to exert equal pressure in two perfectly opposite directions. Otherwise, work would have been impossible. A normal hammer is a good example of why special tools are needed. Hit something with a hammer in a reasonable gravity field and you'll stay in place, pasted down by your own weight. Do the same thing in zero-gee and you'll go flying. Without gravity to hold you, the force of your swing not only will drive a nail down, but you up: an equal and opposite reaction.

So zero-gee tools have counteraction balance weights, counter-rotating collars driven by gears, and so on. The power tools especially look like the results of drunken binges at an inventors' convention.

The second flaw was that the *J.M.* was boosting at two gees toward the calculated transition point for the jump to the New Finnish system. A zero-gee spanner is more a weapon for use against one's self than a tool in two gees.

There was a third flaw, of course, We were boosting toward the New Finnish system—and neither of us wanted to go.

"Mac, easy with that thing! You've got it tight now, don't strip the bolt."

"Sorry."

"Let's take a break. We're ahead of schedule anyway."

"Sounds good." I tossed the spanner aside and it clattered to the deck with a satisfactorily loud noise. Without further discussion, I followed Joz down to the wardroom for a cup of tea. She puttered about with the makings while I sat and brooded.

"I cannot believe this," I suddenly announced.

"What?" Joslyn asked, her mind more on the tea than me.

"The mission. The whole harebrained thing. And the way we got into it."

"The way we got into it. You're right. That's the worst part of it," Joslyn said as she brought the kettle to the table and sat down. There were advantages to constant boost: you had homey things like kettles instead of squeeze bulbs. "If I had a chance to do it," she continued as she poured, "I honestly believe I would have volunteered to help the good people of New Finland. I truly do. But I feel so *compelled* by the way it happened, as if I were a piece on a chessboard that had no choice but to go where it was sent."

"I don't think Pete liked doing it that way, but I don't see what choices he had, either. No one did, since the Finns were attacked. Once that happened we were the only thing the League had. Good old Pete," I said ruefully.

"He certainly pushed every one of your buttons, from the debt you feel to him as your substitute father, to duty. . . ."

". . . To the chance that we *might* get a lead on our missing classmates." That was the first time I had called those lost on the *Venera* "missing," not "dead." I realized I was convinced they were alive.

"Don't forget the fate of the League is in our hands," Joslyn said, with just a hint of a smile.

"I haven't, but I'll keep trying." I sipped at my tea and we sat quietly for a minute. "What gets me is there's nothing to stop us from saying the hell with it and pointing the *J.M.* away from the trouble. If we turned and ran, or just destroyed the drone and showed up a year or two from now and claimed we had never found it—if we chickened out, no one could do anything about it.

"Against that, the only thing making us go in and risk our lives for strangers is the feeling that we have to do it." I paused. "And it's enough, I guess. Thanks to the sense of duty they've bred and beaten into us. And I know what you mean about having no choice."

"And now that it's all out of your system, let's go finish the go-cart," Joslyn said, rumpling my hair.

The "go-cart" was what was left of the torpedo we had started with. Joslyn and I had pulled down the entire nose section. I had been working on installing a crash-couch onto the front end of the torp's motor housing while Joslyn pulled the guidance system out of the nose section and hooked it back up to the decapitated torpedo. She left off the frills: it would pick up a downloaded trajectory from *Stripes*'s guidance system and run with those numbers: that was it. The control panel was one button marked "ON."

The crash-couch looked more like a lawn chair, and folded up like one, but it was extremely strong. The *J.M.* carried about ten of them, in case she ever had to carry passengers.

The go-cart was the key to our grand plan for getting an agent (me) down to talk with the locals and arrange for the little matter of the transmission of 5,000 combat troops.

Along with Pete's message to us had come other recordings, full of such information as our side had.

Most importantly, the League had some information on the enemy. When the alert came in from the New Finns, every intelligence outfit in the League had gone to work, digging into old files, cross-checking, trying to figure out the Guardians. It didn't take long to find out who they were—or at least who they had started out being.

About 110 years ago, at the turn of the 21st century, a collection of fascist and right-wing groups in Britain and the United States combined their forces and called themselves the Atlantic Freedom Front, or just the Front—apparently deriving the name from something in 20th-century England called the National Front. They staged demonstrations and caused a riot or two, and during the slump at the beginning of the 21st century, began to get some attention. They were willing to sign up just about anybody—people like the Ku Klux Klan, The New John Birchers, the remnants of Afrikaaners in Exile. They got to the point where they thought they were a lot bigger than they really were.

On March 15, 2015, they attempted to overthrow the British and American governments. Never, at any moment, was either government in the slightest danger—the Front did not number more than a few thousand members on either side of the Atlantic. What was supposed to be a brilliant double coup ended up as little more than a pair of bloody scuffles in Washington and London. Their street thugs were called Guardians of the Front, and they managed to kill a few police and soldiers, and a few innocent bystanders. Mostly, the Guardians just got themselves killed. The leaders, and such of the others as could be caught and convicted, were thrown in jail. That was the end of the story, or should have been.

Colonization laws were pretty loose back then—and I guess they still are. Pretty much anyone who could hire a ship and get the needed gear together was allowed to launch and go pick a planet.

The Guardians, or what was left of them, set out to do just that. Not secretly, either—the intelligence kit we got included reproductions of old ads calling for volunteers to start "a New Order in the Skies." They were ready to launch their ship—the *Oswald Mosley*—by June 2018.

To no one's great surprise, the Guardians tried to bust their leaders out of jail before leaving Earth. The authorities had been expecting an attempt, but not such a well-organized or well-executed one: the Guardians had been learning. Simultaneous raids on prisons in England and the United States got the chief hoods out and left a lot of good men dead.

Two hours after the raids, the Guardians and their head men were launching ballistic shuttle craft toward the *Mosley*, and an hour later, the *Mosley* boosted from orbit, soon entered C^2, and was never heard from again. No one was sad to see them go.

The planet the Guardians had claimed to be headed for was searched some time later. No sign of past or present human habitation was found. The *Mosley* was listed as missing and presumed lost with all hands, and good riddance. Last of the Guardians.

Until New Finland. Unquestionably the same people. They called themselves Guardians. The insignia matched, and so did the brutality.

Against them, the League had provided us with only a sketch of a plan: get the receiver down to the planet's surface at the right place and switch it on at the right time.

The League did provide sets of maps, and diagrams of the New Finnish system, drawn up at the time the planet was settled. There didn't seem to be much current information.

There also were language-lab gadgets and a complete set of tapes and recordings on Finnish.

No program of hypnotic teaching, sleep teaching, audiovisual gimcrackery, or anything else is going to change the fact that learning languages is tough for some people, and I am one of them. I came very close to rebelling against sentences like "The cat is on the roof of my grey-haired maternal grandmother's house of flats." That once came out "Grandmother's mother is on the roof with the grey cat on her head."

But Joslyn is one of those people who pick up languages the way my dress uniform picks up lint. She would be. In any event, she was there to see me through it all and help me get great-grandma and the cat off the roof.

Joslyn tried to use my language problem to say she should be the one to contact the New Finns. But that was clearly impossible. The reports the League had passed along were very definite on the point that the Guardians were barely allowing the Finnish women out of the house. No women were allowed in positions of even minor authority. The only Guardians any Finns had seen were men, though there were rumors of a "comfort corps." Whoever went down there would have to play spy, pretend to be one thing or another at one time or another. That would be merely tough for a man, but it would be impossible for a woman. I had to go.

Alone. Up to that moment, alone had meant alone together for us. Now I might die, or Joslyn might, and the other would be truly alone, surrounded by nothing but people, or perhaps marooned in space.

That was the thing we worked hardest at not thinking about.

We came to the transition point and skittered through the skies for a long minute or so of C^2 flight, the longest jump either of us had ever taken. C^2 doesn't feel any different than normal space, since what the C^2 generator does is drag a bubble of normal space, big enough to contain the ship, into C^2 conditions. The only disconcerting thing was that the outside cameras didn't work. A camera looking at the ship showed it normally, but any lens or port pointed outward showed . . . nothing. At least that was the theory. It didn't look like nothing. Empty space, *that's* nothing. What you saw in C^2 wasn't that. It had no color, no detail, no substance, no evidence of any energies human instruments could pick up. But it wasn't nothing. I feel sure of that, but I couldn't say why. How could eyes evolved to see light make anything of what theory said C^2 required—light that, well, moved faster than light, so to speak.

That doesn't make any sense, which is another attribute of C^2.

But then we popped back into normal space in the outer reaches of the New Finnish system. Working as fast as she could, it took Joslyn half an hour to check our position. That slice of time I spent watching every passive detector we had. If the New Finns were wrong, and they had gotten the anti-ship missiles deployed out this way, we were already dead. The missiles supposedly came in so fast there wasn't any point in trying the laser without radar, and we couldn't use radar without being spotted ourselves. Even so, I had the laser primed and ready to go.

But the hours passed, and we were still in one piece long past the time it would have taken a missile to find us if there were one looking. We were inside and, for the moment, safe.

Joslyn finally spotted enough of the system's planets to triangulate our position. We were on course: we were going to fall straight into the sun. We'd brake our fall and roll out into a safe orbit first, of course, but keeping the sun between us and New Finland was the most obvious way to avoid being spotted: a sun makes a pretty fair shield. The easiest maneuver to keep us hidden was a direct fall. By the time we had to fire our main engines, we'd be completely screened by the sun.

Joslyn intended to put us in a solar orbit exactly opposite New Finland's, moving at exactly the same velocity, so that we'd remain hidden by the sun, always 180 degrees away from the planet, but in the same orbit.

But we had about a week of falling into the sun before we needed to maneuver. That time was private. I won't speak of it, except to say that we were as happy as we could have been, with things the way they were.

At last, it was nearly time for Joslyn to drop the *J.M.* into the proper orbit. We had to get me ready to jump ship before that. I would ride one of the two smaller ballistic landers, *Stripes*, on in the *J.M.*'s current trajectory for a while yet. We wrestled the go-cart onto one of *Stripes'* exterior cargo clamps, swathed it in reflective material and heat-proofing, and stowed my gear aboard the auxiliary ship.

And there was no more time. I had to hurry. If I lost the race, 5,000 troopers would be trapped for all time inside a timeless bubble of rotated C^2 space, with no receiver to find the bubble and pull them back. If C^2 was un-nothingness, that was undeath. If I lost the race, this solar system had no hope, and others might follow it.

We said our last in-person goodbyes in *Stripes'* airlock. We were at war. The odds were that we would never see each other again.

We held each other tight and said things that wouldn't interest anyone else anyway, until another moment more would mean Joslyn missing her burn window and losing fuel we couldn't waste.

Hatches clanged shut, I slid into my command couch, took the controls, and jogged *Stripes'* thrusters. I aligned my little ship and edged away from the *J.M.* The bigger ship's engines jumped to life, and the fusion jet took my wife away from me.

I slipped a set of tiny plastic headphones on, and squeezed them tight against my ears, as if that would keep Jozzy a little closer. "Goodbye, kid," I said softly.

"Good hunting, Mac. But save a few of those bastards for me."

"Why bastards? What have they done to you so far?"

"Well, you're not here any more, are you?"

The great power of the *J.M.*'s engines created a strong plasma, a super-hot gas-cloud formed of fusion exhaust particles. It caused static in radio frequencies. As the big ship slowed and I fell onward, the plasma served to jam radio signals perfectly. We were cut off from one another.

The *Joslyn Marie* slowed her fall and eased into orbit behind me, to wait there in the loneliness of space for word from me. If I survived to send it.

I too had to perform a pair of rocket burns, the first one speeding my fall into the sun, the second shifting my path into a tight loop *around* the sun, a gravity-assist maneuver that would flash me across the diameter of New Finland's orbit in less than a month.

It was a tricky manuever, and might even cook poor old *Stripes* a bit—and me with her if the cooling system gave me any problems—but I had to move as fast as possible. There was no hope of using C^2 this close to a sun. I'd be more likely to end up in the center of the star than where I wanted to go. I had to stay in normal space for another reason: the Guardians were looking for ships entering from C^2, and I'd be hard to miss.

Still, it was a long wait, and an unpleasant one, more so as I came near the star. I was only 40 million kilometers from New Finland's sun at closest approach. That violated the warranty on *Stripes*, but she kept me safe through it all. Good ship.

The worst of it all was the boringness of space travel. There is very little to do on a ship by yourself. Added to that was the tension of all the unknowns ahead of me; it was not a pleasant time. Mostly I studied my Finnish.

Finally, it was over. One hundred eighty degrees around the sun from the *J.M.*, I arrived at the vicinity of New Finland, albeit travelling at a great relative speed. I couldn't use *Stripes'* engines to slow down: Joslyn and I didn't want the aux ship to get within two million klicks of the planet. Closer, and there was a chance someone might spot her. I had to abandon ship.

That was what the torp, the go-cart, was for. I was to jump ship, climb into the fold-out crash couch, and ride the torp's motor in. *Stripes* would continue on her present course for a long while yet, until she was far enough from New Finland to use her fusion engine without risk of detection. Then she would turn back toward the sun, going into a solar polar orbit that would keep her in line of sight of both New Finland and the *Joslyn Marie* for many months, if she was left undisturbed by the Guardians. While in line of sight, *Stripes* could serve as a relay station for laser messages between Joslyn and myself.

I had an interesting trip from there on. I collected all my gear and checked my suit over a half dozen times. I would be counting on it for a long while. Then I gave the guidance pod on the go-cart a download from *Stripes'* astrogation computer. Now the torp's computer would know where it was and where I wanted it to go.

Before I abandoned *Stripes*, I wrote Joslyn a brief note. Nothing meaningful. But if I got myself killed, as was very likely, and Joslyn recovered the aux ship, I wanted her to have something, some words, that had passed from my hand to hers.

And then I was out the hatch. It took some huffing and puffing to get my oversized, pressure-suited self, my maneuvering backpack, and my equipment bag onto the go-cart in such a way that it would be properly balanced in flight. When I had, I stretched a finger toward the cargo-clamp release button, and a rattling vibration told me I was free of the ship. I reached a little farther and shoved hard against the ship's hull. The go-cart and I drifted slowly away. I checked the chronometer in my suit's helmet—an hour until I had to push that single button marked "ON" and get this show on the road. Plenty of time for *Stripes* to get safely distant. I hadn't shoved with great precision: the go-cart was tumbling gently. It didn't matter. I spent the hour watching the gently receding *Stripes* drift around my field of view, to be replaced by a splendid view of New Finland and her single large natural moon, Kuu. I was too far away for any hope of spotting Vapaus, which was my eventual target. I was lucky in that the sun remained pretty much at my back as I tumbled.

And then it was time. I pushed the "ON" button, and

the torp's gyros began to whir busily. I felt the vibration through my suit. The guidance pod spotted New Finland and set itself up to home in on the planet.

Without any warning, the engine lit up ten gees at my back and that go-cart *moved*! It was a short life but a merry one, and the torp engine died as suddenly as it had opened up. Without the burn, I would be following *Stripes* as she slowly drifted away from the planet. Now I was moving straight for New Finland, and at a pretty good clip. The torp began to rotate itself along its long axis for the retro-burn about 30 hours later. If the retro-burn didn't work, I was going to drop right into the atmosphere and burn up. I had enough confidence in the torp that I wasn't worried, but I had something else that annoyed me enough to avoid boredom: I was now pointed straight at the sun, almost forced to stare at it. I slapped my sunshield down and set it to OPAQUE. Otherwise I would have been blinded.

I had a good bit of waiting to do. I spent part of it chewing over the plan Joz and I had cooked up for my getting inside the hollowed-out asteroid world Vapaus.

I had read up on the place. Vapaus had started out in life as a rather routine lump of stone and rock floating through space on an orbit that brought it within easy range of New Finland. The Finns had dragged it into orbit of the planet and set to work making an orbiting industrial base and shipping port out of it.

The first step was to hollow it out, and trim the oblong lump of rock into a cylinder.

The New Finnish system had several gas giant planets in its outer reaches. The closest-in giant had a small ice moon far outside its gravity well. This moon was mined for ice, which was towed to the asteroid's orbit.

The interior of the asteroid was by then a cylindrical hollow, which the Finnish engineers proceeded to pack with ice. The mine shafts were sealed with pressure locks, and the asteroid was then set spinning.

Giant solar mirrors were brought into position around

the asteroid, and tremendous amounts of light and heat were focused on it.

The stone melted like butter.

The heat-pulse hit the ice-filled interior. The ice boiled off into super-heated steam and inflated the asteroid the way a child's breath inflates a balloon.

The engineers having done their math properly, the pressure locks blew off at the right moment. Ninety percent of the water escaped to space, and then the pressure lock resealed. The rest of the water was retained to become the basis of Vapaus's artificial ecology.

When the molten rock cooled, the Finns had an inside-out world about six times the size of the asteroid they had started with. They had been the first to try the technique with a stony asteroid. (Others had "inflated" iron-nickel asteroids, but those satellites had annoying problems with magnetic eddy fields and electrical effects brought on by spinning up megatons of conductive material.)

The scrap rock was dragged down into a lower orbit and the solar mirrors melted it all down into one lump of slag, which never got any name other than "The Rock". The Rock made a good base for a lot of processes that relied on zero-gee, and was also a handy orbital mine.

Joslyn and I had worked out a plan that was based on the fact that Vapaus had been inflated. It was known that the rock had bubbled in places. It ought to be possible to find a bubble, dig in through it, and reach the interior.

I hoped so, anyway. Otherwise, I was dead. I sighed. Best not to worry about that little possibility. It was going to be true of just about everything I did for the foreseeable future.

When my helmet was opaqued, it could be used as a reading screen. I had carried a few tapes along, and now I put them to use, as I learned another ten new words in Finnish.

It didn't make the ride seem any shorter.

The 30 hours slid away in studying, sleeping, and worrying. Riding with the helmet opaqued was tough: besides the readouts and telltales inside my suit's collar, there was nothing to see. The blacked-out glass of the helmet was dark and featureless, inches from my face. I hung in the middle of space with only my suit between me and infinity, feeling claustrophobic. That made my worrying all the more effective. A dozen times I reached for the black-out control to lighten the helmet so I could *see*, and just barely talked myself out of it each time. The sun would have blinded me. Period. That was a convincing argument, even under the circumstances.

The torp was programmed to bring me about 100 kilometers off Vapaus and then fire its motor not quite enough to bring me into orbital velocity. My backpack unit would make up the difference, and the torp was to fall on into New Finland's atmosphere and burn up.

I was alseep when the burn came, dreaming about flying *Stars* through a coal-black cave, trying to get to Joslyn, though she fell farther and farther away. I came awake badly disoriented, having a lot of trouble sorting out the dream from the reality, until I remembered it was okay to kill the blackout control now. The planet of New Finland popped into existence in front of my face, and then slowly swung away and got behind me. Its job done, the guidance system had shut down, and the torp was tumbling without gyros.

I wanted to get away from the go-cart as soon as I could; I wasn't eager to share its ride down to the surface. The backpack unit, comprised of a maneuvering jet unit and life-support system, was stowed underneath the crash couch, along with other equipment I expected to need. I pulled the hose connections that had attached me to the life-support unit, as they were snaked through the crash couch, wrestled myself free of the couch's straps, and pulled my gear out from beneath it.

Working as fast as I could, I shoved clear of the torp, dragging the gear with me. I wriggled into the backpack unit and re-attached the hose connections, then swung

on my brow, and I shook my head to clear my vision.
The droplets flew off my face and dried instantly against
the side of the helmet.

I was now only ten meters above the surface, watching
it rush toward me. I was seconds from my landing. Now
I had to try and match my lateral speed to the satellite's
spin. I had to be moving at the same speed as the bit of
rock I landed on. Too slow and I'd be bowled over, and
probably thrown out into space. Too fast and I might fly
past the asteroid altogether, and have to try again—this
time badly short of fuel.

I clenched my teeth and went in, aiming to fly slightly
toward the center of the rock. I fired the jets so as to
match speed with the spin. The whirling rock seemed to
slow, and slow more, and with my feet a bare five
meters above the surface, I matched the spin, released
the maneuvering controls, and pulled the spike shooter
from my belt, rushing as fast I could. I was about to hit!
I shot the rocket-powered spike into the rock below me.
Even as it bit into the rock, my lateral velocity began to
show up again. I swung up short against the line attached to the spike and landed neatly on my feet, balanc-
ing on my free hand.

The asteroid was spinning to create an artificial gravity by means of the centripetal effect. The farther out
from the axis you got, the stronger that gee force would
be. I wasn't very far, but I was far enough. I felt a very
slight tug *down*, and as far as my inner ears was
concerned, "down" wasn't through the surface of the
world anymore—it was toward the horizon, toward the
rim of the world.

Suddenly I knew in my gut that I wasn't on a slight
rise in the middle of a flat plane, but hanging by a thin
line from an overhanging cliff three kilometers high. A
cliff that had at its top—and at its base—nothing. Nothing but empty, empty space. Just as I made the mistake
of looking *down*, the sun swung around the horizon at
manic speed. The photoreceptors on the helmet dimmed
a bit as the sun hit. I watched, fascinated, as the dark-

ened sun sped around that gloomy plane and swept *under* me. The raging inferno of the sun was directly *beneath* me. . . .

My foot slipped.

In an instant, I was dangling off the sheer face of the cliff, held only by the one length of line clipped to my waist. I was going to fall! Into the sun! My hindbrain screamed and gibbered. I looked down again to see if the sun was really there, and saw the planet, New Finland, whip beneath my feet. Closer and bigger than the stars, it seemed to move even faster. Then it left my field of view, and the empty, empty stars were there. Worse, a thousand times worse than a fall into the quick death of the sun. A million year's worth of monkey ancestors yowled in my head. I was going to fall, and to fall now was to fall forever, forever into nothing, always to fall, fall. . . .

I passed out, only for a few seconds, I think. When I came to, I took as long as I dared to calm my instincts. My throat hurt, as if I had been screaming. I tried to steady my shaking body. I breathed deeply, relaxed and tensed every set of muscles, I tried to sing a little song to myself. Above all, I did not, repeat DID NOT, look down or open my eyes.

All the fears that normally protect us from foolhardy gestures—fear of falling, fear of the dark, fear of the unexpected and the disorienting, the dangerous surprise, had conspired against me. If the rope had been in my hands, where I could have let go in fright, instead of clipped to my waist, those fears would have killed me.

It took long minutes to conquer that fear.

When the trembling ceased, I slowly and carefully opened one eye, making sure to look only straight ahead, struggling to convince my inner ear that it was all right, I was only hanging in front of a very ordinary cliff that was only a half meter away. Just like in training. I waited a bit, then opened the other eye just as carefully. Okay so far.

Slowly, gently, I swung my legs back and forth, working up a pendulum motion that got me in reach of the surface.

I grabbed for handholds and, clinging for dear life, very gingerly peered down to look for my rock bubble. I breathed a sigh of relief. My marksmanship had been good: I was almost directly above it, and only about 15 meters away.

The surface sloped away toward the crazy sideways horizon, and Vapaus's rapid rotation brought the sun around to hang directly beneath me again.

Everything considered—the shakes I still had, the sweat that lined the inside of my suit, the aches of being in that suit for almost two days now, the idea I got that the helmet glass just had to crack, sometime, probably soon—and you'll agree I wasn't climbing down that insane cliff under ideal, or even hopeful circumstances. The only advantage I had was that, in being rather near the axis of rotation, the artificial gravity produced by Vapaus's spin was low. I could not possibly have made that climb in normal gravity.

Climbing, especially rock climbing, is composed of pauses and lunges. You look over the rock face and rehearse, time and time again in your mind, which limb you will move first, and which will follow. You wait, and work up the will to do it. Perhaps you try the very beginning of the move a time or two, not even moving your hand or foot from the rock, just relaxing the hold one arm has on the rock, trying to see if your other arm or your legs can hold you in place until the first arm can get to where it's going. Maybe you find the move can't work, and you sweat out the close call for a moment until you try some other way. Then, finally, when there is no reason left for pausing, you lunge, and move as quickly and smoothly as you can to the next set of handholds and footholds, hoping they will support you. Sometimes they do.

It was crawl and clamber, climb and hang, pause and lunge. Twice my handholds and footholds weren't good enough; I fell off the inward sloping cliff and had to swing up like a pendulum again and get back onto it. Then I would cling to the rock, wait out the shakes, and proceed.

Finally the rock bubble was directly below me, half a meter away. I fired a rope spike into the face of the cliff, shot another into the side of the bubble, clamped the two reels short, and clipped the ends of the two ropes together. I fired another short rope to hold myself to the cliff more securely, then took a five-minute break and got to work on the bubble.

I pulled my hand laser from its holster, set it on narrow beam, and fired it straight into the bubble. It took about a second and a half for the beam to pierce the bubble's surface, and then the trapped gas that had formed the bubble jetted out, carrying with it a fine cloud of rock dust that quickly dispersed. I cut along the surface of the bubble in a rough circle with a rope spike in its center.

In 15 minutes I had a manhole-sized piece of rock free of the bubble. I holstered the nearly exhausted laser and pulled on the line that held the manhole cover. With a bit of straining and effort, and a screeching like squeaking chalk that was transmitted through the rock and carried into my suit, the rock cover came off. When I released it, it swung back and forth for a few seconds, then hung quietly off to counterspinward, held oddly off center by the unsettling Coriolias effect of the satellite's spin.

I pulled the hose connections to my backpack again and detached myself from it. I shoved the backpack into the hole first, then crawled in myself.

I was in. I had made it this far. At least I was off that cliff. Rock under my feet, instead of off to one side.

I unclipped myself from all the lines that held me to the cliff, and used one of them to lasso—on the third try—the rope holding the manhole cover. I pulled it back in toward me, fired a rope spike into its inside surface, and wrapped the line around my forearm.

Steadying the cover with one hand and wishing I had

three hands, I pulled out the can of rock sealant and sprayed the thick gunk on the cover and on the lip of the hole.

I ducked back into the hole, switched on my helmet light, then pulled the cover back into place and gave it a good hard yank to give the sealant a chance. For good measure, I sprayed another coat of the stuff around the inside of the cover.

It took the sealant a few minutes to set. I used the time to get the life-support unit detached from the maneuvering backpack and strapped to me by itself. I hooked the hoses up after being off them for about five minutes; that is about the practical limit before you start seeing spots in front of your eyes from lack of air.

I dug one last tool from the gear bag hooked to the backpack—a rockeater. It was a simple, powerful device, and by far the biggest gadget I had taken with me. I set it agaiinst the wall opposite the one I had come in. On the other side of that wall lay the interior of this world. I switched it on. Three sets of spinning, industrial diamond-tipped teeth bit into the rock face. The rock was reduced to a fine dust and funneled into an exhaust tube. I paused for a moment to shove the end of the tube into the far side of the bubble.

Gritting my teeth, I started up the drill again and dug it into the rock. The sound, transmitted through the surrounding rock and into my suit, was the devil's own shrilling, keening racket. It dug a round tunnel about half a meter in diameter. In spite of the exhaust tube, the dust soon managed to cover my helmet, and I had to pause frequently to brush it off.

The hole grew slowly. In 20 tooth-rattling minutes, I had dug about a meter into the rock. I had no idea how thick the walls were, and was prepared to spend long hours with that screaming machine and the rock dust.

But it was less than an hour later that the rockeater almost skipped out of my hands and the last of the rock wall collapsed in front of it. I shut it off as the interior atmosphere of Vapaus whooshed into the vacuum of my rock bubble, jetting up great clouds of dust that took a few minutes to settle. I worried that the dust cloud might be seen, but when it cleared, I saw the satellite's interior was dark. It was night in Vapaus.

I pulled the rockeater back down the hole it had made and stashed it in the now rather cluttered bubble, then crawled up the smooth-sided tunnel and poked my head out. I cracked open my helmet and breathed in Vapaus's sweet air.

It was 42 days—1,000 hours—from the moment the signal beacon had awakened us from a sound sleep.

I was inside Vapaus.

Now came the hard part.

CHAPTER FOUR

I crawled back into the rock bubble and stripped off my pressure suit. It felt remarkably good to be out of it. I had been inside the thing for nearly two-and-a-half days by that time, and was looking forward to smelling something besides myself. I peeled down to skin and realized that I was still going to be smelling essence of me for a while. I needed a bath pretty badly. I had brought along one set of coveralls to change into once I ditched the suit, and I got into them now, reluctant to put clean clothes over dirty skin.

The rock bubble was not a good headquarters. It was impossible to stand up without using one hand to balance myself. The inside of the bubble was sort of egg-shaped, with the narrower end at the bottom. It was half full of sneeze-making rock dust, and the rock dust was full of abandoned gear. It was easy to fall over.

The seal around my manhole cover seemed to be holding, but I gave it an extra dollop of rock sealant anyway. I didn't like the idea of taking chances with somebody else's air supply—I had spent a large portion of my life breathing canned air, and that made me very sensitive to the problem.

A growing flood of light was pouring into the tunnel from the satellite's interior. Day was coming to Vapaus.

It was clearly impossible to risk being seen climbing down the interior cliff in broad daylight. I would have to wait for nightfall. That meant I could sleep now, and I needed it. I detached the legs (pants, I guess you'd call them) from my pressure suit, rolled them up into a pillow of sorts, and stretched out to sleep in the tunnel.

Toward evening, I woke, as stiff as a board, and retreated to the bubble to do some setting up exercises. Then I prepared to leave.

I set a steel spike in the roof of my tunnel and attached a line, which ended in an electromagnet, to the spike. The electromagnet was switched on and off by a radio link switch. I gave the button a test. The magnet and the line attached to it fell away from the roof. I caught them before they could go over the edge, reset the magnet, set it back in place, and gave it a good hard tug. It would hold.

I had climbed the outside of the cliff the night before. Now I got ready to start climbing down the inside of the same wall. I left behind my pressure suit, backpack, the rockeater, and all the other gadgetry, and took just the coveralls and what was in their pockets. Before I went down, I looked out across the face of Vapaus.

Dusk was just setting in that great cylindrical plain. Light was provided to the interior by a powerful spherical "sun," made up of thousands of individual lamps, which hung at the exact center of the world, floating in the zero-gee zone at the axis. It was anchored to the fore and aft cliffs by strong cables, which did not support its weight (in the axial zone, it had none), but simply kept it from floating off the centerline. This interior "sun" was dimming now and was the red of a true sun seen at dusk. Houselights were coming on in the plains below.

I was surprised by how easily I accepted this inside-out world. Maybe this was because I seen photos of other such places before, but I think it was more because it *looked* right, and natural. The scale was too vast to think of it as man-made. It was just as magnificent a vista as the Grand Canyon or Valles Marineris, but far more hospitable.

The greensward girdled Vapaus completely. Gentle hills were covered with lush grasses and graced by the hint of color lent by flowers too far off to be seen. Trees grew in profusion below my feet, in a sweeping arc of forest that climbed the sides of the world and continued unbroken over my head.

Rivers flowed in the sky as well, one directly above me. I could not see its origin, as it was shrouded in cloud, but I traced its progress toward the sea, which wrapped itself around the middle ground of the satellite's interior. Twin bands of clouds, which, like the central sea, ran clear around the world, hid the ground level from view at either end of the plain. These cloud bands started flat up against the fore and aft cliffs and extended about a quarter kilometer in toward the middle of the cylinder, steely grey boundaries to the green and blue splendor they framed.

As I started down the aft cliff, this band of cloud was below my feet. These clouds, and the gathering darkness, were enough to shield my movements from observation.

The fore and aft walls, or cliffs, were hollow dome-shapes. Measured along the axis of the world, Vapaus was about 11 kilometers from end to end. Measured at the base of the cliffs, it was about 10 klicks. This meant that the climb down the outside had been against a constant overhang, but that climbing down the interior wall brought you down a steadily gentler slope. By the time I reached the end of the line, I was able to scramble down with a fair degree of confidence, even in the dark.

I used the radio relay switch to shut off the electromagnet that held my line, and it instantly started to drop in the most peculiar fashion. As I've said, the apparent gravity inside a rotating cylinder like Vapaus increases from zero at the axis to its maximum at the walls of the cylinder. This meant, of course, that the top of the rope fell more slowly than the bottom of the rope.

There was another odd effect as well: the spin of such a world isn't imparted to a falling object inside it. The object falls in a straight line toward the surface. But to an observer on that surface, who is carried by the spin of the world, a falling object seems to sheer away from the direction of spin. These two oddities came together to give that falling rope the strangest snake dance of a fall I've ever seen. I coiled in the line and stuffed it in a crack in the rock.

It was silly, I knew, but I felt safer climbing down the inner wall than I had climbing down the outside. It was, in some insane way, reassuring to know that if I slipped, I would tumble "only" a kilometer or so down the inside instead of out into empty space on the outside.

It actually was fairly safe. The cliff wall was full of cracks, nooks, and crevices: I had no trouble finding handholds. I quickly descended into the band of clouds that clung to the cliff wall. The wall grew clammy and slippery, and soon I was low enough for rain to start falling. The mist and rain soaked clear through my light coveralls. I noticed the air was a bit cool for my tastes as I got nearer the surface. That made sense—Finns would *like* it cold. The air grew denser, too. The last 50 meters or so of the climb I just slid and skidded down the pile of loose rock and pebbles that had accumulated at the bottom of the cliff.

Finally I reached level ground and looked back up the way I had come. It is always satisfying to look back at pulling off a hare-brained scheme once it has worked, and I felt sure no one could possibly have anticipated this one. The Guardians would guard the airlocks at the forward end, not here.

I squelched my way through the rain-soaked grass at the base of the aft cliff and headed in, toward the inhabited parts of the satellite.

There is a man who lives on the end of a pleasant lane near the aft cliff who may be wondering to this day what happened to the pants, shirt, and food that vanished that night. Whoever he is, thank you. It all went to a good cause. League of Planets Survey Service issue coveralls were not the thing to wear in those parts, and the black bread was delicious. After the snack, I buried the coveralls and moved on.

Soon I found myself at a transport station of some kind. I hung back and watched the proceedings. It seemed simple enough. Brightly lit rail cars were running along a ground-level monorail, arriving about once every five minutes. They stopped, opened their doors, waited about 30 seconds for passengers, shut their doors, and zipped off into the night.

Looking up into the sky, or rather at the land that hung over my head, I spotted the lights of other rail cars sliding silently along in the darkness here and there, like glowworms far off.

One of the cars crossed the central sea, and its cabin lights were caught and reflected by the water, casting a soft burst of light that vanished almost at once.

At this time of night, there were no other riders at this remote station. I stepped aboard. The doors slid shut with a whoosh and a click, and the car rolled forward smoothly.

I stared out the window, eager to see as much of the strangely upside-down landscape as I could in the darkness. Other passengers got on at the next stop. In the tradition of rapid-transit riders everywhere, I ignored them, and they ignored me.

No one was waiting at the next few stops, and we drew near a cluster of lovely towers that stood by the shore of the central sea.

The car stopped, and two surly-looking men in dark grey uniforms shooed other passengers away and stomped on before anyone else, swaggering with their thumbs thrust into their belts, their hands near vicious-looking laser pistols.

The enemy! Up until this moment, the Guardians had been academic, unknown. Now they were here, real, in front of me. I was sitting in the seat nearest the door. One of them came up to me and hooked a thumb toward the far end of the car. I didn't respond. Maybe I was too intent on looking him over. In any event, I nearly blew the whole game right there.

"What's the matter, boy?" the soldier growled. He spoke English with a flat, hard, clipped accent. "Don't want to share your seat?" He stepped closer, leering at me. "Huh?"

I got out of the seat and moved to the end of the car, the other passengers looking at me oddly. The two soldiers flopped down on the seat I had vacated.

"That's a lot smarter, boy," said the one who had spoken before. He pointed at a patch on the wall of the car that partially hid what looked like a scorched laser burn. "Don't want no more holes or bloodstains on these nice trains, do we?" The two of them laughed loudly. The other riders studiously ignored the whole scene. The soldier waved the back of his hand at me in dismissal and spat on the immaculately clean carpet.

The train eased to a smooth halt at the next stop, and I got out at once, before I did something angry and stupid, something that would get me burned down in my tracks and waste all the effort that had gone into getting me there. It was close, nonetheless.

A fellow passenger got off with me, and as the train pulled out, he touched my arm and spoke in rapid Finnish I had trouble following. "Be more cautious and careful, friend. Do not throw your life away over their childish mocking. Tomorrow, or the next day, or the next, will be the time to fight them. Die today and you cannot fight them tomorrow." He nodded and limped away, disappearing behind a turn in the path. The trees that hid him from view were burned and blackened, and the sidewalk was shattered before me.

Yesterday had been a time of fighting, too.

For the rest of the night and the beginning of the following morning, I wandered over the surface of Vapaus. I saw a good deal, but learned no more than I already knew. Here was a world not simply conquered, but brutalized. Soldiers were everywhere, shoving past pedestrians, sauntering down walkways, cursing and insulting the Finns. Vapaus's night life centered around the cluster of towers by the side of the central sea, and here the soldiers were out in force, grabbing produce from streetside stalls, "impounding" and guzzling stock from a liquor store, shouting vulgarities after young women.

The soldiers never travelled alone. From the hatred I saw in the eyes of the Finns, I doubted if even the soldiers who travelled in pairs were all that safe.

I took a look at a map posted at one of the rail stations and found that the hospital was in a tower near the central sea. The next part of the plan Joslyn and I had cooked up called for being near a hospital, so I rode the train one last time, crossing the central sea as the artificial sun started to brighten directly overhead. The water was a fantastic sight from the bridge. From a perfectly flat plane below me it swooped into the sky like a single titanic wave frozen over the curve of the world. All along its coastline were craggy inlets, small sandy beaches, and narrow fjords. Here and there were the wrecks of brightly colored pleasure boats, but the sea itself was empty. I left the sea behind and walked from the train to a spot about a hundred meters from the hospital, in the burned-off remnants of a small park.

I took the tiny tranquilizer capsule from my pocket and swallowed it. I walked on as casually as I could, waiting for the pill to hit. It did, like a load of bricks. I fell to the littered sidewalk.

The drug was a depressant as well as a relaxant. It dropped my body temperature and slowed my heart to a crawl, enough to scare the hell out of anyone who came upon me.

The pill wore off a few hours afterwards, but I slept on. The snooze I had had in my tunnel the night before hadn't been very restful.

I awoke in a clean, private hospital room, according to plan. The nurse who watched me was tall and slender, with short blonde hair and grey eyes. She saw I was awake and pointed a pocket laser at my forehead.

This was not according to plan.

She spoke good English, with a slight lilting cadence. "You are a very bad spy, did you know? No Finn is allowed to carry a laser, but you won't have the chance to report my having this one here. Your drug was so obvious it made our doctors laugh. Your head Guardians think you can get into the hospital without our noticing things like that? What did you think getting here would do for you?"

There was one bright spot. As Joslyn and I had figured, the hospital staff had been allowed to remain at work after the fighting, in the face of the many casualties. We had hoped to find a staunch group of underground workers here, both because it was one place that Finns would be allowed to remain in an organized group, and because the doctors and nurses would get a firsthand look at the Guardians' murderous handiwork.

It seemed we had figured right. Now all I had to do was convince my nurse here not to drill a hole in my skull.

I asked her a question, in very bad Finnish, trying to keep calm. "Is this room bugged?"

It startled her. She replied in Finnish that was too fast for me to follow easily. Don't believe the ads for the hypnotape courses—you don't become fluent, no matter how long they tell you to stay under. Especially Finnish.

I waved my arms to stop her. "Please! Go slow. My Finnish is not good."

Her forehead furrowed, and she repeated herself, talking more slowly. "What do you care if the room is bugged, Guardian? It would be *your* friends listening." She grinned malevolently, an unpleasant change for her pretty face. "As a matter of fact, they *think* they are listening to this room. We changed a few wires here and there, however. They will be listening to what they think are your noisy snores."

Good. At least I could talk freely. But something occurred to me. "How do I know you're not a—a Guardian?"

No one under a hundred years old should be able to look that angry. Her finger got a little closer to the trigger. "Okay, okay." I had slipped back into English. I switched to Finnish and said, "Never mind. I'm convinced."

She sneered at me. "*You* don't convince *me*, fool. If you want to spy on us here, at least send someone who speaks Finnish like a good Finn."

"I'm not a spy! I work with your side."

"Nonsense! We have no record of you. You are not from here. I'm beginning to lose patience with you, spy."

If this was her version of patience, I was in deep trouble when she got annoyed. "I'm from the League! The League of Planets! They sent me!"

She snorted. "And your starship is docked at the airlock complex next to the Guardian troop transports?"

"Terrance MacKenzie Larson, Commander, Republic Of Kennedy Navy, attached to LPSS 41, *Joslyn Marie*. ROK Navy ID four niner eight two four five."

A hint of doubt showed in her, and the laser lowered just a hair. I thought she was beginning to believe me. "You lie," she said after a moment's hesitation. Well, maybe not yet. "If you are from the League, why didn't you show yourself three months ago when these monsters descended on us?"

"I have been in—or on, or whatever, this world less than 20 hours."

"What did you do to get in? Use your own private airlock?"

I began to lose patience myself. "As a matter of fact, yes."

At that, she burst into laughter. "Spy, you are very bad," she said through the last of her giggles. "You are very, very bad at whatever it is you are trying to do."

I sighed and flopped back down into the bed—and noticed the view out the room's large picture window.

Spread out before me was the rearward end of Vapaus: I could see the cliff I had descended, and had the feeling I could pick out my route down.

I turned to the nurse. who was still smirking at me. "Could you bring me a pair of high-power—oh, what is the word—binoculars!"

That almost set off the giggles again. "But, spy, don't most spies carry their own?"

"Look, lady, you can sit there and laugh at me, or you can get the binoculars. If you get them, I will show you my private airlock. If you don't, you won't get to see it."

"You are wasting my time. But so this nonsense will stop, I will humor you and call your bluff. Then we can get to what it is you are really doing."

"Fine. Great. Just get the field glasses."

Keeping the gun pointed at me, she pushed the talk button on the room's intercom and spoke rapidly and quietly into it. Then she sat back down and we waited without speaking for a few minutes.

A big, burly man in an orderly's uniform came in carrying a pair of binoculars. Without a word, he handed them to the nurse, who gave him the laser. He pointed it at my heart instead of my skull. Not much of an improvement.

She tossed the binoculars onto the bed. I reached down and handed them back. "No, you look."

Coming no nearer than she had to, she picked them back up. "Where do I look?"

"Do you know where Roos Place is?" That was the street I had walked onto when I had gotten to the bottom of the cliff. I congratulated myself on remembering the name.

"Yes."

"Good. Now, find it with the field glasses, then look directly behind it at the aft cliff. Okay?"

"Yes."

"Move straight up the cliff until you're about halfway between the cloud cover and the axis." She did so, and I watched her as she looked over the cliff, stopped, and moved back down a bit, as if she had seen something worth looking at. "Now. What do you see?"

"Some sort of hole in the rear cliff. Right at the top of it is some sort of glint, like off metal." Her voice was shocked. I seemed to have convinced her.

"My private airlock. If you wait until tonight, and send your raiders or commandos or what you might call them, you can look at my hole there. You'll find it leads to a rock bubble that has a hole cut in it that has been patched shut. Also, you'll find a standard League-issue long-duration pressure suit, a worn-out laser, and some other gadgets. My ship is hidden on the far side of your sun."

"Are you truly from the League?" There was amazement and hope in her voice.

"Truly."

"We never really dared to think you'd come...." A sudden thought came to her. "How many men do you have?"

I thought of the experimental matter transmitter. "If we're lucky, about 5,000."

She rushed out of the room. I could tell I had made her day.

There was a general bustle of activity, during which my orderly calmly kept the laser aimed straight at my chest. Someone came in to photograph me and take my fingerprints. I never did find out exactly why.

My nurse seemed to be trying to get someone in charge to pay attention to her. She was in and out two or three times, pacing indecisively and trying to figure out if I was telling the truth.

Finally the door swept open and a very dignified, calm sort of medical man came in. Clearly, Someone In Charge had arrived. He shooed the orderly out and drew up a chair alongside my bed. "Nurse Tulkaas has said some extremely interesting things about you, Commander," he said in very precise English. "Where are these men you spoke of?"

"About four light weeks away, I'd guess."

He didn't bat an eye, but I could see Nurse Tulkaas's face collapse in disappointment. The doctor said, "You are not aware of the missile system?"

"We should be able to get our troops around it."

"How?"

I hesitated. "Doctor, could I get out of this bed and discuss this at a table? One with a big lunch on it? This is a bit complicated, and I haven't had a real meal in days."

"Of course."

"Great." I hopped out of bed—and hopped right back in. Finnish hospital garb does not include pants. The doctor almost smiled at my discomfort. "Nurse, could you get Commander Larson a robe out of the closet?"

The nurse got one and performed some maneuver with it that got me into the robe without getting me out of bed. Long practice, no doubt. I tied it around my waist and got out of bed again. "One other thing," I said. "Could you have a hypnotist join us? I didn't dare carry any paper or film, but I have a lot of information. If I was caught by your Guardian friends, we wanted to make sure I didn't talk. The information is blocked from my conscious by about three separate post-hypnotic commands. You'll even have to put me in a light trance to get the keying words out of me."

"I'll have Mr. Kendriel attend us." The doctor led me out into the hall.

"This is the final keying, Commander. When I speak the appropriate word, you will awaken with full conscious memory of the information you have been carrying."

I could hear the voice from far away, but it didn't seem to mean much to me.

"I will count backwards until I reach one, and then speak your key word. Five, four, three, two, one—Mannerheim. Now, then, Do you remember it all?"

Of course I did, I thought dully. "Yes."

"Good. Now, I will count forward to three and tell you to awaken. When I do, you will awaken and still remember everything. Ready? One, two three—wake up!"

My mind switched back to the ON position and I opened my eyes, somewhat out of it for a moment. Then I blinked and turned to the hynotist. "Could I have paper and pencil?" He handed them to me, and I scribbled down a long column of numbers, writing quickly before I had a chance to forget anything. Antenna position, power levels, that sort of thing. Then a condensed box diagram of the receiver unit's auxiliary equipment, from which a good electronics engineer could build the required circuitry.

"Commander, if you could explain what all this is about?"

"In a moment, Doctor. I have a lot of details to remember. Please hand me that map of the planet's surface, if you would."

The last thing in the hypnotic memory had been the coordinates of the point where the receiver had to be built: latitude and longitude. I examined the map for a moment, then ran one finger down the right longitude line and another done the right latitude.

Then I did it again.

And again.

The coordinates were wrong—45°W 15°N was under water.

I sat and stared at the map. I closed my eyes and concentrated. Yes, I had remembered the coordinates properly. I checked the map again. Said a few choice phrases. Bit my nails. But it was still under water, nowhere near shore.

"Commander! What is the matter?" the doctor asked.

"This map is accurate." I didn't even bother to make it a question.

"Yes, of course."

I turned and faced the doctor—who still hadn't given me his name. "This will take a moment to explain. The League developed, very recently, a matter transmitter.

It is still experimental. But they had enough confidence to take the chance of using it. My ship was intercepted by a drone that carried the key components of the receiver unit. I was ordered here. The transmitter is a much more precisely designed system, and requires a great deal more power. The United States Space Craft *Mayflower*, which has the transmitter itself aboard, has used it to beam 5,000 men and their equipment toward us at the speed of light. They were transmitted from far outside this solar system. They were aimed to be received at 45°W 15°N. They *must* arrive at that point, or they cannot arrive at all. That point is under water, nowhere near land."

"There is no Finnish shipping. The Guardians control it all."

"And no ship could be big enough for 5,000 men," I said.

"This is amazing! They have really transmitted those men toward us?" He turned and asked the hypnotist, "Is that truly possible?"

Mr. Kendriel shrugged. "In theory, yes. The idea has kicked around since the invention of the C^2 drive. It would be an application of the same principle. To oversimplify, the effect that puts a ship into superlight speed is rotated through 90 degrees, producing a normal C^2, except that it is static in space, or more accurately, adjacent to every point in our space. The stumbling block has been to find a way to lock on to that bubble, track it, and pull it back into normal space in a controlled manner. I imagine that they've licked that problem." Mr. Kendriel had done some reading, it seemed.

"Remarkable. What a wonderful invention. . . ." The doctor seemed to consider the possibilities for a moment. Then he came back to the problem at hand. "But why can't they arrive anywhere else? Is the beam that carried them that tight?"

"It isn't the width of the guide beam that is the trouble. It's the Doppler shift. The point from which the guide beam is sent and at which it is received *must* be dead in space to each other. Exactly so. The point 45°W 15°N will be moving at exactly the right speed at the moment the radio signal arrives at New Finland. The rotation of the planet around the sun, its revolution around its own axis—even the perturbations caused by this satellite—were all accounted for precisely. If the signal is at all distorted at reception, the men will be—distorted."

Would they appear as giants? Pygmies? Inside out? With sine waves imposed onto the cells of their corpses?

We couldn't receive them. I shut my eyes and wondered what it was like to step into a machine, expecting to appear magically on a new world . . . and never come out. A quick and painless death, but one that easy, in a frightening way, unknown to those who died. Would they be truly dead, frozen for a moment of subjective time that would last for all eternity? Or just—gone?

Nurse Tulkaas knit her fingers into each other and stood, staring at nothing. "We had hope for a brief moment. Now it is gone. Your League must learn to read maps before it sends men over radio waves."

"Karina, that is unfair," the doctor objected. "It was the coordinate shift that did it. It's quite simple, Commander. When we first mapped this world, we assigned a rather arbitrary set of coordinates to it. When it came time to build, one of the prime city sites lay square on what would have been the planetary dateline. Rather than give up the site, it was seen as a better solution to shift the assigned lines of longitude. Your troops are targeted to what is no doubt an excellent site—as located on an old map."

"And now the men are as good as dead," I said.

Nurse Tulkaas suddenly burst out, "Why have you done this mad thing?"

I looked up from the table I had been trying to stare a hold in. "Huh?"

"Why didn't you mind your own business instead of coming all this way to raise false hope and kill so many men with a stupid mistake?"

"Because, Karina," the doctor said testily, "the Commander is an honorable man sent by an honorable League of which we are members, and this Commander and that League are sworn to try and rescue us. As for stupid mistakes, it was we who made whatever erroneous maps they worked with—and we who lost this war long before he arrived."

"But we screwed up," I admitted. "We should have known about the map. That's the sort of thing they needed a Survey for. Since we didn't bother setting up until six months ago, the war is lost and those troops are dead. A lot of dead men have died without knowing it."

The doctor was about to answer when a forgotten voice cut in. "Those men are *not* dead." It was Kendriel, the hypnotist. "From what I know of the theory, and what I can see from the diagram you have made, it is obvious that once the radio signal has locked the receiver into the C^2 bubbles that hold the troops, they can be pulled out of C^2 at our leisure. We do this by hooking the signal-capturing device up to the rather simple receiver you have sketched out. Your *ship* can match velocity until it is, as you put it, 'dead in space' relative to the guide transmission. It can be received without distortion. Then we carry the capture device to wherever we wish to receive the troops."

There was a dead silence.

Short, balding Mr. Kendriel smiled shyly and spoke in English for the first time. "You see, Commander Larson, I have the hobby of electronics."

CHAPTER FIVE

With that, we were back in business, and the Finns got to work. For an underground, they were a pretty slick outfit, and seemed to operate remarkably free of interference from the Guardians.

The doctor finally broke down and told me his name was Tempkin, and admitted he was the leader of the underground. I think even at that point, his people were only about 90 percent convinced of my bona fides. Everything I had done *could* have been faked, but the saving point for me was that there wasn't any clear motive for such an elaborate deception. Even so, I was sure that they were perfectly prepared to make me disappear if I slipped up. Whether I was a plant or legit, Tempkin could be sure I wouldn't talk to anyone on the other side. That made him willing to describe how they had managed to deceive the enemy so completely.

"First off," he explained, "the hospital was a natural focus point for loyalist activity. In the same building are the administration and executive offices for the whole satellite. Fully 30 percent of the interior of this building is given over to electronics of one sort or another: computers, communications, the usual sort of things. Fortunately for us," he said with a smile, "one microcircuit looks like another. We have placed a great deal of clandestine equipment here in the control center. Mr. Kendriel is not our only electronics hobbyist by any means. We have tapped their taps, bugged their own facilities, and misdirected their own surveillance.

"Also, when it became clear that Vapaus would fall, every map, building directory, transport diagram, and information service was 'revised.' There is a good deal hidden from the Guardians, simply because their computers have not told them it is there. I won't go into details at this point, but there are quite a number of large installations they don't have a clue about. Some are ready to fight when the time comes, some are already at work.

"I'll trust you far enough to give you one small example. There is a perfectly normal pedestrian tunnel under this building, that once led in a perfectly straightforward way to nearby buildings. It still leads to them, but by doing a bit of masonry work and taking down a few signs, it vanished from sight. It is often very helpful to us."

I had been escorted back to my room. While we were talking, clothes suitable for a well-to-do Finn were brought to me, and I changed. Tempkin soon went off on some errand, and I had little to do but wait until he returned. I clearly wasn't yet trusted enough to get to see such things as that hidden tunnel.

In fact, I was more or less politely left to wait until the following morning. I suspect that the delay was put to use sending some climbers up the aft cliff to check out the hole I had poked in the satellite. By morning, they should have had a genuine rockeater, Republic of Kennedy pressure suit, and League-issue laser with a nearly exhausted charge in their possession, and my entrance tunnel disguised (at least I couldn't find it with binoculars later). In any event, the Finns seemed more satisfied after keeping an eye on me for a day.

The next morning Tempkin guided me to an office that we entered through the back of a broom closet. It was the radio room. Tempkin, the radio operator, and I spend several hours in a three-way, two-language discussion on how to hit *Stripes* with a message laser, and what the message should say. It took a bit of computer time, some patient translation by Tempkin, and a ream or two of scratch paper, but the communications officer seemed satisfied that he could find *Stripes* with a beam once he knew where to look.

I asked Tempkin how they managed to hide the message laser from the Guardians, and he explained. "Because Vapaus is spinning, and ships were constantly flying through the vicinity, with the chance of interfering with the beam or, worse, crews being blinded by the beam, the message laser had never been kept here at all, but was always kept on The Rock. We have merely camouflaged it a bit better. The Guardians have searched for it many times, and we have let them think they found it once or twice, but so far it is safe.

"We have used the laser constantly to contact our people down on the planet. In fact, they already know about you. Unfortunately, they have no easy method of talking back. We have also a number of small relay transmitters hidden on the exterior of Vapaus. A few of these have been found, as well, but we haven't been put out of contact altogether . . . so far. As you know, it is impossible to detect a laser beam in vacuum unless you are directly in its path. This has helped a great deal."

I spent about another hour putting our message to Joslyn in a standard League code, on the very long chance that the Guardians did intercept it, somehow. As briefly as possible, it told her what needed to be done with the signal capture device, and instructed her to stand by for further word as to how to get the capture device to Vapaus.

With that, the ball was in Joslyn's court.

After a bit of thought, it was clear to me that the 5,000 League troops could not be "received" on Vapaus. There were only 4,000 people living there as it was. There simply wasn't any way the satellite could provide housing, food, or even air to the troops. Also, there wouldn't be much employment for them in space. They could certainly knock out the garrison that held the satellite, but then what? The Guardians on the planet nuked the satellite and were done with it, that's what. Or simply shot down any ship that left and waited until everyone on the overpopulated satellite died of asphyxiation. No, the troops would have to get to the surface of the planet, that was clear. How wasn't so clear. The Guardians controlled everything that moved in space. Worse than that, no Finn was allowed to fly through space except for reasons of great importance to the Guardians, and then only under extremely heavy guard and with examinations that didn't stop at stripping down to skin. They searched with X-rays and microscopes.

The Finns had tried smuggling tiny ships and cargoes back and forth from space, but the Guardians, for whatever else you could say, were excellent shots. They knocked down every aircraft and spacecraft that flew without their authority. Nothing escaped.

It all boiled down to the fact that the capture device would have to ride a Guardian ship down. It was also pretty clear that someone would have to ride down with it. I was the logical candidate for that job.

We had a brilliant plan: we were going to get the Guardians to build the receiver for us.

Step one of the plan was to get me woven into Vapaus's population. Someone did some skillful kiting of computer records and built up the fictional identity of Dr. Jefferson Darrow, recent immigrant from the United States. Darrow had married a Finn and had followed her here when she had immigrated. She died soon afterward, but Darrow remained on Vapaus. He worked in his own lab on various communications projects. Dr. Darrow was a highly skilled electronics technician, quite uninterested in politics—a fact which made him rather unpopular with his neighbors. He was, in point of fact, a recluse.

In short order, I was installed in a prefab bungalow near Forward Cliff, a picture of my deceased wife on a side table, the furniture wounded with a few old stains and spills, and, for the benefit of anyone who looked, a pair of underwear lodged under the dresser that had clearly been there for months, at least. I was left on my own with the job of making the place looked lived in, and pretending to putter about in the electronics lab that took up one room of the house.

No one knew exactly when the Guardians might take an interest in me, but they were confidently expected to do so. Communications workers were high on their list of useful subjects, and there would be some question as to why my file had only come to the surface now.

So I rummaged around and waited for the enemy to spot me, getting the kitchen properly dirty (work that Joslyn would confirm is right up my alley) and taking it as easy as I could.

For ten days both Finns and Guardians completely ignored me. Tempkin's organization vanished completely.

I don't know who told them what, but even my neighbors pretended I wasn't there.

Then, one day, things began to happen.

I came back from a walk around the neighborhood to find the Guardians waiting for me in the living room.

There was a head man and a couple of hoods in uniform. The boss sat in my best chair, flanked by the two goons.

I saw him, and knew I looked on the enemy. He was blatantly overweight, so obese it had to be a declaration of his penchant for high living, an obscene proof that he ate and drank more than others because he had a right to more, a right to all he could take.

His hair was iron grey and cut so short it couldn't fall flat. His eyes were dead and old until he locked his gaze with mine. Then they came to life—murderous, hateful life. Those eyes were nearly lost in deep folds of fat, but they gleamed from their depths like deadly jewels. His wide, lipless mouth was very slightly open, as if it were ready, at a moment's notice, to gobble up anything of interest that came into its owner's path.

His uniform was not the standard grey, but a deep, brooding scarlet with death-black epaulets and pockets. The bright colors of his chestful of ribbons took on a malignant cast against that background. He stood, glared at me, and spoke in English with a typical Guardian accent, harsh and nasal. "I am Colonel Bradhurst, Special Interrogation Branch. Your records say you are Jefferson Darrow. We find that you have rather belatedly appeared on the list of skilled subjects of the Protectorate of New Finland." He paused for a moment, then spat out a sudden question. "Where has the computer kept your name up to now, cretin? Did you just appear out of thin air?"

"I—"

"Quiet!" He stalked across the room to the window and glared at the lovely view, as if he were angry with it. "How long have you been in the New Finnish star system?"

"I arrived with my wife about ten months ago—6,000 hours or so."

"Very poor timing on your part, wasn't that? Your wife died, too, and left you quite all alone. Such a pity." He turned and glared at me again. "One thing we have learned about this noisome people of yours is that they are excellent gossips. No one knows anything of you. What do you hide?"

"I just—just keep to myself. I'm not hiding anything."

"Of course you hide nothing. No one ever does." His face hardened. "For long. Not from me. What are you working on, here by yourself, Darrow?"

I decided Darrow had better play this as a coward. It was going to be pretty easy to act scared. The trick was to concentrate on feeding Bradhurst the bait instead of standing there being petrified.

"I'm . . . wor-working on a special transmitter, very advanced, that can—"

"You lie! This place has been searched top to bottom in your absence. Your lab is full of meaningless toys, nothing of any real use. 'Very advanced' devices? Nothing!

You all try so very hard to impress your new masters. Trying to earn favor, clamoring over each other to gain special privileges and steal what is left for yourselves. Yours is not a loyal people, Darrow."

"These aren't *my* people! My wife was a Finn, I'm not. I don't owe them a thing! My new transmitter is up *here*." I pointed to my forehead. "I can't get any equipment, or computer time to test things, or any chance to design or build. But I *know* I could build a working, practical matter transmitter!"

He suddenly looked suspicious in a new way. It seemed I might be of value. "Matter transmitter? What are you talking about?"

"A device that could move material objects through space from a transmitter to a receiver using radio waves." That was bait enough, I thought.

He stopped. Not just stopped talking, but all of him stopped. His face lost all expression, and in his opulent uniform and stiff posture he looked more like a machine than a man. I thought I could almost see the gears turning. *Matter transmitter! That would be quite something, if he is telling the truth. Delivering such an invention to our use would be greatly to my credit. And I can test his claim at low risk. If he is lying he can be killed by my men, so none need know I was fooled. I can gain but can't lose.*

"Can you prove your claims? You will work with Guardians to do so?" he demanded.

"Yes. Just give me a place to work! And give me the credit."

"Of course we will." He stared at me thoughtfully. Cooperation is something a tyrant rarely sees. "If you are not lying. I will send some of our technicians. You will describe this transmitter, and the principles involved. If you are attempting to fool them, or trick us, you will be killed very slowly and painfully. If you are telling the truth, and if you can build this device, there will be credit and benefit enough for all. The Guardian is not ungenerous to those who contribute things of value." He made ready to leave. "But there is one more thing. It is

possible you arrived here ten months ago. I will waste
no time interrogating you now. If the record lies, you
will have had a hand in it and will pay the penalty. We
shall examine you most carefully now, your present and
your past. If we find you are lying, you will die, transmitter or no." And he left, moving quickly for a man his
size, escorted by his two goons.

I slumped down on the couch in a pool of sweat. The
con game was on.

CHAPTER SIX

"Hey, be careful with that!" The grey-suited private had grabbed up a delicate metering device as if it were a hand grenade. Jefferson Darrow, Ph.D., was moving, with a little help from his friends. I had insisted that, without actual tests, there was no way I could safely compensate for the Coriolis effect on Vapaus. Of course, the spinning of New Finland on its axis created the same effect, but not as strongly. My keepers believed me, and so the test device would be built on the planet's surface. It had been ten weeks of conning the Guardians' technicians without actually giving anything away. They were quite willing to believe the transmitter would work. I was lucky in that the people I was fooling were good engineers, but with even less grounding in theory than I had. They were curious to know *how* the matter transmitter would work, and weren't much worried over *why* it should work.

The con had been helped by the fact that the public had been aware for decades about the possibility of a matter transmitter. There had been a lot of loose talk of splitting of the atom in the 1930's, long before it happened. Once people had heard of the idea, they were prepared to believe in it. My ground had been prepared in the same way. With that support, my explanations and proofs could be pretty vague, to say nothing of misleading. While I was out to build a working receiver to a matter transmitter, I certainly didn't want the Guardians to know how it was done. By the time my theories got to trained people on the invader's home planet who could spot the fallacies, it would be too late, if our side was lucky.

It had been a long ten weeks of deception. The computer forgers of Vapaus were true artists, and I sometimes thought they were going to give the banks a real headache if and when this was over. In any event, by the time Colonel Bradhurst began his inquiries, my past was put together with near perfection. Not absolute perfection, for that would have been suspect. But the holes in the information were artfully made and easy to explain. The obscenely fat Colonel Bradhurst was by profession and inclination a viciously suspicious man, and he gave me a few bad afternoons. As a hungry dog will chew on a bone rather than search for fresh meat, so was Bradhurst willing to threaten me over slightly questionable acts. While I was on Vapaus, he never went after big game.

It had been ten weeks of learning, and of growing revulsion. In bits and pieces, from tight-lipped and embittered Finns, from boisterous and sneering soldiers, I learned the story of New Finland's defeat.

It had not been as easy for the victors as they had expected. The plan had been for a small fleet of ships to enter the system, bomb a few minor towns, laser targets in the larger ones, and have the craven civilians capitulate without further resistance. The ships had come. The bombs were dropped on three towns, and the lasers had burned a dozen buildings and plazas in Mannerheim and New Helsinki down to slag.

The surrender demand had been made.

The invaders had expected an unarmed world. But the Finnish memory is long, and the Finns recalled the long, long centuries with always an enemy at the border, and foreign soldiers always near. They had fought the

Russians, the Germans, the Swedes, the Danes, and even, in the dim past of the 13th and 14th century and beyond—each other. Their past did not let them trust to light years of vacuum as a sufficient defense.

The Finns waited until the occupation troops had begun to arrive. Few of the first wave survived long enough to land, and few who did land lived long on the planet's surface. But the Guardians were too great in strength; they had kept coming and coming. They took the planet's surface.

However, in space, the Guardian ships found themselves being cut to pieces. The Finns had been far better prepared than their invaders had ever dreamed. Finally, the Guardians resorted to terror tactics: nuclear weapons were exploded in space a few kilometers away from Vapaus, and the satellite, with its high civilian population, was threatened with destruction. The satellite had controlled the orbital battle, and when it was forced to surrender, the planet's last hope was gone. The Guards almost succeeded in preventing word from reaching the League, as well. Once the Guardians arrived, no manned ship escaped the New Finnish system—and only one drone made it out.

But what should have taken two or three days to accomplish had taken 20 days, and even as I fussed over the transmitter, Finn and Guardian continued to trade acts of sabotage and reprisal. "Light casualities" had grown into slaughter on both sides—on the ground, in the air, and in space.

But the Finns had gained time. Vapaus became a mass of hidey-holes, secret tunnels, disguised arms factories. Taps were placed on computers and communication, reports and data banks were erased or falsified. An explosion was faked on The Rock, and a convincing show made the Guardians think it was reduced to a radioactive deathtrap. They steered well clear of it, and the shipyards there went on working, slowly, very quietly, to make the ships needed to fight, someday.

Even in defeat, many Finns had refused to surrender.

The Guardians believed that fully a third of Vapaus's population had died in the riots, carnage, and reprisals that followed the garrison's arrival. But the confusion was used to full advantage by the defenders. More than half the apparent casualties had gone underground, their deaths faked. They were out of sight, working on a hundred projects toward the day when they would fight back.

Not all the deaths were faked. From my windows I could see a black scar on the land halfway up the curve of the inside-out world. Overhearing a conversation at the local store, I learned that the entire family, save one son, of the satellite's administrator—Dr. Tempkin—had been wiped out in a single bomb blast. The corpses of the wife and the children were identifiable, but Tempkin's corpse was nothing but a charred cinder.

I wondered if I would have had the nerve, the courage needed, to come home to a blazing ruin, see my family murdered, and yet find in myself the cunning and gall to take advantage of the situation and vanish. Could I have worked a grisly piece of subterfuge, found a dead man and thrown him into the flames to take my place? Tempkin had seemed such a gentle man. What nightmares did he have?

The invaders had not permitted "Tempkin" and his family to be cremated, and guards stood over the ruins of their home night and day. The stench that came from there was the perfume of barbarism.

It had been ten weeks completely in the dark. There was one day I noted in my head; the day when, if all our plans were to have any hope, Joslyn would have flown one of the auxiliary ships—*Stars*, probably, because it used the least fuel—and positioned the capture device at the right point and velocity in space. If she had succeeded in receiving the troops' signal and if she could get the capture unit to the Finns, somehow, we still might win through.

I had constructed a device the size and shape of the real capture unit, wondering if the switch could be made for the real thing. One evening I left the fake on the bench with its back panel off. The next morning I walked into "my" lab to find the genuine article. I took a screwdriver and replaced the back panel. The power light was on. I didn't know if it had indeed made the capture, or how Joslyn had gotten it to Vapaus, or how the Finns had collected it, or how it had gotten into my well-guarded lab.

The Finns were good at what they did. Maybe cloak-and-dagger was natural to their temperament. I don't know. But they were a bit over-mysterious for my tastes.

Long before I had taken on my part as Darrow (whom I didn't like much) Tempkin's staff had decided on an exact moment for the troops to be deployed, and for a general uprising to occur at the same moment. Not only would the 5,000 League troops arrive, but a planet and satellite's worth of hell would break loose, a vast underground ambush. The Finns would concentrate on crippling the enemy's transport. An army that can't move can't fight. It was vital that I stick to the agreed-upon timetable, which was what chose the moment I announced I was ready for the "experiment."

And so the thumb-fingered privates were loading my equipment, some of it vital, some of it window dressing. Finally everything was packed and I rode a passenger lift to the docking port of my transportation: a Finnish ballistic shuttle rocket painted over in the Guardian colors: black and red.

As I entered it, I saw that the civilian passenger fittings had been pulled out and military-style interchangeable pallet clamps put in. It was a sloppy, hurried job. Sharp projections, poor welds, scratched paint, and stripped bolts were much in evidence. That was the way the Guardians always worked. They were cut-and-cover engineers, shoddy workmen. Everywhere I spotted hints of overextension, a hollowness behind the conqueror's shining facade. Privates wore uniforms made of half a dozen materials, none of them very durable. A patched pair of pants was common on anyone below the rank of sergeant. The Guardians preferred the confiscated weapons of the Finns to their own. Few officers wore anything but a Finnish pistol. The guards on my house had complained that their issue lasers couldn't hold a charge more than a week.

Guardian repairs to war damage were rough and uneven. Rebuilt walls were crumbly, and the work on one bridge over the Central Sea had to be done over twice. But they had won.

So far.

Even as I boarded the shuttle, which bore a strong family resemblance to *Stars, Stripes,* and *Uncle Sam,* I didn't have a precise idea where I was going. The problem had been foreseen, and the Finns had assured me that I could expect—or at least hope for—help at any of the bases I might arrive at.

I rode down under extremely strong guard, and any service *I* was willing to fly with would have grounded that ship's pilot without hesitation. We lived through the landing, but a number of my guards were too busy making a mess of the bulkheads to bother about me.

I came out of the airlock to find a dozen troops pointing laser rifles at my head. There were times it was easy to play the part of a coward like Darrow, and that was one of them. I froze, utterly shocked. They had found me out, and for some reason had waited until I was on New Finland to arrest me.

But then I saw a figure in a lieutenant's uniform striding calmly toward me, a smile on his face. He came up the passenger ramp with his hand outstretched. I numbly stuck out my own and he took it. "Dr. Darrow. Welcome to New Finland. I am Lieutenant Grimes. I am to escort you to Base Demeter." He shook my hand warmly. "Will you come this way?" He led me down the ramp and toward a jeep that had just pulled up. The laser rifles stayed trained on my head.

"Is it safe to. . . ?" I started to ask, my voice trailing off.

"Oh, the honor guard? Quite safe. They won't fire

without commands. Orders, you see. A great many of these Finns tried to escape as they came out of the hatch. It was felt a show of force was needed. But you've nothing to worry about, I'm sure. Come now, this way."

He led me to the jeep and we drove off.

We rode away from the landing pad and out the base gates, headed north. We traveled for about four hours. Finally, we came to the gates of Base Demeter. The gates were hastily opened, and we headed down a wide, unpaved road that ran the length of the central camp. We took the second right down a narrow road that doubled back slightly, then made two more right turns, into a single-lane road that ended in a circular court about 30 meters in diameter.

The court was ringed with massive, hangarlike buildings painted gun-metal grey with camouflage-green roofs. Grimes' driver drove us directly into the largest building through large barnlike doors. Its interior was utterly empty and gave the feeling of never having been used. It was of rough prefab construction, unventilated and unheated: it was meant to keep the rain off, nothing more or less. It was cubical, 30 meters in every dimension. There were no windows.

Grimes turned to me. "Well, Darrow, this is to be yours. We'll set a cot for you in the corner, and meals will be brought to you. There is a latrine across the court, which you will be taken to no more than three times a day. The materials you requested, and the cargo from your landing boat, will start to arrive within the hour. My commander expects a demonstration of your machine within ten local days." There was no cordiality in his voice now. These were orders, to be obeyed, no questions. He turned to leave.

"I was promised two weeks! I'll need at least that much time!" But it was too late, he was gone. The two weeks was a lie, of course. I expected to be ready within a week, and the attack was set for then, but greater speed than promised seemed like a good idea for keeping the brass happy.

The doors clanged shut, cutting out the daylight. I was alone with a duffel bag, two dangerous-looking guards, and a nutty scheme that seemed like to be my obituary.

I slumped back down against the far wall of the building from the guards and sighed. Time to do some waiting.

It was not one but three hours before my equipment arrived. Two corporals with patches identifying themselves as being assigned to 135 Customs and Inspection Corps rode a cart into the building, towing a trailer full of my gear. One of them hopped down and handed me a clipboard.

"Sign all six copies," he said. "This amount of luggage is far in excess of what is normally permitted. Clearance and inspection were quite difficult." He reminded me of the librarian at the orphanage back on Kennedy. The old fossil had been convinced that in a *properly* run library, no book would ever leave the shelf. I signed the forms willingly enough, and smiled cheerfully at all the regulations he saw fit to remind me of. I tried to be cheerful and cooperative enough to spoil his officious little day.

There were plenty of forms to rustle through, too. Receipts, acknowledgements, statements of declarations, waivers, denials of visible damage, a chit for wear and tear on the shuttle craft and all ground vehicles.

There is something beautiful in the routine lack of imagination a bureaucrat brings to his work. To such a person, beauty is order, as pure as an untouched and fragile flower. Muss the slightest corner of one regulation and the bloom is gone forever.

The beauty was still there for the 135 Customs and Inspection Corps. All the forms were filled out, every single regulation complied with, every buck passed perfectly. In spite of all the difficulties, the "luggage" had been delivered properly, including the capture unit, its power lamp still glowing.

Never mind that I had just become the first man in history to smuggle a fully armed and equipped 5,000-

man army past customs. It said right over my signature that I had nothing to declare.

There wasn't much point in unpacking what I had brought from Vapaus. It represented the last stages of the job, the delicate electronic work. Before any of that could be done, I had to get the big structural part of the receiver built. However, the man who was supposed to meet me at this end hadn't shown yet. More hurry-up-and-wait.

Along toward sunset, I was awakened from a light doze when the barn doors swung open and another wagon rolled in, dragging loads of steel and a number of electronics racks. I got up from my seat on the floor with a crick in my neck as a good-looking, cheerful, slightly pudgy young man hopped down from the driver's seat and walked over to me with a light step. He reached out and offered me his hand. "Dr. Darrow. George Prigot. The big brass seem to think you're on to something pretty big."

"I might be at that." I took an instant liking to George. He was of medium height, with a thick mop of shaggy brown hair. His eyes were calm, almost sleepy, and yet had a bright spark hidden in their depths. His handshake was firm and solid, and his hands would have done a surgeon credit—big, long-fingered, and used with a graceful economy of motion.

This was no military type, uniform or no. It barely was a uniform he had on. The insignia was faded, and the shirt was rumpled and washed to the point where it was a completely different shade of grey from the pants, which were too long, almost making him trip over his unshined shoes. Every outfit has one of George's kind in it—the tolerated talent, too good at what he did to be done without, and therefore given more freedom, more license, than anyone else.

"A matter transmitter. I used to hope I'd get the chance to work on one. I gave that up when they sent me here. Not much research on this planet for a while."

"Well, you'll work on it now. Did you get a look at the blueprints they wired down from the satellite?"

He pointed to the cart full of girders and sheet metal behind him. "That's it, right there. All prefabbed. We just finished up the last of the cutting an hour ago. In fact, my plan is to get the basic structure up tonight, while you get caught up on your rest. You look pretty done in. Where are you billeted? I'll run you over."

"Short trip. I'm not supposed to go farther than the privy, three times a day. They're bringing in a cot."

"Brilliant. You can't do design work sleeping on a piece of canvas in the middle of a machine shop. Heinrichs!"

"Yes sir?"

"First thing on the agenda is to get the doctor here a place to lay his head. We'll build him a soundproof cubicle over there in the corner. Get some soundproof wallboard and so on. I want it up inside of three hours. Pound the quartermaster over the head until he issues you a decent bed and bedding. Also, we'll need working tables and chairs. Brass didn't think we'd need any office space to do this. Got it?"

"Okay. Do I check with you if I need anything else?"

"Use your judgment. Better still, use Steve's. He knows what we can get away with. Learn from the master."

"Yo." Heinrichs neglected his salute (but George didn't seem to expect one), hopped back into the wagon, and drove off.

"That should settle things. Oh! They think to feed you?"

"Nope."

"And I forgot to eat, myself. Tell you what. You get freshened up a bit and I'll find us some food." And George was gone.

The privy detail marched me across the courtyard. By the time I had my shower, shaved, brushed my teeth, and generally gotten closer to feeling human, Heinrichs and a few others were already putting together my bunkroom. George appeared, bearing a pair of stacked trays, and, as George put it, "some of the boys" started to rig work lights.

The lighting was stark and cross-angled, like searchlights in a dark field. Brightly lit figures would scurry in front of a light and then vanish completely into huge shadows. Great misshapen beings would appear in silhouette on the walls and then transform themselves into normal humans as the original stepped closer to the wall and straightened up.

There is a magic about a rush job at night. The barn doors were left open as men came in and out after tools or a sandwich from the mess hall, and cool night air spilled into the brightly lit hangar. The previously untouched room lost its virginity. Men were at work, and litter appeared on the floor—scraps of paper full of rough sketches and calculations, sandwich wrappers, bits and shims of steel from pieces that needed a trim, tools strewn about, and cables snaking everywhere in entangling webs.

In the center of it all, the shell of the receiver grew like a ruin coming back to life. The first bracing appeared, and the wide curve of a half cylinder grew across the floor. Parts were welded together, and each joint was closely scrutinized by George. He was a tough man to please, and no job was done until it was done over and done right. Soon, the skeleton of the beast was complete, and we started putting the skin on.

Sheets of narrow-gauge steel were flush-bolted to the inside of the frame, and the pieces joined with a precision Finnish laser welding unit. You could run your hand over the seams and never find them.

This was a proud crew, a tight crew. George ran them hard, but they knew how good they were. The lowest-ranked laborer had just as much of a chance of winning a technical argument as his superior. Here the job was important, and to hell with the paperwork, we'll patch up a story later.

The Guardians I had been **up** against so far had been robots, or sadists, or barbarians, or simply boors. Here I was part of the team, since I could handle a screwdriver, since I could help Get The Job Done. After all the long weeks of isolation, starting the moment I set foot aboard *Stars*, this was just what I needed.

I nearly forgot whose side they were on, and the strong chance that this machine would result in their deaths. It's easy to rationalize killing the bad guys, but here was George offering to loan me his tape deck for the duration, and I might be arranging for him to be lying in a pool of blood in a week's time.

One line of thought could have cheered me up as far as that went. The plan might fail. The transmitter could go blooie. Guardian intelligence might catch up with me. I might blow the schedule. Could I speed up the work, or stall, if need be?

The great shape grew and solidified in the middle of the hangar, spotlit and backlit now and then by the welders. They were down to finicky alignment work by the time exhaustion caught up with me, and I crawled into my bunk, morning just peeping in the door. I slept long and well.

Outside my comfortable little room, a machine of death and salvation slowly grew.

CHAPTER SEVEN

"Jeff, if this things works, things are really going to change. I mean *really* change." George downed a big gulp of New Finnish vodka and grimaced at the strength of the stuff. He handed me the bottle and I took a slightly shorter pull off it. I nodded a somewhat hazy agreement.

"Cars, planes, hell, even intersystem spaceflight—all of it obsolete. Push a button and there you are!"

"And then once you're at the other end someone hands you a bill for a gigawatt or so of electricity."

"Just a question of efficiency."

"Think it can be made efficient?"

"Sure. I think you can make it efficient."

"Me. Hmmmm."

"You. Jeff—why is it you always talk about it as if it wasn't *your* work?"

"I dunno." I realized I was on thin ice again and tried to retreat. "I guess the idea has been floating around so long I can't take credit. Or else I don't really believe it will work."

"Oh, it'll work." George was no more a theorist than Terrance MacKenzie Larson (alias Jefferson Darrow) was. His opinion, no, his certitude, was based on faith. Faith in me, ol' Doc Darrow. I took a longer hit off the bottle.

Judas. I felt like Judas. George so clearly liked me, respected me. I had found it harder and harder to play the part of Dr. Darrow, prize chicken and quisling, around him. Here I was, posing as the brilliant inventor of the gadget he had dreamed of as a kid in the children's barracks back on the Guardian's planet, Capital. And I was to betray him

We were sitting in my little private room, and the boys from George's crew (or, more formally, 9462 Construction Battalion) were throwing themselves a little party to celebrate the completion of the basic structure. From here on in it was finicky work with oscilloscopes and test calipers. One of the boys opened the door, stuck in a rather red nose, yelled "C'mon! Th' party's ou' here!," and nearly slammed the door on himself as he left, without waiting for a reply.

George grinned and sipped at the bottle. I shook my head at him. "You sure don't seem the military type, George. How'd *you* end up here?"

"Hell, Jeff, on Capital, *everybody's* the military sort. There isn't anything else. That's the whole point."

"What's the idea of calling it Capital, anyway?"

He shrugged vaguely. "They figure it's going to be that. Someday. The Capital. Capital of everything, everybody."

"Everybody? Earth? Bandwidth? Europa?"

"I guess."

"Jesus H. Christ! *Why?*"

"Thought you didn't care about politics."

"Politics, no." Booze, and my guilty friendship toward George loosened my tongue a bit. "But you guys have killed a lot of people here. There'd be a lot more killing if you take on the others."

"Yeah, they have killed a lot. . . ." He grunted to himself and smiled grimly. "And I know what you're thinking, and you play too fair to say it: 'Why do you always talk about it as if it wasn't *your* work?'" He laughed without any humor behind it, and looked through the wall in the direction of the matter transmitter's receiver. "And what work will *we* do with *that*?"

George suddenly seemed very upset, and I remembered just a little too late that I wasn't supposed to be at all concerned about what the Guardians were like. "C'mon," I said. "You guys aren't any worse than other governments have been. Don't be so hard on yourself. Besides, *every* invention has military potential." Blearily, I thought about what a flaming bastard Darrow was, about how slimily perfect his powers of rationalization were. Then I remembered Darrow was me. Which gave me plenty more to think about. Suddenly I felt like I hadn't bathed in a long time.

George grunted. "There are things . . . things you don't know about us. Things all of us know about ourselves, that the Central Guardians have declared state secrets, anyway. If I told you, it would be the firing squad for both of us." He paused. "It isn't just that we fight wars. You're right, everybody does that. But my people have done things. . . . If you knew what we've made ourselves into, what we allow ourselves to remain—Sometimes I think the war we're really fighting is against our own past. And we're losing." He took a long haul off the bottle.

There was something in his tone that made my skin crawl. In that moment, I *knew*, I knew deep in my gut, that the Guardians had kidnapped my classmates. And I *knew* that to the Guardians, kidnapping was as nothing, that there was more, and worse. I tried to change the subject. "Look, George, take it easy. We're supposed to be celebrating. We finally finished the job."

He smiled faintly. "Yeah, I guess we did."

"And it's one hell of a machine, isn't it?"

"Hell of one." George noticed I was starting to get a little fuzzy. He slapped me on the back and stood up. "You get into that bed and get some sleep. Lots of work tomorrow."

Lots of hangovers the next day, too. *Mine* was impressive, anyway. I had been hanging around engineers too long: I felt a strong urge to disassemble my head and fix whatever the hell was the matter with it.

We went on with the work.

Then, one day, tomorrow was *the* day. I had been fooling with phony circuits for a day and a half by that time. Now it was time to quit stalling. All the gadgets lashed together on Vapaus, all the impressive blinking lights, were in place. Most of George's men were back at other work again. Just George and Heinrichs were still assigned to me.

I closed down the inspection hatch I had been diddling with and sauntered over to one of the guards. "If you would, please get a message to the base commander. Tell him we'll be ready for a demonstration at 2000 hours tomorrow."

"Yes sir!" This *was* a big moment; the first time any of my guards had called me "sir"—or anything at all, for that matter.

By now, a hundred plans were being put into effect around this world, and in Vapaus. With luck, by the time the League troops arrived, the Guardians' forces would already be half crippled. A host of mysterious flat tires, shorted out engines, strange cases of food poisoning, delays and problems from civilian suppliers, a rash of fires.

The Guardians' intelligence units were going to notice fast. Chances were someone had been picked up and interrogated already, someone who knew more than he should have. Conspiracy is a highly skilled profession, practiced only by amateurs. There was sure to be some warning that something was up.

Would someone make the connection between my bogus machine and the sudden flurry of headaches from a population that had seemed subdued?

Time started to drag toward deep night. I felt alone and afraid.

The remaining guard watched me closely, but allowed me to step through the doors of the hangar and breath in the fresh cleanness of the mild autumn weather.

I looked out to the crystal clear sky, the old familiar stars, seen in strange new places from a different world. Not for the first time, not even for the hundredth, I thought of Joslyn. She was out there, somewhere, and only if I lived would I see her again. That alone was reason for this fight. I thought back to those good days, before the drone came into our lives with its frightful news, and farther back than that, to the days of training, before the *Venera*. How had I come from all that to this sorry place? How had it come to me to try and break the yoke the Guardians had hung on this world?

I realized that I had never had a choice, that I had had to come. The thought that, even for a moment, back in the comfort of the *J.M.*'s wardroom, I had thought it might be understandable to cut and run.... No. this was my fight, now, by right of duty, honor, and anger. For what they had done to Tempkin's family, if nothing else.

And Joslyn. She was in this fight, too. There was a hell of a reason. If we won, she would be safe.

The fate of a world was more or less in my hands that night, but it was Joslyn I thought of.

I looked at the stars, and loved her with all my heart.

I spotted a portly figure in a greatcoat marching toward me in a studied sort of hurry, leaving a jeep behind him. He walked through a light, and my blood froze. Bradhurst. Intelligence. He walked straight toward me, opened his lipless mouth, with a sort of basilisk's smile, and spoke.

"Good evening, Commander Larson."

Oh my God.

Poker face. Ignore it. You are in it *deep*! I stood there and looked at him. "Hmmm? Bradhurst? It's me, Darrow. You've got the wrong guy." My heart was pounding so hard I thought I could hear it.

"I have the right man, Commander."

A dead, silent moment passed between us. He stared at me with those vicious, dead eyes and all I wanted to do was run.

"I don't know what you're talking about. I'm Darrow."

"Of course you are. Come along, anyway." He gestured to the guard that he was taking me for a stroll. "The guard seems to trust you, letting you stand in the open doorway like that."

"No reason not to trust me. Besides, where would I run?"

"Precisely." Bradhurst was enjoying this, a cat playing with a bird who can't get away, letting it try, anyway.

Bradhurst slipped his hands into his pockets and drew out a pair of fine leather gloves. He carefully pulled them onto his fat fingers. "Imagine my position. Thanks to me, a man is put in a place of trust, put in charge of an important new weapon. The weapon is excitingly useful, very tempting. The man's records are satisfactory. Very convenient, isn't it? Especially since this man simply popped out of the woodwork, no explanation of why he was missed before." Bradhurst smiled at me, a hungry gleaming of teeth. "There is, however, a flaw. If something goes wrong, things have gotten out of control to the point where *I* might be blamed. So I checked. And I checked again. Most slowly. Most carefully. I even check a memory file that includes a listing of the personnel of the League of Planets Survey Service. The records, and the fingerprints, were of interest.

"I don't know how you got here, Larson, but you are here. That machine in there—I don't know what it is, but I know what it isn't. And it isn't here to do the Guardians of Capital any good."

Bradhurst stopped and turned toward me. I thought of running, but he was right. Where could I run?

He glared at me and kept talking. "There seem to be an untoward number of accidents and problems with the locals tonight. I wonder if you know anything about that? But it doesn't matter now. We've walked far enough. We go back now, and tear that machine to pieces—we'll find out what it *really* is. And then, after we have shredded every single fact from the remains of your brain, you will die."

No matter how long the odds, I had to try to get away in the dark, circle back, try and activate the transmitter early. I had no chance, but I had no choice, either. I shifted my feet to run—

"Don't try to escape, Larson." Suddenly, his voice was as hard and cold as granite in a cave. I backpedaled a bit. I *had* to try.

He pulled out his sidearm. "I'm warning you—"

A ruby beam sizzled through his neck, slicing through the flesh, and he collapsed against me, gurgling, already dead.

A pair of boots came crunching up, and a dim figure appeared, reholstering a laser. "I had to stop the transmitter. I couldn't let 'em keep killing. I was going to kill *you* until I heard this guy talk."

George Prigot. He grabbed at the body and pulled it off me, shoving it to the ground. I gulped, blinded for a moment by the splash of blood that had struck me in the face. I looked down at the broad, puffy face. A thin line of blood oozed up from behind its lips. Now the face was as dead as those glassy, murderous eyes.

"He's no loss," George said. He looked at me sharply. "That night we were drinking, I realized Capital isn't a good place. There's a better life in this stinking camp, just being away from Capital and a little nearer to people who used to know peace. I couldn't help it spread, and that machine, what it could do. . . . You really from the League?"

I remembered to breathe, gulped air, let myself go to the shakes. It had been that close. "Yeah. Yeah. Terrance MacKenzie Larson, ROK Navy. The League."

"Good." He prodded the body with the toe of his boot. "What do we do with the body?"

"I don't know."

"Wait a minute. I know a place. Give me a hand." We each grabbed one of Bradhurst's arms and pulled the still-warm body up. We dragged it about 50 yards through the dark to a toolshed. George leaned the body against it, fumbled with a bunch of keys, and opened the lock.

We shoved the body inside. I ran back the way we came and did what I could to scuff up the gravel where the body had bled and where we had dragged it. No one who wasn't looking for blood would find it. I hustled back to find George hiding in the shadows of the toolshed.

"Now. Talk," he said. "What the hell is going to happen when we push that button?"

"Not what. Who. It really is a matter transmitter. The League is beaming 5,000 troops at us."

"My God. Is it going to work?"

"I have no idea. I hope so."

"Jesus! But how are—never mind. Later. For now, what do we do about this guy Bradhurst?"

"Let me think. Look. Call the hangar. Tell them to tell his driver you're discussing security for the demonstration with him and you're going to drive Bradhurst back to his quarters. All we have to do is stall them until the test. Afterwards, it won't matter, one way or the other."

"Good enough. I'll be back. Don't go anywhere."

"Where have I got to go?" But George was already lost in the shadows. I sat in the dark for a long time.

George returned. "Okay, I think they bought it."

"Good. Let's get out of here and find a place to talk." I wanted to get away from the corpse.

George led me to an empty building at the end of the camp. He seemed to know how to avoid the sentries. George. What was in it for him? How much was this costing him? Could I really trust him, or would he change his mind by morning? Can you ever completely trust a turncoat?

There was no doubt in him tonight. He asked me questions and we made decisions. We planned and schemed. We were dealing with the death of the men he had eaten breakfast with that morning.

"It's a lot to ask of you, George."

"I know, but you're not asking. I'm doing. I've had it. I've wired up plenty of our nasty little killing gadgets. I went past the far end of camp this morning. A firing squad. I recognized one of the soldiers, and his gun. I had fixed the power feed for him the day before. And they were shooting a 12-year-old girl who had wandered in looking for her daddy. She thought he might be with the soldiers. She didn't think about whose. They shot her for spying."

There was nothing I could say.

It was too much, too fast, too close to the end. If, if, if was all I could think. No one had any idea what would happen tomorrow. The best we could hope was that Bradhurst hadn't told anyone what he had learned, and that the Guardians would know less than we did.

All I knew for certain was that tomorrow, some of us would die.

PART TWO:
WAR ON
THE GROUND

INTERLUDE

The ghosts were with me that night. I dreamed in a pool of sweat, surrounded by faces that stared at me, unsure of me, doubtful I could fulfill the trust forced upon me.

I could clearly see only the *eyes* of the ghosts. Their faces and bodies glimmered, became nearly sharp, distinct, and real, only to fade away again.

A dirty, mud-caked GI with a a baby in his arms; a Cherokee watching in the night for the villains who savaged his world; a frightened, tiny slip of a girl trapped in a bombed-out subway, trying to calm the children imprisoned with her, singing them nursery rhymes, telling stories, half an ear listening for the sound of digging, scraping, the sound of rescue on the way, humming the little tune and wondering if help would ever come. . . .

Forgotten heros peered at me, pointed and prodded, asking if I would fail in this, *my* task.

But, toward dawn, I think, Joslyn appeared among them. She took my hand and smiled at the dead protectors.

They nodded, once each, slowly, and faded into the gloomy mists, to guard at another gate of danger, to peer into another part of the darkness that must of definition surround free men.

113

CHAPTER EIGHT

The next morning it took a long while to realize that the night was finally over, and that this was, indeed, *the* day. I dressed quickly, and, for the last time, went through the daily ritual of the trek to the latrine, closely followed by my two armed guards.

I returned to my room and put on an official-looking white lab coat over my coverall. I dug under my mattress, pulled out Bradhurst's laser, and shoved it into a coverall pocket, hoping the lab coat would hide the bulge.

I ate breakfast—or at least went through the motions of eating it. About three bites actually got down—and barely stayed down. Well, there was plenty to be scared of.

I shoved back the tray, tried to compose my face, and walked out into the hangar. All the debris of our frantic activity had been cleared away, and folding chairs set up in preparation for visitors. I knew there were going to be some visitors, but not that there'd be so many. Another worry, and not one I was prepared for.

The watch on my wrist grew bigger and bigger, and the numbers flashing on it took longer and longer to change. Hours went by as I stood over my control board, checking and rechecking the switch settings, double-checking procedures I knew by heart.

Time dragged on.

Finally, the moment was near. One grey uniform decked with braid, then another, and another, strolled in, found their places, and sat down.

I worried over Bradhurst. Was he expected this morning? How long until he was missed? How long until I was suspected? Had he reported finding this Commander Larson to anyone on his staff?

The grey men continued to file in, the clock crept toward the appointed hour, and I hoped a nervous scientist acted the same way a nervous spy did.

Again and again I asked—Was George to be trusted? He wasn't here yet. Did he have cold feet? Was he already talking to the secret police?

Fifteen minutes before the test, he appeared—the only man from his shop to come. He was in full dress uniform, the first time I had ever seen him in it. It was a formal affair, but that uniform also gave him a chance to wear his officer's sidearm. He nodded to me and tipped the side of his peaked cap with a large cylindrical map case. Poker-faced.

I began to have the presence of mind to think like a soldier. Half of the audience wore sidearms of some kind, and my two guards stood by the door, stiff and rigid, saluting everything that moved. Their boot tops gleamed in the afternoon light. With luck, they would be too busy with the spit-and-polish routine to be of much help in an emergency; however, they carried heavy firepower—laser rifles that could burn holes in steel plating.

Okay, hit them first, *then* the officers, in the few seconds between activation of the transmitter and the materialization of the first League troops.

The League troops were a completely open question as well. Assuming they had been transmitted, and assuming the capture device had done its work, and hadn't been wrecked by some fumble-fingered private in the Guardians' transport service, I still had no idea what sort of soldiers had been sent, or how they would react. All I could hope for was that they were ready for trouble.

At the time the League had sent the drone out to find the *J.M.*, the League's military planning staff hadn't had a chance to get a force together. The reports sent with the drone said that we could expect a combined force made up of troops grabbed in a hurry from half the member states. Since the ship that was to carry the troops to the transmission point was to be launched from Earth, we were told to expect a large proportion of Earthside troops. Political realities (it was broadly hinted in the report) would require a number of small units, token contributions from member states that didn't have the time or money to offer more.

My worrying was interrupted when General Schlitzer, the base commander, arrived amid a flurry of saluting from all sides. Lieutenant Grimes escorted Schlitzer over to me, made introductions, and left us to talk. Schlitzer shook my hand and said, "Good day, Doctor. Are we ready to go forward with the demonstration?"

I gulped and tried to smile, with my heart in my stomach. "I think so, sir."

"Good. Let us hope this is a grand day for us both." He stood and looked over the great machine. "Tell me," he went on, "why is the receiver so much larger than the transmitter cage?"

Damn! He *would* ask that one. The bogus transmitter cage was barely a meter square, while the receiver was ten times that size. "Well, sir, the transmitter is a much more complicated device, and must be built to exact tolerance, while the receiver simply has to be at least large enough to accept whatever it is sent. So as to save time in later tests, we built one large receiver cage, which will be able to accommodate any and all of the big transmitters we hope to build later." I hoped he bought it.

"I see. Well, I suppose we can leave that sort of thing to you technical people." He nodded curtly and turned to face the audience, his back to me. Which killed him, a few minutes later.

The other brass noticed he was waiting for their attention and quieted down. Schlitzer proceeded to give a little speech.

"Gentlemen. You have all heard the basic idea behind this device. If it is successful, it will be capable of transmitting matter over radio waves. The improvement in our ability to strike faster, harder, and more effectively is barely imaginable. In a few minutes we may know that our next conquest shall not only be greater—but bought far more cheaply. We see the transmitter today. Tomorrow, a dozen worlds will see it, worlds that will not be able to face us, except in death. Doctor?"

I nodded, swallowed hard, and started pushing buttons. I energized the system and heard the loud, satisfying *clack* of big relays coming on line. The lights in the room flickered and dimmed for a moment as the machinery absorbed more and more power. Pilot lights and meters came to life. Then there was just one button left to push to start the automatic sequencers. I looked out beyond the sea of faces to the only one that wasn't staring intently at the transmitter or receiver cages— George. Moving very slowly, he had gotten himself directly behind the oblivious guards.

I hit the switch.

The lights dimmed again as power rushed into the capture device. Now we were committed. From here on in, the transmitter operated automatically.

Queep! The first of three audio warning tones. System ready. I slid my hand into the lab coat and felt the butt of the dead man's gun. George had his hand on his holster.

Queep! Capture device engaged.

George killed one of the guards, a silent laser beam boring the life out of his skull.

QUEEP! Receiving objects . . .

A blast of wind slapped across the audience as the

air in the receiver was forced out by the materializing effect.

I pulled out my gun and shot the general. He turned in shock, screaming, and felt his spine opening up under my laser. He dropped like a stone.

There was a flash of light from the receiver that left an afterimage, no, a solid reality of—men!

They were here.

I turned and fired into the crowd of officers. George shot the other guard through the heart. He grabbed the guard's rifle, turned and played the rifle over the crowd, wounding, blinding, killing half of them in a sudden terrible moment. The Guardians were aghast, shocked. Two-thirds of them were dead before one of them thought to fire back at us.

I crouched behind my console—which wasn't heavy steel by accident—and looked at the troops that had arrived. They were here, real. It had all worked. But this was a hell of a surprise welcome for them.

Some of them dove off the receiver stage and took cover, not sure who to shoot at, if anyone. The rest stood there, dazed. It must have been a hell of a surprise.

Queep! The next cycle of troops would be here in ten seconds. . . .

I stood up and yelled, "Get the hell off that platform! Clear out! Clear out!" They came, and I recognized the uniform. Well-armed Republic of Kennedy marines!

"Clear out! Clear out! Get out of that thing! Move it!"

They moved. One of them had the sense to throw something at the people I was shooting at. A loud flash and a boom, and where there had been people—the enemy—was gore and a sudden stench.

Queep! QUEEP! More on the way.

I holstered the gun and stripped off the lab coat. "Soldier! You! Get over here!"

She trotted over and saluted. "Sir!"

"Who knows when there's some artillery coming?"

"Kaplan, Corporal Kaplan has a printout of who's due when, sir."

"Kaplan!"

"Yo!"

Kaplan was in front of me, already fumbling with a thick sheaf of paper. "Kaplan, when do we get some artillery?"

"Just a sec, sir ... ah ... elements of 107th light artillery. British Army. Fifth outfit to arrive. Sir, what the hell happened?"

"Later. Stick by me." I looked up from the printout to see George. "Oh, boy. Hang on, George. It's gonna get worse." George dropped his rifle as if it had turned into a serpent in his hands. He looked bad, very bad. "George! Listen! Artillery. The fifth outfit to come through. Brits. You've got to get them out to the courtyard and show them those targets. Okay?"

"Oh, God. Yeah, okay." He was nearly in shock. Suddenly, he shook himself and answered again in a stronger voice. "Right. I'll do it." He strode, a bit jerkily, to the receiver.

Kaplan and the first private I had talked to were standing with me, just watching their fellows appearing out of nowhere and coming out of the receiver cage.

The first private said, "Pardon me, Commander Larson? Ah, where are we, sir? Weren't we supposed to land in an empty plain?"

"The main office made a mistake. The original site is under water. This is one of the enemy's main bases. We had to improvise. Oh, and it's also mid-October, Earthside. You've been held as sort of a recording for about a month."

She swallowed suddenly and her eyes went pop. "My goodness. How are we getting out of here?"

"Very carefully."

Queep! Queep! QUEEP!

From the hardware on the shoulders, this was the load that carried the heavy brass. These were no desk jockeys; they had the look of field soldiers. I checked their insignia and spotted the commander. He was a big, solid man in a British Army brigader's uniform.

This time I trotted up and did the saluting. "Commander Terrance MacKenzie Larson, ROK Navy."

He looked around himself at the smoky hangar, the mangled corpses in high-ranking uniforms, and the mob of soldiers trying to get themselves sorted out. Then he saluted back and said, "Report!"

"Error in cartography, sir. Original landing site was actually under water. The Finns and I worked out a way to hold your control signal as a recording, then we received the signal in free space and smuggled it to the surface, fooling the enemy into assisting in the construction of the receiver. We were forced to construct it in the middle of one of their largest army bases. Much of the camp brass was here thinking they'd see a demonstration of a matter transmitter. . . ."

"And we've certainly given them that. They got shot up, and so the base doesn't have anyone to give it orders, and perhaps we've got a minute or two to ourselves."

"Yessir."

"Can we get out of here?"

"Maybe. If we can steal enough trucks from their motor pool." I nodded toward George. "This man can show you where it is on a map of the base."

"Roberts! Figure out where it is, take a couple of squads, and get those trucks!" He pointed to Kaplan. "You there! Stand by the transmitter and explain what's going on to the troops as they come through." The brigadier turned back to me. "What about help from the locals?"

"They should be hitting the Guardians—the enemy—on the planet and on the satellite Vapaus, a lot of little dust-ups, right now. Everything acting as mutual diversions."

"Very well."

Suddenly I spotted men pulling what looked like a midget howitzer behind them in the receiver cage. I nudged George and pointed. He finished up quickly with Roberts and took the rather bewildered-looking Tommies in tow, leading them to the courtyard.

The brigadier watched it all rather phlegmatically. "It looks quite a bit like we're in a right old mess. By the way, Brigadier Taylor, British Army."

"Sir."

A loud *crump* came from outside, and a moment later an ear-splitting series of explosions came from the south end of the camp. "There goes the ammo dump, I expect," Taylor said.

"They'll hit the armory next, then work over the barracks and the rest of the camp," I said.

Another series of blasts came from the east, a sharper, staccato series of reports. Taylor looked up sharply. "That's not the shells from our artillery."

One of the Kennedy troops came rushing in from the courtyard. "The camp's perimeter fence just got blown up, a long section right in front of us!"

We all rushed out into the rapidly filling courtyard. It was a disorganized mob. Taylor grabbed the first officer he saw and yelled, "Clear these men out of here! Blow the locks off the hangars and put 'em there. We need this road clear! Lieutenant Roberts is coming back any moment with the trucks we're riding out of here. Fast!"

He strode out into the courtyard, followed by a small crowd that included myself. The fence was down all right, across maybe 100 meters of the perimeter. Men carrying weapons were running toward us. One of them carried a flag—

New Finnish flag! "Hold your fire!" I yelled. "That's our side!" I found my gun in my hand, reholstered it, and rushed out to meet them. I came up to a thin, wiry man of about 50 dressed in a worn old uniform. He saluted as some of his troops gathered in a little knot around the two of us. "It is that we do have trucks and a train," he began in very laborious English.

"I speak some Finnish," I cut in.

He breathed a sigh of relief and switched languages. "Good. We have some trucks and there is a train waiting on its tracks about 12 kilometers from here. We can take some on the trucks and get the others on the train. We heard from the higher-ups that there would be a lot of soldiers here that would need to be evacuated."

"That's for sure. Come this way." I took him to Taylor and explained the situation to the Brigadier.

Taylor nodded and pulled a small communicator out of his belt. "Freiling. Get all the troops you can moving through the break in the fence. The locals are ready to move you." He shut off the communicator and turned to me. "Ask him how many troops he can move."

The Finn understood and answered in English before I could translate. "We can do about two million."

"Two million!"

"Thousand! I'm meaning two thousand. Sorry."

"If you had more lorries, could you handle more men?"

"Lorries? Oh, yes, trucks. Sure, all you want."

"Good." He talked into the comm unit again. "Major Kavanos! Yes, I can hear you, too. Now get some of your men together and follow Roberts to the motor pool. Steal as many lorries as you can. Load them up and head for the break in the fence. Take another detail to make sure we can hold the motor pool. If we lose it, the party's over."

Before he could put his comm unit away, it beeped for attention. "Yes. I see. Well, keep shooting back, try and figure out where they are, and see if our artillery can take them out." He spoke to me. "These Guardians have finally gotten organized enough to start shooting back. We'd better get back to the courtyard."

It was bedlam. The transmitter was still pouring out troops and there just wasn't room for the ones that were already there. Taylor shook his head. "If they have the sense to hit their own camp with artillery, we're sitting ducks."

The first of the trucks was struggling into the courtyard, inching past the masses of troops. Taylor shouldered his way through the throng and jumped up on the running board for a moment. "You! Stop this truck, load it up right here and back it out of here! You men in the brown berets!"

"Sir!" their officer said.

"Get your men into that truck and out of the way!"

"SIR!"

Taylor grabbed a U.S. Army sergeant by the collar. "You! You're in charge of crowd control as of now. Get this madhouse organized, smartly!" The sergeant got to it.

"You there! Get the road clear!" He pulled out his communicator. "Taylor here. Attention all officers in command. Get your troops into orderly columns and as close to the edge of the courtyard as possible. We need the roadway clear. Get dispersed. One good big shell could wipe us all out. Corporal Kaplan, if you would be so good as to relay those orders to the troops coming through."

There was a good-sized firefight to the northeast of the courtyard. The artillery, the 107th, was still pounding the hell out of the rest of the camp. The courtyard was covered in heavy smoke every now and then as the wind kept shifting. I made my way to the center of the courtyard, where the 107th had set its guns. George was still there, working the map with cool precision, his mouth thin and determined. The howitzers were kicking up the clay of the yard, and dust covered the men. George especially had been covered in a dirty white pallor.

"George!" The guns thundered again, preventing conversation for long seconds. "How are we doing?"

He shook a layer of dust off the map and indicated parts of the map covered with blood-red crosshatching, representing about two-thirds of the camp. "We've been bracketing the whole place, block by block, and this is what's, well—gone. Not much left but the mess tents and some of the barracks."

One of the artillery men tapped me on the shoulder. "Are we to expect Brigader Taylor to send out" WHAM "patrols to secure the areas we've hit?" A shell was fired in the middle of his sentence, but he went on as if it wasn't there.

"No, I doubt it. We don't want to hold this ground, just get the hell out."

"Very good, sir."

"Sergeant—can you spare me Mr. Prigot here?"

"Oh, I expect" WHAM "so, sir. We've got the hang of the map now. One of my lads can fill in."

"C'mon, George. We've got to get you out of that uniform."

"Mmm? Oh, yeah."

The sergeant looked over George more closely. "That what the other side looks like, sir?"

"Yes," I said.

"I thought so. Bit of infiltration?"

"Something like that," George said, his voice devoid of any emotion, as if his insides were frozen. I pulled him to his feet and we shoved our way through the throng to the receiver's hangar.

"We'll get you changed in my room," I said.

The crowd inside had thinned out a bit, and Kaplan seemed to have things more or less under control. As we came in, he was giving yet another outfit a rundown on the situation.

I waited until he was done and asked, "How many more to go?"

He glanced down at a long list that was rapidly getting dogeared. "Let's see—that last group was from the Army of the Sixth Republic, the French. After them—just about halfway through, about 40 or so to go."

"Make sure this thing is blown to hell and rubble as soon as the last ones step through."

"Already seen to it, Commander. Oh, and there's several shipments of weapons to hand on to the locals toward the end."

"Good. They're right outside, ready to take 'em, I'm sure."

"Yessir." With a QUEEP and a flash another group

popped into existence on the receiver stage. Kaplan got back to his work. "All right, who are you people? Europa Federals? Right. Now listen up, fellas, and those of you who speak English pass it on to your buddies. Okay. Things have gotten screwed over but good. . . ."

We left him to it and arrived at the room a few of the boys had made soundproof so I could sleep nights. I shut the door on the war outside and we sat down on my bunk.

George let out a deep sigh. "My God. How did I get into this?"

"George. You can get out now. You've paid your dues. Go. Take off. A man can't be expected to calmly go on killing his own people."

"No, Jeff. Or Terrance, or MacKenzie, or whoever you are."

"Call me Mac."

"Mac—don't you see? Yeah, I've maybe, maybe paid my dues for that 12-year-old. Except she's still dead. But *how many more did I help kill*? I don't care how long I worked with the guys I've betrayed. They are killers. Murderers. How many more people were murdered by the cheap guns I fixed and the machines I designed? If I go my whole life, I can't pay that back."

He stared into space for a moment. Suddenly he shook himself and started peeling off the heavy uniform. "Let's get moving." He changed into some of my clothes (a poor fit, but serviceable) and motioned me toward the door. "Let's get the hell out of here and see what's going on."

We walked past the receiver as Kaplan was explaining things to a 101st Airborne Special Operation Commando Unit and went on into the courtyard.

That sergeant must have whipped someone into shape. The trucks were rolling without any trouble, loading up with men and women from I don't know how many military outfits. It seemed like every member state had sent some sort of force to New Finland. About the only thing missing were the Swiss Guards from the Vatican.

The 107th pounded away at the rest of the camp, but the smoke from the fires they had set was already too thick to see if they were doing much besides stirring the rubble.

I spotted Taylor in the middle of the courtyard, talking into his communicator again. "Taylor here. Fine work so far. Keep them moving on." He turned to us as George and I came over. "The Finns have gotten the first troops into their train." He looked over the organized chaos of what used to be an army base and shook his head. "We are going to come through this. Amazing. You and your Finnish friends have done quite well."

Army bases aren't designed to be safe from attacks from inside themselves. We had wiped out the majority of the commanding officers in the first 30 seconds. The first warning most of the enemy had had was the destruction of their own ammo dump. I didn't want to calculate how many men had been slaughtered in the sneak attack, how many had died without any hope of defending themselves. The landing field was a cratered ruin, and the comm center was wrecked, the entire camp brought low and dead.

Kaplan trotted up to me and said, "Get ready for a loud noise."

"The receiver is about to—" BLAM!!!

"It sure as hell is!" Kaplan said. "Good God almighty, I am never going to tell anyone what's going on or where they are again. I did a *lifetime's* worth today."

Trucks were starting to come back from their first trips to the rail line, picking up more men. Taylor spoke into his comm unit again. "All commanders. Lorries on the second trip. Pick a road and keep moving! Just stay in comm range. But disperse. If the enemy knocks out the rail line, let's have some eggs in another basket."

More than just trucks started appearing from the motor pool. Jeeps, halftrucks, even a giant dump truck. They all stopped off, filled up, and moved out through the gap in the perimeter fence.

Random sizzling noises from high-energy lasers and

an occasional ricochet were the only hint of any real fighting.

We had done it. We had actually gotten those troops here, and out of here, against all the odds. And they were going to make it, would survive at least long enough to fight.

The trucks rolled on.

CHAPTER NINE

The trucks ran, rolled, flowed and ebbed, their electric motors humming as they carried the soldiers away from the ruined camp.

Taylor and I watched the procession as the crowd of soldiers shrunk from thousands to a few hundred. Still there was no real opposition, and the Guardian assault we expected didn't come.

Taylor had held back one intact unit—the U.S. Army 1st Battalion, 75th Infantry, a ranger unit. They were posted on the rooftops and along the outer perimeter of the area we controlled. Taylor looked from the rangers on the roof to the crowd on the ground, shook his head dolefully, and looked back toward one of the rangers on the top of the receiver's hangar.

He extracted a rather shabby pipe and got started lighting it as he spoke. "When their reinforcements come, we will be caught with our trousers down. We've got a mob, not a fighting unit."

Except for the rangers, the soldiers left behind were stragglers, cut off from their units. Many units that had gotten away were split up. Even once they got away, they had no idea where they were going.

"Maybe they won't come before we get away," I said. "The Finns are supposed to have sabotaged most of the

128

enemy forces by now. According to Tempkin's plan, all the Guardians are out of it for the moment."

Taylor didn't move his gaze from the ranger as he spoke. "No battle ever went according to plan. Have you ever heard of the American raid on the Ploesti oil fields in the Second World War? Treetop bombing. One of the first times it was tried. But all but one flight of bombers missed the target and had to double back to find it. Hundreds of planes came in over the targets from three different directions at once. Sheer hell. The defending commander, on the ground, thought it had been planned that way; all he could do was watch what he thought was perfectly planned orchestration. No one in the air had the foggiest idea what was going on."

"So what happened?"

"The Americans lost over half the planes." Taylor was quiet for a long time. "Someone out there"—he pointed vaguely with the stem of the pipe—"went ahead and attacked early, or got caught after curfew and was shot full of truth serum. Someone failed to sabotage something. One of the Guardian officers wonders what happened to his friend at this camp and sent a plane over when he couldn't get through on the phone. They'll be here. With amazing luck, we might be out of here by the time they arrive."

"Then what?" I asked.

"I have no idea."

The sun crawled toward the horizon, flirted with the tops of the strange New Finnish trees at the end of the clearing, and slowly left us in the dark. There were only a few hundred of us left by then.

Suddenly Taylor's communicator beeped. I could hear the tiny voice piping out of the little speaker. "Sir, they're here! I'm at about 500 meters due east of you. Spotted them on infrared. I count ten, no, here's a second line coming around the bend. Twenty vehicles, including maybe ten tanks."

"How much time do we have?"

"Five, maybe ten minutes to the camp, then whatever it takes for them to find us."

"Which won't be long. Keep me posted."

"Bayet!" Taylor called.

"Sir!" A tall, gangly-looking woman with frizzy black hair threatening to escape from her helmet jogged up. Lieutenant Colonel Louise Bayet, commanding 1st Battalion, 75th Infantry.

"Louise, a skirmish line 100 yards east of here, if you please. Direct your snipers to expect targets from that point."

"Sir!" She got to it and within moments her troops were scrambling to new positions.

Taylor got back to his communicator. "Roberts! Get everything you can headed this way, and get all your men aboard a truck, including yourself. I want you here in two minutes. In three minutes I want you leading a line of trucks over the western horizon."

He cut off the little radio and simply hollered. "All ranks not of the 75th Infantry. The last trucks are on their way. *Get on them!* If there is no room in them for you, run like hell on foot toward the west! Do everything you can to stay with your unit. Good luck!"

I spoke to Taylor as a new flurry of activity began. "Brigadier, with your permission, I'd like to stay behind and do what I can."

"As you wish."

"Thank you, sir." I grabbed an orphaned laser/projectile rifle and scrambled to join a group of rangers headed to the east.

One of them grabbed my arm and said, "Hold it a minute. Saunders is about to—" BLAM! A stretch of ground 15 meters long suddenly jumped into the air and left a trench behind. "Line of burrow mines. They dig themselves a hole and make it bigger with a shaped charge. Put 'em in a row and they dig a trench like the one we're jumping into." He was a burly, big, deep-brown black man with a gentle, almost childish face. "You're Commander Larson, aren't you?"

"Yup."

"Thought so. No one else around here with a good reason for being out of uniform."

"Krabnowski!" Bayet called.

"Ma'am!" my trenchmate yelled back.

"Spotter says between those two buildings, three trucks coming in about 30 seconds."

"Yo." Krabnowski loaded a mean-looking clip of ten-centimeter rockets into a shoulder-held launcher. He dug the stock of the launcher into the lip of the trench and peered through the sight. The first of the trucks appeared, but he let it come. The second came through the gap, and he ignored it. The third poked its nose in and he fired straight for the engine. The rocket whizzed dead in, and the whole cab went up in a sheet of flame. The third truck stopped dead, bottling up the line of retreat for the others. Krabnowski slammed two rockets into the lead truck, and another pair into the middle one. Screaming men leapt from the burning wrecks and tried to run, only to be shot down by rangers in the trench and on the rooftops.

And by me.

"Krab! Tanks coming, left of where the trucks were."

"Okay, Bob." Krabnowski slapped in a load of thin, needle-pointed, armor-piercing rockets into the launcher. "How many?"

"Don't know. Sal said at least five, then she was busy running. S'getting hot out there."

"Sure hope she makes it back," Krabnowski said.

A furious explosion shook the ground a few meters behind us, throwing dirt and rocks into the trenches, filling the air with dust.

"Here they come. . . ."

The tanks appeared through the smoke, moving ponderously across the field of battle. Krab didn't fool with trying to bottle them up. He fired and hit the lead tank. It kept rolling straight for us, the main gun's barrel swiveling toward us.

He fired into both the right and left treads and they

blew off, but the tank kept coming, rolling off the treads onto its wheels. I shot one, two, three of the infantry men trotting toward us behind the tank, and brought them down, and the tank came on, with the gun's muzzle pointing straight at us.

Krab fired one last shot, squeezing the trigger gently to hold his aim. The rocket hit where the gun barrel joined the turret, where the armor was hinged and complicated, weaker.

The barrel blew almost clean off the tank in a roaring double explosion, twisting around in a crazy angle, and hanging uselessly bent to one side.

"I'll be good and goddamned. I set off the shell right in the barrel."

Another round smashed into the ground behind us, even closer this time. I could hear Bayet's voice. "Pull back! Pull back! Back to the courtyard!" We didn't have to be told twice. With the tanks literally at our heels, we ran like hell for the courtyard.

The last truck full of League troops was rolling out. Roberts was standing on the tailgate, not looking at all happy about leaving. Taylor watched it go, not looking at all happy about staying. "We bought as much time as we could, Commander Larson. Everyone but the 75th got away. Now we find out how the Guardians treat their prisoners."

Bayet stood watching for the tanks. "And how long the Guardians can hold them."

We used one of the sheets from Darrow's bed as a white flag.

I felt ready to cry.

A march under heavy guard that lasted half the night brought the defeated League troops to another camp, where we were loaded aboard trucks and driven off into the night. About ten hours after the last shot had been fired, we arrived at what seemed to be a former civilian minimum-security prison. I wondered if the Guardians had let the Finnish criminals loose on the population or had simply shot them.

They shoved us in, two to a cell, and collected dogtags. I didn't have one, of course. They demanded my name, and I didn't see any point in giving a phony one. I hoped George Prigot had had the sense to ditch his tag and give them an alias. I got a cell with Krabnowski. He was friendly enough, but I felt very, very alone.

The day had been a pretty depressing success. The League troops had gotten here, and had flattened an enemy base. But men on both sides were dead, and any day that ends in prison is not all good.

We were there about an hour or so when a precise-looking corporal unlocked our cell door and yelled, "Larson! Come with me!"

"Lucky me. See you, Krab."

"Good luck, Commander."

The corporal was joined by a surly private at our cell door. The two of them took me into what looked as if it had once been the prison's visiting room. It was a large room with a glass wall dividing it in half. All the original furniture had been stripped out of it, and all that replaced it on my side of the glass was a bare wooden chair, spotlit by fierce, bright lights. There were no other lights on my side of the glass.

A strange device, a set of articulated probes of some sort, sat in the corner. It was a collection of well-elbowed arms that looked like an upended two-meter spider on wheels. Just the sort of thing the Guardians would leave lurking in the darkness.

On the other side of the glass wall I could see nothing but a pair of silhouettes shown up against other bright lights that shown straight into my face. I was shoved into the chair and tied down rather sloppily.

"Let's get straight to it, Larson." The voice came, flat and tinny, over a speaker in the ceiling. Dazzled by the bright lights. I couldn't even tell which of the silhouettes was doing the talking. "We had reports a few days ago that a Jefferson Darrow was to perform some sort of experiment at Demeter today. A Colonel Bradhurst, of Intelligence, was working on a theory that you were Darrow, and you match Darrow's description so closely we won't even bother with fingerprints. The two of you are one and the same. Now then, we are going to ask you some questions, and we're going to get the answers.

"How did those League troops get here, and how many are there?"

"Terrance MacKenzie Larson, Commander, Republic of Kennedy Navy, four niner seven eight two five four."

He sighed. "Don't play games with us. We don't play by your rules. And if you want to play by some limp-wristed antique like the Geneva Convention, I understand that back when anyone took it seriously, a soldier captured out of uniform was legally a spy, and it was considered traditional to shoot him."

Another voice, the other silhouette, spoke for the first time. It was more tired, more sympathetic, far gentler. "Commander, please, let's be reasonable. Name, rank, and serial number we already have. You and I both know that we have ways of getting the answers, and I promise you, we don't waste time making them pleasant. So: How many troops, and where did they come from?"

"Terrance MacKenzie—"

"Yeah, yeah. We get the idea," the first voice cut in. "Now knock off the hero routine. If I decide to do it, in ten minutes I could have you wishing you *had* been shot as a spy."

I didn't reply. I was too scared.

"Last chance, Commander."

I said nothing.

"Okay. We start experimenting. Corporal, if you please?"

I heard some vague noises behind me, and suddenly I was jabbed in the butt with a needle.

In a few seconds my head started to swim and my eyes lost their focus.

The ROK Navy had put a lot of emphasis on resisting interrogation, up to the point of actually using truth drugs on the midshipmen. The teachers had shown us the ways of resisting, and I prayed now that I remembered them.

Even as the drug started to effect me, I began *using* it to defeat itself. A "truth drug" doesn't make you more truthful; it makes you more literal-minded and passive, more open to suggestion. So I *told* myself to be passive, to ignore the outside world, to listen to nothing, to *hear* nothing. I told myself to climb into its navel and stay there for the duration. I could feel the drug making me helpless, and I made one last try to hide the truth behind the dreams and the tortuous web of free association my forebrain constructed.

The teacher wanted me to recite the preamble to Kennedy's Constitution. I shifted my feet and began, but it came out wrong, it wasn't right at all—

    " 'You are old, Father William,' the young man said,
        And your hair has become very white,
      And yet you incessantly stand on your head—
        Do you think, at your age, it is right. . . .''

The class devolved into a chorus of laughs and catcalls, and the teacher, suddenly wearing a grey uniform, slapped me hard. . . .

    . . . My lips were dry and cracked. Someone was trying to tell me a riddle, but they kept giving the answer and wanting me to reply with the question, "How many men can fit in a suitcase?" But somehow, try as I might, I couldn't say it. . . .

    . . . I thought at first the world had gotten bigger, but then I remembered that I was a child. I walked down the long hallways of the hospital where Mom and Dad were doctors, looking for them. I wondered why all the beds were empty, because they had been full of sick people before. I touched my face—I had a surgical mask on. No one could recognize me with that on. That made me feel good. No one I didn't like would know me with the mask on. I walked on and on, up and down the barren hospital, but it was empty through and through. I got tireder and tireder, and finally I sat down in a corner to cry. After a while, I noticed sharp little footsteps coming near me. I looked up and saw an ugly old man in a grey uniform. I got so scared I tried to wish him away. He changed into a pretty nurse, and I looked up and saw it was Joslyn, come to tell me to be quiet and not say anything, just be quiet and it would be all right. . . .

. . . But where were Mom and Dad?

I sat in the ejection seat, waiting for the thing to fire so I could get out of it, that way if no other. Let the next trainee into the damned thing. But the control booth seemed to be having some trouble with the gear. They were rolling in some massive piece of test equipment. I knew then that I'd be stuck there most of the day, and decided to quit complaining, button my lip, and wait it out. I tried to reach and shut off the intercom, but my arms were stuck to the goddamned ejection seat. . . .

. . . seat? The hard lines of the glassed-in control booth shifted, blurred. The ejection seat shape-changed; it was a wooden chair and I was tied to it. Only the test equipment stayed the same, and I recognized it as the wheeled spider-thing that had been sitting in the corner of the interrogation room. Now the arms were unfolded and surrounded my head. At the end of each arm was a blunt-ended probe and a red guide lightbeam, the beams pointed at my head. I had a splitting headache and my nose was filled with mucus and blood.

A man with bags under his eyes and uncombed hair stood in a rumpled uniform, watching as technicians fiddled with the machinery. He spoke, and I recognized the voice of my second interrogator. "It seems as if you've given us a very long night." He nodded at the spider machine and said, "While you were coming to, we injected a very small, in fact microscopic, device inside your bloodstream. It floated up into your brain.

This oversized hat rack is here to get it aligned *exactly* where we want it. Oh, don't worry, the thing is small enough to go straight through any blood vessel, and it will simply dissolve in about 19 hours or so. You won't have any physical brain damage. On the other hand, you won't enjoy the next few hours. I expect you've heard of direct brain stimulation? Well, we've refined it a little."

He turned his back on me and walked away.

A moment later he rejoined his partner behind the glass wall. The first voice came over the speaker, heavy with exhaustion and annoyance. "In a minute, I assure you that in about one minute you will want to beg for the chance to answer our questions— but you may have a little trouble saying so."

"He's telling the truth, Commander. Before we go any further, once again, where did those men come from?"

"Terrance Mac—" The world exploded.

My hands, my eyes, my brain burst into billowing sheets of flame. The world was pain and fire. The room roared with flames and gave off thick, stinking smoke. The guards, standing at rigid attention, burned brightly, the fire sweeping up and down their uniforms.

I looked down and saw my chest aflame, and the smell of roasting meat leaped into my awareness. My *eyes* burned and burned, and I could feel the lids wither away with the awful, searing, killing, heat—

And it stopped.

I stopped screaming without realizing I had begun. I flopped back against the chair, whimpering. I was unharmed. In body.

"What we can do once, we can do many times. The device in your brain has been carefully placed where it will stimulate the part of you that feels *fire* and *pain*." The first man's voice had a murderous pleasure in it now. "Tell us what we want to know, or you will *burn* and *burn* until you wish the fire was real so it could hurt you, kill you, and the pain could end. But it can't end, not ever, unless you answer us. Where did the troops come from?"

Maybe I wouldn't have answered even if I had been capable of speech. As it was, there was silence.

And then there was flame.

It shouldn't have been as bad, since I knew what to expect, but it was worse—far, far worse.

My insides were on fire. I could feel my heart, my lungs, my guts and stomach shrivel up into cinders in the heat.

My legs were twin slabs of roasting agony, pulsing shafts of pain that should have ended in death.

Inside my skull the fires raged, my brain and eyes reduced to black cinders that burned on and on after they should have been ashes—

And stopped. The interrogators must have said something, but I didn't hear them. My hindbrain was in charge, screaming in terror and demanding I escape! survive! But I was tied to the chair—

And the world burned anew. Agony gave me a manic strength, and with a convulsive spasm I snapped the chair to splinters. The knots that held me unravelled and I jumped from the chair, screaming.

I stumbled and fell to the floor, landing on my hands, or what my pain told me must be the blackened stumps of hands, and the impact was new and more violent pain.

I cried out, screamed, yelled, moaned, constantly, without stop for breath.

I rolled to my feet and saw the guards, twin towers of flames, moving slowly, so slowly, toward me.

Snarling in animal hatred, I sprang toward them. I grabbed the first by his throat and *pulled*. His neck snapped under my manic strength. I pulled his laser away from his corpse and played it over the other guard, sweeping the beam back and forth over his body again and again as he fell, wanting to know that one thing, at least, truly burned.

Two grenades on his belt clip went off, throwing the body into the ceiling and smashing a hole in the floor.

I turned and fired through the glass wall. The interrogators dove for the floor, but I followed them down with the beam. The beam sliced a junction box, and the lights, which I saw but dimly through the flame that engulfed all, flared and died.

Clutching the gun, I staggered through the door I had come in, and came upon another flaming soldier. He died where he stood. I ripped his laser from his holster and tore the grenades from his belt, wondering that holding them in my burning hands didn't set them off.

Two more guards, and I blindly cut them down.

The flames went on and on, pulsing and flaring across all I saw or felt. By now I was bathed in sweat, and the *sweat* burned, my sweaty clothes burned. Blood from a cut on my hand burned.

Lurching and screaming, barely knowing or caring what I did, I caromed off the walls, stumbling down the corridor. Something moved and I fired at it, not stopping to see if I hit it. The corridor grew longer and longer, a hideous tunnel of flaming oranges and reds, like the monstrous gullet of some hell-spawned night monster that had swallowed me whole.

Something was in my way, wouldn't let me pass. The cell block door, I realized. I first thought to hold a grenade against it and blow it up, but I remembered in time that that would kill me.

I had to get out, escape. I thought of the laser, and used it to slice clean through the lock. The door swung open. A guard was on the other side, in my way, on fire and reaching for his gun. I killed him with mine.

I saw another locked door in front of me. Burn it open, like the others? But it was already burning. But it might be the way out! I had to get out! I cut through the lock.

"Hey, are you crazy—! Jesus Christ, it's that guy who was with us!"

"Never mind that, he cracked the damn cell block!"

They were coming toward me, so I aimed the gun at them—

—There was a blow to the back of my neck and I fell

to the ground, cringing at the contact with my seared flesh. Why didn't it stop? Dimly I knew I was still conscious, but I gave it up and writhed in my pain. It was too much—why didn't it stop, just let me *die*? But still I heard the voices, they wouldn't go away.

"He fried the guard! Grab the lasers and the grenades and let's break this place!"

"Open up over here!"

"Use the keys, you pyro!"

"Go! Go! There's dead guards all over! Move it, while the power's off."

"That's Larson! My God, what did they do to him?"

I didn't care. Pain is exhausting. It will not go away, let you rest. My body was twitching, quaking, every muscle straining. I couldn't faint, but I could sleep. And dream.

Of fire.

I awoke in the middle of a cold night, delightfully void of warmth. My legs, feet, arms, were masses of cramps and spasms, but they were whole, and wonderfully cold.

Hands lifted me, and carried me, gave me over to other hands. Guns and lasers fired unimportantly behind me, and I was carefully placed in the splendidly stinging cold of a metal truckbed.

CHAPTER TEN

"I said put him down, not drop him!"

"Easy there."

"He's got the shakes again."

Voices. Light and darkness, too indistinct to be called sight. Skin rubbed raw and tired. Muscles in knots. Thirst.

"Hey, his eyes moved. I think he's waking up.".

"Good. Then maybe I can ask some questions." A voice with a gravelly accent.

They were talking about me. A glass of water was put to my lips and I drank automatically. Then my thirst awoke and I gulped at the water frantically.

"Enough for now," said the gravelly voice. An arm in a white sleeve drew the glass away from me. "Strong enough to talk?"

"Ehhhh—yes."

"Good. But we will go slow."

"What happened to me?"

A face formed out of thin air at the end of the arm. The browns and greens of uniforms, rough-hewn figures inside them, came into being behind that face, scuffling their feet and looking at me.

A smile. "I was about to be asking you. I think our Guardian friends have been using their brain machine, yes?"

"Yes." That was it, they had made me think of—fire flame forever and I burned, the flames grew in my mind and I bit into the blood of my lips to quench them to put the smoke and stink away from me—

—SLAP "Stop!" SLAP "Stop thinking about it! It is the brain implants again. The implant itself, that is gone by now, but men have laid where you are and died of the memory. They show people death, and no man can see that for long and live."

A sting in my arm was a syringe. "A tranquilizer. It will relax you." I drew in a deep, shuddering breath, nodded, and thought of cool and quiet.

"If you want to pay them for the implant, first you must rest." Another glass of water at my lips, and I tried to lift my hand to it. A restraining strap held my arm in place. "Relax. Rest. You have earned it. Later, I will teach you how to do the forgetting of these things."

A long time later, I awoke with a ravenous appetite. It was the middle of the long New Finnish day, by the look of the light streaming into the sunny room through expansive bay windows. All was white, or golden sunlight, or pastel green in my room, calm and protective and warm. I lay back in bed, thinking.

Thinking of two things, one very good, the other a torture. It was great to feel the direct responsibility for 5,000 lives off my shoulders. Now they were here, and their own agents. I could take a back seat in the war now; the pros could take over.

Buuas balanced against viciousness, the two teetering on the point of a cruel knife, each rising and falling in my mind.

Yesterday, I had killed at least a dozen men.

There were a dozen families somewhere, waiting for the call, the letter, the visitor in uniform, that would tell them their son or brother was dead, that a stranger had killed him.

I had learned why people shouldn't be soldiers.

The door swung open to fresh hot coffee, buttermilk pancakes, sausages, and the doctor who had been with me before. "A few of your army friends said they were from your world. They made a breakfast they said you would like. Lots, isn't it?"

It *was* a lot, but that was fine with me.

I gobbled down everything in sight. It seemed like months since I had eaten, and my stomach wanted to make up for lost time. Finally, I chased one last sausage around the plate, and leaned back with a mug of the best coffee on three planets.

"Feeling better?"

"Fantastic."

"Good. Now then, brace yourself. I am going to do something that will upset you, frighten you. Try to be ready." He pulled a cigarette lighter out of his pocket. It was an ornate, heavy thing, the color of dull silver. He pulled back his thumb and sparked it.

Fire!

I stared into the flame, fascinated. It turned from a friendly yellow to a bloodcurdling red, and it grew. It leaped from the tiny lighter and licked the ceiling, poured down to burn the sheets and burn at my legs, my arms, shrivelling them down to—

SLAP!

My cheek stung suddenly, and the burning of the sheet vanished as suddenly as the lighter's flame. "That, my friend, will happen whenever you see flame or fire of any kind. A candle, a campfire, a rocket blast, perhaps even the beam of a laser or the sun in the sky. The Guardians like using fire-thoughts. It may go away, it may not. The Guardians abandon those they use the brain implant on, because they are usually insane. Many are brought to me. Your general made a question of our people and brought you here. You are strong, and have been well trained, they tell me, and you escaped early on in the torture. So with luck, it is not so bad. We can hope.

"But it will take a little time, perhaps a day or so, perhaps a week, or a month. If you do not take the time until I think you are cured, then you will die, and it will be the most horrible death I can be thinking of. You will frighten yourself to death. I have been able to cure those who did not die that way first.

"So. We hypnotize you. Lean back, relax, and look— look at the ray of sunlight coming in the window. See how the tree branch outside makes it jump and dance, up and back, up and back. . . ."

"And up and out of it . . . Good! You have the luck to be a *very* cooperative subject. Tomorrow we work more." The little man rose to leave. At the door he stopped, turned around, and smiled almost shyly. "And, for all here . . . thank you for all you have done."

There were twice-daily sessions with the doctor for the next three days, and in the back of my mind, a flame-colored monster gradually lost his hold on my soul.

Beyond that, not much happened to me. I was left with a lot of time for thinking, and a lot to think about.

I worried a lot about the Guardians reinforcing. They had certainly been hit hard when the League troops showed up. It hadn't just been the League forces, though. The Finns had revolted all over the planet, and had done so with at least short-term success in many places. The enemy had his hands full with them.

The dispersed League troops were engaged in various commando raids, and were having good results, according to what reports we got.

But it would all go for nothing if the Guardians could reinforce and we could not. As long as the anti-ship missile system lurked in the outer reaches of this solar system, cutting New Finland off from her friends, we had lost.

The converse was also true: as soon as the missiles were out of commission, the League would have won. Not much was known about the Guardians, but it seemed clear they controlled only two star systems—New Finland's and that of their base planet, Capital, wherever that was. It might be a long and bloody battle, but if our side cracked the anti-ship missiles, then the League's tremendously greater resources could be brought to bear, and that would be it.

The missile system—that was the key. Obviously, it had to be controlled from some central command station. Otherwise the unmanned missiles couldn't be warned of scheduled arrivals of Guardian ships. They had to be under negative control, told *not* to shoot at certain targets. Unless the missiles were programmed otherwise beforehand, they would go after anything they spotted. The speed of light was too slow for any other mode of control; if the missiles waited for a command from base that might take an hour or a day at speed-of-light, the target ship would have time to spot the missiles, defend against them, maneuver, or blip into C^2 again and get away.

No, it had to be a hair-trigger, negative-control system, so there had to be a central control point.

Take it, control it, use it to deactivate the missiles, and the war was won.

Should we fail to take it, the war was lost.

We would lose even if we simply destroyed it. The Guardians had to have had the sense to set things up so they could signal the missiles from outside this star system. Even if the signal took a month to cross the void, they could still time the entrance of a ship carrying a replacement local control device. Until the replacement was ready, the missiles would still hit anything that moved without prior warning.

I was sure the Guardians couldn't get away with having only an extra-system controller, and no control system inside the New Finnish solar system. There had to be some way of defending against jamming, phony signals, or malfunctions.

So far, my logic seemed good. Now all I had to figure out was the location of the control station, and the house of cards would be complete, my logic-castle launched into the air. . . .

Castle in the air.

Vapaus. It had to be Vapaus. And that meant trouble, maybe disaster.

I found my pants and left my sickbed. I had to speak with Brigadier Taylor. I managed to escape the nurse on duty with only a minor skirmish. Between this one and Nurse Tulkaas, I was starting to wonder if Finns only used dragon-ladies for nurses.

Someone had loaned me a set of ROK army uniform fatigues, which fit me as well as most clothes I borrow. Twenty minutes after leaving the doctor's house, I was cooling my heels outside Taylor's office, in a requisitioned school house. My heels were easy to cool, as were my ankles. My borrowed pants didn't make it past my shins.

After a shorter wait than I had any right to expect, I was ushered into the Brigadier's presense.

We got through the pleasantries quickly enough and I got to the point. I ran through my train of thought about the existence and nature of the missile control station. None of it was news to him, nor did I expect it to be; he was paid to figure these things out, and indeed he rather gently pointed out that the planning staff had come to the same conclusions before the League forces had stepped into the transmitter.

"I thought as much, sir, but it can't hurt to confirm these things."

He nodded politely and his hands moved back toward the paperwork I had interrupted. "Was there anything else, Commander?"

"Well, sir, I know where the control center is. Or at least where it ought to be."

That got his attention back. "Where?"

"Vapaus."

"I see. Why ought it to be there?"

"Well, sir. Look at it this way. If we've got the nature of the control center figured out properly, that means that in a last ditch, catastrophic situation for the Guardians, all they have to do is knock out the control center and sit back and wait for reinforcements—and only their side could reinforce."

"And Vapaus is a big, lovely target you could track from any inhabited point on the planet. Even the smallest ship could carry a bomb that could crack it like an egg. Clever.''

"One other thing, sir. I think we were meant to figure this out.''

"Eh?"

"So we won't be tempted to try and take Vapaus. If we did, that would be 4,000 people killed when they knew we were searching for the control center there.''

"My dear boy, we've *already* retaken Vapaus. The inhabitants of the satellite overcame the garrison there the same day we arrived. They were always capable of knocking out the garrison. It was the fear that the Guardians would reinvade that deterred them. When hell broke loose all over the planet, the Vapaus leaders decided the risk was lowered enough to try it. I understand the biggest problem the Finns had was keeping the prisoners alive. The guards tended to look the other way when lynch mobs appeared.''

"Then I respectfully submit that Vapaus, and our only hope of winning, are both in the greatest danger. The moment one Guardian commander feels his side has its back to the wall, he will destroy Vapaus.''

That gave him pause. "If what you say is correct, the only chance we've got is to knock out every remaining enemy aerospace field capable of hitting Vapaus, before they can launch that attack.''

"While signalling Vapaus to begin a very cautious search for the control station. It could be hidden in something the size of a broom closet.''

"True. Commander, my respect for the League of Planets Survey Service has just gone up yet another notch. I think I'd better get my staff to work on this theory.''

"I could be wrong, sir.''

"Yes, you could be. But I'd be a damned fool to assume it. You've shown a remarkable knack for staying alive so far, Commander. That requires luck, or clear thinking, or both. I'm inclined to believe it's your thinking. If you can find your own way out, I think I'd better have a good think myself.''

He was extracting his pipe as I left the room.

Taylor was a good commander. That much he had proved in the evacuation of Camp Demeter. He had chosen the 1st Battalion, 75th Infantry to cover the retreat of the rest of the force. The 75th was the lightly armed force, and, as rangers, were superbly trained in individual initiative and independent action. I think Taylor had expected the 75th to be captured, and had expected they'd break out.

The speed with which they exploited my very random attack showed just how ready they were. Ten minutes after I had burned through that cell door, troops were already capturing trucks and nearly all the prisoners were freed.

Four days later, well-planned raids against the Guardians' supplies and help from the Finns had almost completely reequipped the 75th, and all of it done so quietly that our base was still unknown to the enemy.

Taylor's staff soon proved it was good, too. The Finns had put together a strong intelligence network, and Taylor's people were using it to good effect.

The first thing we learned was very good news. For the moment, the Guardians had only one aerospace base capable of launching a ship toward Vapaus: Base Talon, which the League command code-named Hades. All the other aerospace bases that were operational at the time of the League's arrival were small airfields, little more than clearings equipped with fuel storage tanks. These were wiped out by the simple expedient of blowing up the fuel tanks, or cratering the landing field. Some had been former civilian fields, and of this number, one or two had been captured. However, the enemy still had good surface-to-air missiles and strongly held airfields (which could only operate aircraft, not spacers); the Finns had gotten a few ships shot down and given up space flight for the moment.

Unfortunately, whatever the Guardians lacked in number of aerospace fields, Hades made up for in quality and size. It was huge, and well defended. Without any explanation of why the League was interested in Hades, the Finns were ready to give it a go. With the fighter and air defenses based at Hades out of the picture, they could control their planet's airspace, and launch safely to and from orbit.

The League and the Finns had at least a fighting chance to hit Hades and knock it out. There were problems, though. Our troops were widely scattered and would have to be brought to bear. They would have to move in secret. We would have to accept heavy casualties. But it should be possible to deal Hades a crippling blow. And if the League and the Finns controlled Vapaus and controlled the air, the war on the ground would be quickly won. There were still plenty of Guardian forces out there, many of them in pretty good shape. But if we held space and air, if we held the high ground, they wouldn't have a chance.

It was beginning to look like hitting Hades was the way to win the war, even if the missile control station didn't exist. Taylor changed his mind and decided not to inform anyone about our theories concerning the control station. Too many spies, too many taps on communication.

There was a map of the planet on the wall of the schoolroom Taylor used as HQ, and now geography started to make itself felt. Aside from large landmasses at the North and South Poles, New Finland's land was nearly all in the western hemisphere. There were three small continents there, mainly on the northern side of the equator. Only the largest of the three straddled it.

In a geologic timescale, these three landmasses had broken apart from each other quite recently, and they were rather close together, divided by narrow channels of deep water. The coastlines were rough and contained many fine bays.

The smallest, least settled, and northernmost of the continents was New Lapland.

Both Hades and the League forces were on the largest and most populated of the three, Karelia; the remaining continent was Kuusamo.

Karelia held the largest cities, and probably about 90 percent of the population. For that reason, the Guardians had put their largest bases there, so as to have forces on hand to control the populace.

The cities were nearly all on the seacoasts, and so the Guardian camps were in the interior, both to keep the troops away from un-Guardian influences, and to command the air and land transportation lines.

Karelia's terrain was rough, hilly, and for the most part, covered with forestland: it was not easy to put roads through. Before the war, air transport had been very important. Now the Guardians controlled the air, but were spread too thin to cover the roads very well. The heavy forest cover made surveillance hard—at least, we hoped it would.

We began to pick up information on the rest of the League troops. Pins sprouted wherever they found themselves. A pattern grew, a rough circle centered on the ruins of Base Demeter. Finn and League troops were all over the map, on all three continents, and on nearby islands. We were far and wide, there was no doubt about that.

Taylor's staff decided which groups were worth moving, which would do more good fighting where they were, which would do best joining the fight for Hades. Many forces, both Finn and League, which could have been of great help, had to be left where they were; they simply couldn't get to Hades in time.

Speed was vital. Bayet said her 75th Infantry needed another three days to rearm, and that it would take three nights for them to march to Hades.

Taylor took that six days as his cutoff. Anyone who could make it to the gates of Hades by then, alone or a thousand strong, was given the order to march.

Surprise would be our first line of defense. Preparation must be fast, undetectable. We had to hit them before they decided to launch an assault on Vapaus.

The days wore on in a complication of decisions that were almost totally inexplicable. Guesses were piled on guesses, chains of logic metamorphosed into rat's-nest reasoning, and sheer exhaustion made clear thought a rarity.

But bit by bit, piece by piece, Taylor and his staff made sense of the situation: where everyone was, when they were to leave, how they were to travel, what point in Hades they were to attack.

At the end of the second day since my talk with Taylor, the lights were dimmed in the little schoolroom. The floor was covered with papers, the air rich with the odor of too many people in one room drinking too much coffee. But for one sergeant asleep in a chair and an occasional courier looking for a lost piece of paper, the room was empty.

The map of Hades supplied by Finnish intelligence (at the cost of brave men's lives) was covered with optimistic plastic markers of various shapes and sizes and broad grease pencil lines pointed straight to the heart of the camp.

Fifty troops to take the power room. . . .

Twenty troops to cut fences from perimeter 500 to 610. . . .

A hundred troops to stand by with hand-held anti-aircraft weapons until plus ten hours. . . .

Two hundred and fifty troops to seek out and destroy orbit-capable craft. . . .

Estimated total League and Finnish forces; 4,300.
Estimated total opposing forces: 6,000.

An idle gust of wind came through an open window and blew a few of the markers off the map to clatter on the floor.

CHAPTER ELEVEN

Taylor didn't know what to do with me. He asked me what I should do, and I said, "Scout."

He told his aide that, and the aide told me, "Team Five." I checked in at the ops tent. They told me to wait, Team Five was supposed to be showing up. It turned out that it was Krabnowski who showed up, along with three other troopers.

"Morning, Commander. Sir. Just heard from HQ you were with us."

"Hey, Krab. Call me Mac. I don't know what Navy rank means to you guys anyway. So I guess you're Team Five?"

Krab looked surprised. "Yup. Hey, Bob. Goldie. Joan. This is Commander Mac."

Bob looked at me with bleary eyes suspended under bushy black eyebrows. "So?"

"Hiya, Mac," Goldie said. Goldie was short, stocky, but even in U.S. Army fatigues, gorgeous. Her eyes were big, blue, wide, and clear, with no makeup and not needing it. Her hair was a warm honey-blonde. She had an ample bust, a slender waist, nice hips.

Joan might not have been as openly decorative, but she was beautiful while Goldie was pretty. Tall and cool, with dark brown hair cut very short, slender and languorous. Her eyes were grey and quiet, set in a smoothly sculptured, high-cheeked face.

"Hi, Mac," she said. "That's a private's uniform. What's the gag with Krab calling you 'Commander'?"

" 'Cause I'm a commander. ROK Navy. No one brought me a Navy uniform."

"And you can't shoot up the bad guys in your skivvies," Krab put in.

The other three suddenly looked very unnerved. "Oops. Sir. You're a *real* officer?" Goldie asked.

"Pretty real."

"Oh, boy. Sir. Sorry about the 'Hiya, Mac'. Sir. You just get into the habit of reading insignia. Sir."

" 'S'all right. I'm not going to be too much on giving orders. I'm just along for the ride."

"Well, okay, sir," Goldie said.

"Mac."

"Mac, sir."

"Skip it."

Goldie turned to Krabnowski. "So why didn't you tell us the man joining us was an officer?"

"Figured you'd have the same brains I did and recognize him," Krab said.

Goldie peered intently into my face, subtracted the grime and the three-day growth of beard, and it seemed a light went on. "You're Commander *Larson*! Terrance MacKenzie Larson! The man who got us here!"

"That's right."

Joan whistled and poked Krab in the ribs. "Krab, how do you make friends in high places?"

"Charm, Private. Charm."

"And *you* were the one who got us sprung," Joan added, "and got the brain implant."

"For that, man, we're really going to hunt Guardians. Those sons of bitches. Sir," Goldie finished.

"So let's get this show on the road and give you the chance."

"Groundcar's right outside."

Ten minutes later, the MP and the Finnish town policeman waved us through the perimeter.

A fair dusting of snow covered the ground as we moved out of the town. All was white and quiet.

Our job was straightforward: watch for Guardian patrols and forces that might spot the League forces heading toward Hades. Stop them if we could, warn those who followed if we couldn't.

We crammed into one liberated Guardian groundcar, which mounted a heavy machine gun amidships. That made it a little tight for five, especially when two of them were Krab and myself, but we managed.

There was something that had been confusing me and I decided to ask about it. "Hey, Krab. Maybe you can explain something to me," I said. "Why is it you guys don't have all kinds of fancy gear here? Seems like the brass shipped you off without any of the goodies."

"That's not 'cause they were cheap," Krab replied. "That's 'cause it makes sense. Notice what we're driving here?"

"A stolen Guardian groundcar."

"Right. A groundcar. Not a hovercraft, or some fool walker with articulated legs. A car—a nice, simple machine. A motor in the hub of each wheel. Battery pack under the rear seat to power them. The Guards thought it out the same way we did."

"Which is how?"

"Both armies are on the ends of really long supply lines. Light years. So this jeep ought to be simple enough to fix with a minimum of parts. Also, it's the best machine for the job. This is rough terrain; this road goes up and down more than straight ahead. A hovercraft would just sort of fall off the side of the first hill it tried to climb. H-craft are damned noisy, they make great gargets on infrared, they aren't very stable—like, if the wind is blowing they drift, and if you have to get moving in a hurry you can get your head missing waiting for the ground effect skirt to inflate. They're a *lot* more complicated and more fragile than a car."

"Okay, that makes sense, but why did they send you off with such primitive guns? No self-seeking ammo—"

"Self-missing ammo," Goldie corrected. "The stuff picks *a* target, but it might not be yours. Also, don't get used to it, or it's just too bad when you run out. Think anyone here could manufacture it if we run out? Besides, the rifles we were issued can't fire it anyway."

"There you go again, badmouthing the LUIW," Joan said.

"I am not!" Goldie retorted. "That's just a plain fact—it can't shoot self-seeking ammo."

"Wait a minute," I cut in. "What's a Looey?"

"This is," Bob said, patting the stock of his rifle. "The League Universal Issue Weapon. LUIW. All the rifle troops sent here are carrying them."

"And if you insist, I will badmouth it," Goldie said cheerfully. "You can keep the self-seeking rounds, but the LUIW has too low a fire rate. Only eighty rounds a minute on automatic."

"C'mon, get serious, Goldie," Krab replied, with the air of someone who has had the same argument before. "When you fire on auto, 99 times out of 100 you aren't really aiming to hit anything anyway; you're firing to force the other side to take cover so they can't aim at *you*. If the thing fired 250 rounds a minute, they wouldn't duck any faster, but you'd run out of ammo four times as fast—and do you want to lug half your weight in ammo just to piss it away?"

"Couldn't they just make the ammo lighter weight?" I asked.

"Wouldn't make any sense. The weight of a round is what gives it momentum, range, accuracy, penetration, so it can make nice big holes when it hits something," Krab said. "Lighter rounds get slowed by air resistance, get blown away by a light breeze—no good. I like the LUIW," Krab went on, thoughtfully. "Nice, mechanically simple. Doesn't jam. Just wish they'd trade the laser unit for an extra 100 rounds of ammo."

"What we really have here, Commander, is the

LUIW/L— second L for Laser," Bob explained. "Krab here feels it's just gadgetry, not worth the extra effort of lugging the powerpacks."

I was beginning to wish I hadn't started the conversation. Soldiers are pretty opinionated about their equipment, I guess. My four companions were soon arguing fiercely over the merits of the LUIW, among other things.

On the issue of the lasers attached to the LUIW, they were more or less agreed that they weren't worth the trouble. Lasers don't work well in smoke or fog, the powerpacks are fragile and don't last, and a laser fired at night is quiet enough, but the beam serves to point the enemy right back to whoever fired it. The contractor had made a little extra change selling the laser, but that was about all the good it did, most of the time.

Krab conceded that the U.S. Army had a more sophisticated weapon the rangers could have been issued, but he fought back by saying the Britannics and the Chinese and the Germans and the Bandwidthers did, too—so what if a Yank and a German find themselves sharing the same foxhole and they can't share ammo? The LUIW was a lowest common denominator, and if everyone got the same gun, you were a lot better off than if every outfit went for a specialized weapon no one else understood.

But high tech hadn't been banned from the battlefield: for one thing, there was the Iron Maiden. Bob took the first shift with it. The Maiden was a baby combination radar, sonar, and infrared set that fit over the head and let the wearer watch the world through a pair of video screens about a hand's-breadth from his face. The Maiden was pretty much a guarantee of a headache after more than a hour, and so we switched it off every thirty minutes.

My turn came second, and it took some getting used to. A cheerful little idiot of an imaging computer converted the radar pulses to two parallaxed side-scan images; the result was something like looking through electronic binoculars.

The set usually did a lazy scan of about one rpm—as if my head were spinning slowly around and around on a pivot. Tongue switches let me select radar, sonar, or IR viewing, and also let me override the auto scan if something interesting came up. The Iron Maiden was a royal pain, but a very handy way to keep tabs on things.

We drove on.

Joan took over on the Maiden, and I concentrated on getting the spots out from in front of my eyes. Goldie sat curled up like a kitten under the machine gun mount. "Hey, Commander. You know how to play Ghost?"

"Play what?"

Krab shook his head. "Watch it, Commander. She's a killer at this one."

"Shut up, oh corporal mine, or we won't let you play. Okay, Commander, the first one up picks a letter. Each person goes, and adds a letter to the word. You've got to be spelling a real word, but if you finish a word over three letters you get a letter. First G, then H, and so on. The first one to get "GHOST" loses, and you keep going until all but one person is left.

"Bob, you go first."

"Let's see . . ."

"Now what kind of word starts out M-I-S-O-R-I?"

"It's a perfectly good word."

"You're bluffing. Go ahead, Bob, challenge her."

"If you're after 'Missouri', you're way off. Besides, it's a proper name."

"M-I-S-O-R-I—it's a perfectly good—"

"Krab! Get off the road!" Joan grabbed at the outside of the Maiden, worked the hand controls.

Krabnowski dove the groundcar into the underbrush of the forest, skidding to a halt in the snow. Even as the groundcar was still in motion, the rocket launcher was in his hand. Krab had taken that back from our prison keepers personally. "Where?" he asked.

"Bandit! Coming in low, dead from Hades! Call it— south, southeast. Course—say, 190."

Krab tossed off his helmet and slapped a rocketpack into the launcher. "Bob, raise HQ. Get 'em off the road if they're on it. We'll try and keep the heat off them."

"Scout Five to HQ Comm. Scout Five to HQ Comm. We read a bandit, headed your way, bearing about 190. Possible picture taker."

Goldie was on her feet, the machine gun undogged and loaded.

"Goldie—can that thing pierce aircraft armor?" I asked.

"No, but it'll sure as hell get his attention while Krab's getting a vector on him," she said tersely. "Joan—how long?"

"He's low and slow—call it about 80 seconds. And make that bearing 195—right through that notch in the hills."

"Yeah, he's flying for pictures, all right," Bob put in. "HQ acknowledges. They're under the trees already."

"Lot of good that'll do them on infrared," Krab said, fiddling with the rocket launcher. "Joan—he following the road?"

"Looks like it."

"Goldie, let 'em know we're here."

She let loose a few rounds of explosive bullets in the air. They blew up at the apex of their trajectory.

"He took the bait. Coming in. Visible in about ten."

We could hear the howl of the jet engines now.

"Comin' on in," Joan reported. "Thinks he's gonna burn some local with a pop gun. Give 'em another goose, Goldie."

The jet appeared over the horizon, bearing straight for us. Goldie threw another volley into the air.

The jet suddenly accelerated and screamed in right over us. He dropped a bomb, which went in about a hundred meters away from us. The ground beneath us shook as it exploded, and the air was suddenly full of smoke and bits of burning wood.

Joan shouted out, "He's turning! Gonna barrel right back down the road, from the north." Goldie whipped the gun around and zeroed in on a piece of empty sky right over the road.

The scream of the engines faded for a moment, then roared in our ears louder than ever.

"He's dropping another load! Should fall shor—"

The ground ripped itself apart 50 meters from the groundcar, redoubling the stink of cordite in the air. The jet screamed directly overhead, Goldie dumping bullets onto the fuselage, where they exploded like firecrackers.

Krab jogged out onto the road with the launcher. "One more pass! Joan, when he's at 1500 meters, call out. That'll give the heat sensors time."

"Got it. Goldie, I think you screwed up his tail surfaces—he's turning real wide, might be headed home. No, here he comes—"

"Spotted!" Krab yelled.

"One Five Zero Zero—MARK!!"

Krab fired six rockets at once, and they flared aloft, burning like roman candles, twisting and turning in formation as they chased the jet. One missed the tight turn, but five roared dead into the target; a fireball blasted into violent being where the jet had been, flaming into an orange and black mass of roiling fire. It dropped suddenly into the forest and hit, exploding, throwing us out of the groundcar and lighting the sky with blood-red tendrils of smoke that left behind a shattered pile of wreckage and a sheet of flame.

It was suddenly quiet.

It was back with me. I could feel it. This was *real* fire, true fire that killed and consumed. Horrified, fascinated, I stared for long seconds. This was real, and right here, and it would burn a long time. In some perverse way, I wanted it to.

Suddenly, I realized that *I* was not in flames. It was outside me.

Or nearly so.

With a wrenching of my will, I got to my feet and dusted myself off.

Krabnowski came back to the groundcar, kicking a few burning twigs out of his way. Bob spoke quietly into the radio and hung up the mike. Joan took off the Iron Maiden and shook her head, blinking rapidly. She set the Maiden in her lap and rubbed her eyes.

Krab handed Goldie the launcher. She stowed it, re-shipped the machine gun, and Krab started the ground-car. We rolled on.

Ten minutes later, Goldie and Bob were arguing over whether MISORIENT was a real word. Behind us, a column of death-black smoke climbed into the clean sky.

We made our camp 60 kilometers from the plane crash site without further incident.

The night was cold, sharp, crisp, dark, and quiet. It was my watch, and I sat up in the groundcar, a blanket around me, thinking.

I felt, somehow or another, *safe*—for the first time since I had found myself in this war. Here, tonight, the dangers were crystal clear, obvious, seen far off, as if on th horizon of a vast plain. A man or a machine could appear, and try to kill me. If the attempt succeeded, I would die. Nothing else. No subterfuge, no scheming, no bluff and counterbluff, no tactics or strategy or wonder-ing who to trust.

All I needed was caution, and the higher parts of my brain could sit back and take a rest.

I suddenly felt I understood the quartet I travelled with, and the way they had fought with such calm precision that afternoon.

There can be a moment when a struggle becomes a simple, obvious choice of YES, I will survive, or NO, I will not. The choice is elemental, automatic. Even a suicide is careful crossing the street on the way to jump off a building.

Make the right choice, choose the right path, and you live. Otherwise, you die.

I cradled my rifle in my arms and calmly watched over the cold night.

Two day later, the dangers got complicated again.

We were driving down that same road, enjoying the day and watching for trouble, when Krab suddenly pulled off the road and drove into the brush.

"What—" I began. He cut me off, motioning for silence.

I shut up, and heard the high buzzing of a groundcar's electric motor.

With sharp hand signals, he urged Joan, Bob, Goldie, and me into positions behind cover. The moment we were set he jogged about 20 meters back the way we had come and made rare use of his laser rifle to slice through a tree trunk. The tree toppled across the road with a loud crash.

Krab pounded back and dove into the brush near me. We waited.

About 15 seconds later, we had company. A groundcar, the twin of the one we had stolen from the Guardians, zipped up the road. The two occupants had heard the tree's crash and had their weapons at the ready.

They stopped the groundcar a few meters back from the downed tree and started to step from the groundcar, cautiously searching out whoever had done it.

They never made it out of the groundcar alive. I nailed each of them with a slug in the chest.

No one moved for a long minute. I had shot without thinking, and done it right. Now I felt sick.

We crept out from the brush carefully, wondering if the dead Guardians had any friends following behind.

"Nice shooting, Commander," Krab said.

"Yeah, just wonderful," I said bitterly.

"Bob, radio this in on our next report," Krab said, shouldering his rifle.

Soon we were putting miles behind us in two ground-cars.

We were ahead of schedule, and we wanted to keep more or less on station with the main body behind us.

There was very little point in reporting a stretch of road "clear" and then leaving it unused for 48 hours.

With that in mind, Krab decided to set camp early.

We made camp at the top of a gentle hill that looked out over a broad valley. Not only was it a nice view, but we could see anyone who was coming. We camped in the center of a wide hollow near the brow of the hill, which kept us out of the wind.

Being warm in the middle of a cold night is a satisfying thing. The five of us huddled close to the fire and relaxed over our meal. Goldie was officially on watch; she ate with her laser rifle across her lap. The Iron Maiden was set to give out a frantic beeping tone if anything awoke its idiot radar brain. We were covered.

Bob finished his meal and strolled over to the ground-car we had grabbed. He came back with a bulky canvas sack that landed with a heavy thud when he dropped it.

Krab peered at it across the fire. "*Now* what?"

Bob squatted in front of the bag, picking at a clamp on the bag's drawstring. "Mail call."

Goldie suddenly looked interested and started to help him. Joan sighed in exasperation, a kindergarten teacher whose charges kept spilling the fingerpaint—on purpose. "Commander, I *was* hoping your presence would put at least a slight damper on those two. Just tell me whether this rates a dishonorable discharge apiece for them."

I grinned. "I haven't the faintest idea, but a D.D. sounds about right."

Bob spoke with a tone of injured dignity. "We are *not* snooping. We're scouting, aren't we? Well, here's a whole bag full of intelligence to go through."

"Plus, we won't have to search for firewood the rest of the night," Goldie put in.

"Now, we can't go destroying evidence," Bob said.

"Hey, Commander," Goldie said, "if we find any checks or money or anything, can we impound it?"

"Bright, Goldie," Bob said absently. "Just stroll into the First Bank of New Finland and ask to cash a Guardian payroll check. They'll be happy to take your head off at the door."

"Yeah, I guess you're right. What else have we got?"

"Not much. Hmmmm. Boring. Boring. God, the Guards get dull mail."

Krab had a thought. "Hey, any care packages in there?"

"Good question," I said. I pulled out a small box, about 10 centimeters on a side. I cut it open with my knife. "Paydirt! Chocolate, cigarettes, some kind of cookies. . . ."

Bob and Goldie immediately gave up on the letters and checked for more packages. In a few minutes, the two of them were surrounded by a pile of food, cigarettes, some cold soldier's long johns, and a collection of pornographic novels printed on lightweight paper—"packaged especially for space travel to save *you* money," it said on the box. Bob decided he was on a streak and kept digging.

"Hey, now, this looks interesting."

"What did you get, Bob?" Krab asked.

"Military pouch or something. Says TOP SECRET."

"Watch it, Bobbie. Might be booby-trapped," Goldie warned.

"Just a sec." He pulled out his pocket flash and clasp knife. "Hell, if they think I can't get past *that*. . . ." He started to work on the pouch's lock, holding the light in his mouth. After a minute or two of jiggering, Bob twisted the blade of his knife slightly to the left and the pouch unfolded itself with a click.

Bob smiled to himself as best he could, with the light in his mouth, and started to rifle through the papers inside.

He started to read, and the color left his face as if a switch had been thrown. He swallowed and spoke quietly, but the tone of his voice was enough to silence the rest of us. "God's own holy shit. We're going to die. Commander, Corporal Krabnowski, we had best damn well say to hell with the schedule and break radio silence.

"There's—there's a ship coming. A hell of a big one. One that can come through space and enter an atmosphere. It's some kind of aircraft carrier, or spacecraft carrier. The damn thing must be the size of an asteroid, and the *guns* it must have. . . ."

I reached over, dug into the military pouch, found a piece of paper and a number. I read it out loud. "Ship's complement: 2,000 men."

There were other numbers that I had to read out loud, that said hope was lost. "Service facilities for supplemental support of 80 Comet space-going fighter craft, 50 Revenger multi-entry aerospace fighters, and 40 Tornado aircraft are required."

There was more, much more. It was an information kit for the dead commander of Base Demeter. Schlitzer. I had killed him myself. The package was sent to advise him of what services might be required of him.

Bob fingered one of the documents nervously. "They call her *Leviathan*."

"Commander! Groundcar coming!"

"You sure that's the one from HQ?" It was still night; New Finland had a long one. I trained a pair of IR binoculars on the bend in the road.

Krab patted his rocket launcher, loaded and ready in his lap. "If it's not, I've got a reception planned." But when the groundcar popped out from behind the trees, the League's Flame, Ship, and Star ensign was flying from its gun mount. There were two people in it, a woman and a man. I recognized George. The woman must be the intelligence officer Taylor had sent us when we reported on finding the *Leviathan* report. HQ had sounded as alarmed as we were.

The groundcar pulled to a halt.

"My God! George!" He looked like death warmed over—wan, tired, spent.

"Hello, Jeff." His voice was flat, laden with exhaustion. When had he slept last?

"Krab! Get over here!" Krabnowski yelled to Joan to take sentry and hurried to the groundcar to help me lift George from the seat.

"George, what happened to you?" I asked. Krab and I held him up. I was sure he couldn't stand on his own.

"J-just can't sleep. Haven't eaten. Dunno."

I turned to the woman. She stepped down from the driver's seat, shaking her head. "*Bonsoir*, Commander. Lieutenant Marie-Francoise Chen, Army of the Sixth Republic of France. 899 70 12 28. I do not know why they made this man travel. Expert on Guardian technology or not, he is not well enough to do so. I am sorry."

"I quite agree." Damn it, wartime or not, they couldn't expect to squeeze any more use out of George when he was in this shape. "George, you've got to eat. We've going to get some food into you and get you to sleep."

"Don't want to eat. Tried sleeping. Can't."

"You eat, like it or not. Goldie—get some chow whipped up. And dig up some sort of sleeping pill from first aid."

"Right."

Krab and I half-led, half-carried George to the campfire. Goldie was already busy getting food together. Bob and Lieutenant Chen grabbed some gear from the groundcar and followed us. Chen started looking over the material while we got some food into George. Goldie got a powerful sedative down with the last gulp of soup she had heated from freeze-dried stores. Soon the drug took hold in spite of him and he slept, fitfully, through dreams that should have wakened him a dozen times, but for the strength of the drug.

"Why don't you sack out, too, Commander? Everyone else got at least six hours last night. You didn't sleep at all, and we've still got some waiting to do," Krab suggested.

Chen looked up. "Yes, Commander, do so if you have tiredness. It will be several hours before I have any results."

"You talked me into it. Goldie—let me see one of those knock-out pills." I couldn't afford to waste sack time lying awake worrying.

*   *   *

"Commander. Wake up." Joan shoved a cup of coffee under my nose and broke up my dream. I took the coffee and downed it in one gulp, searing my tongue in the process. "Arrgggh. Thanks. How long have I been out?"

"About three hours."

"How's George?"

"Sleeping like a baby. He finally quit tossing around and settled down."

"That's something, anyway." I had slept in my clothes except for my shirt, belt, and shoes. I wriggled out of the sleeping bag and put these on, getting into my clean shirt a bit reluctantly; it had been "clean" for the better part of a week now.

"Chen got anything yet?"

"She says so. That's why I woke you."

Joan retreated from the tent's entrance and let me out. We walked to the fire. Lieutenant Chen sat by it, not even noticing she was shivering slightly. She had wrapped a blanket around herself, a mug of tea by her side. She had fine, delicate, oriental features on a round, high-cheeked face. Her hands were long-fingered and graceful. She moved quickly, precisely.

The night was cold, clear, and quiet. The slightest hint of light in the east warned of the still-distant dawn.

As I approached, she saw me, stopped her reading, and closed her notebook. She sat, staring at nothing, chewing on the end of her pencil, for a long time. Then she rose, and saluted me. She spoke quietly. "Commander Larson, I have completed my first analysis."

"Well?"

She hesitated. "Let us step away from the camp for a moment. Come."

I followed her as she led me away into the darkened clearing.

She began. "Technically, I suppose I should be making this report only to General Taylor. But I think you and your friends have the right to know. Forgive me if I cause *you* to tell *them*. This is very difficult, even just to one person. I have learned most of what I can about the enemy ship, *Leviathan*. The good news is that she was launched from their planet, Capital, long before we attacked. It is chance that brings her here now, not news of a counterattack. When our assault began, *Leviathan* was certainly in deep space many light years away. No warning could have reached them over radio in time, and we watch all the places they could launch a message drone from: none have been sent. The commander of *Leviathan* will arrive expecting a subdued, peaceful planet. But once they arrive in this system, they will learn of our presence quickly. We can't depend on surprise. And I must warn that I do not know exactly when she will come, but soon, soon.

"I have considered the state of our own forces, such as they are. I have balanced this with what is known of the enemy's other bases.

"*Leviathan*, she is awesome. On the face of it, she could defeat us all, easily. But there are flaws in the giant's armor. Indeed, I think much of the armor is not there at all. There is hope, a slender thread of it, for us. There is a slight chance that we can win through and defeat this *Leviathan*.

"In my profession, I deal in numbers, in facts, in probabilities. Sometimes to remember that those numbers are people of flesh and blood and souls is a most difficult thing.

"But I force them to be numbers, in my head, because then terrible things are not as terrible. But this time, for me, now, it is impossible to think of them but as people who laugh and cry.

"It will be most difficult. It will require great luck and nerve. But perhaps we can beat *Leviathan* and win this war.

"In that effort, it is all but certain that most of us will die."

CHAPTER TWELVE

At first light we again contacted General Taylor. He ordered us to stay put: by now we were within a few hours' drive of Hades. There was little point in risking the information we had gained by getting much closer.

By now the positions of League and Finnish forces were in the shape of a rough half-circle around the northern side of Hades. Little incident had marred the approach of our forces. With luck, the Guardians wouldn't spot us until it was too late.

So now we waited. When George awoke, I suggested that he and I go for a walk and stretch our legs a bit. We needed a chance to talk. He looked better than he had the night before, but he didn't look good.

"Jeff—I mean, Mac. What's going to happen?"

"I don't know, George." The two of us sat down on a fallen log.

"If you— if we— if the League forces win ... what will happen to me?"

"Whatever you want to happen, George. You've got skills, talent, and there's a lot of room out there."

"I've been with those American soldiers, mostly. They told me a lot about Earth. Do you think I could go there?" He blew out a great puff of air, and watched his breath swirl for a moment in the cold air. "I'd like to see Earth."

"It's something to see."

"They used to talk about it a lot back on Capital, but it sounded all different. The Americans talk about big cities and all different kinds of people in one place, and on Capital, they tell you about all the evil, corrupt people and how disorganized it all is."

"Well, I suppose they're both right."

"But don't you think I'd have trouble there, being from Capital and the Guardians and the war?"

"Yeah, probably." I looked out over the valley. Ahead there, somewhere, lay Hades. "You're a good man, George, and I've got to be honest with you. I don't know where it'll be easy on you."

"I know. I also know no one has the slightest idea what will happen after the next 12 hours or so."

"I will promise you this. I'll get you off the planet, out of this star system. Maybe I can talk to Pete Gesseti, a friend of mine. Get you Kennedy citizenship. They're terraforming a moon called Columbia. Maybe they could use a good technician."

"Hmmmmm. That'd be nice. If I live to get there."

I didn't have any answer to that one.

We sat quietly, looking over the peaceful valley.

"Commander! They're here!" Goldie ran up to us. "Joan spotted the column headed this way!"

By the time we got back to camp, Taylor was there with Lieutenant Bayet and a tall, redheaded officer wearing a British Army uniform. Behind them, soldiers marched and vehicles rolled down the road. Taylor acknowledged my salute with a nod. "Commander. Lieutenant Chen here tells me that it might be possible to defeat *Leviathan*."

"Yes, this may be. But only from space," Chen said. "From the ground is hopeless. And those in space need the information we have here."

The British officer I didn't know spoke. "We can't possibly transmit it by radio. The Guardians would be sure to listen, and know exactly how much we knew about this thing."

"Do we have message lasers with us?"

"Nothing powerful enough to hold a good, tight beam to Vapaus without worrying about detection. Every time Vapaus reports, we hear about new spies and snooping equipment the Guardians left behind."

"And we have a great deal of information here," the Briton went on. "We have no encoding equipment, no video equipment. We'd have to *read* that encyclopedia to them. It would take the better part of a day, even ignoring line-of-sight problems. The Guardians would track the transmission long before we'd made a good start. No. We must send it by post."

"Very well, Stanley. You've convinced me," Taylor said unhappily. "Oh, excuse me, Commander. Major Defforest, this is Commander Terrance MacKenzie Larson, ROK Navy. George Prigot, who has been of great help on technical matters. Major Sir Stanley Defforest, commanding a detachment of the Royal Regiment of Fusiliers."

"Delighted to meet you," Defforest told me. "Heard a great deal about you, all good. Now then. We agree we must send it by post. By hand. That means we must hijack one of the aircraft we intend to smash."

"I agree," Chen put in. "That is the conclusion Commander Larson and I reached last night."

"Mmmmm. Mr. Prigot. What types of craft that could reach the satellite are at Hades?"

"Well, of course I don't know what aircraft are where, but the only Guardian ships that could reach orbit are the Revenger ballistic ship or the Nova-class attack ships. The Novas launch more or less like a normal plane, then fly to appropriate altitude and launch themselves from mid-air into space."

Chen spoke up. "According to our Finnish informants, of those two, only the Nova is there. No Revengers."

I objected. "I was under pretty tight wraps at the time, but I think it must have been Hades that I landed at when I first came to the surface. What about the ballistic job I came in on? It was a converted civilian ship."

"No. That would be one of the *Kuu* spacecraft," Chen said. "All are accounted for. Some recaptured at Vapaus, others blown up or sabotaged. There are none at Hades. That leaves only the Nova."

"Pity it couldn't be one of the ballistic craft. You say this Nova takes off and lands like a normal aircraft?"

"Yes, horizontal launch."

"Then what we must do is hold a runway while we get one of them in the air, carrying some of our people to Vapaus."

"How much would that add to our other problems?" I asked.

"Not a great deal, I think," Taylor said. He spread out a chart of Hades on the hood of a groundcar. "This is our most up-to-date information on the place, Lieutenant Chen?"

"Yes."

"Then the Novas are almost certainly in these hangars aside the longer of the two main runways. The hangars are dispersed pretty widely, one every half kilometer or so, to prevent one lucky hit from us wiping them all out. Now our current plan is to come in from the north and sweep straight across the base, blowing up anything that looks worthwhile. Then we simply keep going and run like hell out the south side of the camp, praying the enemy is in no shape to pursue. A raid. Now what this hijacking idea requires is that we contain the main garrison and thus hold that runway clear long enough to get the plane off, and *then* run like hell."

"We just sit there and soak up casualties until we get a signal that the ship is away?" Bayet asked.

"Yes. I agree it is a pretty grim circumstance. But unless we get that ship off, get the information on both *Leviathan* and the missile control center to Vapaus, we have lost, and the Guardians will simply kill us sooner rather than later. It is our only chance to win, and go home."

Bayet clearly didn't like it. "We don't have any pilots with any hope of flying that thing."

"On the contrary, Lieutenant," Defforest said. "First, Commander Larson here is an experienced spacecraft pilot. Mr. Prigot is an expert on Guardian technology, and their way of doing things."

"And, included in the forces that came with us are 30 Navy fliers," Chen reminded the group.

"What Navy fliers?" Bayet asked.

"Thirty fliers from the U.S. Navy. Experts on flying unfamiliar aircraft. They were brought along in the event of just this sort of case, or unless the Finns needed more pilots."

"So they were, Chen. My memory is going. Find them, and get them here. Or at least enough of them to fly that plane," Taylor said, and then turned to me. "Commander Larson. We must do this, though none of us like the idea. I am afraid Deforrest is right: *you* must be aboard the ship we hijack. Not only as a pilot, but as the ticket in. The Finns on Vapaus know you. They will trust you, listen to you. Mr. Prigot, if you are willing, I must ask you to go along. And Lieutenant Chen, you will act as the actual courier. You are our resident expert on *Leviathan* now, and I imagine the Vapaus Finns will have more use for an intelligence expert than we in the days to come.

"And you'll need help getting to that ship, obviously. Not too large a force, no need bringing attention to this project. I think the scout force you've been with has proved its ability," Taylor went on. "Commander Larson, I leave it in your hands. It is up to you."

"I'll do what I can, sir."

"I think that will be enough. Good luck. Do your best, and while you're doing that, I've got to manage the rest of this war. Stanley, Bayet, let's not keep that driver waiting."

They crossed the clearing and got into the major's groundcar. They returned a last set of salutes from our little force, and drove away.

I wondered if I would ever see any of them again.

*   *   *

The troops continued to come through, sometimes in large numbers, sometimes the flow of soldiers reduced to almost nothing. We waited for the fliers to show.

Two hours later a quartet of young officers in blue uniforms arrived in the clearing, looking not quite sure of where they were supposed to be. Goldie waved them over to us. "You must be the flyboys," she said.

The one woman in the group grinned ruefully. "Yeah, we're the flyboys. Captain Eva V. Berman, United States Navy, Deep Space Special Forces Detachment. This is Lieutenant Commander Randall Metcalf, L.C. Bob Emery, and Lieutenant Edward Talley, United States Marine Corps. Lieutenant Colonel Bayet said you had a job for us?"

"Well, for two of you."

"And two for backup. Our crew is so hungry to fly, you're lucky all 30 didn't show up. We drew lots. These three won, and I cheated."

"I thought so," Metcalf said. He spoke with a slight drawl. He was tall, lanky, pale with a thin face, wiry black hair, and a pair of bushy eyebrows that made him look surprised. "I counted about 20 slips in the hat with your name on them."

"Quiet, Randall," Berman said. She was toward the short side of a pilot's height. She had chocolate-colored skin and dark brown hair, cut short, and a smart-aleck's twinkle in her honey-colored eyes. "Pay him the slightest attention and you're lost. Just let him be first into the bar, let him fly a plane once in a while, and keep him fed. Now then, what is it we've got to do, and when do we do it?"

Long hours later, well after dark, we were at our jump-off point, half a kilometer from the base perimeter, and about three times that far from the nearest hangar that could hold a Nova, according to George. We were a motley crew: Bob, Joan, Krab, and Goldie, U.S. Army; Metcalf, Berman, and Emery, U.S. Navy; Talley from the Marines; Chen, French Army; me from the R.O.K.; and George.

Metcalf and Berman were the prime pilots for the job. If they didn't make it, Emery and Talley were it.

Attack was timed to start about three hours before the late rising of New Finland's large natural satellite, Kuu.

"Commander. It's getting close to time," Krab whispered.

"We ready? Both groundcars okay?"

"Enough juice to make it. We're ready. 'Bout five minutes."

"Okay." The signal for the attack was an opening barrage of artillery, which would be followed immediately by the launching of blindingly bright flares. The League troops were supposed to know to look the other way. The flares were expected to dazzle a large number of the defenders for the first minutes of battle. The blind-lighting would last two minutes, then drop to a useful intensity.

We waited, sitting in the two groundcars.

Then—BLAM; BLAM; BLAM; we shut our eyes and hunkered down. Seconds later, we felt the silent burst of light from the flare through closed eyelids. Even without looking, it was awfully bright.

They must have known *someone* was out there—there was return fire immediately. Too immediately; they couldn't possibly have taken time to aim.

Bob was listening, too. "What the hell do they think we've got—bombers? I hear anti-aircraft fire!"

"Well, they're throwing high explosive, too," Krab said.

A shell landed behind us with a *boom*. "Yeah, Krab, but artillery fired *blind*?"

"It can kill you just as dead."

Suddenly it got darker inside my head. "Flares dying! Let's move it!"

But we were already rolling. Krab drove the lead groundcar. Goldie, Berman, Talley, and I rode with him. Bob drove the second groundcar carrying the others.

Krab cut the lights on, and the perimeter fence sprang into existence not 30 meters away. He got us a bit closer and slammed on the brakes. Joan and Goldie were out of the groundcars and moving toward the fence, carrying flexible bangalores. They unrolled the charges, shoved them down at the base of the fence, set the timers, and ran for the groundcars.

The fence went up and over as they regained their seats. It landed, and the ground exploded underneath it.

"Mines, dammit!" Already the roar of the battle around us was loud enough that Krab had to yell. Explosions and shouts filled the night. "Goldie! Saturation fire, fore and past fenceline!"

Goldie took up the groundcar's deck machine gun and sprayed bullets into the ground around and beyond the gap in the fence.

Three more mines went up, and we were through the fence before the ground had settled.

The hangar we were looking for was on the farther of the two parallel runways. We were coming in from the northeast corner of the base, and the runways ran east-west.

Krabnowski killed the lights the moment we were through the fence and drove straight south into the darkness, careering wildly, bounding through potholes and hummocks in the rough ground.

Here and there in the darkness on either side of us, we could see other parties moving forward, toward the center of the camp.

Now League forces mortar and artillery started to be felt. Ahead of us, buildings started to go up, the noise of the individual explosions lost in the roaring noise of the battle surging forward around us.

Krab slammed onto the paved runway and the ground-car nearly flew out of control as the tires hit their first decent traction of the night. We overshot completely and ran over the far side of the pavement. Bob saw it and moved fast enough to swerve hard and stay on the pavement. Krab cut the wheel hard and got us back on the runway.

The flares had given a lot of light until now, but they began to gutter out. In the flickering half-light thrown by the flames of battle fire, I spotted the cross-turn onto the south runway, and pointed it out to Krab. We took the turn on two wheels and jounced down hard on four coming out of it.

"There!" I yelled. The hangar was dead ahead. As we came closer, the lights died. Someone had had the sense to cut the power.

Goldie and Joan lay down covering fire with the deck guns as we squealed to a halt outside the hangar. Krab and I were the first to reach the buildings on foot, running like hell. We were in front of the open roll-out doors. And there she was. From what George said, that had to be a Nova. A laser cut through the air and reminded me I didn't have time to look. But Krab nailed the guy before I could take a bead. I spotted a second on a catwalk and cut him down with my rifle.

Movement at the back of the place. Krab and I both fired at it, and heard screams in return.

"Hold your fire! Clear at the back!" A crash of heavy boots on a sheet-metal door, and Bob had kicked his way in the rear. "We blitzed three of the bastards out back."

I kept moving. There was a steep open staircase, almost a ladder, halfway down the left side wall, that led to a loft overhead. I charged straight up it before I could give myself a chance to think, firing slugs wildly to cover myself. I heard a noise and shot at it. A thudding noise told me I had hit. They cut the power back in from below, and I saw I had killed him.

Moving fast, I checked the rest of the loft. Clean.

Time. We had crossed the perimeter 10 minutes ago.

I got back down and counted noses. Emery was gone.

"Where's Emery?" I asked Metcalf.

"I looked next to me in the jeep and he just wasn't

there," Metcalf said. "Must have plain bounced out of the seat on one of the bigger bumps."

"Damn!" For some reason, it suddenly struck me I didn't remember his first name. "Jesus, I hope he makes it back to our lines. Bet he's safer out there than we are in here."

"Don't remind me. So let's work on getting out of here."

"George! Is this the bird we want?"

"This is it." Something of the old George was in his tone of voice. He was near a complicated machine again.

"Then let's get busy. George. There are offices upstairs—"

"Tech manuals."

"Right."

"I'll look. I hope they have real books and not some damn data file we have to plug into the computer we don't have." He headed up the steep stairs.

"Commander, aren't you a little worried about showing so much light?" Julie asked.

"Yeah, but we need it to work by. Besides, I don't know if light or dark will attract the most attention. Look, I want you four to post some sort of watch. But keep close, keep low, and don't do anything exciting."

"Don't worry."

"Chen, Berman, Metcalf, Talley—let's get to it." We looked for a hatch into the ship and found one over the starboard wing. The Nova was a big, black, mean-looking beast, a hulking mass of brute streamlining. It had no grace, just power. We went aboard.

Metcalf got in first and found the lights. He looked around with a disapproving expression. "Well, it's home, but it's not much."

"Thing must fly like a lead brick," Talley put in.

"Look, if the thing gets us into the air and stays there, I've got no argument with the design," I said.

"What design? Brute force and a set of fuel gulpers. You could put those engines on the hangar and fly just as well," Metcalf said.

The three of them were already in command seats, looking over the controls. Berman had taken the pilot's seat. She flicked up a series of switches and the control panels came to life. The cabin was full of whirring and clicking as machinery woke up.

"Pretty lights," Metcalf said. "Hope they're attached to something.

"Can you people fly this thing?" I asked.

" 'Thing' is the word, but I think so," Metcalf said. "Controls are more or less standard. Give us a little bit of time to look it over."

Suddenly, the whole plane, the whole building, rattled as the battle moved our way for a moment. Another load hit even closer a few seconds later. "Well, get on it. I'm going to see how they're doing out there," I said.

Talley shook his head as he toggled a few switches. "No sense worrying about them, sir. If they don't make it, we won't be far behind."

"Well, somebody get a seat warm for me. I'll be back."

I got out of the plane and met George as he was climbing up on the wing. His arms were full of thick volumes with boring titles. I patted him on the back and kept going.

I headed toward the entrance of the hangar. Abruptly, it was lit with the brightness of a lightning bolt. A roaring explosion deafened me for a moment, and I was thrown to the ground.

As I scrambled to my feet I saw Krabnowski hunkered down by the corner of the doorway. "Krab!" I went over, squatted down next to him, and looked out over the night.

"Getting hot out there," he said.

"They gunning for us?"

"They're gunning for *everybody*. Damn, it's cold. Here we are freezing our buns off waiting to see if we get burned alive."

"How long we got?"

"No idea. Ten minutes, 50 years. Depends on how they manage to contain the Guardians down the other end of the base. If the Guards can counterattack, they'll do it right down our throats."

"Jesus."

"So you get back there and get that ship in the *air*. Maybe we can't beat 'em, but we can fade away. Time is what we're up against."

Two minutes later I was back in the ship, doping out the navigator's station. Could we fly it?

If Chen and the Navy fliers could figure out what all the buttons did. If I could get the computer to figure an air-launch program that would get us to Vapaus. If the dials weren't lying and it really was fueled and powered.

I got to work on the nav station. George and Chen were helping the others by cross-checking the controls against the tech manuals.

The navigation system wasn't that different from what I knew, and I got it chugging along after a fashion. Vapaus was a pretty standard mission, so there was plenty of data in the computer to play with.

No, the machinery wasn't so bad. But the numbers. . . . I liked what I saw less and less. The window—the slice of time and the piece of sky we had to hit to make rendezvous with Vapaus—was awfully tight, and fuel consumption was outrageous.

It was tighter than I had ever dreamed it might be. I struggled to lay in a solution. I finally got one, but I didn't like it. Not with an amateur crew and hostile airspace all the way. Still, we might make it. . . .

Krab shoved his head through the hatchway behind me. "Commander! If you're not out of there in ten minutes, you're not going! Damn it, we're three klicks away and I could *see* our lines get broken."

Berman yelled, "Tow cart! Get the damn tow cart hooked up or we're not getting out of the hangar! Talley, you and Larson. C'mon, Randy, let's get it lined. We'll skull out the rest in midair."

Krab, Talley, and I rushed out of the hatch. It took a nerve-wracking three minutes to find the tow cart. If it had been taken out for maintenance, that would have

been it. The only way the Nova could move under its
own power was jet or rocket power—and firing up inside the hangar would have caved it in on top of the
ship like a puff of wind knocking over a house of cards.
But Talley found the cart parked just outside the hangar
in the darkest corner.

The battle was headed this way, our side in fighting
retreat. The fight would move right through this spot,
and soon. The flash and roar of the firefight grew closer
and closer. "That's one hell of a nice mess," Talley
said.

"And getting nicer," Krab said. "Let's haul it, man!"

We didn't argue. Talley jockeyed the cart around and
we got the tow bar hooked up to the forward landing
gear.

And the war reached us. Talley's chest dissolved into
a red pulp and he fell clear of the cart. Bob appeared
out of nowhere and was in the driver's seat, gunning the
engine as he poured fire into the darkness. But the
uniforms he was shooting at—

"Is that our side?" I yelled.

"It doesn't matter, damn it!" Krab screamed. *"Get
that ship in the air!"*

A shell, stray or aimed, sliced the rear wall off the
hangar. Krabnowski dropped to the ground. Bob was
screaming at me. "Go! Go! Get the hell out of here!" He
raked the ground ahead of him with fire as the Nova
started to roll out onto the runway. Goldie and Julie
were ahead of me, hugging the ground, returning the
hail of fire that came out of the darkness.

I jumped onto the wing and dove through the hatch,
bullets clattering past me. I slammed the hatch and
sealed it.

"Tow bar clear! God bless you, Talley!" Berman called.
"Rolling free! Main air engines start, one, two, all
engines."

The powerful jets exploded into life. "Engines, full
power, mark." Metcalf said. "Watch the nose-up on this
sucker, Eve."

I saw it out the nav station window. Three tiny figures, already a hundred meters back, firing into the darkness.

They all died that night. They must have. God knows how many of us did, all told.

"I christen thee the United States Commandeered Spacecraft *Bohica*!" Metcalf yelled.

Berman sang out "Full throttle—
and we are AIRBORNE!"

We flew out of the wreck of Hades toward the line of dawn, out of burning night into the day.

PART THREE:
WAR IN THE SKY

INTERLUDE

That moment. It all changed then, for a very brief spark of time. So many people died that night, and I moved to a new place and a new fight so suddenly, that it was as if the people I had known weren't dead, but simply somewhere else. Not dead, just gone away.

That moment. As our fugitive ship scrabbled into the sky, I felt the fire again. Just for an instant, it returned. And now I was its master. Inside me, I had conquered that monster. I knew it was to be a capricious and dangerous servant. In my fancy, the flames beneath and behind me saluted my departure.

Death unreal, and fiery destruction my slave. The pure warrior. Then that moment was gone, and I belonged to myself again.

CHAPTER THIRTEEN

"Altitude 10,000 meters, climbing to cruise at 100,000 and steady on course. Keep her pointed that way, Randall," Berman said as she unstrapped herself and climbed from her couch.

"Will do, boss." Metcalf guided the big plane with a careful delicacy; by no means did he trust this ship yet.

"Commander Larson? Could you come forward a moment?" Berman asked.

"Just a moment." By my board, Metcalf was barrelling us right down the line; there wasn't much for me to worry about at the moment. Still numbed by the horror on the ground, I was moving slowly, almost feebly. I climbed out of my crash couch and moved forward to Berman. She was crouched in front of the weapons control station, where Chen sat. George was seated in the comm officer's station, across the tiny aisle from Chen.

"What is it?" I asked.

"She must have been hit by a ricochet. Creased her scalp. I don't think she's going to make it."

Krabnowski hadn't made it. Was anyone I had left five minutes ago still alive?

"Commander?"

"Mmmm? Sorry. Let me take a look." Berman moved out of the way, and I knelt down in front of Chen. She was pale, limp. A thin line of blood dribbled out of the corner of her mouth. A vicious broad slash marked the path of the slug across her forehead. Could the bullet have caused a concussion? Could it have cracked her skull a little bit? What of the blood in her mouth? Another bullet through her lung? I opened her mouth and probed with a finger. No, it looked like she had bitten open the inside of her cheek. Probably a spasm had jerked her whole body around when the bullet hit.

I wiped her blood off my hands onto my coveralls and opened her left eyelid. I moved my hand to shade light from the pupil, moved it away. I tried it again. Her pupil didn't react, didn't expand or contract. "Christ, I think she's concussed."

"What do we do?"

"How the hell do I know! I'm no doctor!" What did they all want? What was it I was supposed to do? "For God's sake, leave her alone!"

"But she might die!"

"And if we clean the cut and put a goddamned bandage on her forehead we could dislodge a hunk of bone right into her head and watch her brains squirt out her ears! Strap her in as best you can, leave her be, and get back to flying this thing—or we're *all* dead!"

Berman shot me a venomous glance and tended to Chen. I stalked forward to the cockpit and sat down next to Metcalf. Why had she asked me? She should be in command, she outranked me. Ah. I was in the Survey Service. I was supposed to have extensive medical training, I guess. She had wanted medicine, not commands.

"Damn it," I said aloud. "I don't remember the last time I ate or slept."

Metcalf's eyes scanned the controls and the skies, and he spoke without looking at me. "What happened on the ground?"

"They're all dead, Randall."

His jaw muscle worked. "Praise God in Heaven. Praise almighty God, but sometimes I wonder if He's paying the slightest damn bit of attention. Better get Eve back up here. We're coming up on the coast, and there's supposed to be some sort of Guardian airbase down there. Could be a problem."

She heard him. "Coming, Randall!"

She and I brushed each other in the narrow aisle. Her pretty face and hands were smeared with unnoticed blood. She glared at me, hurt and angry. Neither of us said anything.

She strapped into the seat I had just vacated and took the controls. "Now at 14 minutes into the flight. Passing coastline in approx 90 seconds." Her eyes were cold, her hands and knuckles white with their grip on the control yoke.

I sighed inwardly and felt tireder than ever. I trudged the few steps to my nav station, set the belts around me, and looked into my radar screen. Adrenalin shot through my system. Three of them!

Metcalf called them first. "Commander! Bogies, six o'clock low and climbing fast!"

"I got 'em, all right, but there aren't any bogies up here; just bandits! George! Can you pick up any radio from them?"

"Just a second. Not sure of this rig yet—"

George threw a switch and a hard voice blared out from the overhead speaker. "—peating, this is Skycoast Leader to Nova Fighter, acknowledge. You have no clearance. No clearance. Respond or be fired upon."

"Well?" George asked doubtfully.

"For Christ's sake get on the horn!" Berman shouted back. "Kid 'em along until we get out of range."

George fumbled with the control panel for a moment, then hit the right button and pulled a headset out of its niche. He put it on. "Call—calling Skycoast Leader. Come in Skycoast Leader."

"Skycoast Leader. Identify yourself!"

George looked out the window and read the number on the wing. "This is Nova 44-8956NF, 44-8956NF. "We are attempting escape from attack on Talon Aerospace

Center. We have sustained damage. Bad damage." Talon was the Guardian's name for Hades.

The voice from Skycoast was still very suspicious. "What sort of damage? Can we assist?"

Metcalf turned around and mouthed *landing gear* to George. George nodded and spoke. "Landing gear jammed —we were fired upon while trying to fly the ship out."

Now the trio of Guardian jets was visible in the infrared TV pickup in the tail of the plane, three tiny dots rapidly growing. I put on my own headset and cut in the intercom. "Navigator to pilot. Can we put on any speed and leave them behind?"

"Negative. Not and reach rendezvous. We can't afford the fuel. Besides, if we try and high-tail it, no way we could outrun a missile at this range."

"Terrific." The *Bohica*, or whatever Metcalf had named her, had launched unarmed.

George was still talking with the enemy pilot. Now he switched to intercom and told us, "They're coming in for a fly-around to inspect our damage. They've instructed us to cease climbing, level off, and match speed."

Metcalf swore under his breath. "Well, boss?"

"Do it, Randy. They've got the guns," Eve said.

Guns, I thought. *There was a gun right by my side. . . .* I spoke into the intercom. "Does everyone have a sidearm, a laser?"

"Yo." Metcalf.

"Yes. So what?" Berman asked.

"I don't," George said.

An idea was coming to me, but damn it, it was a long shot. "Okay, Metcalf and Berman—who's the better shot?"

"I only qualified Marksman," Berman said.

"I made Sharpshooter," Metcalf said.

"Okay, Metcalf. You get your pistol out, set to laser, fullest power, tightest beam." I did the same to mine. "And switch seats with Berman."

"Just what the hell have you got in mind—sir," he

asked as they traded seats. The ship burbled in flight for a moment and settled down.

"We wait for the right moment, when at least two of the fighters are in range, then you and I fire our laser pistols direct at the pilots, at their faces, and blind them. These are visible-light lasers. The beams should be transparent to the glass in our windscreens and theirs."

"You're kidding."

"If you've got a better idea, we're all listening. Eve, be ready to give it the gun."

"You *are* kidding, right?"

"No. Eve, you want to countermand?"

"I can't think of anything either. I wish I could."

"George, will it work?" I asked.

"It ought to," he said nervously. "It shouldn't melt down the glass, anyway, and we won't be much worse off it it does."

"That's good enough for me. Eve, be ready to floor it and head for orbit."

"Commander, on our original flight plan, we still have 17 minutes and 1,000 kilometers to go before air-launch," she said.

"I know, and we can't cut anything out of that. Launch sooner and we can't possibly reach rendezvous with Vapaus. But if we don't shake these guys, we're not going anywhere. One thing at a time."

"They're closing for the fly-around," George reported.

I looked at my radar. "Two are, anyway." One plane, the leader, probably, was hanging back, holding station two klicks back. The other two planes scurried forward. They were dull black, with angular forward-swept wings and windscreens like dark, massive insect eyes. "George, you know that ship at all?"

"Not one bit. New to me."

"Two fighters coming up."

George cut in. "They request you attempt to cycle landing gear."

"At these speeds?"

"We weren't planning to use them, anyway." Metcalf was always ready to be helpful.

"Okay, I'll give 'em a show," Eve said. She flipped the landing gear switches back and forth, so the gear would go in and out fitfully.

I watched the screen. "One of them had to see it. One of them is now directly above us, one below. George, patch the radio into the intercom."

"—isible damage, Nova Fighter. No visible damage."

George gulped and spoke again. "Believe it's in the hydraulics somewhere."

"Possible, Nova fighter. But we see no leakage."

"Boss, slump back or something! If they see a woman flying this thing—" Metcalf said.

"God, Randy, you're right." Berman pulled in from the window, trying to keep herself small and still reach the controls. Our uniforms weren't exactly regulation either, but there was no help for that.

"Commander! My bird's in the slot!" Metcalf said.

"Nothing on my side. He's coming down from on top of us—" I replied.

"Now my plane's drifting forward, easing back in a bit."

Metcalf and I watched our targets sliding in and out of position on either side of the *Bohica*.

"He's coming in . . . okay, I can fire—" I said.

"He's drifting back. C'mon, you bastard, look this way!"

"Can you fire? This guy's sitting there waiting for—"

"Almost—almost—FIRE!!"

We fired at the same moment. From my viewport I could see the thin line of ruby cut through the sky.

The beam slapped at the pilot's face. Instantly his visor began to melt and flow. He reached for his ruined eyes in a spasm of pain, and suddenly his jet dropped away, out of the sky and into the sea.

"Eve— Gun it!"

The big engines throttled up hard and we clawed for sky. "Metcalf—did you—"

"Yeah, I got him."

I watched the radar. "One still on our tail." I looked into the IR from the rear viewscreen. Far behind, two contrails plummeted down, down, down in crazily twisting spirals. Between them, an angry black speck was growing behind us.

I cut the radio back in. "This is Skycoast Leader. In pursuit of renegade Nova Fighter. Sanders and Hampton are downed by Nova. Renegade bearing—" and the radio began to squeal and chirrup meaninglessly.

"He kicked in his scrambler. We won't hear anymore," George reported.

"We've heard enough," I said.

"Commander Larson, we cannot achieve rendezvous with Vapaus. We'll overshoot the entrance to the launch window."

"I know, I know." Daylight grew stronger. We had flown into the sunrise quickly. I killed the IR view and went to normal vision from the TVs. The sky was bright, but the sea below and land behind were in darkness. We still climbed, and now we could see the curve of the globe at the horizon.

"We have to try for orbit, any orbit," Eve said. "There isn't an airfield held by the League that could handle this crate, anyway. And if we turned back toward land they'd shoot us down for sure. We don't have the jet fuel to try for anything else but orbit. It's that or fall into the sea."

"A rock and a hard place," Metcalf put in.

"That it is. Randall, watch the radar. Larson's got to bollix up some sort of course."

It couldn't take long. Minutes before, we had been shooting for one tiny piece of sky. Now I would count us lucky to hit any orbit at all. I started to crank out the numbers for a minimum orbit, lowest energy delta-vee, no change of orbital plane, never mind the sunlines—

"Missile fired! Two missiles!"

I cut away from the nav system and checked on my own radar. Maybe 30 seconds had passed since we had hit the two downed fighters. I cut back to nav. The computer had solved the problem, such as it was. "Pilot! Let's get out of here! Heading 98 degrees, yaw zero, pitch 35 up, roll zero!"

She swung the ship's nose hard, snapped into the heading, and pitched the plane up, making it climb. "At heading!"

"Fire orbital insertion burn, full power fusion engines, at altitude 50,000 meters."

"Orbit engines, full, 50,000."

I cut back to radar. "Missiles closing." Dammit, Chen was unconscious in front of the weapons control station. The radars for this sort of job were there. I upped the magnification.

"Holding heading 98, 0, 35 pos, 0. Altitude 25,000 meters—mark!" Eve's voice was hard and cold, but now fear was behind the calm.

"Missiles closing—range 14,000 meters. Closing at 650 meters a second."

Metcalf's voice cracked. "Altitude, 30,000 meters."

Eve spoke. "Larson—call out missile ranges. Randall— give me a countdown to air launch altitude."

"Ten seconds," Metcalf said.

"Oh my God. . . ." Almost forgotten in the fight, George stared at the TV pickup, his hands balled into useless fists.

"Range, 11,000 meters," I said.

"Nine seconds."

"Ninety-five hundred meters." Now, out of the rear TV pickup, I could *see* the missiles, tiny white circles of fire with dark points at the center.

"Eight seconds."

"Stand by for air launch," Eve called. Would Chen make it? How many gees could she take with that wound?

"Seven seconds."

"Seven thousand meters." My voice was high and weak over the roar of the engines.

"We won't make it."

"Shut up, Randy—give me data!"

"Forty-two hundred meters," I said. He was right.

"Sweet Jesus, five seconds."

"Missiles at 3,000." Suddenly one of them slowed, fell back, and dropped off the screen. "One missile out of fuel."

"Please, sweet Jesus. Four seconds."

"Second missile closing faster—1,200 meters."

"Three seconds."

"Five hundred meters!"

"EVASIVE!" Eve yelled, and wrenched the ship into a deep, shrieking dive that snapped my jaw shut. I tasted blood. An explosion slammed after us, shaking the ship, and I heard the scream of metal shearing away. Eve pulled out of the dive and began to climb again.

"We're hit. Lost some rudder control, and we're leaking somewhere," she said.

"Yeah, but my God, we're alive. Thank your Aunt Martha it wasn't a nuke."

"We've got a yellow light on the orbital engines. Randy, can you read it?"

"Fuel leak."

"Can we make orbit?"

"Missile on screen!" It came out of nowhere, the moment I switched back to low magnification.

"Randy! Altitude!"

"Forty-five thousand meters!"

"Missile impact in three seconds."

Eve pulled back on the yoke, brought us to a dangerously steep climb. Somewhere in its guts, the ship shuddered and there was a dull thud.

"Forty-eight thousand meters altitude."

"Impact in two!"

"Fifty thousand meters—"

"AIR LAUNCH!"

The huge motors exploded into ravening life. On the TV screen, I could see a ghostly image of flame reach out and touch the missile, and it vanished, vaporized.

The noise was fantastic. The whole ship was shaking frantically. George seemed to say something to himself, but it was impossible to hear. He seemed to shake with reaction more violent than the ship's.

Through the headset, I could just barely hear Berman and Metcalf.

"Red light on fuel leak now, boss."

"I hear you, Randy. We gotta cut our mass."

"Passing Mach one." The shaking, the vibration remained for a moment, but now the roar of our flight faded away. Then, as we came out of the atmosphere, the vibration faded, too.

"Okay, pumping fuel from wings to main tankage."

"Eighteen seconds into burn."

The tension had broken, vanished completely. We were still alive.

"Fuel leak looks worse than I thought. We might have trouble hitting even minimum orbit," Metcalf said.

"How bad is it?" I asked.

"Look out your port."

Here, above 90 percent of the atmosphere, the wingtank hydrogen vaporized immediately. There was a stream of thick, ropy vapor spewing from a hole the size of my thumb at the base of the wing.

"Jesus," I muttered.

"You said it," Metcalf agreed. "I'm pumping the wingtanks into the onboard tanks as fast as I can, but I gotta pump from both wings at the same time to keep the ship balanced."

"Will we make it?"

"I never try to predict a leak."

"Thank you, that's very helpful."

The cabin was quiet for a moment, then a tiny, weak moan came from Chen. She was still with us, for the moment. But how long could she take three gees?

Now it was three and a half gees. As the ship burned fuel and thus lightened itself, the rocket engines could push the lightened load faster and harder with each passing second. We would hit peak acceleration of about four gees and a whisker.

"Sixty seconds into burn. Commander, have you taken

a look at dropping the wings?" Metcalf asked. "Once the wing tanks are pumped dry, it'd be nice to dump the weight. Can we get away with it, or would it louse up our trajectory?"

"What trajectory?" I said. "We've settled down to the right heading schedule, but we didn't start that way. We ought to hit *an* orbit, but I have no idea which one. Let's see. Why don't you run the pumps ten seconds after the tanks are dry, just to be sure. Then shut them down, kill main engines for two seconds, blow the wings, and throttle back up?"

"Why not, indeed?" Metcalf said. "We're not going after the precision flying award, that's for sure. Eve, can you handle that?"

"I can," she replied, "but I don't know if this heap will hold together."

"If it doesn't, we all hit the drink," said Metcalf. "With that leak, we definitely don't have the fuel to make orbit carrying the wings."

"Hasn't been one of our better flights so far, has it?" Eve said unhappily.

"No, boss-lady, it hasn't," Metcalf agreed. "Should have the wing tanks pumped dry at 120 seconds into the burn."

"Okay, stand by for two-second engine stop at 130. Randy, I'll do the flying, you make with the bolts on the wings. Blow 'em clean."

"I've got the safety off already. Just one button to push."

There was a sudden whirring sound as the pumps ran out of anything to pump. Just then, the ropy jet of vapor from the wing sputtered and vanished.

"And there go the wing tanks at 105 into the burn," Metcalf said.

"Okay, stand by for wing and tail jettison," Eve warned.

"Okay, Eve, all explosive bolts armed and ready. You hold onto this sucker when I blow the wings and tail. It's gonna want to spin out in ten different directions."

"I'm on it. Let's get it lined."

"George, you and the Commander call the wings when they're well clear. I'll watch the tail through the rear TV," Metcalf said.

"Stand by," Eve called. "One hundred twenty-five seconds, 126, 127, 128, 129, SHUTDOWN!"

There was a leaping off of pressure as the engines cut out. Then, out my port, I could see brief flashes of light. There was a squeal of metal on metal, and then the wing drifted silently away, sidling off into the sky.

"Port wing clear!"

"This one's clear, too," George said.

"Tail assembly clear. At least this ship works properly when you want to blow it up. Gun it, professor!"

"Engines restart!" We were kicked back into our couches, harder than ever. We were topping four and a half gees. Was Chen going to make it?

"Mac, do you have any idea where this orbit is going to take us?" George asked.

"Which orbit? The one we were supposed to hit, the orbit we tried to launch into, or the one we're *actually* boosting into? We were coming out of evasive action when Eve hit air launch. I don't even know which way we were pointed then! Eve corrected and got us pointed the right way, but I've got no way of figuring the effect of those first seconds on our flight path, or what losing our wings will do. Should put us higher, but I don't know by how much."

"Makes things a little tougher to figure," Metcalf commented.

"But we are going to make orbit, aren't we?" George asked.

"Oh, probably," I said, "but it won't last long—two or three revolutions we'll be so low in the upper atmosphere that we might even have been able to use the wings, a little. Not enough for it to be worth it."

Berman and Metcalf were pilots. They had worked this out already. George, however, was distinctly uncomfortable. "So we get this far and wait to fall down?"

"Just hope someone up there is willing to pick up

hitchhikers," said Metcalf. "We won't come within two thousand klicks of rendezvous with Vapaus."

"Oh." George sat there, bewildered for a minute. "So why is everybody so calm?"

"When we courageous flying types get *really* calm, that's the time to start worrying," Metcalf explained. "Personally, I wet my pants when that first missile went halfway up our tailpipe."

"C'mon, it wasn't *that* close!" Eve said with a smile in her voice.

"So why are my pants wet? Two hundred forty-five seconds into burn."

A few seconds later a buzzer went off. "Dammit! Ten-second fuel warning. Burn time 250, 251, 252, 253, 254, 255—past this it's all bonus time—257, 258, 259—"

The engines bucked once, twice, growled, flickered, and died. We were weightless.

"Engine stop, 259 seconds. Maybe a hair more with that last rumble. Commander, are we going to stay up here?"

"Gimme a few minutes." The only things I knew I could handle without spending two hours with the manual were a sextant and an altitude radar. I got a rough ground speed with the sextant and bounced a series of pulses off the planet with the radar. Then it was a matter of fiddling with scratch paper. "I make us doing 7,400 meters a second, roughly, at 162 kilometers, and it looks circular. We made it, just barely."

That rated a ragged cheer.

"George," I went on, "get on that radio and give Vapaus a call. If you can convert from Guardian settings, they're on UHF channel two."

"Piece of cake. Ah, Lieutenant Metcalf, what was it you named the ship again?"

"United States Commandeered Spacecraft *Bohica*. It's a long story."

"Be careful or he'll tell it," Berman warned. "Commander, let's see to our patient."

I unstrapped myself and guided myself over to Chen, Berman right with me.

Chen was still out, completely. Now, in zero gee, the oozing cut in her forehead hardly seemed to bleed. Instead of pouring down her face, the blood ballooned from her face in a tiny sphere that trembled with her breathing. Eve kicked past me into the rear of the cabin and returned with a compact first aid kit.

"This is the United States Commandeered Spacecraft *Bohica*, the USCSC *Bohica* calling base station Vapaus. Come in, please. We are derelict and carrying wounded. Come in Vapaus. This is the USCSC *Bohica* calling. . . ."

George's thin, cheerful voice droned on in the background as Eve and I tried to tend Chen. I gently sponged the blood away from her forehead and gingerly tried to clean the cut. It didn't seem too deep or too bad.

There was a small flashlight in the first-aid kit and I tested her pupils again. This time they responded, a little. She coughed, and a few drops of blood gurgled out of her mouth and floated out into the cabin. Eve corralled the blood between her hand and a sponge. That cut in the mouth was still nasty. In zero gee, the blood could pool up and block her lungs—she could drown in it.

"Mac, we don't need two pilots right now, and you must be exhausted by this time," Berman said. "I'll do what I can with Chen, and you take it easy. We'll need you to be sharp when we talk to Vapaus." She started to bandage the forehead cut.

"Commander, if you could spell me for a minute, I'd like to step to the head," Metcalf said. The *Bohica* was a long-duration ship, and had a tiny washroom.

"Okay." I climbed into the copilot's couch and Metcalf headed aft. The legs of his pants were darkened and an acrid smell followed after him.

George paused in using the radio. "I thought he was kidding about wetting his pants."

"Not a hot pilot anywhere who couldn't use a diaper

now and again," I said. "Some parts of my training were a little messy, too."

Metcalf returned in a few minutes, his pants wetter but cleaner after being rinsed.

"Randall, maybe you'd better see if we can't keep our nose through our direction of travel." Already, the *Bohica* was beginning to tumble. Tenuous though it was, the atmosphere was still with us, and if we could keep our cross-section small we'd last in orbit a lot longer.

I didn't need to tell Metcalf any of this. He took one glance out the port, saw the planet's surface roll past it, and whistled. "I'm on it."

"This is the USCSC *Bohica* calling base station Vapaus. We are derelict and have wounded. We request aid. Dammit. This is the USCSC *Bohica*, calling anybody. Help. Over."

George went on and on. I tried to sleep. I had had about four hours sleep in the last 52 hours. I tried to doze for about an hour, but I was too restless. I gave it up and went forward to see how Metcalf was doing.

"How's it look?" I asked as I settled into the copilot's seat.

"Not so good. The gyros are from some bargain basement somewhere. Pitch is okay, but the yaw isn't much and the roll is nothing at all. They must have been ripped up by that near miss."

"So what're you doing about it?"

"Hosing it out the attitude jets and waving our fuel supply goodbye. Thank God the bozos who built this crate at least gave the att jets a separate fuel source, or we'd have lost them when the main engines ran out of juice."

"What about the jet fuel?"

"What? We can't burn that up here. No air to burn it with."

"No, but there must be some way to vent it."

"So?"

"So, if you vent it, you cut the mass of the ship, and—"

"With less mass to push around, the att fuel will hold out longer. Well, let's see." He pulled out the pilot's manual George had rescued from the hangar. "Vents, air—fuel. Page 456. Hold it, diagram, page 444. Hmmm. Well, that's something. If they haven't bent all out of shape, the vents are positioned so the thrust from one venting cancels out the thrust from the other. Probably still get *some* tumbling from it, but what the hell." He checked the manual for the appropriate switches, then punched some buttons. There was a far-off *whoosh*ing and suddenly the *Bohica* was surrounded by a cloud of white vapor that dispersed instantly. The ship started to roll around its long axis, but Metcalf let it ride. "I'm just going to worry about holding that cross-section. A roll doesn't matter. Thanks for the idea."

"Any other problems?"

"Well, I think we've got a battery problem. Power seems to be draining pretty quick. I'm going to have a few words with the ground crew about that when we get back. In the meantime, maybe you could power down stuff we're not going to need."

"Do what I can." Which wasn't much. I shut off lights and powered down boards we weren't going to need— mine and Chen's, for starters. But these were the most trivial uses of power. The real crunch came where we couldn't do anything about it: the radio, the life-support system, the attitude-control system. I cut back the thermal controls a bit, but even being a bit colder wasn't going to help much.

It was a dark, cold, quiet ship that fell through the sky around the bright planet, the war planet that spun silently around the ports. Soon, we again entered the shadow of the world.

"This is the USCSC *Bohica*, calling anyone, calling anyone. We are derelict and have wounded. This is the USCSC *Bohica* calling. . . ."

We drifted on through space. George's voice gave out, and I spelled him for a while. We came out of the planet's shadow, and then, dead ahead of us, the bright star that was Vapaus rose above the swelling curve of dawn on New Finland. We had passed it before in orbit, but never at dawn. It was lovely. As the light poured into the now cold cabin, it seemed a new warmth, a new hope came to us all as we looked at that shining point of light.

I switched from the broadcast antenna to narrow beam and aimed the squirt antenna straight at Vapaus. "This is the United States Commandeered Spacecraft *Bohica*, calling base station Vapaus. Come in, Vapaus base. We are derelict and carrying wounded. Please come in, Vapaus base."

There came, finally, an answer. I couldn't understand the words at first, until I realized it was Finnish.

There was expectancy in the faces around me.

"Well, what did they say?" George asked.

"They told me to surrender or be fired upon."

"Oh, my God."

I hurriedly took up the mike again. "This is *Bohica*. We are a League ship. We're on your side!" I said in bad Finnish.

"Surrender or be fired upon."

Suddenly, on either side of us, there were bright flashes of fire-yellow light, and a clicking on the hull. Explosive shells had gone off very near us and small fragments bounced off the ship.

"That was a calculated miss," Metcalf said.

"Yeah, a shot across our bow—but they had to have fired those shells before they radioed us," said Eve.

"This is *Bohica*! Vapaus base, we request you cease fire! This is an unarmed ship! We are unarmed—carrying wounded!"

The star that was Vapaus flickered at its edges for a moment. "They're firing again," Metcalf said.

Long seconds later, more flashes of light, brighter, closer, and this time it was the sound of steel smashing through the hull. The ship began to tumble, skewing end over end. An alarm sounded.

"We're losing air!" George cried. He shut off the alarm.

"Vapaus, your fire has punctured our hull! Please cease fire! We surrender, for God's sake!" Now the bulk of the satellite was beginning to swell as our orbit overtook hers. There was no reply, but no fire either.

George scrambled for a bulkhead and grabbed a red box out of a cubbyhole. A patch kit. He pulled out an aerosol can and sprayed a grey smoke into the cabin. It hung there, pulled nowhere, then slowly drifted toward the ventilator. He shook his head. "If the leak was in the cabin, this stuff would suck toward it in a straight line. It's somewhere else in the air system, where we can't get at it."

Eve watched the growing shape of the satellite. Now it was close enough that we could see its spin. "Why don't they finish us off? What are they doing? Those shots bracketed us perfectly. If they had wanted to destroy us, they could have had us on the first shot."

"I don't understand." I paused for a moment, then transmitted again, speaking Finnish. "This is *Bohica*. Calling Vapaus. We are derelict. We have wounded. We are your friends. We stole this ship to escape the enemy. Please do not fire. Please respond."

The speaker remained silent.

Slowly, the satellite crawled across the sky as we overtook her in our faster, lower orbit. Then she drifted behind us to fall behind the curve of New Finland.

We were in sight of the great satellite for over an hour, with no more words and no more attacks.

But then something came to me, an idea that I had blocked into the deepest part of my mind. I examined the radio's frequency controls and shifted them to a new setting. Then, hardly daring—for some reason, even afraid—I broadcast again.

Deep in my crawling fears I thought I knew what had happened: somehow, the Finns on the satellite had been overthrown a second time by the enemy. They had attacked, then examined our orbit, found it would decay in a few hours, and decided not to waste effort to destroy us.

In that case, if she had survived this far, there was still one person, one ship, who might be able to save us.

"This is Commander Terrance MacKenzie Larson, aboard the USCSC *Bohica*, calling the League of Planets Survey Ship *Joslyn Marie*. We are derelict, carrying wounded, and under fire from the satellite. If you can respond safely, come in, *Joslyn Marie*." I paused and bit my lip. "This is Mac. Joz, are you there? Please, Joslyn, are you there?"

But there was only silence. Vapaus drifted below our horizon.

We kept trying. There was little else we could do, other than curl up and die. Marie-Francoise Chen seemed near that anyway. Eve had long since run out of anything that could blot up the blood from her mouth. Now she was using a small sponge, blotting the cut in Marie-Francoise's mouth, then wringing out the blood into a plastic storage bag to keep it from floating out and spattering around the cabin. She had not been entirely successful; the area around Marie-Francoise was covered with splashes of blood—some dry, some still shiny and sticky-black. Eve seemed unaware that there was far more blood on her face than on her patient's.

The cut on Marie-Francoise's forehead had stopped bleeding, but Eve was forced to impede the clotting in the mouth in order to sponge up the oozing blood. Even so, the cut seemed to be closing slowly.

It was something like three hours since we had launched.

We transmitted again and again, both to the satellite and to the *Joslyn Marie*. There seemed little hope in either, but no hope at all elsewhere.

"This is Terrance MacKenzie Larson aboard the *Bohica*, calling Survey Ship *Joslyn Marie*. For God's sake, Joz— answer. Mac to Joz, come in, please. . . ."

* * *

Randall was staring moodily off into nothing. The *Bohica* seemed to have stopped tumbling, at least. He had nothing to do, except watch the batteries drain, watch the air gauge show our air slowing vanishing out some pinhole, and stare at the sky.

"This is Mac Larson, calling the LPSS *Joslyn Marie*. Joz, can you read me? Come in. Calling—"

Suddenly Metcalf yelled out, "Radar! Something coming up on us retrograde—and fast!" I kicked in my radar, and saw two tiny pinpoints slide out of the east, climbing over the curve of New Finland.

They were coming fast, damn fast, retrograde, flying the opposite direction from normal orbit. An immense amount of power was needed to hit retrograde orbit—at least 10 kilometers a second, delta-vee.

"They must be doing eight gees," Randall said.

"Missiles. God damn missiles," Eve said hollowly.

It was too much. To make it this far and be blown out of the sky by our own people. "They think we're a bomb, a nuke," I said. "They think we're a booby-trap and they waited until we were on the other side of the planet from them to shoot us down.

The two fierce knives of light drove toward us, rounding to hard dots of brightness as the missiles arced over toward us.

"Two blips, closing at like 10 kilometers a second, accelerating."

"George—Eve—Randall. Thank you. You all did your best. As Marie-Francoise did," I said, very quietly.

Eve looked at me sadly, intently. Her face was covered with bloody splashes. "Goodbye, Commander."

All was quiet for a moment.

"Two blips still accelerating, dead for us. Thirty seconds to impact," Randall said. "We're going to die."

We could see the missiles plainly. No escape.

And then there was a bright shaft of light that gleamed dimly through the thin air there at the edge of space. It lanced to one missile, and it blossomed into incandesence.

The laser reached for the second bomb, and it, too, vaporized. The blobs of expanding light rushed past us in weird silence, into the blackness of space.

A third blip came speeding over the side of the planet, from the same direction as the missiles.

The radio burst into life. "Mac, are you there? For God's sake, are you there? Mac?"

I began to laugh and cry and my muscles began to shake all at once. The others were frozen where they were, still not understanding. I switched on the mike.

"Joslyn, I have always admired your sense of timing."

"Oh, Mac! Thank God!"

CHAPTER FOURTEEN

Joslyn wasn't going to be able to help any more for the moment. She had heard just a few seconds of one of my transmissions to the *Joslyn Marie* through the repeater pick-up she carried when away from the ship. It was, thank God, enough to convince her.

The *J.M.* had been docked at Vapaus for some weeks now.

They *had* thought we were a bomb. The great satellite we thought was ignoring us was on full alert, everyone in pressure suits. Joslyn had taken about half a second to decide what to do, and then broken all records getting through Vapaus airlock control to the *J.M.* She had undocked *Uncle Sam*, our cargo lander, just in time to see the missiles launched into retrograde orbit.

She followed without a glance at her fuel gauge. To catch the missiles she had to accelerate 24,000 kilometers an hour! That meant something like five minutes at eight gees. It was a hell of a ride, but finally the missiles came above her horizon, and that was that.

Now *her* tanks were dry.

A very apologetic Vapaus command was sending a tug to each ship.

The catch was that the tug headed for *Uncle Sam* planned to be able to get back. Instead of the brute force flight Joslyn had followed, the tug was launched on a

207

trajectory that would take 15 hours each way to match between the two orbits. No reunions just yet.

We couldn't even really talk. Her orbit put her above our radio horizon about four minutes an hour. And an open radio channel used with three or other people in the room isn't really my idea of privacy.

A tug came for us inside of four hours. Metcalf used the last of our att fuel to kill our tumble, and the Finns docked with our ventral airlock, came in, got Chen on a zero-gee pressure stretcher, hustled the rest of us out, and slammed the hatches shut in ten minutes. Then the tug backed off about 30 klicks and shot a missile right into *Bohica*'s hapless self. That was one bad-luck ship.

Our entrance to Vapaus was more routine than the first time I had arrived. The tug docked at the central docking collar at the axis of the satellite. From there, mechanical arms grappled the ship and guided it along a tracked entrance system to a vast airlock chamber about a third of the way down the axis. Instead of bothering to pressurize the lock, the ground crew extended an accordion-pleated flexible tunnel about four meters in diameter. This was set up around the tug's side hatch and inflated. We disembarked, walking gingerly in the reduced gravity of the dock areas. A doctor and orderlies were waiting to transport Marie-Francoise to the hospital center.

Dr. Tempkin himself was there to meet the rest of us. He greeted us politely and hurriedly, and then led us through a maze of corridors to an elevator which carried us down to the central cylindrical plain of Vapaus.

The elevator had a glass wall, and at one time the view of Vapaus's interior must have beautiful, magnificent. Now it was the picture of a near-ruin.

The vast greenness was scorched to sullen brown. The lawns, the trees, the parks were all more than half-dead. Here and there were patches of green that seemed to be fresh and new, as if the plants were staging a struggling return. But this was more a dead place than a live one. The central sea was no longer a sparkling blue, but a ring of dark, murky, greenish-brown. No pleasure craft could be seen. Here and there, stolid, dark trawlers plied its surface.

Clambering up from points every 90 degrees around the interior, straddling the central sea with broad legs on either side of it, was a giant construction of open girders, the whole unit symmetrical, each pair of legs supporting a long central arm. The four arms met at the exact center of the world, the midpoint of the axis. Four giant Ys upturned and joined in the center by their bases. In the center of the vast thing, along the axis of Vapaus, we saw what looked like great, gimballed turbines.

"What in God's name is *that*?" George asked.

"That," Tempkin said, "is 'Hydra.' The entire unit is there for the purpose of holding the gyroscopes you see at the precise center of the world. It took five days to assemble it, using every man, woman, and child we could spare."

"*That* was assembled in five days?"

"It was long ago designed, built, disassembled, and stored in case of just such an emergency as we now face. It was intended for rapid assembly. And do not forget we are a major shipyard, with many automated construction machines to help us."

"What is the emergency?"

"The Guardians launched a bomb against us a week ago. It failed to destroy the station, but it nearly cracked the shell of the satellite. It was a near miss. We spotted it and it set itself off prematurely to prevent our deactivating it. Even so, it had enough force to throw a tumble into Vapaus's spin. The whole satellite is wobbling. Shrapnel was thrown from the bomb and it hit at tremendous speed—it was like an earthquake.

"When Vapaus began to tumble, we lost much of our power network, and the temperature control scheme was thrown awry. There were great, sudden rains, which washed much of our topsoil down into the central sea.

All this, and our green plants died. Of course, we rely on them to exchange CO_2 for oxygen.

"We have done all we can to refresh our oxygen, but our reserves are near gone. We have seeded the central sea with algae to produce oxygen while we recover. The trawlers are working to recover the topsoil."

He paused for a moment. "Also, there was fighting, burning, sabotage, as we overthrew the Guardians' troops. This, too, fouled the air, and repair machinery was badly damaged.

"We will most likely survive, but it will be no small matter to restore this world."

We rode the elevator down in silence.

As we left the elevator, I noticed a low, intense humming that seemed to pervade everything. It was the gyros, whirring and humming high above, working to wrest this world back into its proper rotation.

The air smelled of smoke and dirty soot. It was stale and stuffy.

As we walked, the people looked at us with mild curiosity, but their expressions all seemed dazed, shocked, tired. As Tempkin led us to the administrative center, we passed burned-out buildings, charred fields, smashed and broken places.

At Tempkin's office, the debriefing began, all of us from the *Bohica* barely able to keep our eyes open, wishing we could change our clothes. A recorder was set up, and we sketched in the story of the war on the ground. I emphasized George's role in all that had happened. Tempkin was tremendously suspicious of George anyway, and insisted, gently but firmly, that his fingerprints and photograph be immediately "sent down." Midway through the debriefing, an orderly came in with a slim file folder. Tempkin examined its contents and nodded to George, saying, "Well, you don't seem to be on any of our lists, and the Commander is willing to vouch for you. Welcome." He didn't seem very happy about it.

I described the discovery of the mailbag, and what was found in it, and our deductions concerning the existence and location of the missile control station. I described the decision to bring the information to Vapaus, and our escape to orbit. Tempkin interrupted with a question now and again, but for the most part, he listened quietly.

Finally, the story was finished. Tempkin sat in thought for a while. "I am stunned," he said at last. "From orbit, we watched the destruction of the spaceport you call Hades, thinking that it meant we had won. With Hades gone, the Guardians could be starved out. We thought nothing was left but the mopping up, the setting to rights. Then the supposed second bomb came—which turned out to be you. We thought this time they were trying to be clever and fool us into inviting the bomb into our home.

"Already, we have assigned technicians working on ways to punch holes in the missile system. It is thought it might take years, but we are patient, and self-sufficient enough.

"Now, this mighty ship, *Leviathan*." He stopped and shook his head.

"But Commander Larson, Lieutenant Metcalf, Miss Captain Berman, Mr. Prigot. For now, you have done your part and more. Little more can be done now except to study the information you have brought. Take the time to rest." He stood up and led us from the office.

Vapaus had been a garden world, and perhaps would be again. Now it was a grey, dirty ruin. Having seen it more nearly whole, it was worse for me. But I knew my companions were saddened by the shattered, grimy look of the wounded satellite. I invited them all to be billeted away from the sad landscape, in the *Joslyn Marie*. There was room to spare. The *J.M.* had been built for a crew of nine.

It was good to get there. That ship was home.

The four of us had a quiet meal together, refreshed

ourselves, and retired to bed. George, Randall, and Eve settled down for the night in a stateroom apiece. I entered the captain's stateroom—our room—Joz's and mine. I got into bed, looked around the peaceful room. Home. I luxuriated in the comfort of clean skin, a full belly, and zero gee to sleep in.

The room was warm, cheerful, and cozy. I could see Joslyn's clothes, her hairbrush, I could smell her scent. Not just the smell of her perfume, but her own special, private scent, a delicate hint of fragrance that reminded me of clear blue skies and love in peaceful springtime.

A thousand times I had imagined our reunion, picturing us rejoined upon the wreckage of a battlefield, or in the deep green coolness of a secret corner of Vapaus, or in the depths of space. But never this way. Reunited with a Joslyn still missing, a joining with what seemed her ghost, surrounded by hints of her existence, Joslyn herself gone.

A horror I had kept locked away from myself as best I could in all that time slithered its way to the surface of my brain: she was dead. I had never dared admit to that fear, against all the risks and flames of war, that she might have been killed in some battle here in space. I was exhausted, I was drained of all emotion, facing a grim future darkened by the coming of *Leviathan*. There, in the darkness, the conviction formed, cold and certain, that Joslyn *was* dead, that she had sacrificed herself in the rescue of *Bohica*, that the tug had failed to pick her up, that her ship had crashed, that disaster had overtaken her in the complicated dance of the orbits.

It is hard to cry in zero gee. The tears don't *go* anywhere, they simply well up in your eyes and turn your vision into a shimmering cloudiness. I shook my head and the foolish tears were flung from my eyes.

It was reaction to too much danger, too many fears, too many close calls. Here, now, safe for the first time in uncountable days, I collapsed into horrifying tremors of fear and sorrow, caught between wakefulness and nightmare.

Awareness ebbed from me. Gradually, I descended into my nightmares, my memories—of my mind and body and world on fire, of cold nights of fear, of broken and bloodied bodies, friends destroyed by unseen murderers before eyes, of always running, always nearly trapped. Always the vision of Bob, Julie, Goldie, and Krab as I last saw them, as they were eaten up by the war and the darkness.

Thus Joslyn found me, and came to me, and understood, far into the night.

"Mac, what have they done to you?" Josyln held me in the darkness, shifted her arms and held me tighter. She could see the clouds and the fire still between us, the darkness of the war. "Grim, frightened, so fierce—oh, Mac. I do love you so."

I shook my head and kissed her, barely able to speak. "Oh, Joslyn, thank God for you."

"And for you." In the dimness of the stateroom I could barely see her face, but her expression was clear and indescribable. Love, passion, desire, relief, confusion, and trust contended in her eyes, the set of her mouth, her knitted forehead.

Finally we slept. I knew that Joslyn had saved my life many times before the *Bohica* escaped those missiles. I remained as whole as I did only because I knew she loved me.

"Welcome to breakfast, oh mighty Commander," Randall said.

I sailed into the wardroom and smiled ruefully. "Hello, folks." Joz was playing hostess and serving up an English breakfast to Eve, Randall, and George. "Somebody sure let me sleep." By my watch, about 13 hours.

"You needed it, Mac. Hungry?"

"You'd better be," George said. "Mrs. Larson, ah, Lieutenant Commander Larson, I mean your . . ."

"Call me Joslyn."

"Thanks. Joslyn sure doesn't do cooking by half."

"Oh yes she does. Tomorrow is my half. My turn."

Joslyn said, "And the day after that, and after that, and after that, and—"

"What?!"

"I've been doing the cooking for this ship ever since you jumped overboard in *Stripes*. You've got a lot of catching up to do."

I laughed and made a rude noise. Then my stomach woke up and I discovered I *was* hungry. Joslyn's cooking at breakfast can take some getting used to, but I had done that long ago. Joslyn had clearly been dickering with someone for fresh food from Vapaus's surviving farms. I faced a "good British breakfast" of bacon, sausage, baked beans, friend eggs, strong black tea, orange juice, and thick-sliced ham. It vanished quickly, to Joslyn's obvious delight.

While I was still eating, the others had gotten to the coffee-and-chat stage. Randall was fiddling with the viewscreen controls. After a bit, he managed a view from our sternward camera, nestled between the *Joslyn Marie*'s main engines. The *J.M.* was docked to Vapaus by an airlock on the side of the ship, so the stern cameras had a clear view, unobstructed by Vapaus. The curve of the planet was plainly visible to the rear of the screen, and here and there, tiny ships could be seen drifting through the maze of stars that entangled the sky. "Nice view," he said. "But where is *Leviathan*?"

That was the question we lived with for two months. There was no clue anywhere as to when *Leviathan* would arrive. It might be tomorrow, or today, or next day. In the meantime, we tried to get ready. There was enough work to go around.

With Hades out of the picture, it was possible to fly somewhat risky missions to the planet's surface in the *Kuu* class ballistic transports the Finns used. These ships could go in, pick up personnel or supplies, and get the hell out fast. The Guardians were still a serious enemy, still had an air force, still fielded more soldiers than we did. The *Kuu* missions were dangerous, and we lost a few of them. But we needed them. They lifted the remainder of Eve and Randall's group of fliers to orbit. Their commander didn't make it, which left Eve in charge.

The *Kuu*s brought in needed repair equipment, technicians, spies. They were invaluable for getting our people to where they were needed on the planet. Vapaus was the acknowledged headquarters of the Finnish and League forces. With our ability to observe any point on the planet, we could know when to hit, when to fight, when to protect what was left of our forces.

The troops that had hit Hades had taken about 30 percent casualties. We had wounds to bind.

The repairs to Vapaus went forward, and the satellite slowly healed. There was half a day of celebration when the wobble had been worked out of Vapaus's spin and Hydra could be shut down.

But ahead of all other work were the preparations for meeting *Leviathan*. Marie-Francoise recovered quickly and worked endlessly with the Finns to squeeze every drop of information out of the documents we had. The Navy pilots and the Finnish pilots trained together and made frequent trips to The Rock, where the major shipyards were located. There, frenetic efforts were being made to mass-produce orbital fighters.

There were a thousand strange schemes for space-battle weapons: exotic acids, clever limpets, robot mines to be placed in orbit, drone ships, and so on. There simply wasn't time for them all. The engineers set out a rigid series of priorities for what could be done in what amount of time.

George and I worked on battle tactics. Mostly, I think, because the Finns didn't know what else to do with us. We were given a fairly free hand and a large auditorium with a big hologram tank in it to play with. I think we surprised them by actually accomplishing anything.

We were so badly stuck for a while there, I think we surprised ourselves. The first thing we did was program the hologram display to present New Finland's globe,

Vapaus, The Rock, New Finland's natural moon, Kuu (which means "moon" in Finnish), and so on. Then we taught the computer what the performances of our fighters were, what the abilities of *Leviathan* were, what we thought the likely performance of the fighters *Leviathan* carried would be.

George took command of the League forces, I of the Guardian ships. Which orbits benefited which craft? What traps and decoys could we lay for them, what tricks could we anticipate and avoid from their side?

All of this was of use, of course, and we passed a lot of information on to the people who could use it.

There was one problem, however, that no one could figure out: *Leviathan*'s reentry. Obviously, the thing was expected to enter the atmosphere and there perform as a gigantic armored airship. Yet there seemed to be no possible way the great ship could hope to survive entry into New Finland's atmosphere.

There had to be a way. Otherwise, the ship was useless. But *Leviathan* hitting atmosphere from orbital speed would be like asking a soap bubble to survive a hurricane. Any ship intended as a lighter-than-air craft had to be far too lightly built to be able to hit atmosphere at eight kilometers a second.

"Dammit, George. They've got to have some stunt maneuver, some brilliant trick to get them into the air. If we can dope it out, we can be sitting right on top of them when they try it."

We were sitting in the auditorium, each of us with a portable computer terminal in his lap. The holo tank was frozen into one moment in time, the planet, moons, and ships locked into that one moment. We had gotten tired of playing space games and come back to the central problem.

In the presence of a whole new set of gadgets, George had staged a major recovery of his former spirit. He was taking a lively interest in the coming battle, not because it was an event that might decide the fate of a world, but as a fascinating puzzle to be solved.

He thought over the *Leviathan* problem again. "All right, they have to enter the atmosphere. They can't do that from orbital speeds. So they can't be entering from orbit."

"That's perfect George. What does it mean?"

"Beats the hell out of me," he said brightly. "That's as far as I've gotten."

"Terrific." I sat and thought for a bit. "Maybe *Leviathan* is an elaborate hoax. Maybe the mailbag *was* a plant."

"Makes sense. All the Guardian generals got together and decided to concoct a phony weapon that would scare the enemy into setting new records for producing fighters and weapons."

"I see your point. So let's take what you said, and work it from the other end. If they attempted reentry, they'd be torn to pieces. So: what is the maximum velocity they could deal with and hold together?"

George worked with his computer terminal. Finally he said, "If you're waiting for things to make sense, keep waiting. With the best materials at hand, careful flying, real precision, and amazing luck, they could just about manage Mach two without leaving the vertical stabilizer behind. Also the wings. And that is a very optimistic upper limit."

"It's *got to* be a fake!"

"But it doesn't make any sense as a fake, either."

"Let's take a break," I said with a sigh.

"Sold." George punched some buttons and the images of New Finland and vicinity vanished as the house lights came up.

We left the theater and headed back to the *Joslyn Marie*. We found a note from Joz in the wardroom: *Visiting Marie-Francoise. Back soon.* George shrugged. "Does that mean we risk your cooking again?"

"It's my turn tonight anyway."

"Easy on the garlic this time, okay?"

"Spoilsport." I started digging out cooking pots and latching them to the stove. Cooking in zero gee is no trick once you get used to it. It isn't hard, just different. "So, what is it we've got hold of here?"

"A ship that can't land, can't reenter, but has to pop into the atmosphere and float there."

"*Could* it do that? Sort of a matter transmitter with no receiver?"

"Yeah, right," George said. "If they could do that, why bother building the ship? They might not even need aircraft, let alone a carrier."

"Okay, it was just a thought. Where's the soy sauce?"

"On everything when *you* cook," a cheery voice said from above us. Joz floated into the wardroom head-first from the upper deck. "How can you put that stuff on every piece of food you get your hands on?"

"Same way you can serve three kinds of pork for breakfast." She spun herself around to be right side up and I gave her a kiss. "How's Marie-Francoise?"

"Getting on quite well. They won't let her out of the hospital for a week yet, but she's turned that hospital room into an office. Papers and computer gear everywhere. And the view from there! Even with the whole inside of Vapaus ripped up, the window looks out on—"

"The whole satellite. Remember how I got into this place the first time?"

"It's no good trying to tell *you* anything. I shall have to talk to George. George, what did you clever lads manage today?"

"Well, we made the League's ships show in blue and the Guardian ships show in red, but then we decided we liked it better the other way and switched it back. Then Mac finally got the scoring system to work properly. I took all five hands of gin during our lunch break, and then we decided to show the League ships in yellow, but non-propelled facilities, like Vapaus and relay satellites, in blue. Before we knew it, it was time for dinner."

Joz gave us both an odd look. "That's certainly giving your all for the war effort."

I clipped the lid on my pan of peas and sighed. "What

George is trying to say is that we're stuck. We've got the display system down perfectly. . . ."

"Well. . . ."

"Okay, almost perfectly. Battle Control on The Rock will be getting a duplicate program to display the real thing, when it comes. But now that we've got the system, we can't run any realistic simulations until we know how *Leviathan* is going to approach the planet."

"I'm starting to think we won't figure it out till the real one shows."

"The rate we're going, you're right. Dinner in 20 minutes."

I fussed over dinner, the problems still spinning around in my head. It was a riddle: how can something be next to a planet in space without being in orbit around it, and yet be practically dead in space relative to the planet? Put it another way—what has exactly the same orbital characteristics as a given planet in a given orbit. . . .

"Son of a bitch! I've got it! Josyln, you mind if I put dinner on hold for a while, maybe all night?"

"What for?"

"I know where that damn ship is going to come from! At least I think I do! I want to get back to the Battle Theater and see if it makes sense."

We were there in 15 minutes, and I immediately began working the computer keyboard.

A diagrammatic view of the inner New Finnish Star System lit up the screen, the planets in exaggerated scale—otherwise, they could not have been seen at all. "Okay, great," I said. "Now, this is a dynamic display. I'm going to speed up the time scale." The tiny specks of worlds started to zip around the bright point that represented New Finland's sun.

"*Now*, I'm going to tell the computer that New Finland no longer exists. Watch what happens to Kuu, the moon."

Abruptly, the blue and white marble of New Finland vanished. The grey dot Kuu burbled briefly, then continued to follow the same orbit about the sun that the planet had.

"So what does that mean?" George asked.

"We've been forgetting that *New Finland* is in orbit around its sun."

"We accounted for solar gravitation in our programs."

"I mean the big picture. Look at Kuu! It doesn't give a damn whether New Finland is there or not! It's the *orbit* that matters, not what is *in* the orbit."

Joslyn stared at the display. "So that means *Leviathan* has to end up being in exactly the same orbit as New Finland, thrusting in some very precise way to compensate for New Finland's gravity, and come in on a trajectory that lets them match the planet's velocity exactly—"

"And they'll just float down into the atmosphere—"

"Since they're matching its velocity anyway."

"It's crazy!" George protested. "No parking orbit, no margin for error. If they go wrong by a tenth of a percent, they'll either plow right into the side of the planet or roll right off into space again."

"I wouldn't want to be the pilot," I agreed, "but it ought to be possible. They do have some fairly heavy maneuvering engines."

"Jesus," George said, staring at the display.

"Okay," I said. "Let's work out the details." This was it. It had to be. It made sense, if a fairly desperate sort of sense. It felt *right*.

"It's a terror weapon. It's incredibly inefficient most ways, but it sure would scare the hell out of me. Just imagine the damn thing *parked* right over the capital, blocking out the sun, not letting anything else fly, or even move, without its permission," George said, hours later, late into the night.

"Yeah, but it's more than that. It's an extension of power. It can go anywhere to dominate any place over land or sea and sky. It's part of a grand plan. One *Leviathan* to a world, and that world is under your thumb. It can't revolt without the site of the rebellion being smashed to rubble. Also, according to what Marie-Francoise has figured out, it's half offices inside. A flying office building. A capitol building, an administration center."

"The soldiers conquer and move on. *Leviathan* moves in and controls," Joslyn said.

I set the holo tank back to the view we had built up of how *Leviathan* might enter. The tank became a tangle of ellipses, hyperbolae, and parabolae. The basic requirement was that *Leviathan* achieve New Finland's *precise* orbital velocity *exactly* at that point in the sky that the fringes of the planet's atmosphere occupied. That didn't eliminate as many possibilities as one might think: we had limited things down to four families of approaches, but each family had at least 20 major members; there was an infinity of variations overall. Now it came down to tactics. From a military point of view, which was the best way of doing things?

Twelve hours after I forgot dinner, we left the battle theater. We had made a lot of progress: it seemed possible that *Leviathan* would want to sneak up on the planet, with as little warning as possible. That had to mean—almost literally—diving out of the sun on a tight, hard hyperbolic or parabolic course that whipped in close and hard to the sun, getting lost in the glare and the radio noise a star throws. In that way, there would normally be almost no way to detect the ship. But once the Finns knew where to look, it would be a different story.

Day after day we plugged away at the simulator. George and I were there ceaselessly, and Joz split her time between the battle theater and working with Marie-Francoise. Marie Francoise was more or less mended, though still woozy at times. She ignored that, working every moment she could on finer and finer evaluations of *Leviathan*. Joslyn shuttled back and forth between Vapaus and The Rock, where the fighting ships were being built with frenetic haste. She talked with Eve, Randall, and the other pilots. What tactics made sense?

Leviathan's defensive fighters did such and such a thing this or that way. Was there a weakness? Could it be exploited? Then the pilots usually said well, maybe. Could you run a simulation? And Joslyn came back to us.

The fighters that came off The Rock's production line were ugly, mass-produced, cylindrical tin cans of space. The standard type was called a Hull Three by official Finns, and a "Basic Fighter Vehicle" by the fliers. Basic Fighter Vehicle became "BFV," then "Beefie." Other pilots decided the things were better named for their shape, and tagged them Lead Pipes, which lead to some strange names being painted on the hatches: *L.P. Cinch, No Moving Parts, Down the Tubes.* Some of the Beefies got names no one dared write down.

There were some variants, two of which were important. The Basic Fighter Vehicle, Stretched Tankage. BFV/ST: The Beast. Beasts were the long-duration ships, trading more fuel, more air, and more food for somewhat lower performance. There was also the communication ship, the eyes and ears for Battle Control: the Attack Tracking/Reconnoiter/Command ship. AT/R/C. *Hatrack.* We had two of them. The *Hatrack* also earned its name by virtue of all the antennae hanging off it in all directions. *Hatrack* had better radar, better radio, better computers than a normal ship would need. It was supposed to run the battle and help fight it at the same time. To make up for the mass of all the extra hardware, Hatrack had two sets of the modular main propulsion system set up in tandem, and a set of stretch tanks off a Beast.

God, were those ships ugly.

All carried powerful lasers and missiles. A few had specialized weapons carriers welded on top of all the other modifications.

At the same time, New Finland's existing craft were made warworthy. Some of the *Kuu* class ships, which had already done heroic service, were armed more heavily. The space tugs were armed with lasers; drones were turned into robot kamikazis.

Except for skeleton groups of shuttle and maintenance craft, every ship was rebased at The Rock. If it was at all possible, not a shot would be fired from Vapaus. The Rock was just that, a solid mass of stone. It made much better armor for itself than the fragile, spinning shell of Vapaus ever could.

We could not afford to lose either satellite. If we won through, they were vital lifelines between New Finland and the remainder of mankind. If we could not smash *Leviathan*, the satellites might be the last bastions of free people in this star system. If need be, they were the launching places, should we be forced to retreat and hide in the depths of space, vanishing into the dark orbits of the outer planets.

But for all of us, those who knew exactly what was expected of the enemy, and those who knew only that danger was on the way, there was one thing we did over and over again. People looked to the skies—with eyes, with viewscreens, with radar, with telescopes—and asked, *When are they coming?*

It was two months after my second arrival on Vapaus that the company of the *Joslyn Marie* was awakened suddenly in the middle of the night.

From almost the first moment the crew of the *Bohica* had arrived at Vapaus, the search for the control center had commenced. There were teams crawling over the entire satellite, searching with sonar and radar, sharp eyes, record checks, and hunches.

Tremendous preparations for battle had been made since Dr. Tempkin had been disheartened by the news of the great ship. Our ships were ready and the crews were eager to fight. Deep inside the sheltering mass of The Rock, Battle Control was operational, the crews trained, the computers up and running. The wounds of Vapaus were not healed altogether, but her hurts had been greatly eased, and precautions taken against the dangers of wartime. Hydra had not been taken down—it might be needed again.

New weapons appeared every day, it seemed. It was possible that we had an actual chance to beat *Leviathan*.

The *J.M.* was getting to be a crowded ship: Marie-Francoise Chen had accepted our invitation of a billet on board. Randall Metcalf and Eve Berman slept there when they were on Vapaus. George Prigot, Joslyn, and I were permanent. We were settled into a life that seemed happy and comfortable in the face of the urgent work we were all engaged upon.

All six of us were aboard the *J.M.* the night the intercom buzzed to life next to Joslyn and me.

" 'llo?"

"Commander Larson!" It was Tempkin, sounding very excited. "We have found it!"

"Found what?"

"The missile control center! Bring that Prigot and the French officer. Rauman Park Station, on the red transit line. Have your party wear their pressure suits." He broke the connection.

"Pressure suits?" Joslyn asked sleepily.

"Don't ask me. I just took the message. Let's get this crowd moving."

Eve and Randall invited themselves, of course. Fifteen minutes later we were aboard one of the transit cars, moving through the strange darkness of Vapaus. Here the lights in the sky weren't stars, but streets, houses, people carrying flashlights. It was eerie for what you had unconsciously decided was a star to commence swinging back and forth with the easy motion of a night-walking stroller.

There were few other passengers aboard, and that perhaps was lucky. It is generally considered gauche to wear pressure suits in a habitable area: not only do they attract stares and tend to crowd up a place, being rather bulky, but a person in a pressure suit is a sight to start rumors about leaks. . . .

There was a car waiting for us at our stop. The driver

hurried us aboard. He immediately started off at a great pace through the darkness, driving on large balloon tires over the countryside, ignoring the roads. After a few minutes, I could see the dim outline of a large tent, lit from within. We pulled up and the driver urged us inside.

Dr. Tempkin was there in his own pressure suit, which had been put on over his pajamas. "Good evening to you all. We have indeed found what we were looking for." He gestured to a knot of men clustered around the center of the tent. "There is a hatchway there, cleverly sealed. They are working to open it. There is a vertical tunnel beneath it, leading straight through the bedrock of Vapaus. We sent a tug to examine the area from the outside. At the end of the airlock tunnel is a well-camouflaged platform, open to space. On it, racks of equipment and radio antenna. It *must* be there to control the cursed missiles. It was found when a nearby resident remembered seeing Guardians working here. Sonar soundings located the tunnel precisely."

A murmur of conversation from the knot of men was followed by a brief smattering of applause. The hatch was open.

Tempkin locked his helmet in place and we heard his voice over our suit radios. "Let us go take a look."

Floodlights were brought to bear, pointing straight down the tunnel. It was square in cross-section, about a meter on a side. Bolted into the bare rock on one side was a metal ladder. Tempkin went down first, and I followed.

"The airlock at the bottom here is really tiny. Better take it two at a time," I said.

Tempkin and I shuffled into the lock and cycled through it.

We cracked the exterior hatch and moved out onto the platform. We stepped out of the hatch onto . . . something.

Our feet, our sense of balance, the utter silence, all told us that we were on solid ground that was perfectly still beneath our feet. But that ground was a wide-mesh metal grating. Below us the stars, the sun, the planet, and the sky wheeled.

The platform was welded to heavy I-beam girders at its four corners, the beams set into the solid rock. All was painted the exact dirty grey of the surrounding rock that was Vapaus's exterior.

I imagined how it must look from space—a tiny patch of hard-to-see rectangularity, whizzing past the eye in a moment as the world spun by. No wonder it was hard to find.

In the exact center of the platform was an elaborate two-operator control system, locked inside a wire cage. By the door to the cage was a featureless rectangular solid, the size and shape of a coffin.

"Ah! The antennae hang through the grating beneath it," Tempkin said, kneeling to look through the floor. "We can hang an atmosphere bubble around this platform. Then we can work on it more easily."

George and Marie-Francoise came through the lock. George stopped and looked hard at the coffin-shaped box. "Mmmmph," he said. "I know this machine, the big box outside the cage. I helped design it. It's a shield box, an entrance control. It's a standard device for protecting valuable machines that must be left untended."

He walked over to it and pushed at an unmarked, featureless point on it. The front panel swung open smoothly. Inside was an array of unmarked heavy-duty switches, each with a safety cover. Above the switch array was a single, large toggle switch. George pointed to the lower array. "One hundred switches. When they are set to the proper combination of on and off, you flip the top switch and the cage door opens nicely."

"If you set it wrong, or if you try and force the cage door or something, what happens?" I asked.

"Dunno. Depends on what kind of bomb they put in it. Might just melt down the machinery, might crack the satellite open. But I can open it safely. I'll need tools. Induction meters, very sensitive. Radiation checkers, so maybe we find out about the bomb. Screwdrivers, wrenches, magnifiers, work lights, micro tools, labels, note paper. . . ."

The tools arrived and George got to work. The bubble crew came with their rappelling gear and started climbing over the rock to put the bubble together. Tempkin and I returned above ground and Randall and Eve took a look. Joslyn and I wandered off to scrounge a cup of tea and came back to the site. Soon a message came through that George wanted to talk to me. I got back into my suit and returned to the control platform. "How is it going, George?"

"Not good. This is not fun." He traced a circuit painstakingly as he spoke. "You know the old bit about the attack dog who was trained to nail anyone who came near his master's place? Well, the guy goes off and comes back, and there's his dog, just laying for him. I ran this project maybe five years ago. They wanted a *real* safebox no one could get past. We thought of all sorts of crazy, complicated ideas. So complicated they could be fooled, or broken, or gotten around. So we came up with this nice, simple idea instead. One gimmick, though. This is one hell of a weak inductance field I'm using. A few less gauss and it wouldn't register at all. A few more, and up it goes."

The bubble crew finished up and I shooed them off the platform and back up into Vapaus. I closed both airlock hatches after them. George never said exactly why it was he wanted me. Maybe just someone to talk to so he'd be fairly calm. Maybe as a good luck charm. Whatever the reason, it was an honor I'd have been happy to forego.

With the bubble ready, I opened an air tank and the slack plastic soon billowed out from the platform. I cracked open my faceplate. George took off his helmet and gauntlets.

Finally, George sat back on his haunches and sighed. "That's it. All circuits traced. The switches are set properly. Unless those bastards booby-trapped it, or someone is playing games. Here we go."

He threw the switch. The control cage door opened smoothly. "Very nice," I said.

George grinned happily. "Sheer luck." He clumped over to his pile of gadgetry. "Next up." He carefully cut two wires leading from a fat cylinder just inside the cage door. "That's the self-destruct unit. That was the bomb the entrance control operated. Probably was wired in some other way, too. Harmless now."

A fat spark jumped between the two cables he had just cut. "Jesus! That couldn't happen! There's no delay circuit. There must be some signal from the outside!"

"George! Below you!" The control antennae were slowly swiveling to a new heading.

"*Leviathan* must have sent the destruct signal! She's here! Let's get the hell off this platform!" George yelled. We rushed for the hatchway and I shoved it open hard, slamming down my faceplate with my other hand.

There was a deep, rumbling roar in the rocks above us. I dove through the airlock and hit the spill valve. The higher air pressure from Vapaus's interior gushed through the open lock and into the plastic bubble.

The rocks above us rumbled again, and jets of fire lashed down from the girders that held the platform to the satellite. Then, incredibly, the platform itself sheared away from the girder attachments and began to fall out into the depths of space, tearing the bubble's plastic away as if it wasn't there. Our air exploded away into space, and the gushing of air from the interior became a hurricane. We were pulled half out of the lock. George was on his feet, propped up by the wall of the airlock, unconscious. He must have been stunned by the pressure drop, his helmet and gauntlets sailing off into space with the platform. The hurricane roared on.

And stopped. The hatchway on the inside, on the surface of Vapaus, must have slammed shut.

George crumpled up and fell out of the airlock. I grabbed for him and slammed my forearm into the edge of the hatch. I caught his suit collar, braced my feet inside the lock, grabbed his arm with my other hand, and dragged him into the chamber.

I slammed the outer door, dogged it shut, and opened the faceplate of my suit. It was the only air I could get to George. The lock was in vacuum and the suit's air blasted past me to fill it. The suit's airpump whirred wildly, dumping all the reserves it had out of the backpack tank.

That didn't put much air in the lock, but enough— about a quarter of an atmosphere. George gurgled and started breathing. His nose was bleeding.

"Mac!" Joslyn called over my suit radio.

"We're both more or less all right," I said. "We're okay, inside the airlock. Get the upper hatch open and we'll come on up."

"Commander, this is Tempkin. Tracking reports—"

"They report a gigantic spacecraft appearing from behind the sun. We know." I paused for a moment. I was dazed, short of breath, and my arm hurt. "*Leviathan* sent a signal to the control station here, the second she came out from behind the sun. George had already cut the cable on the bomb that would have melted the platform, but they had charges in the I-beams, too. Those went off and they cut it all loose. The whole platform just fell out into space.

"*Leviathan*'s commander took over the missile control system the first moment he could, and why the hell didn't we figure out *that* part of it? They're here."

PART FOUR:
LEVIATHAN

4 Thine enemies roar in the midst of thy congregations; they set up their ensigns for signs.

7 They have cast fire into thy sanctuary, they have defiled by casting down the dwelling place of thy name to the ground.

8 They said in their hearts, Let us destroy them together: they have burned up all the synagogues of God in the land.

13 Thou didst divide the sea by thy strength: thou brakest the heads of the dragons in the waters.

14 Thou brakest the heads of leviathan in pieces, and gavest him to be meat to the people inhabiting the wilderness.

18 Remember this, that the enemy has reproached, O Lord, and that the foolish people have blasphemed thy name.

20 Have respect unto the covenant: for the dark places of the earth are full of the habitations of cruelty.

23 Forget not the voice of thine enemies: the tumult of those that rise up against thee increaseth constantly.

—The 74th Psalm

CHAPTER FIFTEEN

Four hours later, the group that had swarmed around the tunnel shaft was scattered. Marie-Francoise had demanded that Joslyn attend her to help in the gleaning of new information on *Leviathan* from direct observation. The ship was still not much more than a dot on a radar screen, but at least the intelligence types had something tangible to work with for the first time.

George and I were hustled off to the hospital. My arm had a greenstick fracture, and George had a mild case of vacuum shock. Neither of us was seriously hurt, but the doctors wanted us kept overnight. They weren't worried about our recovery; they just didn't want to take chances with personnel valuable to the war effort.

I didn't fight it. I was short on sleep and they even gave me a private room.

Soon after the doctors and nurses left me to my own devices, a soft knock came on the door. "Come in," I called.

Eve came in and rather hesitantly took a seat by my bed. "Hello. How they treating you?"

"Hello. I'm okay. I'll be out of here tomorrow morning. What's up?"

"They gave me the fighter command."

"Oh." There wasn't much past that I could say. Eve and I had started off on the wrong foot on the *Bohica*, and things had never improved past the peppery stage.

234

"None of the Finnish naval officers past the grade of lieutenant are still alive. Executed by the Guards or dead in action. They decided they needed someone with command experience," she explained.

"Why come to tell me?" I asked.

She blushed slightly, her deep brown skin darkening, and she looked away. "I thought you might figure you deserved it."

"Nope. As you said, you're the senior officer."

"I've got a feeling the Finns could patch together a brevet command under some League regulation if they wanted to."

Had she come just to rub it in? No, if anything, she seemed embarrassed to be here. "Eve, I don't want it. I never wanted it."

"Dammit, Larson, neither did I!"

Bingo. "I see."

"I'm a fighter pilot, not a strategist. I could spend the next ten years over in Battle Control, and I'd *still* be a fighter pilot."

"I sympathize, but I ask you again. Why tell me about it?"

"Because you are the only other officer remotely qualifed for the job. Joslyn's good, but she's a grade below you, and she's got the same problem I've got— she's got a pilot's point of view, not a god-damned chess player's. If I could refuse the appointment in your favor, I'd do it in a second."

"No." That much I was sure of.

"Why not?"

"I could ask you the same question. Eve, I've taken whatever they handed me in this war since way back when I was minding my own business. I've faked it. I've winged it. I've improvised. I could take what they gave me, because I was the only one for the job, but I can't take your fight. *You're* the one that's got the training, the rank, the fliers who know you. This is your ticket. Not mine."

"Dammit, Larson! Mac. Don't you get it? I *can't send my kids out to die!*"

"No? Neither can I. But you have to, so you will. If I thought I'd be a better fighter commander, that I could keep more of them alive, I might be tempted. But I don't think that. And I can't take it just so you could sleep better nights. I've already got my own nightmares."

No more words. She rose, turned, and stalked out the door.

I killed the lights. I didn't sleep well *that* night, anyway.

The Finns managed to send a space tug after the missile control station and retrieve it. When it was examined, it became clear that if George hadn't cut that last set of cables, the thermite charges would have incinerated everything on the platform before the girders were blown to throw it into space. As it was, we recovered the control station virtually intact. The controlling software had all been wiped clean. There was no hope of recovering the control program and taking command back from *Leviathan.* The hardware was intact, though. The Finns immediately got to work tracing the circuitry and learning how to run it. Inside a day, we knew which button was supposed to do what, even if the buttons didn't work anymore.

It was valuable information.

A terrible truth was upon us. We could no longer simply defeat *Leviathan*: we had to board her. She now controlled the missile system. If we had located the Vapaus control point just a day or so earlier, we might have had a chance to hash out the code needed to order the missiles to self-destruct. One thing we learned from the recovered Vapaus control station was that the missiles would indeed remain on patrol, still attacking anything that moved, indefinitely, even if their owners could no longer control them.

The Finns also got a nasty shock. It was soon very clear that the missiles were a lot smarter than had been thought. It might take 50 years to override them. Unless the Finns were, at best, to be bottled up in their system for that long, we had to kill the missiles.

The only way to do that was to get aboard *Leviathan*, get to the control station, and use it to tell the missiles to blow themselves up.

That wasn't going to be easy. It called for a redrawing of all our plans on very short notice. Now that *Leviathan* had been spotted and tracked, we could tell with a great degree of certainty what her course would be. From where she was, there was only one path that led to a safe arrival in the airs of New Finland. She would reach the useful range of our fighters in 360 hours, and arrive at the planet in 500.

One thing was a great help. George was utterly certain that the control station aboard *Leviathan* would be completely identical to the one we had. The Guardians tried to standardize people; they certainly didn't custom-design machinery. Working with speed and determination, the Finns hooked up the recovered control station to a simulator and set to work training teams of two in the use of it. The controls were on two panels four meters apart and set up so the two operators stood back to back. It was impossible for one person to work it alone.

Joslyn and I were one of the teams they trained. If and when (mostly if) we got onto *Leviathan*, each of the teams was to head for a certain part of the ship. There were about six areas of of the ship that Intelligence (in other words, Marie-Francoise with Joz kibitzing) thought might hold the control station. There were two teams for each site. We'd be lucky if one made it. There wasn't time to train three sets of teams: *Leviathan* was on the way.

Joslyn and I got to the point, after long, weary hours of being drilled by the Finnish simulator team, where we could have run the station in our sleep. At times, I did.

A few nights after Eve offered me the command, I still worried over it. Joslyn and I talked it over.

"As far as I can see it, Mac, you were offered the chance to make a bad situation worse. Her making the offer hasn't gotten around, but if it did, it would certainly be pretty rotten for morale, and worse if you went through with it. I wouldn't want to fly for a reluctant commander."

"But could I have said yes? Should I have said yes?"

"I don't quite see how. There isn't any way your taking command would make matters better. What scares me is that she made the offer at all. She must be so afraid. It doesn't make me expect brilliant command decisions. But so much damage would be done to the morale of the fliers if they knew she was unwilling. . . . You'd have to be good enough to overcome that. Mac, you're not. You couldn't be. If you were, you'd be 30 years older and an admiral instead of an explorer."

"I know. I guess the offer scared me, too."

"One other thing, my love. Remember that even if our ships are held in reserve, we're some of the 'kids' she has to send out to die."

Waiting was tough, but after a long time, it ended. *Leviathan* was in range.

Joslyn and I were overseeing a Finnish crew that was stripping the *J.M.* for battle. George was on The Rock, working at Battle Control. He piped in the radio from the first strike to us as we worked. The *J.M.* had to be made lighter, her weapons had to be prepared.

With the battle in our ears, it was hard to concentrate.

We heard the first transmissions as the fighter team approached the enemy.

"—ord, that ship is big."

"Oh, my God! It's too big. We can't fight that thing."

"We already are. This is Able Archer. I am being fired upon by laser. No effect on fighter at this range."

"This is Able Baker. I'm getting it, too."

Eve's voice came in. "Jesus, they're eager. Archer, Baker. Fire a Redeye missile each. Hatrack, give them miss vectors. Let 'em think we're screw-ups. We need to see how they'll react. Hatrack, launch sensor probes in their wake."

"This is Hatrack. Missiles and probes launched on near-miss. Boosting toward target."

"Bandit! I see bandit launch, from the port side."

"How many?"

"Hard to read, radar is pretty jammed up. Visual poor at this range with the sun at their backs. I count one, two, three craft."

"This is Hatrack. I have tracking on bandits. They are ignoring missiles and headed for our fighter group."

"Battle Control here. Flights one and four, lateral flank maneuver, space to 100 kilometers, ecliptic."

"Able Baker. They are firing on the Redeye missiles. Lasers from the main deck. Archer's Redeye is homing. Baker's is sliding away. Looks like you didn't put enough miss on it, Randall."

"How about that?" Randall radioed from the lead ship.

"Battle Control. We are receiving from five good probes, but not for long. Four is overheating—laser damage. Four is out."

"Hatrack here. One fighter still heading for us. Other two turning to hit the probes."

"Able Archer here. That un-miss of mine is heading straight for their main laser array, looks like. The Redeye's shielding worked. I guess. And whambo! That didn't do that laser cannon any good."

"Hatrack. That fighter nearly in range. Permission to engage?"

"Battle Control here. Negative! We have to draw out more than three lousy ships."

"Hatrack here. You just got 'em. Here come—on, lordy lord, 18 blips, half to a defensive shell, the other half heading our way."

"This is Baker. I can scope the defensive shell zapping the probes and the other Redeye. Cleaned 'em out."

"Hatrack. Another flight launching. I count at least ten blips."

"Dammit. This is Battle Control. Withdraw. If they chase you, let 'em. Don't hit the fighters so near the big ship."

"Well, that was exciting."

"Stow it, Lambert. All according to plan, and you know it."

"Oh Jesus. Maybe not. There are five of the bastards on intercept with me. Eve, I gotta fight it out. Going into firing pass—and there we. . . ."

There was dead silence on the feed for a moment. Then: "Hatrack! This is Battle Control. What the hell is going on!"

"Nothing anymore, Batcon. But Lambert got two of them, first. All other fighters withdrawn safely."

The Guardians gave chase, and the first wave of our fliers withdrew. The word was passed to the second wave to trim up their orbits, and as the Guardians came in behind the first wave, the second wheeled out from behind the planet and pounced on their rear. They were cut off from their main ship, and she was too far off to offer assistance.

None of the Guardians escaped. Four of our fighters didn't make it. And that was the last thing that went right, the last piece of tactical planning we followed through on.

No one ever saw that battle. There could be no eye-witnesses. Only by sheer chance did anyone actually see his opponent, and then only for split seconds as two warring ships whizzed past each other. This was a battle of distance and speed, of long hours of boredom, brief moments of mind-wrenching action, and danger sandwiched into them at random.

Those who directed the battle watched symbols and numbers and orbit projections, translated into holographic displays. Joslyn and I watched, when we could, on the repeater monitor receiving from Batcon. The whole affair seemed a large and elaborate game. In the center of the hologram was the planet, represented as a plain, featureless ball, or actually two balls, one centered inside the other—the inner showing the physical planet, the outer showing the practical limits of the atmosphere.

The planet was shown as transparent: one could see the tiny midges of light that displayed the fighters as they whirled behind the bulk of the planet.

A great, blood-red arrowhead bore in on the planet, slowly, ponderously: *Leviathan.* Two blue ovoids, Vapaus and The Rock, ambled round the planet in a stately dance, Vapaus orbiting three times each time The Rock orbited twice.

The midges, the fighters, were the color of their bases. A gossamer thread held each object, to show its present orbit.

Now and then, the flashing dot that represented a missile would sprout from one ship and move to another, and the second ship might wink off the screen. A voice would call, "Nailed the bastard!" or "Jesus, they've torched Edmonds."

I was shocked by *distance*. It made no sense—I had travelled dozens of light years to get here, and these little ships were flying but a few hundred thousand kilometers. But in spite of accelerating constantly at one standard gee, and building up incredible velocity, these ships took long hours to reach each other.

The Guardians sent a second wave of their own after us. Our attacks had been carefully planned, long in advance, up until that moment, but sooner or later, something had to break. The Guardians' ships cracked our formations. We still did well, but not as well. We destroyed another eight of their ships, but lost another four of ours.

Eve seemed afraid to risk the forces needed for whatever challenge was at hand. She sent two ships where five could do the job, or one instead of a pair. Out of fear, she was letting us lose, letting us die, a little at a time. The battle degenerated into one-on-one slugfests between pairs of ships, or three ships against two, a battle of stragglers and predators.

Patterns started to develop. Both sides learned, paying for knowledge with the lives of their pilots. The enemy ships were lighter, smaller, shorter duration ships than the Beefies. Their very lightness gave them an edge in acceleration over the short term. Crudely put, they put bigger engines on smaller, flimsier ships.

Their lightly built ships would lose in a laser duel, but had a better chance of outrunning a missile. The Beefies and the Beasts carried a lot more fuel and breathing air.

I watched the display as a Beast chased a bandit up out of orbit. By then we knew very precisely how much fuel the bandits could carry, and thus how long, all told, they might fire their engines.

The pilot of the Beast worked it out in his head. He chased the bandit at his top acceleration, 2.6 gees. The bandit could do 3.1, and he started out 1,000 kilometers ahead of his pursuer, gradually edging farther and farther ahead. But even if he had wanted to, he couldn't have turned back; the Beast would have had him.

After three quarters of an hour at 3.1 gees, the bandit was moving at a speed many times faster than the planet's escape velocity. The Beast turned around and headed for home at an easy one gee. The bandit was as good as dead. He didn't have the fuel in his tanks to get back.

He tried. He not only had to shed his speed, but shed it fast enough to get back to the planet, where he might hope for rescue. Maybe his engines finally melted to slag, maybe his tanks dried sooner than they should have. He didn't make it. He's still out there, somewhere.

A bandit and a Beefie chased each other into opposing orbits, the Beefie only 50 kilometers below the bandit. One travelled east-to-west, the other west-to-east: every 42 minutes they made a pass by each other. Their closing velocity was nearly 60,000 kilometers per hour. They ran out of missiles first. The missile's tiny on-board computers couldn't maneuver quickly or accurately enough to make a hit at those speeds.

Then it was lasers.

The two ships flew past each other, having about 10 minutes line-of-sight on each other every half orbit, every 42 minutes. The two beams lashed out at their opponents, both ships heating and overheating as the ships bore down on each other, each tracking the other. Then the two would have a half hour to cool, to check damage, to recuperate and watch the readings on the battery gauges.

Then another pass, another half-orbit's rest, then back at each other, the two ships gradually dying as they were cooked. The radios died as the antennae melted off. The ships tumbled as paint bubbled off and safety values vented, causing tiny side thrusts. Low on fuel, the pilots ignored the tumble. Both ships had tracking devices for their lasers, so the beam could be aimed no matter where the ship was pointed.

The batteries drained, the lasers grew weak.

In the middle of a pass, the Beefie's laser overheated and blew up. The ship itself survived for the next pass.

The bandit must have thought he had the kill. The two ships came back at each other. The Beefie pilot used the last of his fuel to very slightly raise his orbit, and then fired his engine once again—with the bandit passing straight through the fusion flame. The bandit came out a puddle of metal. The Beefie's orbit went unstable. He reentered.

He hit atmosphere over the night side of the planet, when, by chance, the *J.M.*, docked at Vapaus, was almost directly overhead. A field of darkness, then suddenly a spot of light, a long fiery tail careening through the night, then the darkness undisturbed again.

Death and the threat of it were everywhere. I looked, watching the tiny sparks circle the battle monitor, watching relayed transmissions from the cameras on the fighters, on Vapaus, and The Rock.

A fighter out of fuel, out of weapons, its pilot capable only of watching the missile coming toward him from an orbit just barely faster and lower than his, the missile just *waiting* there for long hours until it drifted close enough. The pilot could *see* the missile 15 minutes before the end. He aimed his camera at it, a tiny dot that grew larger and larger in the screen, and then the picture went dead.

A bandit's power system must have died suddenly: he was headed back toward *Leviathan* at high velocity. He reached the point where he should have put on the brakes to make a safe docking, and kept going, falling like a rock straight for the ship. *Leviathan* fired on her own fighter with a great flurry of missiles, and the bandit turned into a cloud of dust that swept past *Leviathan*.

Space was littered with broken machines, derelict ships and missiles, debris, clouds of vapor that dispersed into vacuum from broken fuel tanks, and the broken bodies of dead warriors. Some hit the atmosphere, and New Finland was graced for many days with the pretty sparks of more shooting stars than usual. Others drifted out into distant orbit of the planet's sun, or out of the system entirely, to be lost forever.

It was carnage in slow motion, hours or days of struggle for advantage, climaxed by death that came in the blink of an eye.

And we were losing.

I could see it when I tore myself one little part of the picture, from some small, fascinating horror, and looked at the whole battle at once.

Whoever had ships left, when the other side was wiped out, would win. For each two ships of ours that died, three of theirs were killed. But the Guardians had more ships than we did, and their commander was cautious. He held his ships back deep in the holds of *Leviathan*, as the great ship bore inexorably down toward the air.

Eve couldn't do it. Maybe it was a hopeless situation, maybe a wiser or older commander could have kept us out of trouble.

She tried. But all her machinations and provocations had failed to strip *Leviathan*'s flight decks.

So she played her hole card.

Us.

"Berman to *Joslyn Marie*. Please come in. Over."

"This is *Joslyn Marie*. Come in, Battle Control. What have you got for us, Eve?"

"Stand by, Mac. We're piping numbers to your computer. Okay, call up file *Bushwack* and slave your monitor to my computer."

I typed in the commands, and the battle model vanished from the hologram generator. *Leviathan* appeared.

"Okay, Mac, Joslyn, this is our best information on *Leviathan*—what Marie-Francoise and Joslyn cobbled together, plus watching through the scopes, plus guessing.

"You guys get to attack her," she said.

"Y'know, I had a feeling you'd bring that up."

"Sorry, Mac. But listen. We can't get the ships up from the hangar decks to kill them—so we have to bottle them up. Now, here are the targets." Four spots on the hologram started blinking red. "These are the launch sites for the fighter craft. A pair forward, a pair aft, port and starboard, out of the hull itself."

"Nothing off the main deck?"

"Nope. We figure the topside is for use in atmosphere. They fly fixed-wing right over the side, and we can see what look like ballistic launch cradles, for use in gravity. Okay, we've logged this course into your onboards." The image of *Leviathan* shrunk to a tiny dot. The planet reappeared, and *Leviathan* was faced away from it, thus directing her engines precisely toward the planet for braking. A looping red line popped into existence. It leaped away from where the *J.M.* was now, shot toward

Leviathan, crossed her stern, flew by the ship's port side, then petered out, headed nowhere at all.

"That's goddamn hairy, Eve. What thrust levels?"

"Six gees the whole way. That's why you're in it. No other ship has enough jump in the engines to fly that long at those power levels. You're only the ship with the delta-vee to get in and out fast enough with a chance to survive."

Joslyn stared at the plotting thoughtfully. "Captain Berman. Could you include the jets of *Leviathan*'s thrust in the image?"

A pink plume a hundred kilometers long popped into the image. It cut directly through our course.

"My God!" I said. "Eve, you're sending us through a fusion flame!"

"Dammit, I know that! I know, I know, I know. But there isn't a single other damn way to do it. The fusion flame creates a gigantic plasma shadow their detection gear can't see through. It provides the cover for you to get close enough to hit them."

"What is our time in the plume itself? And what temperatures can we expect?"

"We figure the time at between four and ten seconds. We're trying to keep you to the edge of it, where it's a bit cooler. In the fringes, the temperatures are no more than 6,000 degrees absolute. The plasma particles are thinner there, too—lower density."

Joslyn's voice was flat and hard. "We cannot survive that."

"With *Uncle Sam* docked in place, using *Sam*'s heat shield to protect the nose of the *J.M.*—"

I whistled softly. This was insane. "That will help, but not enough. The heat's way too high to handle."

"It's not just heat. It's more like flying into a nuclear bomb as it goes off," Joslyn said.

"Let me finish. We're going to insulate you. You'll make it, probably. You have *got* to smash the launch stations. *Leviathan* hits air in 58 hours. My kids are too hard-pressed. The way this fight is going, I won't have a fighter left by then. *Leviathan* will hold the sky—and then they can deal with Vapaus whenever they want. They'll win. If those launch sites are wrecked, we'll still be in this one. And you're the only ship with a ghost of a chance."

"Eve, it can't work! Why not have us fly through the sun, for God's sake?"

"Mac—Commander Larson. Lieutenant Cooper. You have your orders. The insulation crew is to start on you right away. I suggest you get your ship cooled down as far as possible. You launch in three hours. Berman out."

I pointed to the thin red line that showed our course. "Notice something, Joslyn? They didn't even bother plotting a course back for us."

"I know, Mac. But that bit I'll attend to right now. Hell. Right about now I'm wishing we hadn't agreed with each other quite so much about doing our duty."

"Tug captain here. Please now undock your ship and take up station-keeping 100 meters from satellite."

Joslyn did so. Then we waited. We heard scratches and thumps on the hull, and then silence.

"Tug captain here. We have done the attaching of the end of the mylar to your ship. Please, using gyros only, no thrusters, commence to be rolling at one-half revolution a minute."

The *Joslyn Marie* began a long, slow roll along her long axis. We watched the view from a camera on Vapaus. Hanging beside the *J.M.* was a stubby cylinder, the tug. It held what looked like a giant roll of aluminum foil between two of its work arms. As the *J.M.* rolled, the foil played out. The tug moved itself along our ship's axis, so that the foil was wrapped over the ship. Normally, mylar was carefully bonded to the side of a spacecraft slated for work close to the sun. There was no time for careful work now. The mylar was rolled right over the attitude jets. If we *had* used them, the stuff would have been blown off into space.

Finally, the entire ship was covered. A tiny spacesuited figure who had been watching calmly from a perch on one of the tug's arms used a machete-like knife to cut through the mylar as it continued to roll off the reel. The cut was sloppy, but he managed to cut it free. He grabbed onto the end of the strip that wrapped around the *J.M.* and hung on. He picked up the spin of the ship. He used a sprayer to squirt adhesive all over the end of the mylar, and then used his backpack jets to push him down onto the hull, dragging the foil with him. He set his feet against the outside of the film. When the end of it hit the hull, it stuck and he bounced.

"Remind me never to try that," I said.

"I doubt you'll have trouble remembering," Joslyn said.

"Next step," I said. The tug captain touched up his attitude fussily and then moved the tug slowly back down the length of our ship. A thick stream of goo spewed from a hose held by another arm. The goo fizzed and bubbled as it hit vacuum, then spluttered against the mylar over the ship's hull and hardened into a foam casing for the ship. It was ablative shielding material, used to beef up heat shields. Heat would dissolve it away, but the ablated shielding would carry the heat along with itself.

It was a cockeyed, haywired solution to flying into a fusion plasma, but it was comforting all the same. It was an ugly jury-rig, but the shielding upgraded the mission from "suicide" to "risky."

Except for a single radio aerial and the main engines, the entire ship was sealed in. That aerial was expendable—the fusion flame would vaporize it anyway. All our other communication and detection gear was stowed away.

"Cooling system shunted through engine bells and on full," Joslyn reported. We needed to start cold. Even without going through the fusion flame, we needed cold. Heat was generated constantly by a working spacecraft. The shielding made excellent insulation. Now we routed super-cold liquid hydrogen from our fuel tanks into the cooling ducts of the ship, and then through the engine bells. The bells were cold now, and made good radiation surfaces. Once we lit up the fusion jets, there would be no way to cool the ship until the shielding blew off.

If we lived long enough for the shielding to blow off.

CHAPTER SIXTEEN

The clock went to zero, the *J.M.* launched herself away from station-keeping at an easy one gee, and we throttled up to six gee in about three minutes. We could hear the creaking and groaning of the ship's structural members as they took up the load.

More and more quickly, Vapaus fell away from us. Joslyn and I were crushed into our acceleration couches more and more deeply. The couches had been adjusted to high-gee configuration, which basically meant they were now sacks of viscous jelly inside thin, very flexible membranes. The jelly was some exotic organic compound, and the membranes tended to be very slightly permeable; in other words, the cabin soon stank to high heaven. I didn't cut in high power on the ventilation system, though—it would get a workout soon enough.

In fact, the temperature was already rising. We had cooled the entire ship down to 4°C. Now, though the engines were isolated so as not to contribute much heat to the system, there was plenty of other heat inevitably produced by running the ship, and no way to get rid of it. It started to warm up again. Slowly, but we'd have to watch it.

Our velocity increased at a frightening rate. In less than three minutes after hitting six gee, we had passed New Finland's escape velocity. If the flame under our tails decided to go out, or the astrogation system went blooie—well, we weren't coming back. We'd fall into the sun.

We had no cameras outside the shielding to see it, but there was another glowing point of light between us and the sun. Much smaller, much closer—and much brighter. From here, it would be a sloppy point of light to the naked eye. *Leviathan.*

Six gee was wearing, to say the least. By the end of this day, in spite of all the protection and cushioning we had, Joz and I were going to be covered with bruised skin, capillaries popped and broken. Both Joslyn and I were awash in various drugs and vitamins to bolster our bodies against the killing pressure. And it could kill. If it did so, the *Joslyn Marie* would go on as a robot and try and carry out the mission on her own, with two corpses along for the ride.

I *felt* like a corpse already. I couldn't turn my head to look at Joslyn, but each of us could see the other through the ship's camera system. She looked like someone had dropped a ton of bricks on her face, which wasn't so far from the truth. She moved her eye toward the camera and flicked the corner of her mouth in an attempt at a smile.

On we roared into the depths of night. This was no close, safe orbit. This was out into the great emptiness.

Five hundred seconds: 7,350 kilometers from launch point. Velocity 29 kilometers a second.

Seven hundred seconds: 14,406 kilometers out—41 km/second.

Nine hundred seconds, the halfway point in the initial burn: 24,000 kilometers from launch point. Fifty-two km/second—190,000 kilometers an hour.

Now the gee forces were getting noticeably higher as we lost the mass of our fuel. Ship's programming accounted for this. At 1,000 seconds, the first of several throttlebacks occurred.

Faster and faster we fell deep into the sky on a roaring tower of fusion flame, atoms dying and aborning in the violence of our passage. My body was already exhausted with nothing more than the effort to stay alive when it suddenly weighed 600 kilograms, but my soul revelled in the awesome power of the skybeast we rode, a blazing torch in the empty black. The power, the might, the incredible velocities were no longer frightening, but enthralling, invigorating to my spirit. My wife and I rode a mighty chariot through the skies to wreak vengeance on our enemies and tormentors.

That last idea must have been partial oxygen starvation— *Leviathan* massed about 1,000 times as much as the *Joslyn Marie*.

But, damn all that's holy, she was a *good* ship. Her engines didn't falter, she held true course, she streaked across the skies.

Twelve hundred seconds into the mission: 42,000 kilometers from launch, 70 km/second—over 250,000 kilometers an hour. Our speed itself was a shield. We were moving too fast for any but the most sophisticated radar to have the slightest chance of tracking us.

We flew blind, on into the deep.

Fifteen hundred seconds, 25 minutes into the flight: over 66,000 kilometers from launch, roughly 30,000 klicks to fly—88 klicks a second.

Sixteen hundred seconds. The numbers stopped meaning anything. Now it was time to get ready to fight. Cameras left inside their protective nacelles, but powered up. Radar ready, but not switched on—the mylar shielding would have fried its brains.

Joslyn and I worked the controls carefully, barely speaking, moving as little as possible. Every time you lift an arm in six gee, you're doing the same work as chinning yourself on Earth.

Eighteen hundred seconds. Course true. One half hour from launch. Velocity relative to target, 121.21 kilometers/second, bearing zero two zero.

Then: engine shutdown. Zero gee. Camera three on, nacelle open, camera remaining under shielding.

We suddenly floated at our ease, the engines stopped, our hearts wildly pounding against the terrible pressure that wasn't there any more. Then our stomachs did flip-flops as the gyros whirled into action, rotating the *Joslyn Marie* to the safest attitude, placing our nose dead ahead.

Head first, we fell into the fire.

Camera three showed us the darkness under the layers of mylar and shielding. Then the darkness was suddenly dark no longer, but a dull, sullen red that grew violently in intensity and brilliance, finally exploding into nothingness as first the shielding, and then the camera, vaporized.

An alarm clanged shrilly.

Joslyn called out, "Skin temperature 500 degrees and rising."

"Emergency cooling system on and full."

"Skin temp 600."

"Okay, coming up on weapons launch!" I called.

"Attack computer launching weapons, cycle begins, launch torp 1, 2, 3, 4, 5, 6 away, cycle to load, launch 1, 2, 3, 4, 5, 6—torps clear!"

"Joz, I see all external thermocouples ablated—no reading."

"Right-o. Last of shielding gone. Hot spots in stern bulkheads, cooling at 95 percent capacity."

"And rising. We got problems."

"Skin temp now 1,200. Damage lights on, more coming."

"Cooling overload!"

"Now seven seconds inside plume."

"Cooling overload, all units, all units over maximum."

But then we were out of it.

The computer grabbed at the ship, spun it on thrusters this time, pitching the multi-megaton ship through 100 degrees in half a second.

The interior of the *J.M.* was a hellburning hurricane as the cooling system hauled out the superheated air, full of the smells of burnt insulation and melted plastics and the stinkings of sweat. The air temperature briefly hit the boiling point of water and dropped quickly again as the heat pulse moved through the ship. The cooling system was pumping liquid hydrogen from the fuel tanks through the emergency cooling coils and boiling it off into space. The temps came down quickly.

We didn't even notice. The camera clusters came out and, at that moment, we saw *Leviathan.*

Gigantic. Huge. Monstrous. No machine, no spawn of man's hand could be that vast, that great, that *awesome.* It had to be a monster, a *thing* of nature, some nightmare child of a dark sun, a great beast the shape of a hunting manta ray.

It was a mass of brooding metal that *grew* as we looked in shock at its brutal, grotesque massiveness.

The ugly monster swelled as we rushed closer, then vanished and reappeared in the rearward screen as we flashed past. By the numbers, we were alongside her less than a second, but surely it must have been longer.

But then we were past, and the cameras zoomed in closer as we flashed away, skewing away under an easy, one-gee thrust at 90° from our former course. Bursts of light flared against the side of the great ship. One, two, three. . . .

"I count five hits," Joslyn said.

"Coming up on second firing sequence."

"Torps fire: 1, 2, 3, 4, 5, 6 . . . recycle to load—1, 2, 3, no 4, no 5, 6 fires."

"I read 4 and 5 as misfires."

"Disarming and jettisoning misfires on manual. Duds away."

Flares of light appeared in the screen and shrank to nothing as the torps blasted away from us and zeroed in on *Leviathan.*

The great ship's lasers opened up on them, but we counted three more hits.

"Can you spot any launches against us?"

"Hold, monitoring . . . negative. Oh, Mac, my darling, we're clear!"

"Hot damn! Are we on the line for your escape-and-return course?"

"Certainly are, dearie. All set to crash into Kuu!"

"I'm afraid to ask if you're kidding." I looked at her. The grin was too pleased with itself. "No, you're not kidding. Okay, stand by to crash into New Finland's moon."

With the ship directed to a new heading, the engines roared back to six gees, and we were squashed back down into the acceleration couches. After the brief respite, the crushing agony of that thrust seemed worse, if anything.

When Joslyn had worked out a course away from *Leviathan*, she knew she couldn't head back the way we had come—*Leviathan* wouldn't be surprised a second time, and we weren't on her blind side anymore anyway. So we had to get away from the ship, which was directly between us and New Finland. However, we also had a hell of a lot of velocity to shed: we had to decelerate. Joslyn fired our engines to accelerate us 90° away from our previous course. We were still moving out, but now we were also moving sideways. Once this sideways motion had gotten us well away from *Leviathan*, we could put on the brakes.

In essence, we had to put on the brakes along one axis and accelerate along another, simultaneously.

However, we were simply moving too fast and our tanks were too nearly empty. We had to have help slowing down.

That was were Kuu came in. We would fly around it in a tight curve, using its gravity to brake us, or, more accurately, to send us moving in the opposite direction at the same speed.

This sort of maneuver had been used for a century, but the catch for us was that to get redirected, we needed to coming frighteningly close to Kuu's surface—about 13 kilometers. That was close enough to be called a crash if we were off course by more than .01 percent.

Kuu wasn't much, just a ball of rock, a small and useless world. But there is no such thing as a small world when you're dropping toward it. Every detail of that low-budget planet swelled disturbingly in the viewscreen. It was cratered to saturation; any rock that dropped wouldn't add to the number of craters—the new crater would simply erase an old one. There might have been mountains and valleys and plains at one time; now there was nothing but the cratered rubble of their destruction. It was the dead, ugly bones of a world, without the benefit of distance or atmosphere to soften the harsh cruelty of that landscape.

We sweated out *Leviathan*'s revenge on us, but no attack came. Perhaps we had crippled her launch cradles, perhaps we had been moving too fast to be caught, perhaps they were too hard-pressed in the battle with the League fighters.

The harsh black moonscape swept ever closer. Our radar told us we'd miss by zero, but the distance we hoped to miss by was smaller than the margin of error the radar had at this range.

"Mac! Camera five!"

I switched over to five, and swore under my breath. *Leviathan* was launching. One, two, three bright sparks popped away from the ship. A fourth spark came into being, but suddenly turned into a fuzzy patch of brilliance.

"Something went up on the launch cradle!"

"We didn't stop 'em, but it looks like we slowed 'em up." No more sparks jumped away from the ship.

I flicked back to the main view camera and saw Kuu dropping in on us like a boulder on an ant. The sphere grew even as we watched, and I had to jog back the magnification to pull the whole globe into view.

Radar showed us still 30,000 kilometers out and closing. We watched the dead planet grow, its image wavering now and then in the plume of our exhaust.

By the time we were 10,000 klicks out, our headlong rush was noticeably slowed. By 8,000 we seemed to be barely crawling. All was relative, though; we'd still need every gee of thrust we had to get out of this. Kuu's gravity took hold of us and pulled us in. We gained velocity again.

Now we seemed not only to be moving toward the moon, but around it, the surface sliding along underneath as our trajectory led us around the limb of the world. The *J.M.* kept her engines pointed dead at the landscape that rolled forward beneath us. It seemed as if we were in a long, steep glide now. Swiftly sailing down toward the rubble of the crater field below us.

I told the computer to bring up the impact predictor program, call up data on Kuu from memory (the Finns had supplied the *J.M.* with up-to-date information on their star system when she had first docked at Vapaus) and show it on my main monitor. The program gave me three displays.

One was a simple meridian grid map of Kuu. A tiny red "x" rolled slowly over it. If the engines crapped out right *now*, that x would be the site of our very own crater.

The second was a number, now up from 0 to 15,350— our peripoint in meters over the average radius of the planet.

The third was a burbling black line, which shifted and flickered from moment to moment—it was a radar display of the visible limb of Kuu; a cross-section of the landscape ahead of us. It answered the question—seeing how our peripoint is 15 kilometers, are there any 16 kilometer high mountains in the way?

Peripoint would be almost exactly at the center of the far side of Kuu—the area that was most poorly mapped.

If the engines held out, and *if* we lived to the point where the red "x" vanished, it would mean that, *if* Kuu was a perfectly round body with no mountains or valleys (which it wasn't), and *if* its gravity field was uniform (which it wasn't), we would miss the satellite's surface.

Then the peripoint figure started to drop. 15.3 km, 15.25, 15.15. "Damn it!" I said. Kuu's gravity field wasn't uniform, all right. Below the surface we passed over was an area of greater density, and hence with a stronger gravitation pull than the average for Kuu. It was pulling us down.

Now there was no sense of sailing, of a long glide—we were falling, no two ways about it.

Kuu's ugliness whizzed past our cameras.

That burbly line got more burbly. "We are coming up over a highland area," Joslyn remarked. That was a neutral way to put it. "Ohmigod, we're about to pile into a mountain!" would have done just as well and been just as accurate.

"All right, Mac, I'm taking manual control. Give me countdown to peripoint and peripoint in meters."

"Twenty seconds. Peripoint 12,500. Nineteen seconds—12,400. Eighteen—11,900."

Joz was glued to her own displays, watching the engines, the limb radar, and the TV pickup of the real estate below.

"Fifteen seconds," I went on. "11,900. Fourteen seconds—12,000. Thirteen—12 seconds. Holding at 12,000."

"Cut! Go to digital, limb altitude maximum," Joslyn ordered.

"Maximum elevation, 10,500 meters. Rising . . . 10,600 . . . 11,800—scramble! No data!"

"It's all right, Mac. We're through. The radar's trying to read empty spa—"

WHAM!!

The lighting died for a moment and I remember thinking it made no sense—if we had hit there would have been time to notice we were dead. Emergency lighting came on and the readouts unscrambled themselves. Suddenly I realized we were in zero gee.

"Joz, what—"

"Shut up!" she yelled, urgently throwing switches.

I sat there in the middle of the air when I should have been weighing six times too much, waiting for the hot pilot in the next chair to save my skin and explain.

The lights flickered again, and the ship lurched sickeningly as the engines relit under us. The ventilators brought a new odor to the sweaty ooze we had long ago forgotten—the smell of burnt insulation and melted wire.

"I've got some control back, Mac, but we've lost engine number two—and we're riding the idiot backup computer. Get the prime computer back on line."

I was already keying in the start-up commands. The prime system was back on line in ten seconds.

"Okay, Joz, see if you can get it to take commands."

"Laid in. Whew! When things go wrong!"

"Are we out of it yet?"

"I think we'll hold together, more or less. Engine two is right out and gone—I believe the bell isn't there at all anymore. Cooling failure, and the poor thing went poof."

"What happened?"

"I think the last tall ridge we passed over made the computer think we were going to crash. It ran an automatic evasive maneuver, throttled the engines up full, then decided we weren't going to hit, and dragged the thrust level back down again, hard. All in about half a second. These engines have had a bit of a time of it already. They were hit with this super surge and it was just too much for them. Engine two blew, and that caused a *second* power surge that had circuit breakers cascading out through the whole power loop—including the propulsion system. Out go engines one and three."

"I've brought one and three back up, and gimballed them to compensate, but as soon as I can, I'm throttling them back down to about two gees, from six. They probably aren't feeling too well either. The cooling situation isn't very good at all," said Joslyn, concluding with a masterful understatement.

"But can we get home at two gees?"

"Oh, yes. We lost the engine, not the fuel. But it will be a longer trip by some hours. And of course, *Leviathan* is still out there."

The *Joslyn Marie* swung from behind the dead world that had so nearly claimed her, and headed back down toward her base, her friends, her enemies, and her fate.

CHAPTER SEVENTEEN

Our limping ship came up from around the far side of Kuu and fell down toward the inner orbits of New Finland.

Joslyn worked quickly to decide on a new orbit for us. With one dead engine and two questionable, she was not going to try any grandstand maneuvers.

She settled on a highly elongated near-equatorial orbit that brushed The Rock's orbit and rolled out ten times farther out from the planet, to a 50,000 kilometer point. "If we get stranded in that orbit, someone from The Rock or Vapaus ought to be able to come and get us, sooner or later," Joslyn explained.

"You're forgetting *Uncle Sam*," I said. "She'd make a pretty good lifeboat—and she can fight."

"I'm sure *Sam* could take care of us, but my interstellar namesake here is a valuable piece of hardware and we should be sure she's kept handy. As it stands, I want to get us into that orbit and settle down to do some damage checking before we go one bit farther. This is a good ship, but the poor dear is likely to blow up on us if we ask too much more of her without a chance of repair."

"Which I suppose I should get on with." I got busy with the damage control diagnostics. Most of what needed doing could be done sitting at a computer console. The computers checked out the ship's dozens of systems and hundreds of subsystems. When something didn't come up to the standards set for it, the computer presented the situation as best it could to me. I would note it for later manual repair, or maybe just a visual once-over, or tell the computer to switch over to a back-up system. Many of the problems were so clear-cut the computer simply informed me of switchovers—the primary was in a hopeless mess.

Then I had to go through the whole shebang with the backups in place. Glitches develop in complex equipment.

There were no lethal failures. There were dozens of minor breakdowns, though, which made it an urgent job. Usually disaster in space isn't the result of one overwhelming failure, but a series of small, related failures that sneak up on you in unexpected circumstances.

That was why the *loss* of an engine was so nearly fatal, even though the *absence* of an engine wasn't. The designers of the ship had included an excellent collision avoidance system. Quite reasonably, that system hadn't counted on anyone trying to get that close to a planet at such velocities.

It wasn't that we were in danger of crashing. It was very close, but at the moment all hell broke loose, we weren't actually about to hit. The margin of error was simply too close for the anti-collision system. Avoiding collision is important, to say the least, and the system has a very high priority over ship control and a very inflexible margin for error when guarding against a hit.

What was nearly deadly was the intercession of this very good system at exactly the wrong moment, under unforeseen circumstances. What was dangerous was the throttle-up, with the engines already straining; that throttle-up being caused by the anti-collision system panicking. When the engine blew, that caused the ensuing power surges, which set up cascading power and control failures throughout the ship. *That* series of failures was what nearly got us.

We weren't going to let something like that happen again.

When I finished at the computer, I started on my inspection tour. Several trips to the parts storage compartment later, I had replaced many of the units the computer hadn't trusted.

Even after I was done, long after we reached orbit, the control boards showed that our ship was at war. What should have been in the green was in the amber, or even the red. Outboard cameras rolled out on telescoping booms and looked at the exterior of the ship. They sent back a picture of a badly cooked hull. The shielding for the pass through *Leviathan*'s flames had been barely enough. There were a dozen spots where the hull had discolored and deformed. Leak meters showed we were losing air. I sealed the hatches leading to the after decks and depressurized them. No sense letting air leak out of cabins where no one was breathing.

The camera that had nestled in the center of the thrust bulkhead had failed when the engine had. We managed to guide a camera on a boom down to take a look at the main engines.

There was a mess. Engine two wasn't broken down—it was gone. The fusion flame must have vaporized the engine bell and most of the innards of the thing within milliseconds of the cooling failure.

One and three were still there, but with some unnerving dents and dings in them. The engines were meant to withstand such a disaster to one of their fellows, but it had obviously been close.

Neither Vapaus nor The Rock contacted us for long hours. We squirted several brief ID codes over our comm lasers, essentially saying "We're here!" We got back automatic responses from the communications computers, that said, "So are we." It seemed that the people there were too busy to deal with us yet.

Space was largely quiet. We didn't use radar, so as to avoid detection if we could, but IR, radio, and long-range cameras could tell us something. Few engines burned, few lasers fired, few warheads exploded. The battle seemed to have worn both sides down to the nub.

By this time, all of the repeater satellites that relayed information between ships and satellites were gone, all of them long ago shot down. We were down to line-of-sight.

If Battle Control wasn't interested in us for the moment, that suited us fine. We worked at getting ourselves—and the ship—set to rights. Clumsy but effective zero-gee showers got the greasy residue of the high-acceleration bags off our skin, and stowing the bags themselves was a welcome chore. With the shape our main propulsion was in, there was simply no possibility of the *Joslyn Marie* accelerating hard enough for us to need them.

Both of us were covered with blotchy red rashes; high-gee-thrust bruised capillaries. The rashes were more uncomfortable than painful, and we stocked an ointment that helped a lot, though it made fresh flight suits a little sticky.

We didn't bother with cooking, but simply shoved some quick-rations down our throats. That, protein supplements, and super-duper vitamins made dinner.

We slept in shifts, four hours each while the other watched the boards.

It was 15 hours after we bombed *Leviathan* when Battle Control finally contacted us by laser. I was on watch and quickly roused Joslyn when the cue light came on.

"—is Battle Control. Come in, *Joslyn Marie*. Do you read? Over." I didn't recognize the voice, but it sounded tired past the point of collapse.

"This is the *Joslyn Marie*. We read. Over."

"Stand by for instructions." There was about a half-minute pause. Then: "This is Berman. Listen to my orders, transmit in five minutes to confirm that you can carry them out." Her voice was utterly dead. There was not the slightest humanity left to it. "You are to clear and kill every available bank of the *Joslyn Marie*'s computer memories. No regard for later restart or operations. Only programs utterly necessary for maintaining the ship inert in orbit, as well as fullest radio control and minimal life support, are to be maintained. All ballistic, maneuvering, and record-keeping functions are to be killed. All memories and computer files not needed to keep the ship barely alive are to be eliminated. You will then stand by to receive and record data transmissions from this location, and you will then assume the function of Battle Control. We will transmit a repeater of the current tactical situation in 15 seconds. That is all. Confirm in five minutes. Berman out."

"Bloody hell. 'Assume the functions of Battle Control'!! What in the world is she thinking of?" Joslyn said in astonishment.

"That, I think. Retaliation." I said, pointing to the screens. The visuals on the tactical situation appeared in the central hologram tank. It was there to read. A line of three missiles were homing in on The Rock. No ship, anywhere, could possibly intercept.

I asked the computer for the status of The Rock's defenses. The computer searched the data just transmitted to us and put the news on the main screens.

ALL LASER STATIONS OUT OF COMMISSION. DEFENSIVE MISSILES REMAINING: 1.

The simplest math. Three missiles incoming, one intercepting missile left. The Rock was doomed. Thus *Leviathan* revenge herself against the attack we had made on her.

"Damn it, we should never have flown this raid!" I said.

"We had no choice, Mac. We had to take the chance."

"Chance, hell. They were bound to retaliate!"

"I know. And Eve knew. And she gave the order." Joslyn sighed. "Now she has given another one. Can we do it?"

I thought for a moment. A long one. The *J.M.* was a good ship, and had good computers . . . but she wasn't a command center. We didn't have enough radio channels. The computers weren't big enough to store all the data on all the ships, friend and foe, let alone track them all. Our radar wasn't up to that, either. We'd have to rely on reports from the fighters. The task was impossible for the ship to perform.

But there it was.

I hit the transmit switch. "This is the *Joslyn Marie*. We are beginning erasure of our computer memories. Please prepare for data transmission."

Well, what else could we do? They were going to *die*. We could at least try to keep fighting.

The ship-handling programs, the ballistics-to-maneuvering routines, the food-prep and inventory programs, the interface programs for contacting the aux ships, the diagnostics, the attack-tracking system, real-time damage control—all of them to be erased, made dead, vanished. The *Josyln Marie* paralyzed, mute, and lobotomized in the bargain. The ship lost attitude control, as the *Bohica* had so long ago (or was it truly that long?), and we began to tumble.

I had the line printer run out a copy of the ship's log before I erased it. If there was a future, someone might find it interesting.

We were stealing the brains of the ship. Just as a perfectly functional arm or leg can be rendered useless by a blow to the head, so was our ship losing, not her capabilities, but the means of controlling and using them.

Joslyn and I worked in a numbing fog. We had to make a hopeless idiot of the ship that had kept us alive, the ship that had been home. We knew it probably meant our deaths as well. Oh, yes, we could escape in *Uncle Sam*, but to where? The Rock would soon be pulverized. *Leviathan* would soon settle into the atmosphere. They would have won. It would only be a matter of time before someone thought to send a missile out into this lonely orbit.

Life support. Kill the sensors in the after decks. Shut down the sensors and the backups forward, for that matter. What point in an alarm system when there was no longer a way to deal with an emergency?

It seemed as if there ought to be a way to do these things by hand, to monitor the dials by eye and go throw a switch or twist a knob. But the sensors and the dials and the switches and the knobs were all linked to the computer system. The computers themselves were backed up by duplicate, triplicate, and quadrupicate machines that could take over, but we needed *their* memories as well.

Within ten minutes, Battle Control started piping data to us over every channel we had.

The single most important program was an emulator routine that let the *J.M.*'s computers cope with programs written for Battle Control. That one they transmitted twice and had us run a comparison drill to make sure the two transmissions were identical.

Our machines had to be able to play the part of their big brothers on The Rock—otherwise, they would have been unable to deal with any of the data coming in on all channels.

And there was plenty of data. Ship positions, fuel and power reports on each one, reports on enemy fighters, on *Leviathan*'s status. A recording of the holographic representation of the battle up to now, in the hope that we might learn something of the enemy's tactics—and, for that matter, *our* tactics.

The job wasn't as bad as I thought it would be. For one thing, there was the grim fact that there weren't as many ships to keep track of as there once had been. Secondly, someone at the other end was weeding out a lot of things it might be nice to know, but which we would never have the chance to use. A few of the blanked out programs and files came through as titles and nothing else—FIGHTER PILOT ROSTER AND BIOGRAPHICAL ... THIRTEEN DIGIT PSEUDO RANDOM NUMBER GENERATOR ... LAUNCH TRAJECTORIES AGAINST PLANETARY TARGETS FROM ROCK'S ORBIT ... and so on. There were other, more subtle cuts. I noticed there were no programs for operations above *Leviathan*'s current altitude. We weren't going to have to go that high, anyway.

The most important data was on the enemy. What did they have left? What sort of shape was *Leviathan* in? What weakness had been exposed? What sort of chance did we have, and what was the best way of exploiting it?

At least it was clear that our attack on *Leviathan*'s launch stations had done some good. It seemed as if they hadn't launched a manned ship since we had hit them, only missiles.

Our side, however, was down to a bare 18 Beefies and Beasts. Both Hatracks were gone. Other than that we had *Uncle Sam*, *Stars*, *Stripes*, and a number of ballistic landers, plus a few tugs, drones, and other non-combatant ships.

We got a giant holographic memory of all that was known of *Leviathan*, and her current condition. Joslyn patched in everything our cameras had recorded as we passed the great ship.

There was a torrent of information. Then it began to slow to a flow, then a trickle, then nothing.

There was more, much more, that could have been sent, but already there was more than we could possibly use. Our computers were full to the brim with data, every usable byte of storage space filled. There was room for the data that would come in from the ships, and nothing else.

All the comm lines were given over to the computers, and there had been no chance for us to talk with the people at the other end. Those who could and would escape had already done so, some in slow-moving tugs unsuited to war, some in pressure suits hoping to be picked up. Some of these made it. Others were never found.

Now The Rock was on a skeleton crew, waiting the last few minutes until it had to die. Eve was there, and dozens of others I will never get to know.

Marie-Francoise and her intelligence crew had already been ordered off The Rock and sent to Vapaus, where they were to continue the job of guessing what the Guardians would do next. Marie-Francoise made doubly certain George came off with her crew. He was the best source of information about the Guards she seemed likely to have for a long time—and she was a bit worried he might decide to stay behind, for a clean death that would let him escape all his doubts.

I don't remember how I said goodbye to Eve. I can't recall what I said, or if I said anything at all, or what she said to me.

All I can remember is seeing her face in those last few minutes as the video cameras beamed their signals to us. She looked so *tired*, so wearied, that it seemed at first that there could be no other emotion in such a face. But it was not so.

I saw the elements of anger, determination, and perhaps a hint of the warrior's lust for battle blended in her face. She had no fear, no time or desire or need for fear.

Then the first missile came, then the second, then the third, and in the flame of purest destruction, then did they die.

The video screen showed us the fusion bombs guttering down to death. The Rock broke up slowly, and tumbled apart. New Finland, Kuu, and Vapaus all weathered a few strikes from newborn meteors. Then it was over.

"Mac. Vapaus reports a missile exploding *exactly* 10 kilometers from the forward docking area," Joslyn said. "That's a pretty clear message—keep the battle control center off Vapaus or we destroy it, too."

"Which makes us the ace in the hole. *Leviathan* probably thinks we crashed into Kuu," I replied thoughtfully.

"I doubt they can find us. They won't look here, and they need their radar elsewhere. It's up to us, Mac. The knowledge aboard this ship is the absolute, utterly, and totally last chance our people have got." She paused. "And, you, sir, command this ship. We are, all of us, in your hands."

It sunk in at last. The chain of command had had each link snapped and cut—Taylor, Berman, and now it cut down to me.

It was all mine. It was up to me. In my hands. I suddenly realized I was *looking* at my hands, intently, as if they could tell me what to do, how to save us from this last extremity. I lifted my hands to my head and cradled my face in them for a moment, then I sighed deeply and looked at the screens, straightening my back and getting hold of myself. Some tiny part of me believed that I would certainly die. It was not fear, it was a conviction, too strong to be called by any other name than knowledge, that I was doomed.

Yet with it came the determination to go out as the others had, with a firm grip on the job, and advancing as best I could, with the last flicker of life I held. Patriotism, fealty to my oath, even self-preservation were gone from me, for at least the time at hand. All that I had was the desire to go out fighting.

Somewhere in myself I found the secret of command. Out there, scattered in space, were men and women who *demanded* leadership. Circumstances left them with no one but myself, and their vast, inchoate, and unarticulated voice instilled in me the power of command.

"Joslyn. We've got to win this one."

"Yes."

"Which means we still have to knock out that antiship missile system, so our side can bring reinforcements to bear."

"Right. Which in turn means we have to get to and use the missile control station."

"Which is in some very secure place in a ship the size of an asteroid. We have to board *Leviathan*."

"That's the sticky part, all right," Joslyn agreed.

"Well, I may have the beginnings of an idea. But first I want to talk to Marie-Francoise."

A big part of what Battle Control had given us was the control over secure communications. Everything possible was sent by laser, and even then it was encoded. In theory, no one could "read" a laser message that wasn't directed at them, but theories had been wrong plenty of times, and there had been plenty of spies in history. We were very careful, for which I was now thankful, as annoying as it sometimes was. If we had been using straight radio traffic I would never have dared called Vapaus, in the fear that a lot of communication traffic with it would finger it as a military target.

As it was, we were reasonably certain that we were not endangering our remaining orbital base. Marie-Francoise was on duty when we got through to the intelligence center. Her face on the video screen showed a certain tired surprise when she saw who was calling. "I thought you were dead by now."

I swore under my breath. Morale was going to hell—and I could have wished to inherit a better informed intelligence chief. Then I remembered that Vapaus had just come up from behind the planet—with the relay satellites out, there was no way she could have known what had gone on in the last 45 minutes or so.

"Mac," she said after a pause. "What do we do now? We have lost our commanding station. We have some fighters left, but no way to guide them. I don't dare use this place for a command center. They'd bomb us in earnest."

"Marie-Francoise," Joslyn said. "The Rock passed the command data to us before they died. *We're* Battle Control now."

A tiny gleam of hope showed in Marie-Francoise's eye. "Enough of the data? Enough so you know all that will happen?"

"Yes," I said, wondering if I was fibbing. Yet as I said it, my idea was shaping up. "Marie-Francoise, you've got to know that damn ship better than her captain by now. Based on what you've got, what is the maximum velocity relative to atmosphere *Leviathan*'s going to face?"

"Mmmmmm. By the time they reach the true, thick air, no more than 550 to 600 kilometers an hour."

"How far outside the atmosphere when she stops braking? Distance and time."

"Give me a moment on this . . . if she were to follow optimum path—turn-over maneuver, to get to glide attitude—no less than 100 kilometers, 25 minutes, maybe 120 and 30 minutes maximums."

"Do you have up-to-date data on our fighters? We should show 18 operational."

"That is right. With The Rock out, I have no further updates, though."

"Right. Now, this one I'm giving to you and to Joz here at the same time. It's tricky. Factor in facilities at that end. I want every fighter to disengage, retreat, and return to Vapaus. Assume that we use the mass of the planet to hide the maneuvers from *Leviathan*. How fast can the last one get back to base? Can Vapaus handle all the ships at once?"

"The last I know the answer for now—yes."

"Good. Both of you get cracking on that. I'm going to run a battle simulation, working on the assumption that you both get good news answers."

"Shall I issue the recall order?" Joslyn asked.

"Not yet. Another thing, Marie-Francoise—find someone with nothing to do and get 'em in charge of rounding up everything that can survive a ballistic reentry with people on board. Don't worry if it can get back *up*— down is all.

"Then get me a breakdown on how many able-bodied types are available for extremely hazardous duty. Volunteers only, and without taking both parents of a child, that sort of thing. Can you run that one fast?"

"Yes, easily. But what is it that you are planning? It would make it easier to know."

"I promise I will tell you. Just let me flesh it out a bit first. It needs it. Get back to me. I've got to do some thinking."

I cut the connection and stretched out—even being back in zero-gee, my muscles hadn't gotten uncreased yet. Six gees takes it out of you. I reviewed my thinking.

It was respect for the dead to call Eve's tactics a plan of battle, but not accurate. I had found myself wondering more than once if I *could* do better. Now I would find out.

She had tried to peel back *Leviathan*'s defenses, without any clear idea apparent of what to do about it once they were peeled back. She had consistently been afraid to commit a sufficiently large enough force to do the job, with the result that smaller forces suffered murderous losses.

That was the situation I had inherited.

I considered what the enemy was up against.

Leviathan's space fighters and missiles were completely unaerodynamic. Her aerial fighters could not fly in space. The only craft she had that could fly in both environments, her Nova-class aerospace fighters, such as the late lamented *Bohica*, would be of no use until the ship was well within the atmosphere, for a very tricky reason: they were too slow.

That's a funny thing to say about a Mach four fighter that could fly itself to orbit, but consider: *Leviathan*'s entry to atmosphere required her to match the rotational velocity of the planet *exactly*. It was a very small needle's eye that the great ship had to thread. *Leviathan had* to be moving tens of thousands of kilometers an hour slower than orbital velocity, or else she would be torn to pieces.

The Novas were a compromise between air and space, and thereby not too efficient in either. Loaded with weaponry and carrying fuel enough to reach orbit, the Novas left the runway able to do no more than 2.5 gees—better as they burned up fuel. The Beefies could take them at launch like shooting fish in a barrel, if the Guardians were foolish enough to launch them. The situation was worse for the Novas if they found themselves at high altitude and low speed: they could get no use out of the wings, and the fusion engines would gulp fuel trying to hold altitude.

What it all boiled down to was this:

Leviathan carried no craft that could defend her in the borderlands of space, where there was not air enough for a jet engine to breathe or for a wing to grab, when she was too close to the planet, moving too slowly for a space fighter to get away without courting disaster.

In the borderlands. When *Leviathan* arrived there, *that* was our window in time. Hit her there, when her missiles could no longer hit Vapaus, when her space fighters would be stranded in orbit if they were away from *Leviathan* when the big ship hit the air, when she was vulnerable. Pull her pilots up off the decks and don't let them back down. *Then* it might be possible to board the ship without being blown out of the sky.

It made sense. My ideas could work. I started on the simulation.

Fifteen minutes later, Joslyn brought me a fresh bulb of tea and a sheaf of print-out paper. She set both of them into restraint nitches and watched my work from behind me. Though I absently noted her presence, it took me a minute to come out of my work and acknowledge her.

"Hello, there," I said.

"Hello there yourself. Drink your tea and tell me what this grand plan is."

"I will. Just give me a minute to unjangle my nerves. How's the ship holding up?"

"It looks like we've a bit of an air leak somewhere. Some impervious seam gave up the ghost or such. We're tumbling a bit, though fairly slowly. Don't try any aerobatics. The far wall will have moved by the time you get there. The tumble will also be a bit of a bother in holding cabin temperatures. Sun angles. We'll have heating fluctuations. The air-cleaning is basically all right, but it may be a trifle murky and damp in here after a bit. I don't want to try and fix it until it's impossibly bad. Without parts, I might make it worse.

"Of course, there's no hope of actually *flying* her, but she'll keep us alive a while longer."

"How long?"

"A week, if your standards aren't high. Ten days if you want to live in a pressure suit—but we'd be in sorry shape by then."

"Can she be repaired?"

"Oh, lordy, yes! Just needs some time in a shipyard, parts, and her computer programs replaced. The poor thing is essentially sound. Just a bit at the end of her tether."

"As are we all."

"Mac?" Joslyn asked, a hint of firmness in her voice.

"Yes?"

"I won't surrender her. I won't leave her derelict and have those murdering bastards patch her up to go shooting people somewhere else."

I looked at my wife. She looked like hell. Her face had blotchy patches of red where high-gee had broken capillaries. Her eyes were bloodshot and puffy. Her lips were dried and cracked. Her voice was strong and calm, but there was a note of brittle anger beneath that.

"This is not just my ship, Mac. This is my home."

"This is my home, too, Joslyn. Joz—I have an idea, a plan. I think it might work. If we try it, we'll have to leave the *J.M.*, but only for a while. I promise you, they shall not take this place. We'll set charges and blow her sky-high, if need be."

She hugged me, and I hugged back, hard. "Thank you, Mac. I know I didn't even really have to say it, except for myself. One gets very careful of a ship, in it for a long time. And I was alone with her all that time you were away. I could not let those monsters have her."

"They aren't going to take her," I said. "They aren't going to take anything. I think I've found the way to beat them."

She pulled back from me to look me in the eye, to see if I was in earnest, if I truly had some hope to offer. Then, at last, she smiled, and suddenly got beautiful again. "Oh, Mac. It's about time someone did. How?"

"You ever hear the first law of offense?"

"Some ghastly americanism, isn't it? 'Hit 'em where they ain't'?"

"Prig. Snob. Some ally. When the chips are down, it's nothing but insults."

"Consider my mood to be duly apologetic and get on with it."

"Well, seeing how it's you—" I said. "But change that rule to 'when' they ain't." I keyed in commands to the computer, instructing it to show *Leviathan*'s entry course. "This is based on the best we've got on *Leviathan*. The maneuver she's got to fly into the atmosphere is complex and must be incredibly precise. Watch the dotted blue line—that's her tracking line, relative to the planet. Unless they crash, or abort the entry and head back into deep space, they have to follow something within a half percent of this plotting. Okay. Now, here. The engines cut out. At this point, *Leviathan* is actually moving slightly *away* from the planet. She's got to balance her own motion very carefully against both the planet's gravity and the fact that New Finland is, essentially, creeping up on the ship.

"*Leviathan* is in a very slightly faster orbit, just one planetary radius plus a hiccup closer to the sun than New Finland. It is just at this very delicate point in time that she *cannot dare defend herself*.

"The ship has to flip end over end. She's been keeping her stern pointed toward the planet so her engines were pointed toward it to decelerate. Once she needs to fly in air, that means getting her wings faced in the right direction. She's really one big wing, of course, a lifting body, but she still has to be pointed the right way.

"That ship is *big*, and can't maneuver all that fast; the planet is *close*, and getting closer. Before they perform the flip-over, they must have every fighter on board and battened down, unless they want them slammed against the bulkheads when the ship goes base over apex. With the ship first whirling around in space, and then immediately hitting atmosphere, it'll be dammed hard to launch or recover anything, anyway.

"Once they begin turnover, that's it for space-going fighters. Any not yet aboard aren't going to get there."

"They'll still have the laser cannon."

"Yeah, I know. But we may be able to get around that. Somehow. Okay, keep watching the simulation in the holo tank. *Leviathan* completes her end-over-end maneuver and lines up for entry. She hits air, more or less in a dive, and speed about 500 kilometers an hour. Immediately, she starts to pull out of it, going into a long, gentle glide down into denser air. She's got to keep her nose well up to do this, holding right to the edge of a stall. She needs to sink into air she can grab quickly.

"Once she hits the dense lower atmosphere, she can bring her nose down and come to her cruising speed, about 200 kilometers an hour. Okay?"

"Right," Joslyn said.

"All right. Once she's at that speed, she's basically just a big, fast-moving dirigible. But *until* she's at that speed, I am willing to bet she can't launch anything. Not in a nose-up attitude at 500 kilometers an hour. The planes would either roll off or get blown off."

Joslyn stood silently, looking at the holo tank. She used the controls to jump back to the beginning of the display and run it again in fast forward. *Leviathan*'s tiny double shut off its engines, flipped end over end violently, dove precipitously into the atmosphere, belly-flopped its way down to about 5,000 meters, and settled down to cruising flight.

"Mac. What you're saying is that from the moment she starts entry maneuvers to the time she's stable in the air she's completely defenseless."

"Except for the lasers, yes. What do you think?"

"I think you're right. My God. We should have held back every ship until right now, attacked en masse and thrown our whole force into the fight at once. We could have forced every spacecraft and every pilot off the ship. They would have hit air without a pilot still on board."

"I know. So why didn't we think of it three weeks ago?"

"Never mind that. The question is, do we still have the ships to force the Guardians up off the decks at the right moment?"

"I bet we can pull this off. I *know* we can. Let's talk to Marie-Francoise and Randall and make plans."

CHAPTER EIGHTEEN

"Mac, you give us some fire control and some decent orbital data, and we'll razzle-dazzle those laser cannon right out of business. Leave it to us," Randall said from the cockpit of his fighter.

"Can you rotate all your pilots through Vapaus and get your ships refitted and patched up in time without *Leviathan* spotting us?"

"No problem," Metcalf said. "The Rock's orbit is full of debris. We gotta fly carefully, but all we do is fly through where it used to be, then do the transition to Vapaus on the far side of the planet from the big ship. No way they'll be able to track 18 little ships through that rubble field. They might suspect, but they won't know."

"And Mac, don't forget we've still got fusion bombs if they take Vapaus out—and they know it," Joslyn reminded me.

"Okay, I guess we've gotta take the chance," I said. "Otherwise it's all over anyway. Go get your refits."

"We don't even need 'em. Our limiting factor was personnel, not ships. There's a spare Beefie for every pilot but two. Vapaus shipyards are getting them checked out now. Including some modifications I ordered."

"You've got something in mind?" I asked.

"Sure. I'm going to lead the first boarding party," Metcalf replied.

"Say again? Is it you or the radio that's crazy?"

"I said I'm leading the boarding party."

"You can't fly that ship in air," I protested. "You'd crash."

"That's why we do it in space," Metcalf replied calmly. "It's impossible—I think. If not, we abort, take some pot shots, and leave it to you."

"You on the level, Metcalf?"

"Never more so, boss man. I owe those bastard knuckledraggers one. Look, we're gonna lose line of sight in a sec. Metcalf out."

I shrugged at Joslyn and cut the line from our end. He had his orders. I knew he'd carry them out. If he wanted to put embroidery on them, fine. I figured he could give *Leviathan* a good-sized headache if he wanted to.

Marie-Francoise had kept her staff busy. What I had wanted was every ship that could carry troops and drop out of the sky onto the deck of *Leviathan*. What she gave me just started there. She also reported that 80 percent of the adult population of the satellite had volunteered for unspecified hazardous duty. That came to about 2,500. All the ships fit for duty could carry maybe 200 troops.

Then Marie-Francoise came up with a wild card: one-man escape shells.

Escape shells are one of the simplest and scariest ways to get out of space. About all they amount to is someone in a spacesuit inside an ablating heat shield, plus a moronic guidance system and a retro rocket. If you're stuck in space, you wriggle into the thing and push the button with crossed fingers.

The guidance gizmo points the retro in roughly the right direction, and with luck it guns properly, you get kicked in the direction of the atmosphere, and the heat shield melts away, maybe without cooking you. You press another button and explosive bolts blow the re-entry shell either away from you or through you and then a chute pops open, which, more than likely, deposits you in the ocean, where you drown.

They weren't *really* all that dangerous, I suppose, but

there were people who rode them as a *sport*. In my line of employment I've been close to killed enough times trying to do a job that I don't see the point of risking my neck for fun.

About 200 escape shells had been stockpiled on Vapaus while it was being built, for the use of construction workers in an emergency. This official stockpile had never been used, and it still gathered dust in a storeroom somewhere.

Marie-Francoise also found a club full of overconfident idiots who called themselves The Meteors, which I thought was all too well-chosen a name. They had held regular drops before the war, and had manufactured their own shells. They hadn't been able to make any drops, or any new shells, since the war began, but they had had their eyes on the old official stockpile for a long time.

The club president insisted that The Meteors could land on the deck of *Leviathan* if they were dropped from orbit accurately. They planned to use grappling hooks and count on plenty of padding in their suits. I hesitated before agreeing to let them go, but we were going to need every overconfident idiot we could get our hands on.

From every side it was the same—everyone wanted to fight, everyone wanted to go, everyone wanted to grab that ship. Marie-Francoise told us Vapaus was a beehive stirred up. Every workshop was full, every gun was loaded, every ship was ready to fly.

The pent-up frustration of cowering inside a hollow moon while others decided your fate, the hatred for the enemy, and perhaps most of all, the nerve-shattering *waiting* to find if you'd ever live free again, or if you'd be killed by a fusion bomb—all of it turned into a sudden manic sense of hope, born of a chance to do something, anything.

Meanwhile, Joslyn and I had our hands full staging the withdrawal from the battle that still filled the sky. Carefully, we ran a fighting retreat so as not to leave our rear unguarded. We got our few ships back to base without further loss.

From the enemy's side, it must have seemed that smashing The Rock had done what it was supposed to do. There were no more sorties against the Guardian fighters, there were no more strafing attacks of *Leviathan*.

We worked out a tight schedule of cycling all our pilots through Vapaus, getting them showered, fed, rested, and put into their new ships.

Maybe *Leviathan*'s captain knew that ships were going back to Vapaus—maybe he lost tracking on them when they hid out in the rubble of The Rock. What mattered was we didn't have any ships coming *out* of Vapaus. I crossed my fingers and hoped that they were satisfied that we were calling it quits.

On our side, the accidents of fate had left me the ranking officer in the line of command. Because of that, people I had never met, people born 50 light years from my home, who didn't speak my language, who had nothing to do with me, were calmly and confidently being handed weapons so that they might take their parts in a half-baked scheme that was probably the result of too much caffeine and not enough sleep.

But the schemes didn't stay half-baked. The amazing thing about command is that it *works*. I handed out vague general instructions on some phase of our attack, and back to me came word that preparations were underway, computer simulations had been run, soldiers briefed, and all was in readiness. Everyone snapped to—with a vengeance.

I wondered about *Leviathan*'s commander. How much did he know about us? Presumably, he had managed to contact some little band of surviving Guardian ground troops holed up somewhere. We at least had to assume that. He must have monitored general broadcasts. Had he spotted his own upcoming moment of weakness as he entered the atmosphere? Had he found some way of countering our moves? Had he closed our window in time? What was he thinking?

All I knew for sure is that we'd give him plenty to think about soon enough.

It started. The first phase of our plan was to raise merry hell on the launch and recovery decks just before entry, trying to prevent the launch or recovery of spacecraft. Marie-Francoise agreed that the space-going fighters almost certainly had been meant for delivery to an orbital base; they'd be worse than useless, adding weight to *Leviathan*'s hull, once she hit air.

Leviathan's commander would be facing some tough choices. If indeed he *could* afford the significant weight penalty of twenty-odd spacecraft, *should* he?

Leviathan might be a flying machine, but she was not a fast or graceful one. Could he afford a helm that responded sluggishly? Could he settle for a faster entry and a lower cruising altitude due to extra ballast? If he did jettison the ships, could he leave them in a parking orbit and risk our capturing the ships? (Believe me, we were working on it.) Or would he decide to drop them into the atmosphere to crash or burn? We set out to further complicate his problems.

From our makeshift control center, Joslyn vectored the Beefies against the Guardian fighters, sending them in to engage the enemy, but also to draw the fighters away from *Leviathan*. It was a delicate cat-and-mouse game: we wanted to present tempting targets to the enemy, but not actually let them hit any of them.

One thing that helped was the mass of knowledge we now had concerning the enemy ships. We know how many gees the Guardian fighters could do, how quickly they could react, how accurate their weapons were. A large part of the data we had inherited was this sort of thing.

The crew on The Rock had compiled such detailed data that we had 15 to 20 clear "signatures"—patterns that certain pilots seemed to follow. We knew that one hotshot who gave his ship about an extra half-gee gun at launch was very conservative about using his lasers. One fellow kept a very poor eye on his rearward radar.

We used this information, and all our skill, and all the skill of our pilots to herd the Guardian ships away from *Leviathan*.

It worked pretty well. The hologram tank stopped showing the little pinpoints of light drifting at random. Gradually, *Leviathan* was left nearly alone in the sky, the fighters being teased farther and farther away.

Whoever was running the show on *Leviathan*'s bridge could see the pattern, too. He started to call in the fighters, and so we upped the pressure, trying to balance our provocations and attacks against the urgency of their attempts to return. The closer their flyboys got, the hotter we made it for them. The pressure of time was finally starting to work for us. Our fighters took more chances than I told them to, and played a little rougher than I planned. I didn't mind. I wanted them to be aggressive. For the first time, we were calling the shots and the enemy was responding to our moves.

But if I was learning fighter pilots were a pretty unruly lot, so was my counterpart aboard *Leviathan*. Long after Joslyn and I had spotted the first movement toward a recall, his force was still widely scattered, engaged in a dozen indecisive shooting matches. Metcalf was ready to tell me about it.

"Boss man, we've got those cowboys so trigger-happy they're liable to shoot themselves," he reported by comm laser.

"If they do, keep out of it."

"I've been good so far—three times I could have smeared one of them."

"I've been watching the tank. I notice the third one suddenly got missing."

"Okay, so I'm trigger-happy, too. Or do you want me help the Guardians look for the guy?"

"Oh, no, have your fun. But if you can hold yourself back just a little bit, I can promise you a real turkey shoot in about eight hours."

"This had better work, Mac. I have an overwhelming urge to paint more little spaceships on my hull. However, I promise to dedicate the next one to you."

"Well, I can't ask for more than that. Get some shuteye. You're out of range of everybody, and you don't need to maneuver for two hours."

"Okay, but put in a call if you want me. Metcalf out."

For long hours it went on, as we sent our fighters to harry the invaders, guiding them in long looping orbits that popped them over *Leviathan*'s horizon briefly and then out again, chasing this fighter, leaving that one behind. We sent our little ships skittering in between and through and around as best we could, trying to keep the Guardians up off their flight deck.

Joslyn and I settled down to hour after long hour of voices buzzing in our headphones, worriedly switching through the frequencies, trying to read numbers that grew fuzzy through bleuried eyes. Too much tea and coffee, not enough food, no sleep.

Around us, the *Joslyn Marie* continued to die. The air slowly grew damp and musty, with a tinge of old, burned rubber to it. Carbon dioxide built up slightly. We had not the time, the energy, or the need to attend to it. Soon we would board *Uncle Sam* to do a job, heading for one fate or another.

And two tiny, shrinking fleets of ships continued to do battle.

Our window in time was beginning to open. Our deadline was that moment *Leviathan* would have to cut her engines.

The hours crawled down into minutes, and then the moment came, and then the flames that marked the great ship's passage faded from the sky.

I keyed in the laser link with Metcalf. "Okay, Randall. Give 'em grief!"

"Way ahead of you, boss man. We're already closing for the planned full-blown attack, by the numbers. We are now firing the beam-riding Redeye missiles from all ships."

"They going to have something to ride?" I asked.

"Oh, I imagine so."

The Redeyes were missiles designed to home in on a laser cannon, following the beam down to the laser itself. The Redeyes were swathed in extremely heavy ablative shielding that could bear up under a tremendous amount of heat and light energy. Metcalf's fliers had loosed a great volley of them, expecting a few to get through while the huge enemy lasers zapped the rest of them.

But the Redeyes needed a laser beam to ride down, and *Leviathan* provided that. Our fighters popped into sight from behind the planet, the Redeyes coming on ahead.

Leviathan's lasers opened up on them. This was the crucial moment for us.

"Beam riders tracking," Metcalf reported. Suddenly the banter was out of his voice. His own craft, and two or three others, were in the focus of the lasers. The Beefies had been coated with the same ablative shielding that the *J.M.* had used to survive the run through *Leviathan*'s flames.

"I'm picking up some heat now." His fighter dodged in and out of the beam as the enemy tracked his weaving course across the sky. "They sure know how to aim that thing. Looks like Vaajakoski's in it too—and there's Takiko in a beam. Some real heat now. The ablatives are helping, but they aren't going to last."

The missiles swarmed to their targets.

"I gotta get out of here. Cooling system in trouble." Metcalf swung his ship around to gun out of range. One of the missiles exploded in space, cooked by *Leviathan*. Another went out. Then one found its mark, and the heat was off Metcalf.

"Whooey. That was some cook-out. Turning now, closing again. Vaajakoski and Takiko still under attack . . . make that Vaaj only. And now she's clear. Three laser cannon fired, all silenced."

"Randall, there are supposed to be *four* laser cannon on *Leviathan*," Joslyn reminded him.

"Yeah, I know. Either it's still out from three days ago, or they are pretty goddamned cagey bastards down there. We're headed in."

The Beefies closed, trying to take and hold the piece of sky between *Leviathan* and her fighters.

"The big ship has ceased fire," Metcalf reported. "If they miss us, they'll hit their own ships at our backs. Hey, boss man, just a note. That deck of theirs can soak it up. The 500 kilogram missiles don't even dent it. Glad the laser stations weren't that tough."

The main body of Guardian ships was now 70 kilometers from *Leviathan*, with Metcalf and his team dead in between them. The enemy was badly caught—they were close to where they needed to go, short on fuel, and yet unharassed only as long as they didn't try to go there.

The Beefies only opened fire if the Guardians tried to move nearer *Leviathan*. They were welcome to move farther away, but they couldn't afford to. They might not have the fuel and they certainly didn't have the time.

I checked our estimated schedule for the big ship and confirmed that *Leviathan* was delaying her rollover to glide attitude. She *needed* the pilots.

All the battling ships were, by this time, drifting toward, or more accurately, dropping down toward New Finland. They were all well under orbital speed.

Leviathan was on her planned course. The Guardian fighters had to stay with her or miss their last chance to get aboard. If the Guardian fighters boosted up to orbital speed, they could never return to base in time.

Leviathan's captain had to wait out our fighters. Would we pull our Navy pilots' fighters out of their crash-landing trajectories in time for the Guardians to recover the fighters?

We gave them a yes on that one. Metcalf's little force suddenly withdrew toward orbit.

Instantly, the Guardians' fighters formed up to recover,

jockeying to establish an orderly, compact formation to get aboard *fast*.

Then we changed our minds. Metcalf's forces doubled back and dropped toward the Guardians.

The turkeyshoot began.

The Guardians could not maneuver, or they would never be recovered. They were forced to hang there, defenseless.

The Beefies soared to the attack with every laser cooking, every missile with a target picked out. *Leviathan* tried to shoot back, but her own people were between her deck and our fighters. Two Guardian ships were blown up by *Leviathan*'s fire. Space was filled with pin-point explosions and wheeling debris.

"Skipper, you were true to your word. This is the best shoot-em-up I've ever been to yet. That's three so far."

"Just don't get zapped yourself."

"Yow! That last big laser is back in business. Oh, God. They've got Greenblat. All ships! Keep below the plane of her topside deck! That last beamer is still with us."

The battle went on, and *Leviathan* sunk slowly toward New Finland.

"Mac, they've got the formation broken. The Guardians that aren't on board are dead. Pull 'em back!" Joslyn said.

"You're right. This is the *Joslyn Marie* to all fighters. You've broken them! *Leviathan* has to start pitchover any second now. Pull back and get to orbit."

"This is Metcalf. I request formal permission to attempt boarding."

"Metcalf! Is that for real!"

"Yes, sir! Permission granted?"

"What about that last laser cannon?"

"They can't bring it to bear on their own deck! Mac! For God's sake, yes or no! We've got about 90 seconds max to pull this off!"

This was desperate madness. Something in Metcalf's voice told me he knew that, too. "Permission granted . . . and God be with you," I said, whispering the last.

"Metcalf out. See you on the down side, *Joslyn Marie*!"

There were still Guardian fighters in the sky, but the Beefies ignored them—the Guards could never return to base now. Later, one of them surrendered to a Finnish tug. Another tried to crash into Vapaus and died beneath her lasers.

The Beefies gathered themselves into a tight formation, banked out from beneath the big ship, and grabbed for some sky. They shot across *Leviathan*'s starboard wing down toward the planet, a mere flash across her viewports as they raced toward the distant ground.

The great, lumbering ship sailed on through the sky, as if all the battling midges that had sparked and died around her meant nothing to her fate. But New Finland's gravity field reached out and grabbed with gentle, impalpable fingers at the great beast in the sky that now gave itself up to the planet. *Leviathan* fell. She moved not only toward her skyfall in the air of New Finland, but toward her tormentors as well.

The Beefies fired their engines again to slow themselves and let *Leviathan* fall toward them.

The ship began her turnover. With amazing speed for such a giant, the massive craft wheeled end over end and lined up her wings with the winds below.

She came upon the Beefies. Her last laser cannon reached out at terribly close range and touched once, twice, among the tiny fleet, and where that finger touched, ships died.

But then the Beefies fired their engines again and leaped toward her decks as hawks would stoop on their prey.

From each ship, slender cables shot out toward the flight deck. At each cable's end, canisters of vacuum-bonding cement split open; instantly, the glue turned hard as iron.

The tiny ships matched speeds with the great one, using their main engines to brake themselves, matching velocity, and then reeling themselves in with power winches.

Now I understood the modifications Metcalf had ordered for his replacement ships. The cable assemblies were standard equipment for asteroid prospectors who wanted to catch hold of a piece of skyrock. Obviously, the rig worked just as well for catching a ship.

Fifteen ships survived to attempt boarding. Two more were blasted by *Leviathan*'s lasers. Another pair had cable attachment failures. They made it back to orbit and eventually got picked up. Takiko brought his ship in all right, but he hit the deck too hard. He lost cabin air and suit pressure and died fast.

But that left ten sets of lasers, and ten sets of eyes and ears and brains on the enemy deck. The Beefies' lasers were meant to cook ships across the reaches of space. With the power of those, we could hold the deck.

"This is Metcalf. Might be my last call for a while. We're down and alive, ten of us. I've already set off glue bags and I'm pasted in here pretty firm. It should be a hell of a ride."

"Metcalf, that was some sweet work there. We're setting you all down for a Distinguished Flying Cross apiece."

"I'll pass that along to the gang, but if you make it a unit citation you'll save on postage. I've gotta button this can up for the ride down. Metcalf out."

"All right, Joslyn, that's our cue. Get *Uncle Sam* powered up and I'll make sure that lights are out here." After transmitting a final update on the battle situation to Vapaus, I started powering down what systems were still in use aboard the *Joslyn Marie*. The transmission to Vapaus was mostly for the record: Our plans were already too far advanced to change, the fighters were finished with their work, and we didn't have much reason to use the *J.M.*—or anything else—as a battle center anymore.

Now, *Uncle Sam* was needed. I used the comm laser one last time. "LPSS 41 *Joslyn Marie* calling Vapaus control. Prepare all boarding craft. We expect to dock in one hour."

Within minutes, the *J.M.* was powered down, an inert hulk. A radar transponder and acquistion lights were left to guide us back to her, eventually. That, and self-destruct devices hooked to batteries and a radio-link were the only things drawing power.

More quickly than I would have thought possible, we were ready to evacuate the vehicle, as the regulation book would term it. We called it leaving home.

Joslyn and I watched the screens aboard *Uncle Sam* as we pulled away. The tiny set of ack lights blinked every two seconds, and would until someone went aboard and shut them off, or until the *J.M.*'s power cells failed in 30 or 40 years. Beyond that, she was dark and dead and lifeless. I held Joz's hand in mine and watched the shrinking, tumbling ship slide away from us.

I couldn't promise myself we'd be back; I wasn't sure of it.

But then there was a course to lay in, and a whole ship to recheck and check again—and a job to do. It felt good to be in a living ship again, where the ventilators whirred and the helm answered crisply under your pilot's hand.

Next stop was Vapaus, where a boarding crew and weaponry awaited us. Joslyn gave *Sam* the autopilot course and we tried to get ourselves in some sort or shape to fight.

First and foremost, we shared a shower—there wasn't time to take turns, and neither of us was willing to go second, anyway. Once again, we had spent days in the same clothes without benefit of hot water, and there had been a lot of reasons to sweat. I can promise that getting clean was the only thing on our minds. Then, more rich protein foods and vitamins, and fatigue killers to hold us together through the next few hours.

But nothing could keep us away from the viewscreen for long. Korsky had been one of the fliers to make it onto *Leviathan*'s deck. She had managed to use a broadcast antenna to transmit pictures from her nose camera, which was pointed straight forward at the bow of

Leviathan. The Finns picked up the pictures, beamed them to us, and sent along their own images from cameras aboard tugs sent out with the specific job of recording the entry of the great ship from orbit.

Even had it not been the skycastle of the enemy, even if our people had not been uninvited guests aboard, even if our fate was not wrapped up in hers, the flight of *Leviathan* was a spectacle worth watching.

CHAPTER NINETEEN

You get used to things being big in space. Fifty years ago they were building power satellites bigger than Manhattan, and things had gotten bigger since. Vapaus had many times the mass of any ship of sky or sea ever built. In space, *big* made more sense than *little*—if for no other reason, then perhaps to give humanity some intermediate scale between itself and the vast emptiness.

But in the air, in the real sky, beyond a certain size, *big* loses its meaning, no longer gives a sense of scale. *Leviathan* went beyond big and huge and gigantic and every other word for large. No superlative could take it in. Nothing *that big* could possibly fly.

But fly *Leviathan* did. Never was there such an entry, never such a flight. "Hitting air," for a spaceship, is all vast speed and violence, the velocity of orbit converted to the red of glowing heat shields and speeding plunges down to a rate where aerodynamics meant something.

Leviathan entered New Finland's atmosphere at aerodynamic speed, and seemed, from the cameras on the orbital tugs, to float in as gently as a leaf.

From Korsky's camera, *Leviathan* rode the maelstrom. The great ship had her prow pointed square at the planet. And she was falling—there was no mistaking that.

*   *   *

Leviathan was a huge manta-ray shape with a swollen belly. Inside her huge delta wings and inside that belly were the large lift cells, full of either helium or hydrogen. Sandwiched in between the cells were decks for men and ships and equipment. Between the two wings was the main body that contained the office decks and workshops.

Along the sides of the main body, at the mid-deck levels, were the launch and recovery cradles for the spacegoing fighters. These had been the targets of the *Joslyn Marie*'s attack run.

At the topside stern was a huge fin, a vertical stabilizer, which served double duty as a control tower for flight operations.

The main aircraft deck was laid out before the control tower. Aircraft were launched straight over the edge of the bow. Our fighters had pinned themselves down in the middle of the flight deck area, blocking the runways.

Six large, cone-shaped spoilers stood out from the bow of the main deck, forcing the air flow away from the deck so that people and machines could stand on the flight deck without being blown over the stern of the ship as *Leviathan* coursed through the sky at hundreds of kilometers an hour.

Korsky's camera took in a wide expanse of flat deck that cut the world in twain. The forms of two tiny Beefies could be seen in the distance. Korsky zoomed to one of them and we could see a flicker of movement— the pilot waving.

The giant air spoilers started to buck and quiver against the sudden slap of air as *Leviathan* finally reached her appointment with New Finland. Her great size and high speed caused a great pressure wave ahead of the ship, a large shock zone that the ship had to punch through.

Wild, violent eddies of air slapped down hard on the decks. We could see the Beefies buffeted by them and see the view from Korsky's camera scramble and clear as her little fighter was rocked back and forth.

Then tortured wraiths of cloud vapor started to whip

and swirl along the decks. *Leviathan*'s passing was heating and concentrating the minute traces of water vapor into sudden clouds at altitudes where clouds had never been.

Like a view of hell, the too-sharp horizon formed by *Leviathan*'s bow began to glow a dull, sullen red as ablative paint started to vaporize and whisk itself away.

Leviathan dove straight down, right for the planet, seeking the levels of air pressure that would support her wings, gathering as much air speed as she could before pulling out.

New Finland ceased to be a disk and grew to a rounded body in space, and still she swelled, until she commanded every inch of sky not cut off by the ship's deckline. There came an indefinable point where one sensed that the camera was no longer rushing toward a place, but already *there* and travelling *through* that place. *Leviathan* became part of the planet, a member of her sky.

The buffeting grew worse and worse, until there was rarely a moment with a clear view for us. The Beefie pilots must have come close to having the life shaken out of them. The planet, stained hell-red by the heat of re-entry, grew visibly as we watched.

Korsky's broadcast antennae sheared off, and we lost the picture. Metcalf, sounding as if he was getting pretty rattled himself, reported Korsky's ship was still holding together.

A picture from an orbiting tug cut in. The long-range lens zoomed in toward the struggling ship. She was beginning to pull out of her dive, leaving a trail of storm eddies behind her as she fought to bring her nose up.

I swore under my breath. With a long, lazy period, as the movement flowed from wing tip to fuselage and back, the kilometer-wide manta wings were—*flexing, bending*.

"Mac . . . The wings!"

"I know. My God, do those bastards know what they're doing?"

Joslyn forgot whose side was conning that ship and talked to it, pilot to airplane. "Come on, you great bloody beast. Pull out! Get your nose up. Dear lord, I think they're losing the port wing. No, thank God, it's still together. Come on, steady on, easily, you great oaf, or you'll have a wing off for certain!"

It ceased, for a time, to be the flagship of our hated enemy. *Leviathan* was truly a great beast, one of the air, struggling against her wounds and the wrath of her element, fighting to live.

With a crawling in my gut, I remembered that if *Leviathan* didn't make it down, neither would the missile control center. If that went, all would have been for nothing.

Again and again, my hands reached for an invisible pilot's joystick. Some deep-seated love of things that fly wanted to grab that struggling beast and guide her to safe haven and calmer air below.

Slowly, ponderously, with the tortured magnificence of embattled greatness, the beast of the air slowed herself, pulled herself up from a dive into the abyss toward a strong, sure, coursing glide. Gigantic contrails and tiny whirling storms formed in her wake. The ship surged ahead and steadied itself as the air-breathing engines came to life, and the flying aircraft started to cruise.

Leviathan arrived.

Joslyn killed the view from the orbital cameras and suddenly the docking complex on the forward end of Vapaus popped into existence on our forward screen. Joslyn had piloted us in on instruments even as she watched *Leviathan* enter.

As Joslyn warped us in, I changed into my combat flak suit—basically a fairly bullet-proof, fairly laser-reflecting coverall with plenty of pockets—and then went to the feelgood cabinet and found another set of pills for us to down. Super-powered vitamins, over-achieving amphetamines that had a label warning about trying to tear walls off, another anti-fatigue number to suck up the exhaustion elements that clog the blood of a tired man, pyscho-depressants to counter the monomania the speed caused, and a witch's brew more. I downed a set myself and brought Joslyn's dose to her.

She winced as she swalled her share of the little ghastlies, and chased them with a gulp of water from a drinking bulb. "Urg and argh. We shall pay for these indiscretions in tomorrow's dawn."

"If there is a tomorrow. Are you quoting something, or did you make that up, and are we docked yet?"

"I made it up, I think, and our guests are already arriving and I'm not even dressed. Could you see to them while I slip into something more lethal?"

I opened the hatchway to the lower deck as the drugs started to hit me. Suddenly, I was more awake than I had been in weeks. I glanced to the metal handrail to see if I was grabbing it so hard it bent. I wasn't, of course, but the surge of artificial endurance helped a lot. More than a few hours that hopped up could put me in a hospital, but for a little while I could feel normal and then some.

As I reached the deck, the inside of the airlock cycled open and men started to pour through it. A pressure tunnel had been linked to Vapaus's interior, so they could get on board without having to wait through airlock cycles. The first one in wore a second lieutenant's insignia. Of the rest, some were army, but many were in civvies— some of my high-risk volunteers. They knew where they were heading, and they were spoiling for a fight. There were a few women among them. All wore heavy flak jackets and were loaded down with equipment. They carried a pistol and a rifle each. Many also carried a number of vicious-looking throwing knives.

I gestured to the second lieutenant. He was a short, peppery little man with an unruly shock of white-blonde hair and a wicked gleam in his eye. It looked like his nose had been broken at least once. Under it hung a droopy, insolent moustache. He gave me a snappy salute. "Second Lieutenant Raunio, sir."

"Welcome aboard, Lieutenant. We've got about 15 minutes to get your people ready for acceleration. Get all your gear into the storage bays, then flatten down against the padded sections of the lower bulkhead here, and try not to drift off. There are hold-down straps to grab onto, so use them. We may have to do some maneuvering, so don't get started getting your gear on until after you hear the all-clear from us. All right?"

"Yes, sir. That is fine. All of these fellows have done plenty of spacing before today. They know what they are to be doing."

"Good. I hope I know what I'm doing once we get down there."

He smiled wolfishly. "I bet that you do."

I chalked up that ambiguity to translation trouble, saluted again, as he seemed to expect it, and left him yelling orders in Finnish, seasoned with a choice string of obscenities.

I was turning to head back above deck when I spotted a familiar figure. "George!"

He grinned and caught me in a bear hug. "Mac, I didn't think either of us'd still be alive!"

I laughed and neither of us said how likely that was to be changed where we were going. It was one of the times when you talk by *not* saying anything. I didn't tell George this wasn't his fight, or that I was glad to see him, or make any of the other speeches I felt like spouting. From the far off days when he had saved my life by killing one of his own people, George had been alone, cut off, part of no man's country. He had lived divided by his own decency from his own people. He had lived, set off by the names *stranger* and *enemy*, from those he aided. In some strange way Mac Larson, the man George had rescued when Mac was alone among strangers, was the only one he expected to accept him. I knew without thinking he was here because he had decided that the two of us would die together if at all.

That sounded fair to me. But it was time to go, time to launch into battle, and no time for words. I led George above deck.

Joslyn, dressed in battle fatigues and armed to the teeth, smiled her warmest hostess smile when she saw us. "George! Wonderful! You *deserve* to be in on this. And I think the party's just about ready to start."

"How does *Sam* look?" I asked.

"Nice green bird, so far. Vapaus Port Control set records topping off all our tanks, and all systems ticking right along. We'll be ready to boost in plenty of time."

I sat down at my console and put in a call to Marie-Francoise. "How does the situation look?"

"So far, not bad. The escape shell team is on station. There are 15 ships of one sort or another ready to follow you down. Metcalf and his pilots haven't been bothered too much yet. Nothing that can get past their shipboard lasers. Good weather down there. *Leviathan* is following a due-west ground-track, headed toward the coastal town of Vipurii, and sunlight is about at local noon where they put her down. Joslyn already has the projected target area logged into her navigation systems. The others will follow your beacon down."

"Any change in our target?"

"No. You'll still head for the main radio room. So have the radio direction finder ready."

All the assault teams were to carry a "black box" that was keyed to electronic "noise" of the sort the control station from Vapaus was found to give off: the *Leviathan* station should give off the same noise.

"Good luck, Mac."

"And to you, Marie-Francoise. *Uncle Sam* out." I cut the connection. There was an unnatural sense of calm aboard the *Uncle Sam*. The dangers were once again clear and clean. Our skins were on the line, the outcome was sure to be decided soon, and for all time. In a few hours we would be living winners or dead losers. As we strapped into our crash couches, it was even a strange and frightening sort of comfort to know that my wife, my friend, and I would die together, if at all.

Then Joslyn pushed some buttons, and we went in.

The instant the engines lit, calm was forgotten. I could feel my heart start to race. The battle was joined, and I found my hands over the laser controls without willing them there.

But there was an atmosphere to punch through first. *Uncle Sam*'s engines roared in the silence of space, and the ship dropped toward the planet far below. Finnish crews in other ships followed in formation, the ships separated by several kilometers.

Stars, *Stripes*, and a dozen unarmed ballistic landers, mostly of the *Kuu* class, lit their jets along with us. The pilots were tug captains, merchantmen without battle training. They were all we had.

If every ship made it down, we could put 200 troops aboard *Leviathan*.

Joslyn took us in at a steady one-gee boost, spinning the ship end over end to start braking as we neared the planet. At constant boost, the trip to the edge of the atmosphere took brief minutes.

At the very fringes of the atmosphere, Joslyn cut the engines. We rode in zero-gee for a few seconds, and then an almost imperceptible tugging from below grew to a gut-crushing force that slammed me into the acceleration couch. I discovered four new places where a combat suit could cut into you. We had hit the air.

Joslyn was taking us in hard and fast, using the steepest possible re-entry angle to get us there soonest, to give *Leviathan*'s radar as little time as possible to look us over.

The acceleration eased off gradually as we shed our great speed. Our formation had floated off a bit during re-entry, and the other ships skittered in closer to us and dove toward our target. This part of the job the tug commanders knew well, and the stragglers zipped back into their slots quickly.

We fell deeper and deeper into the air.

"Okay, Joz, I just picked up *Leviathan* on radar. We're over her horizon."

"Right, Mac. I've got her. Right where she ought to be, give or take a kilometer. We're on course."

High cloud cover was between us and our prey. I tried to raise Metcalf on a radio frequency.

"Able Archer, this is *Uncle Sam*. Come in, please."

"This is Able Archer. Come on in, we're holding your seat. It's getting a little hot, boss man, so step on it, if you please. They're trying to get fighters airborne, but we've cooked three as they came up from below deck. Some kind of troops on deck, too, but we've got 'em sort of under control. Korsky's laser is just about out of juice, and the rest of us aren't far behind. Take the heat off us and maybe we can recharge our power cells. And hold just a sec—*something* scrambled past from below decks just now. They've gotten a fighter off somehow."

"Yeah, must be a drop-launch rig on the underside of the ship. We track the bandit—make that two—headed for us. Can you give us any visual?"

"Maybe. You're at extreme range, but camera on anyway."

A swirl of static filled the screen and settled down to a steady, but snowy picture of *Leviathan*'s main deck. As we watched, a blur zipped past and a third bandit appeared on our screen. We were still 500 kilometers from *Leviathan*, but closing very fast.

The enemy fighters were gunning right for us. I picked them up on our own long-range cameras. I jockeyed around the laser cannon and fired. The first bloomed into a fireball within seconds. I nailed the second just as quickly. The third peeled off suddenly and dove for the ground, then came up from below, straight up our tailpipe.

Our stern lasers were still stowed in the hull. The stern was right in the airstream. If I unlimbered them now, they'd be torn off before I could shoot.

"I'm on it, Mac," Joslyn said calmly. "All ships, break

formation and land at will." She wrestled *Uncle Sam* out of glide and fired the fusion engines. That killed the third bandit.

"Nice shooting, you guys. I think I've got you on visual now," Metcalf radioed. "Wave at the camera and smile. And here come three more of the little devils—no, make that two, and chalk up a bandit to Gilbert."

Our ships scattered as the pilots starting thrusting. The view from Metcalf's camera showed a hazy sky full of tiny points of light moving in fast.

We broke through the cloud layer and there was *Leviathan* laid out below us, an island in the sky, an island under siege. From Metcalf's camera, we saw *Uncle Sam*, the proud stars and stripes painted on her hull clearly visible, sailing on toward battle. The two fighters Metcalf had called rose toward us and then died under my lasers. No more followed them.

The *Leviathan* lumbered majestically through the sky, here and there fires burning on her deck, which was spotted with the burned-out hulks of ships the Beefies had cooked as they tried to launch. The great ship resembled some great monster of the sea as she came boldly on, a satanic magnificence in her lines.

"Shifting to aux engines," Joslyn reported. *Uncle Sam* lurched for a moment as Joz shunted power to the chemical rockets from the fusion engine. The fusion job would melt most deck plates to slag, and slag is hard to set down on, and even harder to walk on. The chem engines gulped fuel more quickly and used it less efficiently, but the temperatures were a lot more reasonable.

We headed for a landing.

And the whole outside world turned red before the camera died.

"Boss man! That last main laser! In the control tower."

Joslyn cut our engines, we dropped like a stone, and in a few seconds were below the great ship. The laser could not hit us without chopping through *Leviathan*'s own deck plates.

"That was too bloody close. Mac, can you hit that tower with a torp?"

"I can try. Gun those jets, while they're on another target." Directly above us, the ruby beam refocused on a new victim, one of the Finnish ships. Her captain tried to boost out of there, but the laser moved faster than he could. The little merchantman went up in a mushroom cloud of fire. I felt a sick feeling at the pit of my stomach.

Joslyn slammed down the manual engine controls, and we sprang back into the air over *Leviathan*. She killed the main jets and hit the attitude jets to bring our nose over until we were exactly upside down, falling straight into the ship's deck, bringing the nose-launching tubes to bear directly on the control fin. I fired every tube at once, dead at the still-firing laser cannon. In the split second before Joslyn maneuvered again, I could see four tiny beams from the Beefies on the deck firing at the tower as well. Joz let the torps get away, then spun us around through 90 degrees and fired the engines again to get out of the way of the deck as it seemed to rush up from below us.

Again we fell past the deck of the enemy ship and toward the planet's surface.

"Randall, how'd we do?" I radioed.

"They're out of business for sure, now. Come on in, Mac. We've got the red carpet out."

"Just a second, Mac. As long as we're down there, let's get that ventral launch tube," Joslyn said.

"Do it."

She braked our fall, more gently this time, and held us in a hover with *Leviathan* directly above us. I spotted a long, tunnel-like extrusion that ran down the center-line of the ship, open at both ends. "That's got to be it, Joslyn." I loosed another flight of torps. I flew them by remote control and scooted them down the tunnel. Bright orange explosions thundered and belched fire out each end of it.

"That ought to hold 'em for a while. Let's get to it."

Joslyn bumped up the engines and took us up over the deckplates.

Three of our ships had landed. Two more came in as we watched. Joslyn jogged the maneuvering jets and we swept out over the giant deck. It was as if we had come to fly over a great, flat plateau, a mountain in the clouds. Here and there across the great plain our ships were coming in to land.

We settled down onto the deck of *Leviathan*. Joslyn brought us in as gently as she could, easing out the landing jacks and coming down smoothly, the hydraulics softening the touchdown.

"Well, we made it."

"So far. Let's see how our passengers took it all." I turned on the below-deck cameras. "Lieutenant, we're on the deck. All clear. How are your men holding up?"

A groggy Lieutenant Raunio wobbled to his feet and waved at the camera. "Not too badly to me, sir. Two or three got the air-sickness, but I will make them do the cleaning up later."

"Sounds fair to me. For now, get them ready to move."

I watched the nose cameras, now panning the deck below us, out of the corner of my eye as I talked, and then switched my full attention to the exterior. "Metcalf, what's going on down there?"

"Hiya, Mac. Welcome aboard. Things have been sort of quiet for a while, but they pulled down a deck elevator a few minutes ago, and I think it's headed back with a reception committee. Call the bow twelve o'clock, and it's about four o'clock, 200 meters from your position. We lost Gilbert a few minutes ago. Someone got in close with a grenade, it looks like."

"Okay, I see it. I'll keep a beamer on it. Joslyn, go ahead with the ground coolers, and let's get that crowd outside."

Joslyn hit a switch and opened the liquid nitrogen valve. The super-cold liquid poured out onto the rocket-heated deck plates and boiled away into vapor, crashing the deck temp down hundreds of degrees. We sat tight for a minute or two, waiting to see if the deck plates held up to the strains of the sudden temperature shift. But nothing cracked and collapsed under us. We unbuttoned the ship.

"Mac! Here comes that elevator!" Joslyn called.

I fired the laser cannon. A jet fighter exploded into flame as it rose into view. The elevator lurched to a stop a few meters short of the deck line. The nose of the jet was lined up on *Uncle Sam.* They would have used the fighter's guns and missiles on us right from the deck.

Another elevator, half a kilometer away, rose into view, a fighter on the platform. As soon as the plane reached deck level, its guns opened up on one of the Finnish ships. Incendiary bullets found the hydrogen tanks, and the Finn exploded. I put an air-to-air torpedo to use ground-to-ground and the Guardian fighter followed its victim into annihilation. "Jesus, how many of those elevators have they got left? Metcalf? Metcalf! Come in!"

I spotted a figure jogging across the deck toward us. I lowered the lasers on it. "I *will* come in, if you get the damn hatch open!" I heard over the radio. There was a sharp explosion from a way off, and the figure—Metcalf, of course—threw itself flat on the deck and covered its head.

The fires of the explosion settled down, and Metcalf got up and started running again. Joslyn popped the inner and outer hatches at the same time, and 30 seconds later Metcalf was past the Finns on the lower deck and in the control cabin, gulping air, leaning again the cabin wall. "Okay, so I cut that a little close," he said. "And by the way, there's a pretty good breeze out there. Those wind-spoiler cones they've got coming up off the edge of the forward deck kill most of the airflow, but there's still enough left to keep you *nice* and cool."

"What did you do, blow up your own ship?"

"Right. We've got to get through that deck and get below. I wanted to knock a hole in it. I overloaded everything and set off all my ammo, too."

I looked at the screen and shook my head. Where Metcalf's ship had been was nothing but a few scraps of smoking metal, and a smooth, undented, perfect expanse of deck.

Metcalf took a look for himself and swore. "Damn! That stuff is *tough*. Their own troops weren't afraid to throw grenades at us and hit their own ship's deck."

"We'll have to take one of the hatchways."

"And they'll be waiting for us."

"Mac! Radar!"

The screen was lousy with blips. "What the hell?"

"That's the escape shell troops!"

"Yeah, *some* of the blips," Metcalf said. "But the big guys are bogies. Shoot first and ask questions later. Call 'em bandits and torch them."

I reached for the laser controls, hesitated, then kicked in a radio frequency we hadn't used yet. A torrent of Finnish thundered down at us before I could reach the volume control. "If those are bandits, they're awfully good actors." I slapped the intercom switch to the lower deck. "Lieutenant, get your man with the best English up here on the double."

"My English is damn good enough, sir!" Raunio announced as he came through the deck hatch.

"Fine, just get on the horn there. It looks like we've got Finnish jets out there and—"

My words were drowned out by the roar of a jet zooming overhead on a strafing run. "Give me taking the microphone," he said. Raunio talked urgently with the flier. They seemed to come to a quick understanding, and the Finnish aircraft pulled out to fly a wide patrol circle around the ship. "Now he knows who's who," Raunio said simply.

"Here come the parachutists," Joslyn said. Tiny parasols dotted the sky and rushed toward us as *Leviathan* cruised toward the piece of sky that held them.

Raunio said, "One of the Finnish pilots to be saying some sort of troops forming up near over by the base of that big control fin."

"Out of line-of-fire for our lasers. This is what they call all hell breaking loose," Metcalf said morosely.

"Well, it's time we contributed. Randall, I hope you've got a gun."

I went down the ladder to the lower deck. The Finnish soldiers were just about ready to go, checking each other's equipment. I grabbed my own weapons, including a rocket launcher, a scaled-down version of one Krabnowski had died carrying. I checked over the direction finder that had been keyed to the control station's noise pattern. There was no chance of a reading out here on the open deck, but I could see that the power light came on. I shoved it into my backpack.

"Lieutenant!" I called. "Over here." We went over to the hatchway. "Here is the situation. The deck is too tough to blow a hole in it. There's a deck elevator stuck halfway up the shaft, with a blown-up jet burning on it. That elevator's our way into the ship. Get a squad to get in close enough to put that fire out. We've got foam bombs on board."

A ballistic lander like *Uncle Sam* tended to set a lot of brush fires; foam bombs that would smother the flames and get rid of the heat were standard gear.

"Okay. Leave it to us doing it," Raunio said. He shouted at his troops, a squad of them grabbed the foam bombs from the racks, and then he stepped to the open hatch, fired a few covering rounds, and jumped to the deck of the ship. I followed out, scrambling down the hatch ladder and dropping the last meter or two to the deck of *Leviathan*. George, Metcalf, and Joslyn came down the ladder.

That scene, more than any other, is etched completely into my mind. There was a crystal-clear air of unreality about what I saw, all the colors brighter, all the distances bigger, all the strangeness of what I saw more alien than it should have been.

As we stepped out of *Uncle Sam*, *Leviathan* came out from under the cloud cover that had blanketed the sun, and everything stood out in bold, clear relief. To the stern, the control fin stood 50 meters high, its apex blasted into twisted shards by *Uncle Sam*'s torpedoes. The wreckage of the control tower and the laser station atop it burned. Finnish and Guardian ships scattered across the broad expanse of the deck were still aflame. The brilliant orange flames stood out against the dark grey hull metal. Inky black smoke poured forth from the wrecks and floated almost lazily up a few meters. There, beyond the protection of the spoilers at the bow of the ship, the smoke was suddenly smashed into wild tendrils that snarled into fantastic knots before vanishing completely behind the fast-moving ship.

As our troops descended from *Sam*, the last of the Finnish ships set down and dropped its cloud of nitrogen coolant. Small bands of soldiers were beginning to come out from the ships. We heard the chatter of automatic weapons.

There was nothing but ship and sky; *Leviathan* flew too high and her topside was too wide for us to see the ground from the deck. The swift ship had left the clouds far behind. The sky was now a bold cobalt blue, laced with thin traceries of perfect white clouds. There was nothing but orange flame, black smoke, grey deck, blue sky, and white cloud. A universe of elemental colors.

Into this world came those who had fallen from heaven to the attack. The ship rushed beneath the vanguard of the parachutists. As they passed over the deck, they fired glue bombs on cables, smaller versions of what the Beefies had used.

Twenty of them came over the deck at the same moment. Of those, one or two failed to get their cables fired off properly and they simply sailed over the stern of the ship to land below on the surface of the planet. The rest caught the deck properly and their parachutes were suddenly great kites as the cables came taut and brutally yanked harness and chute, dragging the chutist forward with the speed of the ship.

Three or four must have been killed by that savage pull, their necks broken, as they did nothing to save themselves, but merely hung in the wind, macabre decorations suspended in the sky.

The others survived to activate the small power winches at the ends of the cables and pull themselves out of the sky safely down to the deck.

More of the chutists came on. Some were too low and their chutes vanished under the keel of the ship. The riders must have been smashed flat by the impact with the hull of the ship, pasted there like bugs on a windshield.

Some of those who came too high landed safely on the planet. One sailed through the billowing flame at the apex of the control fin and kept on going, a human torch aflame. He hung from his chute writhing in pain, until the flames that cooked him melted the chute's shroud lines. He dropped away suddenly, and the speed of his fall instantly extinguished the flames. Just as he vanished under the stern, I saw a reserve chute pop open. I never found out if he made it to the ground alive.

Nearly 200 men and women rode escape shells from orbit toward the deck of *Leviathan*. Something less than 100 actually made it to the deck in one piece. But, God, did we need that 100. We needed every piece of covering fire we had.

Metcalf shook his head and turned to George as we stood, watching the battle before joining it. "Marie-Francoise kept telling us that this was a flying office building, just a military command center," he said. "Designed and built to be frightening, with not all *that* many troops and war planes. She may be right, but on the other hand, it works. I'm scared."

It took less than two minutes for *Leviathan* to pass through the whole of the parachute force. Raunio by that time had his team ready to take care of that burning jet. He led four men toward the elevator at a dogtrot. They got within 10 meters of it when someone below deck started taking potshots at them. They hit the deck instantly. Raunio lobbed a grenade, there was a thud and a puff of grey smoke, and the shooting stopped. Immediately the five men got up and started heaving the foam bombs into the burning wreck. The bombs reacted quickly in the intense heat, expanding into a dense purplish foam that fizzed up over the flames, dousing the fire.

A second team jogged out carrying small tanks of liquid nitrogen. They tossed them onto the elevator stage and shot a few holes in them. The nitrogen boiled out onto the stage and vanished in a cloud of steam as it contacted the intensely hot deck plates. I hoped that would cool the elevator stage down enough to walk on it in insulated boots. Raunio turned toward the ship and gestured *come on*. Leaving five troops behind to hold *Sam*, the remainder of our force ran across *Leviathan*'s terribly exposed deck to the jammed elevator.

The thing had stopped about a man's height short of the main deck, leaving a wide gap for us to enter the ship by. Raunio posted two guards outside and the rest us jumped down to the still-hot, but bearable elevator stage. Someone tossed down a pile of rope ladders, which we hooked over parts of the foamed-over wreck of the jet on the stage.

The ladders were about 10 meters long, which was just about enough to reach the deck below. We climbed down. I saw our sniper. Raunio's bomb had splattered him a little.

The plane had obviously touched off a fire down here when it exploded. The deck was a charred disaster. Five other fighters, in various states of ruin, stood like boggle-eyed monsters in their bays, burned and scorched. I caught a whiff of cooked meat, and my stomach almost rebelled. It had been a flash fire—white hot for a few seconds, then gone. Hydrogen fuel, probably. The sniper must have come in after it was out. No one who was here when it happened was still alive. No one could be.

We were inside the skin, if not the belly, of the beast. We posted a guard to hold our exit and went on.

We were on the port side of the ship, about halfway across the wing. Our team was to try for the most likely location of the missile control system: along the center-line, under the big vertical stabilizer and control fin.

We moved. I set Raunio in the van with the same men he led to the hanger, put myself next along with Joslyn, then the rest of the Finns, then George, and Metcalf in the rear.

It took a minute or two with a flashlight to find an exit in the gloom of the charred hangar deck, but then we spotted it and got set to go through it.

Raunio planted himself in front of the closed hatch and gestured for one of his men to open it. Raunio stood with machine pistol drawn and face set as the door whipped open.

Nothing there.

He dove and rolled into the corridor, jogged down to the starboard cross-corridor, then signalled to the rest waiting at the hatchway.

He gestured us on, and we moved silently into the ship.

We headed down a corridor that led to starboard, toward the centerline of the ship. We started out at a cautious walk, carefully checking each cross-corridor. This part of the ship seemed deserted, untouched, pristine. Yet in the emptiness was something that unnerved, that made our feet move fast, that made us start to hurry, almost running along the corridor. The brightly lit ways seemed haunted, watchful, and we made the best speed we could.

On and on we went, sometimes slowing cautiously, sometimes racing ahead.

The corridors were numbered at each cross-corridor in severely stenciled characters. The signs put us on B deck, corridor 36. The cross-corridors were numbered P-16, P-15, P-14, and so on. I took them to mean portside, X number of corridors from centerline.

A sudden, sharp, explosion from nearby put us back in the shooting war. I almost walked up Raunio's back as he dropped to his belly and sighted sternward along the next cross-corridor. He fired at something, there was another explosion farther off, and he was back on his feet, moving again.

We rushed on our way, always toward starboard and the stern.

"Behind!" I heard Metcalf yell, and the corridor we had just walked past was lost in a swirl of fire and explosion.

We took cover as best we could and shot back until whoever it was stopped shooting. We left two dead, and kept moving.

Again we were fired upon, this time from dead ahead. I realized that the fire had to be coming from the main corridor through ship's centerline. There the Guardians were set to repel boarders.

I pulled my rocket-thrower out of my backpack and loaded in a set of incendiaries. I fired three of the vicious little things and they spurted away. A brief moment later the concourse billowed with flame—then darkness and silence. Somebody behind me tossed a smoke grenade into the dark, and we moved.

The smoke hung there for a long time. We moved into the main corridor, the muffled sound of other fire fights coming from far off.

Joslyn jabbed me in the ribs and nodded off to the right. There was a broad companionway, a ship's stairway, leading belowdeck. Hand signals moved down the line of soldiers and we headed down it deeper into the ship. "C" Deck was quiet. Raunio left two men as a posted guard. Down, in the preternatural silence, to "D," "E," "F," leaving two guards at each level. Raunio didn't like dispersing his force, but it was the best guarantee of our getting back.

We paused at the top of the companionway to "G" deck, and I took a look at the direction finder. The vertical plane indicator was still pointing slightly down; at least one more deck to go.

Whiffs of gunpowder, tendrils of smoke, the burnt-rubber smell of cooked insulation drifted through the air. Off in the distance was the popping chatter of small arms fire, and every now and again, a deep rumble that gently vibrated the deck as a larger explosion went off somewhere. But here, around us, it was quiet. As quiet as a trap about to be sprung.

Raunio peered down the companionway to "G," then tossed a smoke grenade down it. The smoke billowed forth, oozing down the corridor and up toward us. As it spread, small arms fire began, closer, harder. Explosions went off, and a laser hissed somewhere.

Raunio pointed to a faint beam of light betrayed by the smoke. It was at about waist-height in the companionway, halfway down. Joslyn made a snip-snip motion with her hand and took off her backpack. She got a set of wire cutters out of a compact set of tools. She lay face up in the corridor and gestured for me to grab her ankles. I did so and started to slide her down the companionway. Her helmet scraped over the steps. With tiny, fluttering motions of her free hand, she told me how far to slide her down. When she was under the booby trap, she gestured *stop* emphatically.

The wire cutters went click, click, and the faint beam of light died—and the lasers with it.

I was about to pull her up when she gestured to be slid farther down. Another one, and another. Then the third trap was clear and the entrance to "G" deck was open.

Now we knew what to look for. Three other photobeam gadgets were easy to spot as we moved down the corridor.

I checked the D/F unit. No vertical component; we were on the right deck. The thing pointed out a hell of a source, straight back to sternward. We were getting close.

We moved toward the stern. Raunio posted two more guards, and we were down to 12 men. Probably just as well; more would have gotten in the way down here.

Now were we deep, deep within the belly of that beast. For the first time in my life, I began to understand claustrophobia. We were *inside* the enemy. He was before us, behind us, to port, to starboard, above, below. He could come for us from any direction at any moment.

Now, at each crossing of a corridor, Raunio went through an agony of care, kneeling to the deck, sticking his pistol out before his head, holding a throwing knife at the ready in his other hand, checking both directions with a quick, sudden shake of his head back and forth, then again, both ways, before he was satisfied.

On and on it went, stopping our quiet progress every few dozen meters to go through the routine again. Then, finally, there came a time when Raunio stuck his head out and retracted it instantly to look at a bullet ricocheting off the piece of deck where his head had been.

He scrambled to his feet, gathered himself for a spring, leaped across the intersection, spraying the air with fire from midjump. There was a dull thud. I dropped to the deck and fired blindly down the corridor in both directions. There were bodies down on both sides of the intersection. Raunio ran to one, put his pistol to the back of the head and fired, then did the same for the others. I wondered if he was mutilating the dead or killing the wounded. I doubt if he knew, or cared: he simply wasn't taking chances.

I didn't have time to mull it over—I found myself shooting at something without stopping to think. I heard Raunio curse and the whir of a knife flying past my ear. I dropped to the deck and kept firing. One Guardian was down with a knife in his throat, another kept shooting back. I reached for the rocket-thrower and blipped three more of the brutes at them. Too late I remembered I had it loaded with incendiaries. A half second later the corridor was full of the stomach-churning stench of burning human flesh. There was a great wailing scream that stopped as Raunio fired into the flames. A wall of heat and flame rolled down toward us, reaching close enough to shrivel my eyebrows and eyelashes before it shrunk back. There was nothing beside people in the corridor that would burn, and the flames guttered quickly down to nothing.

This was the place. I could feel it. Booby traps, the guards. . . . I pulled the D/F unit out again, and it pointed straight as an arrow down the cross-corridor.

"This is it. Come on." My words broke a silence that, but for cursing and gunfire, had lasted for what seemed like hours. We had been inside the ship 23 minutes.

I led the way and Raunio grew eyes in the back of his head as he took up the rear. I tried to step over the still-smoldering corpses without looking or smelling. Or thinking. The demons gibbered at the base of my skull.

Joslyn raised her pistol and fired as a bullet pinged off my helmet. I felt a numbing shock and looked down at my chest. A second bullet had slammed into my flak suit and flattened into a shapeless mass imbedded in it. Without thinking, I reached to brush it off and burned my fingers on the slug, still hot from the gun barrel and the impact. I stuck the burned fingers in my mouth and sucked at them, wincing at the pain. As I sat there, some part of me yelled to get up, keep moving, get shooting. Suddenly I felt a good swift kick in the rear, and Metcalf grabbed me by the collar, pulled me to my feet, and got me moving.

"C'mon, boss man. He's dead, not you." He nodded to the corpse Joslyn had made as we passed it.

"Thanks, Randall."

"Forget it. All part of the service."

And I pulled him down as another gunner popped into view. We fell to the deck with a jarring slam. The gunner had nothing but a gun, a hand, and an eye visible as he peered out from the cover of the next intersection. My pistol was in my hand. I settled myself into the approved prone firing position and carefully squeezed the trigger twice. On the second shot, that eye died, and the hand dropped the pistol.

I glanced down at the D/F. It was going crazy, whirling its pointer around and around, every light lit. We were right on top of the control station. I walked forward a few meters to an unmarked door. "This is it," I said.

Joslyn handed me a blob of plastic explosive. I jammed

pieces of it into the hatch handle, the four corners, made a guess as to where the hinges were and slapped blobs there, too. Joslyn followed me, jamming tiny radio control fuses into each glob of the stuff.

We signalled the others to flatten themselves against the bulkhead that the hatch was in and did so ourselves. Joslyn hit the button on the radio trigger and KABLOOM happened. We were all deafened by the blast. The hatch leaped out of the frame and slammed into the opposite inside wall with a resounding *clang* that was the only thing loud enough for us to hear. A cloud of dust and smoke jumped out of the hatchway.

Raunio stepped through and fired three times. I went in second and found three dead men. I saw a flicker of movement and blasted at it. Four dead men.

The smoke cleared away quickly.

This was it.

Here, in this compartment, were the transmitters that controlled the anti-ship missiles that lurked in the outer reaches of this star system. Here, if the commands the Finnish technicians had figured out from their examination of the wrecked Vapaus command center were correct, we could order that system to self-destruct, tell the killing missiles to die. The League ships that waited on the fringes of interstellar space could pour into the system, and the war would be won at a stroke.

This was it.

Joslyn and I knew what to do. We had trained on the recovered Vapaus unit dozens of times. Elsewhere in the ship were other teams that had trained just as hard, were just as ready. One other team besides us had been sent to this location. It was never heard from.

I tried to talk to Joslyn, to say, "Let's get started." But I could not hear myself. Joslyn's lips moved, and I heard nothing. I was deafened. It sunk in. So was Joslyn. So were the others. That was bad, that was very bad.

The two control panels were set with their backs to each other, so the only way to synchronize the commands was by calling them out so the following operator could know what the lead operator was doing. If we couldn't hear, the job was impossible.

We spent a long, harrowing ten minutes, first trying to get the Finns and Metcalf to understand the problem, and then yelling our heads off until we could hear each other over the ringing in our ears, while an increasingly edgy Raunio kept watch over the corridors.

Finally, with our throats raw and our ears still sore from the beating they had taken, Joslyn and I got to work.

The Vapaus technicians had provided us with skeleton keys based on the locks on the station recovered there, but there was a more reliable source for keys at hand. We took them from the dead bodies of the two Guardian operators.

We engaged the system.

"Key one in," Joslyn called.

"Key one in," I confirmed.

"Turn key one to first position at my command. Ready, steady, go!"

We flipped the keys over one click and a green light came on over my board.

"Key two in," Joslyn said.

"Key two in."

"Turn key two to first position. Ready, steady, go!"

A second light came on.

"Key one right hand," she called. "Key two left hand. Key one and key two to second positions simultaneously. Ready, steady, go!"

Two more lights appeared and a panel slid open before me. Inside, a new set of controls. Then, off in the distance, I heard gunfire.

"Now grasp Mode Select Switch. At my signal, turn three notches to Full Manual Override. I will count off each click stop. Stop one—now. Stop two—now. Stop three—now." Joslyn's voice came more and more clearly to me, pure and sure in its calmness. Again, in the distance, was the clatter of gunplay. It seemed louder.

"Left thumb over Mode Activate One. Right thumb

over Mode Activate Two. Depress both simultaneously on my signal. Ready. Steady. Go!"

Suddenly, a loud, recorded voice boomed out in a harsh nasal accent. "You have activated the Full Manual Override system. You have 30 seconds to lay in a correct command. If no correct command is received in 30 seconds, the controls will lock, this compartment will seal automatically, and poison gas will be introduced. Thirty seconds—mark."

Joslyn's voice came from behind me, as calmly as ever. "Release safety cover over self-destruct command button. Ready, steady, go. Three inner switches are revealed."

"Twenty seconds, mark," said the recording.

"At my signal, depress leftmost switch. Ready, steady, go. Rightmost switch. Ready, steady, go. Final switch, the center switch, and cross your fingers with your free hand, my love! Ready, steady—GO!"

The control panel in front of me lit up like a Christmas tree. A new recording boomed away in the same old voice. "You have set the anti-ship missile system to self-destruct. If no countermand is laid in within five minutes, self-destruct commands will be radioed to anti-ship missiles. Five minutes, mark. Thirty seconds after self-destruct transmission, this control system will automatically clear all its memory space and operating systems if no countermand is laid in. Four minutes, 45 seconds, mark."

With a whoop of joy we were in each other's arms. Then there was a roar of gunnery, very close. Metcalf yelled to us, "Not so fast, kids. We may not get that five minutes."

Raunio and George were firing in both directions down the corridor from inside the hatchway.

I snarled and slapped a load of high-explosive rockets into the launcher. I stuck the launcher out into the corridor and fired once, each way. The explosions knocked us all from our feet, shook us to our bones, and redeafened us all.

I looked out the hatchway. Not only was there no one left in the corridor to shoot at us, there wasn't much left in the way of corridor.

And we waited through the longest minutes of my life. Toward the end of it, we could hear again.

"Ninety seconds, mark," said the recording.

I toyed with the idea of putting a bullet through that speaker.

Guns and lasers came from the corridor again. Raunio and his men returned the fire. That was going to be a tough way to get out. I decided not to try it. We still had plastique left to play with. The stuff was "directionalized" and color coded, yellow and blue. The force of the explosive was directed in the direction of the yellow side. If you wanted a plain old any-which-way explosion, you kneaded the stuff into a homogeneous green lump.

I climbed up on a stool, took all the directional I had left, and rolled it out with the yellow side against the overhead bulkhead, forming circle about a half-meter around. The overhead was aluminum, not the super-tough material used on the outer hull. We'd get through it. I shoved four of the radio fuses into it and hopped back down.

"Sixty seconds," the nasal robot voice announced.

One of the Finnish volunteers spun around and fell to the deck with her forehead missing.

"Christ," Metcalf said. "C'mon you damn recording, get that signal sent or we all end up goddamn hamburger!"

I pulled the stool out of the way of the coming explosion and watched the fighters at the door. There was no room for another gun there. All we could do was watch the moments die.

"Come on, Mister Machine, tell us about 30 seconds," Metcalf muttered.

I coughed and spat out a mouthful of gunpowder-flavored slime. I noticed my hands were badly cut up and wondered when it had happened.

Finally, the good news came: "Thirty seconds, mark."

"Thought it had broken down on us," Metcalf said.

"Not yet, and you just hope it doesn't for 31 seconds," I replied.

Raunio tossed a grenade in each direction down the corridor. Smoke belched in the door and filled the compartment.

"Fifteen seconds."

"Raunio! We're going out through the ceiling! Be ready to fire your last rounds. George! Get back here!"

"Ten seconds."

"Get in here!" I yelled to the Finns. Raunio shoved his machine pistol into his holster, lobbed one more grenade in each direction, and backed away from the hatchway. He turned and grinned at me. His face was blackened with grime, his hair singed half away, and three long slashes bled freely from his left ear to his chin. "Okay, Mister Larson, sir, get us out of here!" he yelled as the grenades bellowed from the hallway.

George holstered his pistol and scrambled to his feet. He nodded to me and leaned back again the wall, exhausted.

"Five seconds."

"Four."

"Three."

"Two."

Joslyn had her finger on the radio fuse detonator.

"One."

Then there was no sound but the gunfire in the hall. A pause longer than any life.

A click.

The nasal voice returned. "All anti-ship missiles have been radioed to self-destruct. Signals will reach missiles in four to ten hours. Control system will shut down and erase in 30 seconds."

We had won.

We had won the war.

Joslyn pushed the trigger and the charge went off with a wild roar that engulfed the room anew in smoke. For long seconds it was too dense to see anything.

Finally it cleared to show a slab of aluminum hanging from the overhead bulkhead by a single-crazily twisted shred about the size of my finger. I pulled out my laser and slashed it down. It swung down to the deck with a clanging thud.

Bullets spattered the bulkhead opposite the hatchway. A half dozen guns fired as one and an enemy soldier dropped into the compartment, a bloody ruin.

Metcalf and Raunio poured fire through the hatch as I grabbed the stool and set it under the hole in the overhead. I grabbed Joslyn and half shoved, half threw her through it. George followed, then the Finnish privates.

"Metcalf! Raunio! You!" I fired my own pistol into the hatch; Metcalf was through the hole in less than two seconds. Raunio was on his heels, and I was on his.

I looked around me. We were in what looked like an officer's cabin. Then I saw the officer. Very dead. Joslyn had put a bullet between his eyes before he could lift his pistol from his side.

Raunio kicked open the hatch into the corridor and we got the hell out of there.

We tried as best we could to follow the path we had used on "G" deck, one level down, but it seemed "F" was laid out differently.

We were lost in record time. Raunio was in the lead again, wasting no time in caution now. He careered around every corner with his gun blazing in case anyone was there. I looked up at the corridor numbers and swore. We were headed the wrong way. I yelled for Raunio. "You maniac! That's the wrong way!"

We turned and headed back toward the bow.

I turned us to starboard and then back toward the bow, so that we were on Starboard corridor one. I figured Centerline was most likely to be held in force. We hauled down S-1. We needed to get to Forward corridor 36, F-36 and Centerline being where we had left our guards posted.

I remembered something important and pulled out my radio. "All League and Finn troops! Code word

PAYDIRT. PAYDIRT. Mission accomplished. Retreat, escape, save yourselves, mission accomplished and pass the word." I tossed the radio at Raunio and told him to repeat that in Finnish. We kept moving.

The air was acrid, carrying the smell of fire and sweat. F-50. Fourteen more to go.

There was a section of collapsed bulkhead blocking S-1. We jogged starboard to S-2 and kept moving, shifted back to S-1 four intersections down, at F-42.

On and on. I turned us to starboard and then back toward the bow, so that we were on Starboard corridor one. And we found the intersection of Centerline and Forward 36.

Two surprised Finnish guards almost blew us away before they recognized us. We yelled for the guards left on "G" deck and swarmed up the companionway, leaving them to follow.

"F" deck to "B" deck. Four flights of stairs, or companionways, or whatever. That might not seem like much, but try it after the day we had had. The guards from each deck joined us as we passed. By the time we clambered up to "B" there were spots in front of my eyes and I was heaving my lungs to grab all the air I could.

We were lucky up until then. But Centerline, "B" deck was the site of a pitched battle. We were pinned down by fire coming from the direction of the bow. Five meters forward of us I saw a companionway leading to "A" deck; topside, the flight deck, out. It was damn tempting. But we couldn't stick our noses out of the companionway leading up from "C" deck without getting blasted. Ten meters the other way was the corridor we had come down to get this far, less than one long hour ago.

I sat there. My force and I were panting with exhaustion, and exhaustion decided me on which way to go. I knew we could not make it down to portside and then run all that way back on the flight deck. We had to go for the shortcut.

And we had to go. We had to get out now if we were

going to live. We had to fight our way out now, or not at
all. I slapped the last clip of incendiaries into the rocket
launcher. "Raunio," I said. "Signal your men at the
elevator that we're not headed that way. We're heading
straight out that companionway ahead." I kept my head
down and reached over the lip of the companionway
with the launcher in my hand.

Instantly bullets twanged against hull metal. I pulled
the trigger and the first little missile whooshed away.

A bolt of flame lashed out a moment later. I leaped
out onto "B" with a war cry in my throat and stood
with my feet planted, the launcher grasped before me in
both my hands. Before me was an inferno, a corridor
wreathed in fascinating hellfire.

A writhing figure, cased in flame, collapsed to the
deck. I fired straight into it and it exploded into flaming
horror. Burning human gore splashed onto my hands,
my face, my chest.

The fire, the flames, the red-orange monster. I fired
again and again with the launcher, doubling and redoubling the havoc to no purpose.

My little band of fighters ran for the "A" deck hatch
as I covered them, remembering other fire, so long ago.
Again and again I fired, unaware that the launcher was
empty. Look at the fire, exult in the carnage!

"Mac! Hurry! Please!" Joslyn called.

And then I heard the *click*, *click*, *click* of the emptied
launcher firing nothing as I pulled the trigger. I realized
what I was doing, dropped the cursed thing, and ran for
"A" deck.

There, too, was carnage.

Two more of our ships were blasted away. Dozens of
tiny pitched battles raged on the great flight deck, opponents pinned down behind pieces of wreckage, firing at
each other.

Uncle Sam still stood intact, her proud red, white, and
blue paint job looking awfully damn good. There, too,

were the stars on *Stars* and the stripes on *Stripes*, still bold against the Finnish sky.

Leviathan was moving slower, flying lower, listing slightly to port. Now the planet's surface was visible from the deck. Fires burned in a hundred places on *Leviathan's* deck.

I got my radio back from Raunio and broadcast again. "All troops! All League and Finnish troops! Codeword PAYDIRT! Mission accomplished! Withdraw, withdraw, withdraw. This is recall. Get the hell off this ship and save yourselves! Relay this message." I handed the communicator to Raunio again. "Repeat that. Then transmit a recall to those guys guarding the hangar entrance and still below. Let's get out of here before someone notices us."

The exhausted soldiers followed Raunio in one last run for their lives. One young kid stopped running suddenly and fell to the deck with his chest holed. A stray bullet.

From every point of the vast deck, soldiers were headed toward the landing craft. I saw two or three parachustists simply run to the stern and jump overboard, trusting to their reserve chutes. The rest were doing what we were doing, a fighting retreat. Twice we practically ran over Guardian troops who were busy blazing away at our troops with their backs to us. They didn't last long. Raunio ran out of throwing knives.

Uncle Sam seemed to grow no closer as we ran. My heart was pounding, my head was spinning. I dumped my backpack and dropped the rifle I hadn't fired. It had all been too close-in for that. I tossed away my helmet and did all I could to force one foot in front of the other.

Slowly, so slowly, we came toward the lander. A Guardian jet roared across the sky a little ways off, a Finn on his tail. The Guardians had gotten that ventral launcher back in service fast. A missile blurred across the distance between them, and the Guardian blew up, the wreckage slamming into the control fin and bouncing around the deck before it fell off the stern.

Uncle Sam was suddenly close, 75 meters. Fifty meters. Closer. And we were there. Joslyn was first in the hatch and first to the lander's flight deck, but I was a damn close second.

Exhaustion. It was so tempting to take off, get out, get away, and call it over. But we had come this far, and maybe we could end it all.

The viewscreens showed the battle below us and the Finns scrambling into the lower deck. Joslyn cast off her battle gear and dropped into the pilot's chair. I skinned off my own flak suit and let the rest of my guns clatter to the deck. I wiped a bloody sleeve across my face and got to my flight station.

"Joslyn, go to T minus five seconds before lift off and hold. There'll be stragglers. Power up both chemical and fusion engines. I'll want 50 percent of hover power from the fusion side for as long as you've got it."

"But not power to take off on?"

"It's time to finish this thing. I want to see if a fusion jet can slice through this hull metal of theirs." I hit the intercom. "Lieutenant Raunio! Up here, if you please. I'll need some good Finnish spoken. Randall, we may need a spare pilot."

They came up to the flight deck. "Lieutenant. Get on the horn to all ships. Let them launch the moment they have everyone they can carry on board. *Stars* and *Stripes* I want to hold a while longer. We're going to try and punch through this deck and do some damage." Raunio relayed the orders. Metcalf dropped heavily into the empty flight station and started to help Joslyn get *Uncle Sam* ready to move. George, lost in his own shock and exhaustion, his own thoughts, stared out at the carnage below.

I sneaked a peek from the hatchway camera. Nothing moved out there at first, then a sweating soldier staggered into view and threw himself into the ship. Another followed.

The first Finnish ship took off from the bow and headed for any touchdown site he could find. I watched him grab for sky. Below him the New Finnish landscape sprawled out grandly. On the horizon, coming up fast, was the seacoast.

Another Finn launched. The last pair of Guardian fighters in the sky tried to go after him, but the Finnish fighters chased them away.

Another Finnish lander got away.

"*Uncle Sam* is at T minus five seconds, and holding. Fusion and chemical drives at the ready," Joslyn reported. She leaned back in her crash couch with a tremendous sigh. "My God, Mac, we pulled it off."

"So far, anyway. Lieutenant Raunio. What status for *Stars* and *Stripes*?"

He called the two ships and reported. "All systems being go for launch immediately. They both request to take off."

"Denied," I snapped. "We're going to try and nail this beast for good. Let's damn *finish* the job."

"I told them that already."

"Boss man, there goes the last of the merchant ships," Randall announced.

"Good. Everybody, scan the decks on every camera. Anybody see anyone still out there?"

"Nothing."

"No."

"All clear."

I prayed they were right. It looked that way. "Button her up, Joslyn."

"Hold it!" Metcalf called. Three figures were hurrying forward as fast they could with their hands on top of their heads. Guardian troops, surrendering. "Oh, hell. Let 'em comes. Lieutenant Raunio, go below. Three prisoners surrendering and coming aboard. Try to keep your men from killing them." The three climbed aboard very carefully, keeping their hands in view at all times. Through the hatch camera I saw Raunio come into view, give each of them a hard punch to the stomach that dropped them to the deck. He grabbed them by the collars and threw them through the inner airlock one by one, then waved at the camera.

I wondered to myself what sort of work was going to be available to a fellow like Raunio in peacetime. Alligator wrestling, or the local equivalent, perhaps.

"So let's button this crate up," I said. "Half-hover power on fusion jets." The deep rumbling of the fusion engine below us came to life. "Relay same to *Stars* and *Stripes*." From the base of both of those ships a tiny violet-white pencil of light lashed out and flattened itself against the incredibly tough material. For a long time, nothing happened.

Metcalf let out a low, deep whistle. "That deck should be vaporized after five seconds of that."

Ten seconds, 20 seconds, and still the hull held out. But then something seemed to waver and sag beneath *Stars*. At the same moment, the rumble of our own drive fluttered and then deepened.

"*Stars* reports that *Uncle Sam* has pierced the hull," Joslyn said calmly. I glanced at her and saw the light in her eye, the thirst for final victory her voice betrayed.

"Okay, Joslyn, give us hover at ten meters."

The rumble grew louder and *Uncle Sam* lurched into the air. The fusion flame sliced through the normal material below the outer hull like butter, vaporizing the aluminum instantly. A demon's brew of chemical smoke suddenly sprang out of the hole in the hull and spurted up around *Uncle Sam*, blinding us. "Twenty meters, and give us about a meter a second headway toward the stern," I said. "Lieutenant Raunio. Order *Stars* and *Stripes* to do the same at half a meter a second as soon as they burn through."

Uncle Sam's drive sliced through the exterior hull metal nicely once the first piercing was made. She cut a trench in the flight deck out of which spewed the smoke and fire of hell. First *Stars*, then *Stripes* floated gently into the air and started to burn their own slashes into the skin of *Leviathan*.

Now came the real assault. "Joslyn, take us out over the port wing."

Sam upped her speed suddenly and zipped out over top of the port wing. "Okay, hover right here at 15 meters until I give the word. Get ready to bounce out of here at maximum boost."

Joslyn nodded, and our ship took up its new station.

"Mac, we've got to be right over the lift cells here. If that isn't helium down there—" Metcalf said worriedly.

"I know, I know. But it sure as hell ought to work."

"*Stars* and *Stripes* both report two minutes of fuel. They request permission to try and land."

"Damn it. Okay. Granted."

Instantly, the two smaller ships popped away.

"Mac, they'll have to ditch. We're well out to sea," Joslyn said. "We haven't got great lots of fuel ourselves," she added mildly.

The two little ships reached for sky and cleared the deck. They fell toward the sea in formation, engines braking their falls, with no thought of trying for shore, now at least 10 kilometers away. They eased themselves gently toward the sea. The fusion jets touched at the seawater and it exploded into live steam, hiding the two ships from view for long moments.

Randall listened over his headset and reported, "Both ships now landed okay."

Uncle Sam hung over the wing of her great adversary, the lone ship left in the skies above *Leviathan*, but for a few skirmishing fighters long kilometers away. Her drive flame bore in on the unseen piece of hull beneath us. Our ship burbled slightly and Joslyn corrected. "Mac, I think we just hulled her—"

BLAM! A great slap of force threw us high into the air above the ship, flinging us clear of the explosion.

The Guardians had trusted their tough hull too far. They had filled *Leviathan*'s lift cells with hydrogen, the lightest, most lifting, most flammable gas possible.

Joslyn gunned the engines and bounced us high over

the burning ship. The port wing was surmounted by a wall of flame. *Leviathan* lurched and shuddered violently. A great piece of the wing broke clear off and dropped lazily down into the sea. *Leviathan* went out of control and swung about in a great spiralling curve toward the shore, losing altitude and forward speed steadily. We kept station on her, watching the death of that great beast, that great ship, that terrible enemy.

Lower and lower she fell, more quickly now, coming in over the coastline barely 600 meters up. Another explosion ripped off a great megaton piece of the port wing and it fell to the ground, a fireball. The control fin seemed to fold up and collapse. It fell away sternward, still attached to the kilometer-long ship by twisted remnants of girding. It slammed into the earth, throwing up a great shower of soil and sand, trees and boulders. It dug a long, deep furrow in the ground before it dragged the rest of the ship into collision with the planet.

Leviathan crashed with a concussion that shook the land, the sea, and even the sky for a great distance.

Like a mountain unleashed from its moorings to the land, *Leviathan* rolled and bounced and broke apart in billowing sheets of flame that reached kilometers into the sky. Pieces that seemed small by comparison with *Leviathan*, each larger than the *Joslyn Marie*, split off and crashed to the ground.

Slowly, gradually, after many minutes of agony, the last pieces of the tortured monster came to rest and collapsed in flame. The flames spread out and the grasslands, the trees, the very soil burned in the fabulous heat. The fires would burn for hours more.

We watched in horror, in disbelief, in victory at the carnage we had wrought.

We had won, utterly.

I leaned back in my crash couch and stared, in my mind's eye, through the blank bulkheads of the good ship *Uncle Sam* at the clean skies above.

We had won.

"Put her down, Joslyn," I said quietly. "Put her down and let's get some rest."

CHAPTER TWENTY

Joslyn and I walked hand in hand toward the sea, along the quiet shore. Out in the farther reaches of the harbor, we could pick out the outline of *Stripes*, just now being towed into shore. *Stars* floated at dockside a few kilometers down the coast, waiting to be lifted from the water.

It was late evening in the long day of New Finland, and the sun was casting a rich warm glow over the water ahead of us. Joslyn spotted a familiar silhouette a short distance away, and we walked toward it, watching the sky.

The first silent, distant flash came just as we reached George. There it was, high in the sky over the fading sun. George stood staring at it gutter down to nothing as we came nearer. He nodded to us without speaking.

The three of us stood there. Vapaus came over the horizon and moved over us, a friendly watcher in the night. I turned and looked back toward the land, where *Leviathan*'s wreck lay huge and broken across the burned out meadowlands.

The nearby town, Vipurii, was shot up and scared and still there. A few cities—Mannerheim, New Helsinki, were gone forever, at least as they once were. Tomorrow was time enough to begin the rebuilding.

Hundreds, thousands, tens of thousands were dead, and many more horribly wounded. Heroes and cowards alike had fallen—most to be forgotten, a few to live forever in death. A world was scarred, and bent, and bloody, but unbroken.

It was over.

It might be said that the thousands who were dead had lived as much as it was needful for them to live, had contributed to the victory and gone on. One could say that, once again, the tree of liberty had been refreshed with the blood of patriots.

But it was hard, now, to think of a victory, or a defeat, or a war at all. All I could feel for certain was that I was still alive, and free, and just barely unafraid.

Another light flared suddenly, quietly, in the sky, and Joslyn took my hand. The radio waves carried the invisible commands from a machine that was dead, and the killer robots in space were dying. Suicides all—the last resort of the insane.

George sighed, and fumbled at nothing with his hands, as if the engineer in him was looking for something to fix, or build. "There go the prison walls. I helped build them, and thank God I could help to tear them down. Soon the rest of your people will be here, and then you'll—no, *we'll* go off again to fight them on Capital, the home world. And there are a lot more people back home who would be glad to see our side—the League side—win."

"We'll win."

"Mac, Joslyn. This little planet was damn lucky it was you two who came. They'll be naming things for you when it comes time to rebuild. If it had been someone less on the ball, the Finns might have lost for good."

"We would have won, George. The Guardians would have attacked again, and been discovered, and stretched themselves even farther to conquer. They might have won two worlds, or three, for a time, but the threat they posed was the very thing that made the League stronger, and less unafraid, than they ever dreamed it could be."

"Maybe. But you two and your bravery have shortened their time, and saved many lives, and many worlds, maybe even including Capital, if this does lead to winning there."

"That's good enough for us, anyway," Joslyn said. She squeezed my hand in both of hers and smiled.

George sighed again, and I could see that it still cost him to call the Guards "they." He was trying, but his soul was not yet free of their claim on him. "And then they'll be beaten, for good."

"No, they won't be," I said. I dropped Joslyn's hand and walked toward the tideline, letting the cool waves lap at my feet.

"The sky is very large," I said, "and as long as humans travel there, and are free to do what they want, a few will want to rule and conquer and be mighty and greedy. This time, we beat them. And as long as there are men and women, even just a few, who care more about each other than themselves—people who'll die to see a baby live—we will be able to beat them again."

I thought of Pete Gesseti and his theories about our missing comrades, the crew and passengers of the *Venera*. They were out there, on Capital. I was sure of it. They were waiting for us to find them, to track the Guardians down to their home world and free our comrades. The job wasn't over.

AFTERWORD

SPACE FIGHTERS

G. Harry Stine

Science fiction is about to witness another of its futuristic ideas turn into reality. Here in the mid-1980's, both the United States and the Soviet Union are hard at work on space fighters to fly in orbit around the Earth.

The concept of a space fighting vehicle with a crew of one or two has been kicked around in science fiction stories and motion pictures for a long time. As space technology has progressed, the way that science fiction authors have visualized space fighters has changed. But few writers have worked out the basic military doctrines, mission requirements, and justifying rationales behind the space fighter concept.

The artistic depiction of space fighters has also followed Correy's Rule: Space ships are drawn to resemble transportation devices built under current technology. In the nineteenth and early twentieth centuries, the science fiction magazines (they weren't called "science fiction magazines" at that time, of course, because that period was B.G., "Before Gernsbach") were full of riveted space ships that resembled curvilinear steam boilers with bat-like wings. In the 1930 decade, they looked like airplanes. In the 1940s, all space ships resembled the German V-2 rocket. You could tell an s-f illo drawn in the 1950s: the space ship was based on the appearance of an Atlas ICBM. Same for the 1960s, when they were Saturn V moon rockets. Now, they look like the Space Shuttle Orbiter.

The motion picture "2001: A Space Odyssey" had an enormous impact upon the artistic world because it introduced spacecraft with odd but strangely familiar shapes and extremely complex external appearances, a far cry from the slick, streamlined spacecraft examplified by the still-beautiful "Destination Moon" rocket. The basic shapes of "2001" were adopted by industrial designers and showed up as interior of Boeing 727 airliners as well as Volkswagen Rabbits and Plymouth Horizons. The ultimate impact of "2001" on science-fiction spacecraft has been in motion pictures and television, where today the shape of a space craft has absolutely nothing whatsoever to do with its function or with elementary structural engineering.

The missions and operational uses of science fictional space fighters have also been inexorably tied to the past. "Star Wars," "Battlestar Galactica," "Buck Rogers," "Battle Beyond The Stars," and a host of other motion pictures and television shows have portrayed space fighters as nothing more than slicked-up space-going futuristic counterparts of navy fighter planes operating from space-going aircraft carriers, complete down to the catapult launching techniques. It isn't stretching things (although it may make me no friends) to point out that X-wing Fighters, Vipers, and the rest amount to nothing more creative and imaginative than "World War II in Space." This is the Hollywood version of the "Last War" syndrome—i.e., we've always tried to fight the current war with the concepts, doctrines, strategies, and tactics of the last war.

Mind you, I'm not pooh-poohing the concept of the space fighter. Far from it. I've spent more than a few years thinking about what the role of a real space fighter might be, how it might be deployed, and what it might look like.

There have been no space fighters in the real universe to date for several reasons. In addition to the fact that aerospace technology simply wasn't up to the task of building a space fighter in the first place, military planners—whose jobs depend upon coming up with the right weapon system at the right time to counter a real or anticipated threat—saw no justification for such a gadget and didn't have the doctrines or mission requirements for it, let alone the strategies and tactics that would justify such a machine. Because of all the shortcomings evident in the descriptions and illustrations of space fighters in science fiction over the past century, the professional military men have scoffed at the space fighter concept . . . until recently.

Four things have triggered a growing interest in the real possibility of a space fighter:

(1) The NASA Space Transportation System, otherwise popularly known as the space shuttle, proved once and for all that it was possible to orbit a manned winged space vehicle and return it safely to an aircraft-type landing for re-use.

(2) The Lockheed SR-71 Blackbird Mach-3 high-altitude spy plane has since 1962 shown that such high-speed high-altitude manned reconnaissance vehicles had utility beyond what could be accomplished by unmanned orbiting recon satellites.

(3) The Soviet Union began testing a small winged reuseable "spaceplane" in about 1976.

(4) The development of the simple "space cruiser" concept by Fred W. "Bud" Redding, an aerospace designer with the DCS Corporation, caught the eye of the United States Air Force because of an article about it by this author in the November 1983 issue of *Omni* magazine.

These things are leading to the impending birth of the space fighter.

Quite apart from the utility of a space fighter in outer space itself, the vehicle has a definite series of missions it can perform in close proximity to the Earth. Students of aviation history as well as military history knew that early airplanes co-opted the role of the horse cavalry in scouting as well as general harassment of the enemy's rear because of mobility and use of the principle of surprise. Only later did aircraft also assume the role of load-carriers, vehicles capable of delivering either cargoes or bombs over ranges far beyond those of ground vehicles or artillery guns. Helicopters have taken over the tactical scouting and harassment roles today on the battlefields of Earth, but aircraft have kept the art of scouting, harassment, and load delivery alive by doing these things at higher and higher altitudes and faster and faster speeds. The space fighter concept extends them into space itself, but a space fighter must not be considered a load-carrier like the space shuttle orbiter.

The operational requirements for a space fighter, especially the ones we're likely to see in the next 25 years, are simple to set forth and not technically as difficult to achieve as might be assumed. A space fighter should be capable of being launched on a few minutes' notice from the surface of Earth, from an airborne platform, or from a space facility such as the space shuttle or a space base. It should be capable of entering any orbit and making several changes of orbital altitude and inclination. It should have suitable aerodynamic characteristics—primarily a high ratio between lift and drag—so that it can maneuver in the upper atmosphere of the Earth by means of aerodynamic controls, primarily stubby delta wings.

Thus, the space fighter should be able to appear suddenly in the high atmosphere over any nation at any time moving in any direction at a wide variety of speeds. A system of defense against such a space fighter will be extremely expensive in comparison to the cost of the space fighter. In fact, even the detection system necessary to find one and track it will be costly. For operations in the near-Earth orbital region, a capability to change its velocity ("delta-vee") of about 2,500 feet per second is necessary. For operation in the Earth-Moon system, a delta-vee of 20,000 feet per second would be more than adequate.

The space fighter should be a completely self-contained manned vehicle with a life support capability of at least 24 hours. Finally, the space fighter should be able to return to a number of bases or landing sites and terminate its mission in a reusable condition.

In 1965, these requirements were technologically difficult if not impossible. Now they are "state of the art" if clever engineering is used.

It looks as though the Soviet Union has already embarked on a "spaceplane" if not a space fighter program with its small shuttle. France is considering the development of the "Hermes," a delta-winged mini-shuttle intended to be launched into low Earth orbit by the Eurospace "Ariane" rocket. And the United States Department of Defense has embarked upon at least two admitted spaceplane or space fighter programs.

An excellent example of this is Fred W. "Bud" Redding's space cruiser or spaceplane, which is being funded by Defense Advanced Research Projects Agency (DARPA) as a research vehicle. The Redding space cruiser is delightfully simple and brings out the machismo in hot fighter pilots. A slender cone about 24 feet long with a base diameter of about five feet, the vehicle is a scaled-up version of the proven Mark 12 Minuteman re-entry vehicle. The aerodynamic characteristics of this shape are very well known and understood. It's a hypersonic and supersonic airframe shape with good life-to-drag ratio and therefore good maneuverability. And small delta wings, and it becomes *highly* maneuverable. It's large enough that a single pilot clad in a pressure suit can sit in an unpressurized cockpit in the aft end just ahead of a ring of rocket motors. A hatch that can be opened allows him to stand up in the cockpit to look around. In this "open cockpit" space vehicle, the pilot "owns space" around him.

The nose of the conical spaceplane can be folded back to permit it to become a "pusher" or space tug for shifting larger loads in orbit. With a Centaur underneath it as a lower stage, it is capable of taking its pilot *around the Moon and back*.

The simplicity of the Redding spaceplane comes from its lack of design compromises. One of the things that makes the space shuttle orbiter so complex is the requirement that it fly well at subsonic, supersonic, and hypersonic speeds. This was a difficult and expensive technological feat requiring many compromises that didn't contribute to low cost and design simplicity. If a spaceplane is designed to fly at only supersonic and hypersonic speeds, it can be greatly simplified. But how can it be landed if it won't fly at subsonic speeds?

The Mark 12 re-entry vehicle is a fine supersonic and hypersonic airframe but a streamlined anvil at subsonic speeds. The Redding spaceplane is the same. But rather than compromise the design by giving it a good subsonic lift-to-drag ratio to permit a horizontal landing, Bud Redding opted to use another simple and straightforward method: a parachute. Not the simple circular parachute used on early Mercury, Gemini, and Apollo space capsules that dropped the capsule into the ocean in an uncontrolled fashion. Instead, Redding suggests the use of the steerable, flyable "parasail" used by thousands of sports parachutists every weekend. Once the spaceplane gets into the atmosphere and its speed slows to subsonic where it becomes a brick, a parasail chute is deployed, allowing the pilot to steer the slender cone to a soft landing inside a fifty-foot circle. It could be landed even on the deck of a ship at sea.

The Redding DARPA spaceplane is almost a technological reality today. But coming down the line very quickly is something the United States Air Force calls the "transatmospheric vehicle" (TAV). This is not a space fighter or a space cruiser. It's conceived as a vehicle larger and more complex than the Redding spaceplane but smaller and simpler than the NASA space shuttle. The TAV would take off horizonally from the runway of any Air Force base, *fly* into orbit using wings for lift and a combination of turbo-ramjet and rocket engines for propulsion, operate in low Earth orbit, and return at will to land horizontally on the runway of any Air Force base. The TAV may be operation in the 1990s. The Redding spaceplane could be flying in the 1980 decade.

Neither of these space fighter-like vehicles will look anything like what anyone thought a space ship would in the annals of science fiction. They won't look like X-wings, Y-wings, TIE fighters, Vipers, Starfighters, or anything else conceived to date in the minds of authors or illustrators. There is one thing for certain: When their appearances become unclassified (like the appearance of the Redding spaceplane already is), artistic interpretations based upon their designs will quickly come to grace not only science fiction book and magazine covers, but also the beautiful full-color institutional ads of aerospace companies—product ads proudly announcing that "HyperTech's Mark Three Solar Powered Laser Gizmoscope was chosen above all others to provide essential on-board services," and numerous backgrounds for national newsmagazine covers.

Beyond the 1999 space fighter, however, the technological crystal ball becomes cloudy. This is not to say that the wildest hallucinations of a Hollywood art director are a better indication of what futuristic space figters would look like. Probably not, because such concepts are based solely on what looks good and appears to be futuristic. The actual space fighters of the twenty-first century will not only look "right," they will be beautiful in their own way because they'll be designed with a full understanding of the mission requirements of a space fighter based upon realistic military doctrines of space. They will be difficult to operate, dangerous to life and limb, and push human capabilities to their utmost limits just as has every scouting and fighting vehicle (including the horse) throughout history.

Far more important in the long run is the inevitable spin-off of space fighter technology into the technology of civilian and commercial spacecraft. Just as the airliners and general aviation aircraft of 1984 use the engines, electronics, aerodynamics, and other technologies pioneered for military aircraft, so the military spacecraft will also contribute toward the accompanying commercial and private use of space. And *that* possibility is perhaps far more exciting than space fighters themselves.

Move over, science fiction. Another of your dreams is about to become reality!

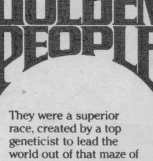